Advance praise for

NEVER CROSS A
HIGHLANDER

"A fascinating, intense love story that Highlander lovers will stay up all night for."

—**Lexi Post,** *NY Times* **bestselling author**

"A brilliant portrayal of diverse characters in the 16th century Highlands, with a hero so hot, the pages nearly burst into flames!"

—**Heather McCollum,** *USA Today* **bestselling author**

"Made my heart sing and is unlike anything I've ever read before. 5 massive golden stars!"

—**Michelle McLean,** *USA Today* **bestselling author**

NEVER CROSS A
HIGHLANDER

THE SHADOW LAIRDS SERIES

LISA RAYNE

Entangled Publishing, LLC
644 Shrewsbury Commons Ave., STE 181
Shrewsbury, PA 17361
Visit our website at www.entangledpublishing.com.

Amara is an imprint of Entangled Publishing, LLC.

Edited by Lydia Sharp
Cover art and design by Bree Archer
Stock art by VJ Dunraven/Period Images,
Mrdoomits/Shutterstock,
Interior design by Toni Kerr

Print ISBN 978-1-64937-095-2
ebook ISBN 978-1-64937-116-4

Manufactured in the United States of America

First Edition January 2023

AMARA

At Entangled, we want our readers to be well-informed. If you would like to know if this book contains any elements that might be of concern for you, please check the back of the book for details.

This one's for Helen Bowman, my high school buddy and class valedictorian. Our sophomore year, she challenged a doubting me to read my first romance novel and handed me a historical romance by Kathleen Woodiwiss that forever changed what I read, and now…what I write. Who knew?

And for all the smart girls and brilliant women who read romance despite the misguided individuals who cluck their tongues and wrongly judge this genre beneath your intelligence.

Read on, my lovelies!

CHAPTER ONE

Ailsa Connery's life depended on the view from Princess Elizabeth's balcony. Her young charge, the second child born to King James VI, had chambers that bordered an inner corner of Stirling Castle. The location of the princess's rooms gave the best angle to view the entire royal courtyard and the approach to the castle's single outer gate.

"Elizabeth!" She rushed into the lass's sleeping nook. "Hurry! The clans begin to arrive for the tournament. You do not want to miss the sight. It shall be grand." Ailsa yanked the covers from Elizabeth's bed and silently cursed the status of the young lady's wild tresses.

Only fifteen summers in age and spoiled to the point of utter uselessness, the lass made it her mission to vex Ailsa on a daily basis. Ailsa had braided Elizabeth's hair into a long, tight plait afore bed last eve, yet here she sat rubbing the night from her eyes with those same tresses tumbling free and untamed. The only way that could have happened was if the bratchet had removed the tie Ailsa had securely wound around the end of her braid. Something she would had to have done apurpose.

Elizabeth knew what a chore it was to brush and style the thick mass of hair that fell to her waist. She also knew Ailsa hated the chore. The chit had done it out of spite. Properly detangling the mess atop the lass's head would cost Ailsa valuable time she did not have this morn, time she needed to be on the balcony so she could locate the warriors who would ride in wearing the glorious colors of her clan, deep red traversed with blue and yellow.

With an irritated shake of her head, Ailsa turned toward the wash table and stepped on something that lay underfoot. She looked down to see the tie that should have been on the end of Elizabeth's braid. Tossing the tie onto the table, Ailsa decided to bypass the needed lecture. In a few short days, she'd never have to worry about serving as lady's maid again. Someone else could worry about the antics of Princess Elizabeth and be the brunt of constant criticism and thoughtless regard. Someone else could worry about how to brush the child's hair just so, which dresses fit which mood, and whether they would be hauled in front of the king for false reports of being mean to his precious daughter.

This day, Ailsa had no intention of letting the lass's antics get under her skin. Her chance at freedom lay somewhere just outside the castle gates, and she was going to be standing on the princess's balcony to watch it ride in. She was going to get them both out on that balcony the fastest way possible. If that meant tugging out some royal hair along with the tangles, then so be it. It didn't matter if Elizabeth was stylish this morn. They were on a reconnaissance mission. At least, Ailsa was. As for Princess Elizabeth, all that mattered was that she also be on the balcony so it looked as if Ailsa was merely dutifully accompanying her mistress. If Ailsa were seen alone on the balcony, someone might suspect what she was about.

Upon the instructions of the captain of the guard, the castle soldiers watched Ailsa closely. She could not leave the castle without Elizabeth or one of the princess's personal guards. Ailsa was limited on where within the castle she could roam alone and during what hours. She had mapped it all in her brain.

Who did what when.

Who went where when.

Who watched her do what at what hour.

She'd memorized it all.

Now, all she had to do was navigate in between the windows of time created by the guards' maneuvers and slip outside on the last night of the tournament set to begin in a few days' time. Her plan required she make her escape right afore the Connery warriors departed. Her clan warriors would protect her. They'd prevent this nightmare of unlawful enslavement from continuing. They'd see her safely home, back to her glorious Highlands. Her heart leapt at the prospect.

Not willing to let the king's spawn steal her chance at getting her first glimpse of Clan Connery plaid in three years, Ailsa grabbed Elizabeth by the wrist and tugged…to no avail. "Come on, princess. Time to put on your finery so all the arrivals can see how bonnie you are."

Ailsa had learned long ago the only way to get Elizabeth to do most anything without opposition was to appeal to the child's vanity. You could not approach Elizabeth directly. The more she knew you wanted her to do something, the more ornery she would be about trying to prevent you from getting your way.

Ailsa had already picked out the dress Elizabeth

would wear. She grabbed it from the hook on the wardrobe door and displayed it across her arm. "Look. I selected the green satin with the full skirt for you. You know how lovely you look in this."

Elizabeth had amber hair. It was her best feature considering what otherwise could have been an engaging countenance and appealing smile if her lips weren't oft misshapen with her mal disposition.

"Why must I watch the arrivals? The fun will not start until the competitions begin." With the back of her hand, the princess brushed a mass of dangling tangles from her eyes, then plopped backward onto the bed. Arms spread wide, the lass closed her eyes and let out a put-upon sigh.

Panic began to invade Ailsa's outwardly calm demeanor. She could not allow this delay. The morn was slipping away.

She rushed forward with the dress. "Tsk tsk, Your Highness. You know your father will expect you to be on the balcony to receive his guests."

'Twas a lie, but the princess did not know that. If she thought she'd incur the ire of the king, she was more likely to do as Ailsa bid. The deception was not guaranteed to work, since the princess had her father firmly enamored despite her constant penchant for mischief and malcontent. Mayhap 'twas no surprise this, given she was the only of the king's three daughters to survive infancy. Still, at times, His Majesty could be quite fickle with his affection, and no one, not even his daughter, wanted to be on the wrong side of his disposition on those days.

Counting on Princess Elizabeth to not want to risk paternal disfavor, Ailsa pressed the fib further. "You must not bring shame to His Majesty by being absent at the start of these most important festivities or by arriving late. 'Twill be thought a sign of disrespect."

Ailsa did not know if anyone would care about Elizabeth's presence one way or the other, but their presence on the balcony mattered immensely to Ailsa's future and her freedom. She could not stand another year, another month, nor even another week imprisoned here as Elizabeth's servant.

Nay, she silently admonished herself, *say it true. You are held as a slave.*

The members of the royal household did not like the term applied to those like herself, descendants of a people stolen from the continent of Africa, whom they held captive to work against their will. While some of her heritage who provided services at the castle were independent and paid in small amounts of coin or sundries for certain services, like Elene More, the seamstress who sometimes visited the castle, or Blak Margaret, the queen's attendant, Ailsa was being held inside the castle as forced, unpaid labor. A status due solely to her dusky brown skin. That transgression against her person easily cleared her conscience of the small deception created by the words she'd uttered to the princess.

Corralling Elizabeth into appropriate behavior had been a constant battle since the day Ailsa had the misfortune to be improperly detained by the captain of the king's guard and forced into servitude at Stirling Castle. Winter's cold had come three times since then, and Ailsa had lamented ever being able to escape this enslavement that had been foisted upon her shortly after she'd reached just a score in years.

She had been born a free woman of the Highlands, the descendant of Caribbean sugar plantation laborers who, during a transfer between islands, had been discovered by Hebridean pirates in the bowels of a Portuguese ship traveling from São Vicente. Unlike many African captives stolen by pirates, her grandparents had been allowed to work off their value and eventually earn freedom instead of being sold to wealthy Scots or Brits as enslaved servants for display as a symbol of prosperity.

Thought to be one such recent acquisition purchased for the king, Ailsa had been detained by the leader of the king's guard. The king had arranged a summer festival to celebrate the allegiance treaties he had procured from several of the then-current Highland lairds, and she'd been with a few of her kinsmen listening to an animated trumpeter. Ailsa had been surprised to see the trumpeter also had brown skin. Fascinated and delighted by the musician, she'd somehow lost track of time and ended up separated from the other Connery spectators. The captain had found her there unchaperoned while she danced and bobbed to the lively sounds of the trumpet and the drums of the two accompanying musicians.

The captain had surprised her when his angry grip snatched her from behind. He'd muttered a stream of obscenities while pulling her away from the crowd. Convinced she had somehow escaped from the group of recently arrived captives he'd herded toward the castle, he'd not stopped his fussing long enough to listen when she'd called him on his mistake or tried to explain her circumstance.

Most of the other captives were so new to the

country they had spoken neither Gaelic nor the king's preferred English, at least not properly. While her use of English may have been twinged with the Highland cadence natural to a native speaker of Gaelic, she'd been certain someone would soon recognize she had been raised outside the confines of captivity. She'd been wrong. Stripped of her garments and forced to wear the inferior linens of servants, she'd been poked and prodded like some wild animal, then hauled before the sovereign for inspection.

The humiliation lived inside her still.

They'd even changed her name.

They called her Anne. Anne Blanke.

All the captives were eventually called by the surname Blanke, as if they had suddenly become some new exotic clan sprung magically from the walls of the castle. How absurd that, no matter what she said or did, she had not been able to convince anyone they had made a mistake.

Being treated as having no worth outside the services she rendered to a vile, unmannered lass had taken its toll. Ailsa was through playing nursemaid, she was through being a captive, and she was through being Anne Blanke. By the time the tournament contests were completed, she'd be in the custody of the Clan Connery army and headed home. Back to claiming her real identity and a chance to rise beyond the limits of her station to head clan healer.

The thought spurred Ailsa to hasten with her dressing of the princess. Mindful that she did not have enough time to release fully the clumps of tangles from the lass's hair, Ailsa sat Elizabeth facing away from the vanity looking-glass afore attacking the mass of

mottled curls. She brushed quickly, ignoring the whines
of discomfort and loud complaints that issued from the
royal bratchet.

After Ailsa had gathered, rolled, and pinned
Elizabeth's hair with such attention one would have
thought she had indeed created a masterpiece, Ailsa
admired her efforts with satisfaction. From afar, no one
would be able to tell the pins held together a veritable
rat's nest. Only someone who came close to the princess would be able to see the details. 'Twould work for
their—*her*—immediate purpose: get out onto the balcony with all due haste. Once the day's procession of
clans was done, Ailsa would find an excuse to have the
princess change attire, and she would redo the coiffure
appropriately.

"There, Your Highness. You look quite fetching.
Shall we retire to the balcony?"

"No." The princess turned toward the looking-glass.
"I told you I did not want to watch the procession. Why
don't you ever listen?" She glanced back at Ailsa. "I
don't understand what's wrong with you blackamoors.
You have been here long enough to be able to understand simple English."

Ailsa flinched at the use of the word blackamoors.
To be reduced to no more than your skin color and
thought less human as a result had been a sobering experience. 'Twas something she had nary become
accustomed to, nor would she ever. While she had always been an outsider in her clan due to her illegitimate
birth and mixed blood, the lack of acceptance had often
been subtle and subversive. This constant subjugation to
ill will, persecution, and accusations of inferiority took a
different toll. She'd learned to read and write—in

secret—late at night in her mother's cottage. It had been an odd undertaking for a lass, especially a common village lass with brown skin, but somehow her mother had managed a tutor. Ailsa would wager her own intellect and ability to understand far surpassed that of the princess, who shunned attention to her studies in the same way she shunned decent behavior.

Not to be deterred from her ultimate goal, Ailsa decided on a different tactic. "I apologize, Your Highness." She bobbed into a brief curtsy. "I thought only that you would not want Lady Sophie to receive all the attention this day, but if I was mistaken—"

"Lady Sophie?" The princess popped to her feet. "Of what do you speak?"

The temporary diversion gave Ailsa time to steer the princess's attention away from the looking-glass. With cunning deliberateness, Ailsa walked to the double doors that led to the balcony and opened them.

"Why, Lady Sophie will be viewing the procession this morn, of course. Know you not of this?"

Lady Sophie, a petite, fair-skinned lass from the Northern Isles, had accompanied her parents to Stirling to observe the tournament and be introduced at court. Her father, a distant relative of the recently imprisoned Earl of Orkney, who was cousin to King James, hoped the trip might secure the lass a suitable marriage offer. Princess Elizabeth detested her. Anyone who garnered attention away from the princess was not to be tolerated.

"Umpf." The indelicate grunt was unlike the princess. She usually hid her disdain better, but perhaps she felt no need with only her *blackamoor* lady's maid in audience.

Without hesitation, Elizabeth strolled onto the balcony with the regalness of the future monarch she was destined to be. As the daughter of the reigning monarch of Scotland, England, and Ireland, the princess's hand was a much sought-after prize. She had no lack of suitors vying for her, but that stopped her not from a miserly penchant to hoard attention solely for herself. Lady Sophie could certainly not be allowed a monopolistic appearance afore the crowds gathered to view the procession.

Ailsa stepped onto the balcony behind the princess, her relief at the lass's unknowing cooperation overshadowed by the anticipation and excitement threatening to overwhelm her. She tried not to fidget, biting her lower lip as she fought the urge to bounce out of her slippers. Slowly, she edged decorously to the side of the princess, so she had an unobstructed view of the front gates and the courtyard.

The first clan had already arrived. Their long line of mounted warriors was nearly through the gates. Not far behind them came a clan draped in plaid of pale browns and gray, the Donnellys. The clan was known for its fierce warriors. Their feats in war fueled many a Highland legend. Several possible tournament champions surely dwelled within their ranks.

Ailsa inched toward the edge of the balcony to get a better view. As she did, she noticed Lady Sophie on the balcony on the opposite side of the U-shaped courtyard. The lady intently watched the procession of Highland warriors using a small spyglass, a monocular device with a glass eyepiece. When looked through, it increased the size of objects viewed in the distance, making them look closer and clearer. The device had only recently come into use by naval officers and ship captains. Coming from the northeastern coastal region of the country, 'twas no surprise Lady Sophie would possess such a scientific treasure, but her apparatus-enhanced observation abilities made Ailsa nervous.

The spyglass lifted from its courtyard target and stopped, pointed in the direction of Ailsa and Princess Elizabeth. Lady Sophie went to lower the glass but then jerked the implement back up to her eye. When she lowered the looking tool again, her gaze focused on Elizabeth. Ailsa was certain the Orcadian was staring at the princess's hair.

A nervous itch crept up Ailsa's back, but she stood immobile, barely risking a breath lest Princess Elizabeth notice Lady Sophie's interest. Ailsa had taken a huge risk this morn, one that she thought she would have time to rectify afore anyone noticed. All she could think about when she awoke this day was that her enslavement ordeal would soon come to an end. Her impatient gamble may now cost her in ways she had not fully considered. She faced certain discipline if the lady had noticed the fiasco of a hairdo Princess Elizabeth currently displayed and spurred Elizabeth to check the unstylish creation or said something this eve when the royals and titled folk supped.

Princess Elizabeth looked up and spied Lady Sophie across the balcony. Lady Sophie gave a genteel nod to the princess, all the while looking every bit as if she were trying not to laugh. Elizabeth gave a haughty nod in return and looked away dismissively, not remotely interested in—or mayhap unaware of—Lady Sophie's suppressed mirth. Once Princess Elizabeth returned her gaze to the courtyard, Lady Sophie made eye contact with Ailsa and cordially tipped in acknowledgment the silk hand fan she'd swapped for the spyglass.

Nearly paralyzed with worry that she'd been found out, Ailsa stared blankly in Lady Sophie's direction. She struggled to decipher the meaning of the lady's gesture. The Orcadian's shoulders began to shake. After another quick glance at Elizabeth, the lady lifted her silk fan to cover the lower half of her face and began to laugh in earnest behind the fan.

A few moments later, having managed to collect herself, Lady Sophie lowered the fan. Sporting a huge grin, she glanced conspiratorially at Ailsa and placed her index finger in a vertical line against her lips afore she rested her fan lightly against her heart. Ailsa then understood the message. Lady Sophie was letting her know the secret of the beehive coiffure was safe with her. Princess Elizabeth had apparently made one too many nips and snipes at the visitor over the last few days, and Lady Sophie was all too happy to simply enjoy this moment of secret one-upmanship.

Finally able to breathe normally again, Ailsa returned her attention to the arrival of the clans. Three more clans marched through the castle gates over time, but to her extreme dismay, the clan she awaited was not amongst them. She tried to stifle her disappointment. The games did not start for a full sennight. Other clans would arrive over the next few days to pay their respects to the king, draw their lots for the games, and enjoy the feast scheduled to last until the night afore the competitions began. Clan Connery must be amongst those who intended to arrive on a later day to make a grand entrance. She would just have to hold on

LISA RAYNE   13

to her patience.

Already bored, Princess Elizabeth turned away from the balcony afore the last warrior cleared the gate. Ailsa turned to follow and nearly collided with the captain of the king's guard. He took one look at Elizabeth and frowned into a double take.

Worry returned to Ailsa full force. From his expression, the captain had noticed the princess's hair. Hopefully, he was one of those men so ignorant of women's ways he'd find the coiffure curious but not enough to remark upon. If not, her chance to return to the Highlands might now be at-risk.

Ailsa held her breath and waited.

CHAPTER TWO

In the Highlands, the dull sky spread gray across the top of the MacNeill clan keep and over the rolling hills that rose behind it to the west. As seemed appropriate for Duff Kallum MacNeill's mood, the clouds spit every now and again. Their droplets misted over the soldiers who had circled around to watch the sparring demonstration he held in the courtyard.

"Keep your bloody shoulder down, for Christendom's sake!" Kallum advanced on the young soldier who'd had the misfortune to draw training maneuvers this bleak morn directly with his pissed-off clan commander.

Ignoring the dampness and the crowd, Kallum swung his broadsword again and again. The weight of his basket-hilted weapon felt good in his left hand. The one-handed sword remained as yet unpopular amongst many soldiers of the Highlands, who still mostly preferred a double-handed grip on a claymore, but Kallum occasionally enjoyed the advantage of having one hand free during battle.

The sword whistled through the air and struck the young soldier's claymore with such force, the lad retreated with each contact. The clang of steel meeting steel fueled Kallum's rage and spurred him to have no mercy on the inexperienced lad, whose face—to Kallum's grand irritation—revealed his fear. The youth stumbled and scrambled to keep his sword up to avoid the mortal arc of Kallum's metal.

"Need you assistance, young Dougal?" Kallum asked with a scowl that nearly crossed into a sneer. He advanced in earnest with a flurry of steps and round-about swings that took complete control of the skirmish. "Perhaps you would benefit from having one of your comrades aid in your fight?"

Kallum's expression was fierce, the taunt no empty solicitation. He spun to his left to easily deflect Dougal's latest attempt at a thrust and, with an abrupt tilt of his head, motioned Odart MacNeill, the lad's lieutenant, into the fray.

The lieutenant took a deep breath but did not hesitate to draw his sword and rush forward. He led his advance with a fierce battle cry, which elicited a satisfied nod from Kallum.

Aye, feuch air noo, Kallum thought, appreciating that now the fight would proceed with gusto. He craved a fight. A real fight. Not the paltry efforts he'd been getting from a laddie-bairn who probably had yet to spill his cods inside a woman.

Kallum feinted away from the lieutenant's charge and moved to keep the two soldiers to his front. Aware the lieutenant posed the greater threat of his opponents, Kallum quickly swapped his sword to his right hand so he wielded the treasured weapon from the side closest to the senior man. Kallum took a stance. His bravado made clear he adjudged the two men no threat of consequence even combined, but he wordlessly dared them to do their utmost.

Angered at the perceived slight given by the challenge Kallum issued—and backed—with his nondominant hand, the lieutenant glared at Dougal with eyes that communicated both his distaste for having been pulled into the training demonstration and an unspoken promise of later retribution if the lad did not improve his performance forthwith. When the two men finally advanced, they did so in tandem. Unconcerned, Kallum used his superior size and weight to shove the younger opponent off-balance while he simultaneously engaged the lieutenant's sword with his own.

The lad fought to remain upright, but he pitched backward and met the ground arse first. He gave an indecorous bounce and slid several meters. To his credit, the foot soldier had the presence of mind to keep his sword up in a defensive position. Only this instinctive move saved him from having Kallum's sword take a slice off his neck instead of stop against the outside tip of his Adam's apple.

The mortified youth gulped. A hush echoed across the ranks of the MacNeill army. Dougal's chagrined glance darted across the soldiers looking on afore it skirted with concern to the clan lasses doing wash down by the loch.

Kallum made a sound of disgust at Dougal's affected interest in the sentiments of the women. The lieutenant, intent on taking advantage of his commander's divided attention, bolted forward. Arrogance mixed with surety spurred his attack. When he slashed downward, toward Kallum's chest, he let out a murmur of triumph. With but a brief look away from the soldier sprawled on the ground, Kallum easily halted Odart's attack by colliding one strong hand against the lieutenant's descending double-fisted hold on his claymore's grip. Kallum captured both the lieutenant's hands aloft with one large palm and held the man's arms, trembling with ineffective effort, in midair.

Not bothering to release the lieutenant, Kallum returned his attention to the young warrior on the ground. He issued a curt rebuke only audible to those within the inner portion of the spectator ring. "You'd do better to mind me, young Dougal, than the women yonder. A soldier who allows himself to be distracted by a lass during battle is a soldier unlikely to live to fight another day."

Without taking his eyes from Dougal, Kallum tightened his grip on Odart, who made several futile attempts to free his hands.

Kallum pressed his sword more firmly against Dougal's throat to accentuate his next words. "Think you any of those lasses will want you if I separate your fool head from your neck?"

Afore Dougal could respond, Kallum tensed as he sensed the arrival of the true source of his ire. Anticipating the confrontation to come, he reflexively tightened his grip on the hilt of the sword at Dougal's throat.

"Think you it not best to refrain from killing our own men?" His cousin and the future laird of the clan, Inan MacNeill, stood but a stone's throw from Kallum's side. Inan leisurely crossed his arms against his chest. "We might have a need come the next battle."

Inan's expression was more amused than miffed, but the mandate was clear: release the laddie-bairn.

Kallum relented and lifted his sword from Dougal's neck. Simultaneously, he gave Odart an abrupt shove. Not satisfied with the way maneuvers had progressed and still nursing some of the anger that had soured his disposition this morn, Kallum placed a foot behind the man's ankle and swept his feet from beneath him. The move might be thought petty by some of the onlookers. But given the lieutenant's poor showing in this sparring match, the man deserved no better outcome than the foot soldier under his command—a place in the dirt.

The lieutenant's arms flailed afore he landed hard in an unseemly sprawl. Dust flew up around him, as did the chuckles of several of the warriors who continued to stand in observance. The sounds of laughter at Odart's expense gave Kallum a small measure of satisfaction. If what the man had just displayed demonstrated the best battle tactics he had to offer, then no wonder the young soldiers under his command could do no better than Dougal.

This would never do.

Kallum would have to restructure the training responsibilities on the morrow.

Odart looked up and caught Kallum's glare, then turned red-faced when he noticed his sword in Kallum's hand. Kallum had divested the man of his weapon with ease afore he'd thrust him dismissively to the ground. A soldier stripped of his sword amid battle fast became a dead soldier no matter the skill of his opponent.

"Your strike when my face was averted, Odart, was an excellent thought. A mite late, but an excellent thought nonetheless." Kallum took a step so he loomed over the lieutenant's splayed-out limbs. "Next time, you might want not to hesitate nor give a warning squeak ahead of your attack."

With a double flick of his wrist, Kallum twirled Odart's weapon twice over the back of his hand as if it weighed no more than a feather, then speared the claymore into the ground at the apex of the lieutenant's thighs.

Odart frowned upon hearing the word "squeak," but his affront at the slight fled with the choked squeal he emitted when he grabbed anxiously for his cods to protect them from being impaled like a wild hare skewered on a spit.

"Aye, like that one," Kallum said matter-of-factly, then turned to head toward the manor.

After a step, Kallum hesitated and glanced over at Dougal. The lad now sat upright but had yet to move from his spot on the ground. He offered the lad a hand. Kallum was known as a harsh taskmaster, but clearly the lad's faults had been due to a failure in proper training, not to personal shortcomings.

The lad glanced suspiciously at the proffered hand afore he finally risked accepting the offered assistance.

Once the lad was on his feet, Kallum gave him a slap on the back of his shoulder. Dougal stumbled a step under the inadvertent force of the reassuring pat and was nearly displaced from his feet again.

Kallum steadied him afore he warned, "I'll expect better next time, young Dougal. See that you double your sparring time."

Looking like he might piss himself at any moment, Dougal responded with a frantic bobbing of his head. The sight made Kallum want to swear in frustration, but he suspected that might embarrass the lad even more. Instead, he simply resumed his retreat to the manor.

Inan fell into step beside him.

They'd only taken a few steps when they heard a perturbed Odart grouse, in a strained voice two octaves higher than his usual, "I'm gonna kill that Dougal."

Several of the soldiers who had yet to disperse chuckled at his words.

"I don't think Dougal is the one to blame for your current unseemly position, Odart," someone quipped.

The chuckles escalated into full-out laughter.

"Mayhap you should be issuing that threat to the commander instead," came an anonymous suggestion.

"Aye!" The combined shouts of the men rang out in unison to encourage the bold act.

Kallum halted and glanced over his shoulder at the man still prone on the ground.

Odart blanched upon seeing the look on Kallum's face. Only a fool would commit an act of such folly, a fool with a death wish. The lieutenant showed himself to be no fool by keeping silent.

The corner of Kallum's mouth lifted in the first semblance of amusement he'd felt all morn, and Odart took a noticeable swallow.

Inan clamped a hand onto Kallum's forearm. "*Kallum…*" he warned, emphasizing each syllable of Kallum's Christian name. "Don't."

Satisfied by Odart's inaction, Kallum glanced down at his cousin's hand on his arm. "What?" he asked with feigned innocence.

With a dramatic sigh, Inan released him, and the two continued on their way. "I know that look. When you give that smirk, it's not a good sign unless one is hoping for all hell to break loose."

Kallum suppressed a smile. Inan's reference to hell breaking loose was not a new observation. A grin from Kallum was not rare but rarely boded well for the person on the receiving end. A truth his cousin well knew and, from the murmurs around them, one with which his men agreed.

"Are ye all trying to get me killed?" Odart snapped in a hushed voice behind them.

From the sound of gravel shifting, Kallum surmised the lieutenant had finally recovered his aplomb enough to unhand his cods and rise from the ground.

Odart continued in a barely audible whisper. "Ye all know that man has a temper to rival the spawn of Hades. D'ye not ken he be known as *Auld Dubh Mahoun*?"

Kallum's expression did not change at the overheard words. He simply kept walking.

"Does that not bother you?" Inan asked with concern.

Kallum had long been aware many referred to him—behind his back—as *Auld Dubh Mahoun*, the Black Devil. No one thought he knew. All were terrified of his wrath should he know of the moniker. Little would anyone suspect how much he liked the title. He descended from great men of *dubh* lineage, Black warriors once reared amongst the magnificent tribes of Africa and a dark king of ancient Scotland who had ruled during the time the kingdom was known as Alba. With the blood of such fierce and majestic men coursing through his veins, Kallum could live with a reputation that equated him with the Prince of Darkness.

"Why should it?" A nonchalant lift of the shoulder accompanied the remark. "I have suffered worse insults from the time I was a boy." His skin, a deep brown from the blood of his tribal ancestors and not merely tanned like the white skin of his adoptive cousin, had made him an early target for the mean lads of the clan.

"I know, but still." A furrow appeared between Inan's brows. "Mayhap if you did not intimidate the men so, they would not think so heinously of you."

"Their thoughts of me are not heinous. They respect me. That is all I need. I need not for them to like me. We are not mates. I need only for them to follow me into battle, guard my back, and give their life, if need be, for the protection of their laird and keep." Kallum took the steps of the manor of the aforementioned keep two at a time. "Besides, the name inspires awe wrapped in scads of fear. Fear inspires mistakes. I prefer my opponents fear me. It gives me an edge."

Truth be told, he preferred them all afraid—alleged friends and foes alike. He'd learned early not to trust any man, save Inan's late uncle, who had raised him after his mother's death; Inan himself; and Inan's father, the current laird. The social abuse he oft suffered as a lad ended only after he'd become physically stronger and more adept with a weapon than his peers. They accepted him now because none dared cross him at the risk of death nor get on the wrong side of Inan as future laird.

"Kallum, our men are not the enemy."

"Until they learn to fight well, they remain as dangerous to me and my laird"—he gave Inan a pointed stare—"as any enemy."

"I am not yet your laird, cousin, but I'm sure my *father* appreciates the thought." The lightness of Inan's mood shifted, and he no longer had the look of one amused by this morn's events.

"We both know 'tis only a matter of formality at this point. The old man is ready to step aside. He waits only for you to step forward and show you are ready to lead the clan by agreeing to wed so heirs are assured to continue his legacy."

A muscle in Inan's jaw began to twitch. The subject was a sore one with him. He'd enjoyed three and thirty rotations of the seasons since his birth. Despite his advancing age, he'd fought for years the inevitable taking of a wife, and currently was at odds with his father over a betrothal negotiated without his input to wed the daughter of a chief of a neighboring clan.

Clan MacNeill was not the wealthiest clan, nor were their lands of significant size compared to clans like the MacDonalds or the MacKenzies, but they had a large fighting force, which would make them a valuable ally for any clan. At a time when the autonomy of the Highland chiefs and chieftains was under attack from the king, the MacNeills were in dire need of allies if they were to maintain control of the lands they had.

"Don't change the subject. We were not talking about me." Inan followed him into the manor. "Or, mayhap, we were. After all, you humiliated those men because you were angry with me. *I* am the one you should have come looking for this morn after breaking your fast."

"I have yet to break my fast this day." Kallum tended to rise afore the sun, and 'twas early still. "And I did not humiliate them. I taught them valuable lessons. 'Tis better they take their beatings from me during daily exercises than in battle where a mistake may cost them their lives." He glanced over at Inan. "I thought it a fitting way to start the day, since one does not simply pound into the dirt the future laird of the clan."

An amused scoff broke from Inan. "You assume you would have won."

Kallum raised his eyebrows in utter disbelief. "'Tis a certainty."

Inan grinned at the blunt statement. "Cocky bastard."

The good-natured slur surprised a laugh from Kallum. Inan was the only man alive who'd dare speak to Kallum that way. Surely because he was the only man alive who could do so and remain unharmed. Leave it to the infuriating bastard to lift Kallum's dark mood even though he'd been the one to cause it.

Though they were not kin by maternal or paternal blood, Kallum had been raised from the time he was seven summers as the adopted son of Inan's uncle. Inan had been just a year older. The two had grown up together as wild young things who ran through the clan grounds and its manor, wreaking all the havoc they could manage—and get away with—over the years. God's truth, they'd grown to love each other more like brothers and were tighter than most men born siblings.

Kallum headed for the high table, where the laird and his senior advisors usually ate their meals. He now had the hunger of four men.

"Will it be so bad accompanying me to the king's tournament?" Inan asked. "You know the bounty for the champion is high. You are our best warrior and our best chance that clan MacNeill comes out the victor. We could use the monies after the recent repairs we made to maintain the keep and the sums spent on additional sentry stations." Inan took a seat across from Kallum. "Plus, there's a rumor the king has promised a fair maiden of marriageable pedigree as part of the reward purse."

"A maiden?" Kallum was appalled. "I have no need for a maiden, fair or otherwise, and certainly not one with marriageable qualities. Why on earth would I want to be shackled with a maiden?"

Inan gave a look that made clear he considered the question absurd. "Every man has need for a maiden at times."

"Sweet Jesu, cousin. I can take care of those needs without binding myself to suffer incessant nagging for a lifetime. I have no need for some weak lass to feed and protect. I am content to take care of my body's needs with the accommodating widows and willing women of the outer village." Kallum carefully avoided dalliances with women inside the keep walls. 'Twas a sure means to a forced marriage.

"Which end of the outer village?" Inan asked with a barely suppressed smirk.

Since long afore the current laird, clan MacNeill had offered refuge to fugitives from enslavement and others of African descent who swore to honor the clan's laws and contribute productively to clan life. Craving a sense of belonging, those accepted into the clan—and their descendants—oft congregated in the same parts of the outer village to establish residences, somewhere along the southern end. Thus, the southern end of the outer village was where most of the ladies with beautiful brown skin that mirrored his own could be found. On the northern end resided predominantly the paler-skinned women of Scots descent.

Kallum gave Inan a look to indicate he thought the answer obvious. "Why, either, of course." He was popular with the lasses. "I care not about their lineages." Nor they his; they were concerned only with the package between his legs and what he could do with it. "I care only that they are willing and give a good tup."

"There is more to life than battles and a tup now and again." Inan lifted his hand to halt Kallum's forthcoming rebuttal. "Even the best of tups eventually finds its limits, especially when shared solely with random wenches. I am not the only one who will need to produce heirs at some point."

Kallum's chest tightened. Just the thought of Inan's words gave him an odd sense of apprehension, a feeling generally unfamiliar to him. "I have no need to sire heirs. I will never be laird of any clan."

That Kallum knew of, only one man of similar lineage had managed to rise to the status of chief of a clan. 'Twas not common amongst the Scots. 'Twere it not for Inan's family, Kallum himself might have ended up no more than the orphan he was, left to toil in some menial drudgery in the southern outer village—or possibly managing to rise to the status of foot soldier.

People of his descent were not always widely accepted across the Highlands or greater Scotland. Life in Clan MacNeill was vastly different. Instances of insensitive hostility or notions of superiority were not completely unfamiliar, but in an odd turn of fate, all the fighting Kallum had done as a lad had honed his skills such that he'd been the incontrovertible choice—and undefeatable candidate—for army commander over each of his ladhood tormentors.

He had found his place in the clan.

"My duty as commander demands I build the strongest of armies to protect our people. One day, Clan MacNeill will be known to have the fiercest army in all of Scotland. That will be my legacy. I have no need to plant my seed and have to father a bairn into adulthood. That is not my lot in life." His lot included an even greater mission beyond that, one that held much risk as well as danger. He had no desire to curtail his secret enterprise due to obligations of the hearth.

And without a wife, what need had he for offspring?

"Have you ever thought," Inan asked, "that I have need for you to produce heirs so my future sons will have as fierce an army commander as mine?" One brow, raised in query, showed above the tankard from which Inan took a long drink.

"You would have to marry in order to have future—*legitimate*—sons."

"Aye," Inan said thoughtfully and took another drink afore continuing. "But in my own time and with a woman of my own choice. And when that time comes, whom will I trust to watch the back of my firstborn son? There is only one such man I trust, and you will not live forever, Kallum. If you have not a care for one woman over the other, possibly the king's prize will be expedient and leave you without the worry of matters of the heart or arranged marriages that barter your soul for offspring." Inan's hand pressed hard around the tankard he held.

Kallum half expected his cousin to crush the pewter vessel one-handed.

A serving lass entered and refilled Inan's cup. Her timid gaze darted to Kallum the entire time she served Inan. She blushed a beautiful rose as she tried to hide her shy smile. Slowly, she made her way to Kallum's side of the table and carefully placed a tankard within an arm's reach of him afore she skittered away, giggling behind her hand.

Inan gave a perturbed glance at the lass's retreating back afore shooting Kallum a disgusted look followed by a baffled shake of the head. "Really? Another one?"

Kallum rolled his eyes at Inan's reaction to the skittish infatuation of the serving maid. 'Twas not as if Kallum encouraged the female attention he often elicited from the clan women of age. They were fascinated by his brawn, his position, and some, he suspected, fetishized the uncommon hue of his skin. Most seemed not the least discouraged by his characteristic lack of flirtatiousness. 'Twas a nice perk of his non-heir status that he had the freedom to dally with any such unattached women he chose, without the need to be concerned with making a *proper* match. Discreetly, of course, and not with any who would expect a betrothal in exchange.

He felt bad for his cousin. 'Twas a heavy weight the man bore with that mantle of chief he was destined to wear as the firstborn of the laird's two sons. The laird had tried for many years to barter terms for alliances and truces between their neighbors to the east but had been unsuccessful. More recently, the laird had finally secured, through the promise of intermarriage, an alliance with their western neighbors closest to the sea-lined coast, who were known for their naval prowess and feats of piracy.

While that might be Inan's fate, Kallum had no intention of following him into the abyss of marriage, family, and heirs.

"Clearly, you think because *you* must take a woman, I must join you in that pain. Have a heart, Inan. 'Tis bad enough you are forcing me to attend this spectacle put on to appease the king's ego. Spare me the talk of maidens and heirs." He gave a noticeable shudder.

As he had intended, the act returned a semblance of a smile to his cousin's lips, so he pressed the concern he truly harbored. "You know I cannot stand being in the king's court. There are so few men of independence there who look like me. I become an oddity to be gawked at, and he's rumored to keep some of my lineage enslaved. How can I go there and pretend I see not that? Think you a maiden will appease my sense of fury?"

"Nay." His cousin's expression sobered. "I do not. I know that which I ask of you. But we are in need of the coin, Kallum. I ask this not as a mere show of Clan MacNeill's might amongst other clans. I ask this for the well-being of our people."

Kallum sighed deeply. He had suspected as much. Inan was not one to make offhand requests or give orders just to throw around his status. 'Twas why Kallum had been so angry when he arose this morn.

After failing yester eve to dissuade Inan from making the journey to court, Kallum had awoken this day with a sense of dread. Inan was unaware of the secret life Kallum oft led between the wee hours of the night and dawn. Kallum had avoided the king's holdings during his excursions, but he did not see how that could continue under the current mandate.

"Aye. I had little doubt 'twas the way of it." Kallum downed the rest of his ale but pushed away the trencher of bread and cheese that had been set before him. He no longer had an appetite. "And you know I will not say you nay."

That he must go to the king's court he would accept, but he'd be damned if he came back with a lass in tow.

On that particular point, he was firm. Still, he had a bad feeling about this undertaking, one unlikely to dissipate with any haste.

Go, become the tournament champion, bring back much-needed coin for the clan. The imperative seemed a simple one. Kallum, alone, understood the falseness of that implied simplicity. The unavoidable jaunt would force him to stand down from his secret mission, and passivity in the face of need required a sense of self-restraint he was not known to possess.

He was a man of action, which meant his presence at court would likely not bode well for him...nor for the king.

CHAPTER THREE

At the king's castle, Ailsa still stood transfixed by the unexpected arrival of the captain of the king's guard to Princess Elizabeth's balcony doors. The soldier continued his slow, curious perusal of Elizabeth's coiffure. The princess seemed not to notice anything untoward in his regard, but Ailsa fought to manage the turmoil that roiled in her stomach at the possible consequences to come. The chance Ailsa had taken when she coerced the princess outside to watch the clan arrivals this morn slowly became wrapped in a distressed regret. The opportunity to catch a glimpse of her kinsmen and hoped-for saviors began to pale when compared to the dangers of the man who stood before her.

The princess retreated into her bedchamber, and Ailsa followed. Ailsa suppressed an outward shudder when she walked past the now-scowling captain. He turned his head to watch her move by, and his eyes held that familiar glint of arrogance and repressed lust they always seemed to have in her presence. Though he had groped and petted her inappropriately on more than one occasion, he had yet to force her to suffer his rutting intentions. Even so, the possible threat of a full taking oft hovered between them as it did now.

The man was cruel and vicious. He had a mean streak that mayhap suited a man of war, but he lacked the finesse needed to adjust in severity the way he handled the simple transgressions that were wont to occur within the castle. Ailsa made sure to avoid him whenever possible. His presence unfailingly made her skin crawl, and she had to push down a sudden wave of nausea at his current untimely appearance.

"Good afternoon, Captain," the princess said from her antechamber. "To what do I owe this early visit?"

The captain returned the princess's greeting with a solemn nod afore once again spearing her hair with a perplexed stare.

A crease formed in the center of the princess's forehead when she noticed the look on the captain's face. "Is aught amiss?" She looked down to verify her bosom was decently covered, then, in an age-old feminine gesture, lifted her hand to smooth her hair.

"Ah, no, Your Highness." He cleared his throat awkwardly. "I, um, was sent to fetch you. The Duke of Lennox has arrived, and the king would like to make introductions."

"Excellent!" She offered her hand with a glowing smile. "Would you be so kind as to escort me?"

The captain looked aghast and made no move to accept the proffered hand.

Ailsa hastened forward. "Princess, I need but a moment to attend your hair. The wind—"

An impatient royal hand waved her off. "Nonsense. There was barely any wind this morn." Elizabeth again ran a hand against the tightly pinned mass atop her head. "I feel not a hair out of place."

Heat rolled up Ailsa's neck. The captain gave her an odd look. Even with her brown skin, she was certain he noticed her building flush.

Luckily, the princess spoke and diverted his attention. "Come, monsieur." Her attempt at flirty French was backed by an added coyness to her smile. "We mustn't keep the duke waiting."

Usually one to entertain the princess's flirting, the captain stepped back from the petite hand that reached for his arm. "Nay, Princess. I think you ought let Anne attend your hair. I'm not sure who assisted you afore, but you are in need of…of…"

While he struggled for a delicate way to make his point, Ailsa cringed internally and tried desperately to keep the chagrin of having been found out from showing on her face.

"Why, Anne assisted me this morn. She insisted I watch the clans' arrivals and always—" The princess broke off upon noticing Ailsa's expression.

From the princess's widening eyes, Ailsa had failed to shield her feelings from the self-serving discernment sometimes gifted to the conceited when their ego was at stake.

Elizabeth ran to the vanity table and peered into the looking-glass. The horrified scream she released should have rattled the stone walls of the castle into rubble. She whirled to face Ailsa. "You…you… How *could* you?"

Ailsa racked her brain for a good excuse, but her normally witty tongue failed her. She glanced at the captain, afraid he'd intervene on the princess's behalf. His brand of admonishment was not one she wanted to suffer ever again.

Stepping over to the vanity table, she picked up the princess's brush. "It is but a small matter to fix, Your Highness. I simply ran out of time earlier, with you wanting to be on the balcony afore Lady Sophie."

At the mention of Lady Sophie, Elizabeth's cheeks turned a bright, blotchy red. Ailsa quickly realized her mistake. She saw the moment the princess remembered Lady Sophie had seen her on the balcony this morn and had thus gotten a good look at her coiffure.

Ailsa raised her arm to block the crystal implement tray the princess snatched from the vanity and swung toward her face. Not to be outdone, the princess swung her other hand and caught Ailsa firmly across the opposite cheek with a hard slap that echoed through the chamber. Ailsa's head snapped sideways, and she palmed the throbbing skin of the abused cheek. She'd seen the hand coming but dared not duck or avoid the hit. She had no intention of letting the princess break glass against her face, but if she had also avoided the slap, the princess's anger would have led to a beating with results much worse than the pulsing pain now coursing across her cheekbone.

"How dare you humiliate me thus." The indignant wench flounced onto the vanity stool, fury making her nearly break the crystal tray nonetheless when she slammed it against the table. "Undo this mess this instant and be quick about it. I will not have Lady Sophie upstage me before the duke."

With a stiff spine, Ailsa walked to the princess's side, put down the brush, and commenced with the removal of the pins holding up the matty coiffure she had created earlier.

Elizabeth dismissed the captain with a wave of her hand. "Captain, you may await me in the hall. I shall be but a moment."

'Twould take more than a moment, Ailsa knew—as no doubt did the princess—to make the royal's hair presentable, but Ailsa dared not correct the misstatement. She also dared not look at the captain, who had been watching her closely upon learning it was her idea, and not the princess's, to watch the clans' entries.

He stopped beside her afore he exited and whispered for only her hearing, "I will attend to you later."

An uncontrollable shudder overtook Ailsa, but she fought not to let the captain see her distress. He took too much pride in the torment he meted out, and this time, he might not stop at a beating or inappropriately wandering hands. After her last transgression, he'd warned he had a sure way of teaching her to remember her place if she could not be trusted to behave suitably for her privileged station. 'Twas common knowledge that many of the enslaved females belowstairs were oft put upon against their will to service males of the household. Ailsa had no intention of being added to their ranks. Once such abuse began, 'twould never stop.

Focused on her task, Ailsa internally vowed there would be no "later" with the captain. She would make sure she was nowhere he could find her for the rest of the day and so indispensable to Elizabeth upon the princess's evening toilet she would not be given leave outside the princess's chambers come the rise of the moon.

She was now in a precarious position. She'd taken a chance this day with her scouting of the clan arrivals and attention to where each clan would camp during the festivities. Her clansmen had yet to arrive, so she had nowhere to run should her plans go awry this early. Even when they did arrive, 'twould be days afore they could depart with her in tow.

Doubt in the viability of her plan threatened to overtake her, but she took a deep breath and kept it at bay. She had not endured humiliation and demeaning treatment for three years to give up now. She was made of stronger mettle than that.

The rest of the clans would arrive over the next few days. She would scope out her kinsmen's location when she could and be ready when it was time. Her satchel was already packed, including the tartan sash she'd salvaged from the rubbish her personal clothing had been tossed into years ago. She'd hid the sentimental garment all this time, wrapped in a worn, rough blanket that no one in the king's household would ever deign to touch, let alone wrap around their bodies.

The leader of the captives' detail had ordered her possessions destroyed upon her capture. They hadn't believed her when she had indicated she was a free Highland lass. No one had wanted to acknowledge her ties to a specific clan and, whether intentionally or by chance, destruction had been decreed for the one bit of proof that might back up her claim. When she had finally been paraded into the grand hall for inspection, those present had easily adjudged her for sale or barter due simply to the color of her skin.

Ailsa took another deep breath. She would not riddle out the circumstances surrounding her current situation any time this day. She had tried, to no avail, to do so over many a sleepless night as she stared at the ceiling from her lumpy bedding.

Why her?

What had she done to rile the God of this land such that he would leave her to suffer the indignities she had faced since her captivity?

She had waited three long years for this moment, a nearly infallible chance to reclaim her freedom and escape the daily subjugation to dehumanization and debasement. To finally shake off the anger she harbored for once again being abandoned and left to fend for herself as if she were worth nothing. One day, she would change that. When she finally returned home, she would rise to the respected status of the laird's chief healer, someone whose worth was without question. She had plotted and planned prior escapes, but an opportunity this perfect and this grand had never presented itself afore.

She would keep her head about her and find a way to do this all again on the morrow and the next day and the next if necessary. What she waited for was coming. She knew not which clans would arrive on what day or at what hour, but she knew one day her liberation would arrive with them. All she need do was last—*survive*—a little longer, and that emancipation was hers.

Her brush hand faltered against the princess's tangles as the captain's words returned to her.

Aye, freedom was hers, unless the captain got ahold of her or figured out her plan first.

• • •

Five days after the altercation with the princess over the matted coiffure, Ailsa could barely hear the clip of horses' hoofs against the stone courtyard above the din of gathered spectators. The increased crowd gawked and gabbed about the influx of more of the fiercest warriors in the land. She had found ways over the last few days to sneak glances at clan arrivals through the window in the west turret, but yester morn, she'd been spied by a royal guard. She dared not use the turret window again for fear a guardsman, mayhap even the captain himself, would be waiting there to seize her.

Instead, she took a risk and headed for the princess's balcony without permission or supervision. 'Twas a gambit she would not usually make, but today the last of the participating clans would arrive, and she had yet to locate her kin. She eased through the balcony doors, careful not to wake the sleeping highness lest she suffer a repeat of the week's earlier nonending rounds of humiliation.

Ailsa gently touched the still-tender spot on her cheek where the princess had slapped her. Alas, the princess had not been satisfied with the single blow she'd landed afore meeting with the duke. She had made Ailsa pay for the hair affront in small ways throughout the remainder of that day. The pettiness had only made Ailsa more determined to escape.

The one saving grace from the public hell she had endured at the hands of the princess was that the chit had been so bent on her revenge she'd kept Ailsa too busy for the captain to waylay her. Ailsa still cringed at the thought of what would have happened if he had managed to get her alone—what still *could* happen. A slight shudder overtook her at the disconcerting image.

One more day and night to get through afore she was completely out of harm's way. On the morrow, the tournament would start. The festivities would be such that the captain would be otherwise occupied making sure no guests overstepped their bounds with the king.

Ailsa peeked over her shoulder to verify the princess still slept, then softly pulled the double doors closed behind her. She searched the courtyard for the guards currently on duty to verify that the captain, or the lieutenant who was his primary spy, were nowhere below afore she eased to the front corner of the balcony. Careful to stay in the shadows, she stood at the waist-high wall and slowly surveyed the courtyard.

The crowd was larger today. More spectators had arrived in time for the feast, and several clans had brought women and children. Currently, it was the arrival of a clan draped in colors of rich forest green interlaced with sea blue that drew the most attention. They made a spectacular sight as they entered the castle grounds with nearly double the number of warriors of any other clan present, but they were not the clan she sought.

Her eyes searched past the gates behind the large contingent of warriors. When the view revealed no other approaching clan, Ailsa quickly looked in the opposite direction. And there they were!

With a tight chest, she fought back a shout of triumph and the flood of joyous tears that threatened. She'd almost dared not continue to believe this moment would come, but there they were, draped in magnificent Connery colors. Her salvation.

I'm going home, her heart whispered.

As she had that thought, a Connery soldier looked back and then up. He locked eyes with her. He'd been among the soldiers responsible for the Connery laird's protection three years ago. She remembered his face. After a long moment, he looked away without a hint of reciprocal recognition. The oversight hurt, but her course remained the same, so she strained to see the direction her kin headed as they progressed beyond the open courtyard. She needed to be able to find them later.

Affected chattering from women directly below the

balcony momentarily drew Ailsa's attention. Something had them all atwitter. Distracted, she followed the women's gazes to the massive army still filing in through the gates. Up front, next to an imposing soldier with sun-kissed, deep tan skin and long, brown hair that flowed loosely about his face, rode a warrior with a complexion to rival the richest brown of the sturdy yew trees of the Scottish woodlands. Highlanders were known for their height and girth, but even for a Highlander, this warrior's size was impressive.

He sat slightly taller on the back of his steed than did his companion. The dark, twisted locs of his hair hung behind his shoulders, secured at his nape with a tied leather cord. He made quite an impression dressed in battle gear, with a sword sheathed at his side and a shield displaying a massive oak tree attached to his saddle.

Ailsa had tended many warriors during her time as a village healer. Several had been some of the fittest of Clan Connery. Yet, as he approached astride his stallion of solid, brilliant black, the unknown warrior presented the most extraordinary sight of strength, power, and... *danger*...she had ever seen.

Gooseflesh pebbled her forearms at the unsettling thought.

The warrior's horse trotted along the path and carried the warrior directly beneath the balcony where Ailsa stood, giving her a better view of his face. A thin layer of facial hair framed his mouth and covered his lower jaw. The tight beard gave him a handsomely rugged look, but the fierce frown he sported tempered the overall effect to make him appear foreboding and unapproachable.

His body language said he'd rather be anywhere but here, which was an odd impression for her to get. Her ability to read the Highland male had clearly been impaired during her stay in Stirling Castle amongst royals, titled gents, and males raised within the surroundings of the nearby capital. In Ailsa's experience, most warriors tended to bask in any opportunity to prove their prowess. Surely, he, too, would find the competitions to his liking. Men were all the same, and warriors were worse than most.

She heard several of the women below voice consternation that the "barbarian" warrior would be allowed to compete in the tournament. Others made no effort to hide their womanly fascination with the size of his hands and the powerfulness of his thighs. Ailsa rolled her eyes at the silly, girlish prattle, but her gaze automatically slid to the massive thighs under discussion, both of which peeked beneath the risen hem of his dress kilt. The man was certainly solidly built. When his horse stopped, her gaze roamed slowly up to the large hand lightly grasping the reins, then up his forearms to the bulge of his biceps.

He dismounted beneath her, and his muscles rippled with the easy exertion.

Her breath caught. *Oh, my sweet Lord…*

His head jerked in her direction, and he speared her with an inquisitive stare. His gaze traveled slowly over her face, down her bosom, all the way to her waist. Blocked by the wall from seeing more, his gaze returned to hers.

"Nay, lass, but close." The rich, deep tone of his voice laced the arrogant remark with naughty suggestion.

Her hand flew to her throat in horror. Had she expressed that thought aloud?

Trapped by piercing dark eyes, she felt the tiny bumps on her skin return and spread, but this time they had little to do with apprehension from a sensed danger, at least not the mortally hazardous kind. The look of appreciation in his eyes, like he'd seen through her clothing to the bare flesh beneath, made heat suffuse her face and spread along the same route as the pebbling of her skin. Decorum mandated she step back into the bedchamber or at least look away, but she found it impossible not to stare back into eyes so dark that, from this distance, she could not see the distinction of pupils.

A spark ignited. His look became a physical touch that burned a central path through her fluttering belly to her core. Her dismay deepened. She knew enough about the human body to recognize her increasing temperature had less to do with the realization the warrior may have heard her involuntary utterance and more to do with a sensual curiosity that could get a proper lass in the kind of trouble that ruined reputations. And he'd caused it all with just one look and four words from his honey-laced voice.

When she failed to look away, his eyes narrowed.

In question? In challenge? As intimidation?

She knew not, but regardless of his intent, she did not look away. Despite her chagrin, she would not be intimidated or cower before him.

Her hand dropped to the top of the wall ledge to brace herself, and she inadvertently brushed the huge vase of flowers the princess insisted be maintained fresh on the balcony during spring and summer. The vase tilted over the edge. She grabbed for it and managed to halt its near crash below, but its contents spilled over the wall. The warrior easily sidestepped the petaled deluge, but a well-dressed spectator was not so spry.

Drenched, the spectator shouted in outrage and glanced up. She shot a quick look behind her to make certain the commotion had not awakened the princess. The last thing she needed was to be caught where she had no permission to be.

Thanks to the unexpected distraction caused by the warrior, Ailsa's venture had quickly gone from risky endeavor to near mission of doom. She silently chastised herself. She had never been one of those lasses who giggled and played coy when a man was around. She had certainly never been clumsy around one, so she was puzzled by her reaction to the warrior.

Catching a man and marriage had never been her goal. She would stand on her own two feet. Once she became the head healer of Clan Connery, she'd have the respect of her people and the protection of the laird. She wouldn't need a husband. Her mother had never had one because her father hadn't bothered to stick around. The two of them had managed on their own without a man. She, too, could do so.

Although her mother had passed, her spirit and teachings lived on in Ailsa. She need not settle for the lot of the other clan women. She would not be subjected to having a man rule over her or selfishly use her body to appease his physical needs or demand her unquestioning obedience as if she had no autonomy or thoughts of her own.

Men could not be trusted to stay in any event.

Women like her did not earn courtship from men of good families or respectable occupations or positions in clan leadership. She had not the breeding of high-born ladies, or a demeanor for dutifully subordinating to the whims of males, or the sensibilities for running a prestigious household. She was not competent in the manners and delicate behaviors that made men of honor pine to have her bear and raise their children. She could expect no more than to toil as some man's cook, housekeeper, and broodmare. If she must toil, Ailsa would do so independently for herself and herself alone.

Such independence sounded earth-shatteringly good, but first she had to escape.

Focus, Ailsa.

She needed to pay attention to the men of her clan so she could follow them to their camp location on the morrow, not stand here like some wench fixated on a warrior whose tartan colors she did not recognize. But try as she might, she was unable to pull her gaze away from the blazing eyes and cocky attitude wrapped in the virile package standing below her.

The Highlander promised a whole lot of trouble. For someone.

Trouble she herself could ill afford. She had enough to worry about with the disturbance the soaked gentleman was about to let loose. His sputtered complaints grew louder and drew more and more attention. Such adverse attention risked spilling over onto her and putting her life in imminent peril.

She took a precautionary step back.

CHAPTER FOUR

Inan MacNeill studied the frown on Kallum's face and shook his head. "You're frightening the lasses again, cousin. Try not to cause a fracas even afore the competitions have begun." He tried to keep his face neutral, but the flicker at the edge of his lips gave away his amusement.

Not all the lasses, Kallum thought as he continued to stare at the brazen creature on the western balcony.

Dragging his eyes away from the lass who, by her manner of dress, appeared to be one of the king's enslaved servants, Kallum returned his gaze straight ahead and ignored the tittering and cowering women gathered along the procession route.

"I care not for the fright of simpleton lasses nor what fracas it might wrought." This was the last place he wanted to be, and his cousin well knew were it not for his vehement request, Kallum would be back at the keep, putting the soldiers of Clan MacNeill through grueling battle exercises. "And my look would not be so off-putting if the mongers did not stare so."

'Twas not only the women who stared. Kallum had caught the curious glances of the local male villagers and the gentlemen amongst the spectators, including the one his balcony lass had given a bath. 'Twas demeaning to be considered a spectacle in your own land. From the time he was a child, except amongst Inan's immediate family, he had never been allowed to forget he was different.

Not quite one of the clan.

Not a true Highlander in the eyes of many.

Never quite good enough.

If not for Inan's early comradery, he may never have known what it meant to have a mate unerringly in your corner. Even as a lad, Inan had had a strong sense of fair and foul and had stood between him and those who would torment him. With an honorable spirit, Inan could never stand by at the mistreatment of another. Those who crossed the wrong line learned early that a negative word from Inan to his father, the laird, would see them severely punished or, worse, their families put beyond the stone walls around MacNeill keep and its surrounding village.

The fair-skinned Scots of the clan eventually had accepted Kallum's place in the laird's extended family—at least, in public—out of personal survival, but Kallum knew he was not considered a true Highlander by many due to his African bloodlines. Though grossly outnumbered, his mother's people had been in country nigh on a century. Many served in honorable professions like musicians and soldiers and seamstresses, even within Clan MacNeill. Nevertheless, many still treated them as outsiders.

He had resented the sideways looks and different treatment as a child. He resented them still. He glanced around. As he had predicted, he could count the number of non-MacNeill people who looked like him on one hand. And that count included the lass on the balcony.

Unable to stop himself, he glanced back up. She was still there, her gaze steady and strong. What struck him even more than her stare was her manner. She stood tall and proud. Her hair was plaited in a thick, dark braid that hung over her shoulder and fell past her bosom. Though she had since moved farther into the shadows, she had stood forward enough earlier for him to make out her features.

She had a lush, full mouth in a face of breathtaking brown mixed with a dash of bronze that oft signaled a mixed parentage. She had eyes an odd color he couldn't quite make out and high cheekbones. One cheek looked slightly darker than the other, which made him ponder whether it was a natural defect in her skin or she had suffered injury.

Intent on determining which, Kallum squinted to get a better look. Her head tilted in question at his continued scrutiny, but she didn't look away. On further thought, she had the willful demeanor more of a royal than a servant, and he considered whether she might be the progeny of one of the king's mistresses.

Inan sighed beside him, which drew Kallum's attention back to their conversation.

"You know many are not used to seeing one of your lineage prepared to do battle and in possession of a stallion such as yours. You have a station well above most *dubh* men of the land. For many, 'tis still an unusual sight to behold."

Kallum's hand tightened on the reins of his steed as he led him toward the stalls where they would draw their lots for the contests. "Then mayhap they should stop forcing those of my lineage into servitude without pay or end so they are free to rise to a station such as mine."

"Do not start this again, cousin. We've been over it. Scotland is not yet prepared to take issue with the enterprises of Portugal. Our king is content to accept the ill-gotten gains of pirate raids and put those liberated from the bowels of Portuguese ships into service for his benefit and the benefit of his kind. We are here to compete in his tournament, not to start a war over politics." Inan glanced over with a stern brow. "I'd appreciate you not putting me in a position to be at odds with the king. We have enough on our hands with the burgeoning divisions in the Highlands. I cannot take on the monarch as well." Inan stopped, and a tense moment passed between them. "Even for you."

They had indeed had this conversation afore. Kallum took issue with most captives who were discovered on slave trade ships not actually being liberated. His mother had fled her own enslavement after one such "liberation," him but a tiny seed within her womb. She'd been alone with no one to champion her and had nearly died trying. She'd firmly instilled in him that every man—or woman—had the right to live free.

If Inan knew what Kallum did on occasion to make that happen, the risks currently facing the clan would get worse. Inan had grave responsibilities to manage. Kallum did not want to increase his cousin's burden or endanger his position with the king. For that reason, he would behave as he must for his kinsmen and future laird while on the king's land, but the constraint sat heavy with him.

"Don't look so stern. It's just a few days. I vow we will stay no longer than necessary upon end of the tournament." Inan glanced his way, then frowned at his non-changing expression. "Forsooth! You have been grumpier than usual this past fortnight. Mayhap you have need for that maiden of your own after all. You seem to have been without female comfort of late."

"You need not worry yourself about my needs. My comforts have been just fine and quite plenty *of late*."

Inan gave a short laugh. "Yeah, which is why you were ogling that bonnie lass on the balcony."

Leave it to the wretch to notice him noticing her. "I wasn't ogling."

Inan chuckled. "Ah, but no denial that she be bonnie. So, you were indeed drawn to her beauty."

Kallum's lips tightened. He had not initially been drawn to the lass's looks, though there was no denying she was strikingly beautiful.

She had spoken.

He'd been surprised to distinctly hear her feminine voice over the noise of the crowd. It had floated to him like a soft siren call. When he caught her staring at him with a look of inquisitive surprise rather than the expected animus, his curiosity had peaked. His interest had not taken a lustful turn. Leastways, not immediately and not more than a teeny, tiny smidgen. He had not been lying about his physical needs. He hadn't visited the outer village recently, but he had no pressing need of a lass to give him ease.

Even as he tried to convince himself of that untruth, his mind returned to the mystery woman, and, thanks to Inan, his thoughts now fully pursued a less-than-gentlemanly path. The thought of her bold stare made him wonder if she brought that brazenness to everything she did and caused a stirring beneath his kilt.

Bloody hell. This was a distraction he did not need.

He looked up again. Her attention was focused on a royal guard who frowned at her from across the courtyard. From the markings on his uniform, he was the king's captain. When Kallum looked back to the balcony, the lass was gone.

Given his commitment to mind his manners while at the castle, mayhap that was for the best. The less he knew about the lass the better. The shadow on her cheek suggested her life at Stirling Castle held dark moments. He should not think on who she was or what she was being forced to be. Such thoughts would only tempt him to do things he'd promised Inan not to do.

He walked on in silence. Mysterious eyes, thick hair, and bronze-brown skin remained foremost on his mind. He pondered whether he would cross paths again with the lass of the defiant stare afore the competitions ended.

And if he did… He gave a side glance at Inan's profile. Would he be able to keep his promise to his cousin?

• • •

A loud cheer went up from the crowd. It was the final day of the tournament, and Ailsa watched the arrogant, brown-skinned warrior duck under the arms of the Donnelly clan's giant. As big as the warrior was, the Donnelly man was bigger. She winced when, afore the warrior could clear the Donnelly, the giant grabbed the warrior's right wrist, yanked him around at the shoulder like a child's doll made of old rags, then tossed him to the ground.

Undaunted, the warrior grabbed for his shoulder and stumbled to his feet. Expecting a look of anger, Ailsa was amazed to find amusement in the warrior's eyes. He acted as if he had enjoyed his short sojourn in the dirt.

He probably did, Ailsa thought.

After all, she'd surmised the other day that he, like every other warrior she'd known, would likely thrill in the barbaric games set up for them to show their manliness. He'd had the look of a beast of war, so she had not been surprised to see him step out for this final match of the competitions. The winner of this contest would be tournament champion and take home a fat purse of coins and precious food staples like salt. Both men were taking seriously their duty to win for their clan.

The giant swiftly attacked, and the warrior, his right arm pressed close to his side, ducked under the big man's arms afore they swung shut in an attempt to grab him. The clansmen dressed in his matching plaid of green and blue—of the Clan MacNeill, she'd learned at the opening ceremonies—sent up a loud cheer. The giant came round for another pass. Again, the warrior managed to avoid the grasp. If he ended up in those arms a second time, the man would surely crush him.

Ailsa watched the MacNeill warrior's face and could almost see the moment a plan formed in his mind. He was faster and more agile than the bigger man, and the man's frustration with every missed pass was evident. The warrior increased his evasive dance. This time he intentionally taunted the huge soldier by weaving close enough to entice the man to go for him but bobbed out of reach afore he could be caught. With each successful pass by the MacNeill, his clan sent up another loud cheer.

The giant began to tire. He leaned to one side as he

walked. The more he slowed, the louder the MacNeill clan became. Shouts of "Kallum! Kallum! Kallum!" rent the air.

The name suited the warrior. It spoke of vigor and toughness and will, and that will showed in undeniable force. The amount of pain he must feel from his injured shoulder had to be severe, but he gave no indication that he suffered any discomfort. With each chant, the energy of his kin visibly shored him up, and he displayed an impressive reserve of strength. He fought with determination, each move designed to wear down his opponent until he could get the upper hand in the wrestling match.

Ailsa couldn't help but admire his fortitude, and silently, she, too, began to cheer him on. Since none of the Connery warriors she'd watched over the last few days had prevailed to fight this day, she wanted the MacNeill warrior to win.

The giant had cut down each of his prior opponents in archery and swordplay. He had been vicious and ruthless in his competitions, more so than she thought necessary. She understood that, in true battles of war, a soldier must do everything he could to survive and win. But in these competitions, a certain amount of courtesy and soldier's honor should be expected.

Whereas every other sword contest had ended with the bested soldier yielding to his combatant, the giant had unnecessarily fatally wounded his last opponent. Amidst a merciless flurry of parries and thrusts, the giant had severed his opponent's arm. The wounded man had spilt his life's blood on the arena floor afore the royal healer could cauterize the gaping wound. It had been a grisly sight. She had no doubt, with this being the championship bout, the giant intended to inflict as much pain as possible on the MacNeill afore he closed out the match.

Ailsa never took sides in these contests. If her presence wasn't required as attendant to the princess, she wouldn't even watch. Today, uncharacteristically, she found herself hoping the dark side to Kallum MacNeill she had sensed the other day included a strong sense of self-preservation.

The distinctive sound of rhythmic stomping began to blend seamlessly with the chants of Kallum's kin. The MacClaren clan, whose warrior had been sent to his death by the giant, were sounding their support. So surprised by this was the MacNeill warrior that he was nearly captured into the vise-like grip he'd been avoiding so studiously. When the giant breezed past him, Kallum gave him an elbow shove to the back. The big man went stumbling and had to grasp the wall of the lower seating area to maintain his feet.

The evasive maneuver, coupled with the supportive chants of the MacClaren clan, apparently snapped the last bit of patience the giant had. He let out a frustrated growl, grabbed the closest man in the stands by his neck, and nearly yanked him from his perch into the arena. With the unsuspecting man dangling upside down over the wall, the giant reached to the man's side and snatched his sword from its sheath. He tossed the gent back into the stands and faced the MacNeill with a smirk. The wrestling competition was over. He planned to end this battle with the meet of steel, but only one opponent had a sword.

In sync with the rest of the crowd, Ailsa let out a gasp of alarm.

Kallum looked at the king to see if the monarch would call foul, but the king merely gestured for the contest to continue.

The men of Kallum's clan roared in outrage and jumped to their feet. The soldier who had ridden in next to Kallum reached for his sword, but Kallum dissuaded him with a subtle shake of his head. Without thought, Ailsa took an unplanned step forward.

What was he thinking?

Without a sword, he was no match for the giant, especially with his shoulder disadvantage. Did all that brawn come with a dearth of brains? He needed to take his comrade's sword.

Her movement caught his eye. He glanced in her direction. His hands tightened into fists at his side, and a look of sheer fury overtook his face. He straightened to his full height, then slid his gaze from her to the monarch. The king raised a brow but otherwise made no indication of what he expected from the end of this match.

A MacClaren warrior slowly stood. Careful to keep a side-eye on his now-armed opponent, Kallum watched the MacClaren unsheathe his sword with exaggerated intensity. The man turned to his chief. In silent petition, he raised his sword in a vertical line, the hilt grasped close to the center of his chest with the flat sides facing outward and against the tip of his nose. The chief, without taking his eyes off Kallum, gave a drawn-out, dignified nod.

Not quite sure what had just happened, Ailsa watched a slow grin spread across Kallum MacNeill's face. The grin held no joy but rather a diabolical resolve that sent a cold wave of apprehension scurrying along Ailsa's spine.

The Donnelly giant stood on the opposite side of the arena and brandished his stolen sword with a flurry of showy flourishes. He finished with one last swing above his head, then charged Kallum with the sword raised high, his intent clearly to slash the MacNeill in two from the head down.

Kallum took off running toward the big man. When he was a few steps away, he slid toward the giant's feet. Realizing what was about to happen, the giant raised a foot and tried to leap over the MacNeill, but Kallum grabbed the ankle of the raised foot and sent the giant reeling.

With a battle cry loud enough to disturb the ancestors sleeping permanently below the ocean waters they had chosen over captivity, the MacNeill sprang to his feet and continued his sprint toward the MacClaren soldier. The soldier tossed his sword into the air. Without breaking stride, Kallum plucked the weapon from the sky. He pivoted toward the recovering giant, twirled the sword twice with a double flick of his wrist, then took a battle stance.

A collective clamor of surprise arose from the spectators, and the king vaulted to his feet. Ailsa gripped the back of the princess's chair with one hand and fisted the fabric of her dress with the other. Why the MacNeill accepted the sword of the MacClaren and not that of his kin was a mystery to her, but his stance made clear he was prepared to face the giant thrust for thrust and parry for parry. Based upon the look in his eyes, he was quite content to make this a battle to the death...if need be.

Sensing the momentousness of the unexpected

turnabout, the remaining crowd leapt to their feet. Cheers, chants, and calls for violence became deafening. The bloodthirsty lust of the people made Ailsa's stomach churn. She did not relish the thought of watching another man die. The knots in her stomach tightened as the duel raged on. The din of metal on metal, the roars of excitement when someone's champion took an advantage, the vicious looks on the faces of the two battling men, all combined to fray her normally staunch nerves.

Then the tide of the battle turned.

The MacNeill got a foot behind the giant's ankle and toppled him to the ground. Giving the man no time to recover, Kallum dropped his full weight onto the giant's chest and pressed the man's shoulder to the ground with one hand. He used the other to lay the blade of his sword against the big man's throat. "Do you yield?"

"Nay." The giant bucked in an attempt to unseat Kallum.

Kallum's arm muscles bulged as he added more pressure to the sword. A line of blood formed on the giant's throat, and rivulets of red trickled down into the dirt.

"Do. You. *Yield?*" The angry words were more demand than question.

The giant refused to yield nonetheless. "Nay!" He struggled harder beneath Kallum and pushed against the hilt of the slicing blade with all his might but to no avail.

When the giant's struggles finally weakened, the MacNeill lifted the sword and slammed the giant in the face with the pommel. The big man fell unconscious.

The MacNeill warrior sat on his conquest for several moments, heaving breaths in and out. When he finally rose to face the monarch, the crowd erupted into cheers and applause. Unmoved by the adulation, Kallum advanced toward the monarch's perch, looking every bit as if he'd like to run the king through with the borrowed sword he still held. The king simply engaged in a slow, regal clap while Kallum approached.

Everyone was so intent on watching what was to transpire between the king and the MacNeill warrior, only Ailsa seemed to notice the Donnelly giant had begun to move. The big man struggled slowly to his feet. He swayed unsteadily back and forth, then silently reached for his sword on the ground. He missed and nearly tumbled back into the dirt. With his disrupted equilibrium, it took him two more tries afore he successfully grasped the hilt of the stolen weapon. On unsteady but stealthy legs, he approached Kallum from behind and lifted his sword.

"Nay!" Ailsa rushed forward. Her throat burned from the piercing shout carried away by the roar of the crowd. She stared in horror at the sword the Donnelly aimed at Kallum's back.

Kallum spun, feinted to the left to avoid the giant's wobbling sword, and thrust his own sword through the man's chest. The big man dropped his weapon and grasped at the blade upon which he was impaled. Kallum grabbed the back of the man's neck for leverage and shoved the blade deeper. The MacNeill did not release the man until he slumped to his death with Kallum's borrowed blade protruding from his chest.

A hush fell over the crowd. Kallum MacNeill stood with hands fisted at his sides and stared at his kill.

Slowly, he turned to face the monarch again and await his judgment.

Ailsa, hands trembling, returned to her place behind the princess's chair. She twisted her hands into the folds of her skirt to subdue their tremors and stood outwardly calm but inwardly unsettled. She, too, along with the crowd and the angry Donnellys, silently waited for the king to speak.

CHAPTER FIVE

Kallum stared at the lass whose expression had given him warning of the Donnelly man's attempt to stab him in the back. She was the brazen lass from the balcony, except today her beautiful face was mottled with bruises of various shades, and she had a blackened eye. Her upper lip had been split at some point, though that injury seemed to be healing. The anger he'd felt upon noticing her face midway through the wrestling contest, when she'd moved on the dais, returned. No man who considered himself a leader of people allowed women to be treated thus under any circumstance, and definitely not under his own roof. Clearly, the monarch ran his household without honor.

The king and his people had the audacity to call Highlanders barbarians. They disparaged the Gaelic language as crass and lower-class, then pushed English as the official, civilized language of the country. Highlanders were already forbidden to educate their children in Gaelic. The clan's offspring had to be sent to English schools in the Lowlands lest the chief risk forfeiture of clan lands.

Despite his royal blood, it was the king who was the heathen. The man was concerned only with his own pleasure and power. No matter the face he put forward to the people, the Highland leaders suspected the monarch truly wanted control of the Highlands. Recent laws attacking Highland language and traditions were but a ruse designed to accomplish the king's desires without initiating direct physical conflict with the clans. The man was a scoundrel.

When the king ceased his inane clapping and raised a golden goblet, Kallum felt no pride in being the recipient of the recognition.

"A toast to our champion." The king took a healthy sip of wine, then replaced the goblet on the table beside the raised ceremonial chair that had been placed at a height above all other seats. He stepped down from his perch and walked to the front of the stand. "You have done well, soldier. You are a credit to your clan, and I will make sure the victor's purse is delivered to your chief."

The king summoned a royal guard.

The guard approached the king, who whispered in his ear. The guard left the stands, presumably to retrieve the promised riches, or mayhap to summon a contingent of soldiers for Kallum's arrest.

Kallum awaited the fallout that would surely follow.

The riches would be delivered to the MacNeill laird. And him? Would he be delivered to the guard for execution? After all, he'd killed a man during tournament battle. The man had deserved to die for his cowardly act. That did not mean King James, who was known for his capricious nature and impetuous decisions, would not take the opportunity to weaken one of the stronger military clans by disposing of its army commander.

Inan must have had the same thought, for he appeared beside Kallum. He wore his sword in its sheath and held his lowered targe, emblazoned with the clan motto "*seas gu daingeann*," stand firm, above a massive oak tree. The MacNeill warriors all stood firm at their seats. Each also held his shield in one hand and sword in the other pointed toward the ground. 'Twould seem his clan intended to defend his life, but 'twas an act he could not allow his kin to undertake.

He had already tried to protect Inan from possible censure of the king by refusing to take his cousin's sword when the battle with the Donnelly warrior turned foul. If the king had seen fit to adjudge Kallum's arming of himself against tournament etiquette, then Inan would have been found equally guilty of any alleged act of MacNeill foul play. No such rebuke would be thought of the MacClaren, whose impromptu gesture could sensibly be attributed to a desire to secure retribution for his fallen kin.

Understanding such, Kallum would not now risk the lives of others simply because he had allowed the temper he oft failed to control to rule his actions at the most inopportune and public of moments. Whatever consequence he must face, he would do so alone. Allowing his soldiers to face the royal guard on the king's grounds would be naught but a losing battle.

The king gave Inan an indulgent smile. He, too, knew any attempt by the MacNeill army to hold off his guard would be futile, and retreat would be near impossible with Stirling Castle perched on its steep rise with only one way in or out.

When the royal guard returned, he handed the king a long, thin pouch. The king loosened the ties of the pouch and withdrew a dagger with a hilt encrusted in jewels. "'Twould seem you deserve to be doubly rewarded, MacNeill. You have proved yourself the valiant champion of my summer festival, and you have rid us of a soldier of a devious ilk who brought dishonor to my court." The king laid the dagger across the cloth pouch and cradled them chest high in both hands. "I believe your Christian name is Kallum?"

Kallum nodded.

"Kallum MacNeill, please accept this as my personal gift to you in token of my admiration for your prowess in battle and as a thank-you for taking care of the unpleasantness caused by the Donnelly warrior."

A hushed grumble echoed across the arena from the vicinity of the Donnelly clan, who began to chafe at the insult to their kinsman.

The king ignored the dissension and awaited Kallum's approach for the dagger. Kallum accepted the gift and bowed to His Majesty. The king motioned for him to wait and brought forth a young maiden with porcelain skin and long, chestnut-colored hair. Kallum outwardly reacted not to her approach or her appearance. Inwardly, he dreaded this moment and racked his brain for a way to turn down the king's female gift without pissing off Inan or making the king rethink his decision to let Kallum live. Not that the woman wasn't comely, but he could not condone rewarding a woman as a prize, as if she held no more importance than livestock. In truth, Kallum suspected the king placed more stock in his animals than he did his women.

Seeing Kallum's nonresponse to his offering, the king chuckled. "Methinks the warrior might prefer a lass of his own lineage." He motioned for the woman from the balcony to step forward.

Wide-eyed, she vehemently shook her head while taking several steps backward. The princess jumped up in protest, but the king waved the princess back into her seat. The petulant lass flopped into her chair, a grand pout distorting her face.

With impatience, the king insistently motioned the reluctant attendant forward. She stepped toward him as if marching toward her own execution.

The king took one look at her face, and an appalled grimace surfaced. "Oh my, I don't suppose this will do." He glanced at Kallum afore grasping the lass's chin and turning her face this way and that. "Tsk tsk, Anne. What a shame."

Even beneath the bruises, Kallum could see the flush of embarrassment rise across the lass's dusky cheeks. It took all his self-control not to jump over the dais and give the king a thorough thrashing. The public display was thoughtless and cruel. Kallum spoke not, but the discomfort from the pressure building in his clenched jaw caused his unoccupied hand to fist.

Inan stepped closer until their shoulders touched. His signal for Kallum to not do anything rash.

The king simply shrugged and released the lass. *Anne.* The name did not suit her.

She caught Kallum staring at her and notched up her chin, a look of censure in her eyes. The defiance had returned. Gone was the face of the woman concerned that a sword would imminently spear him in the back.

She had taken Kallum's silence as a sign of rejection of her, and for some reason, the rebuke stung. The realization annoyed him. He had learned to care little about what others thought of him. He lived his life by a code he did not violate, and those who did not appreciate his ways were of little concern to him. That this slip of a female could make him feel chagrin, when grown men could not, added an additional layer of volatility to his already brewing temper.

Anticipating her husband's desire to find Kallum another substitute with brown skin, the queen motioned a shy lass in the corner to come forward. The king grinned indulgently at the queen afore motioning the lass to stay put. The meek girl had skin of such a light hue she could be naught but of mixed lineage. The look on her face suggested she'd faint if a man so much as glanced at her, but 'twas not her timidity that motivated the king to spare her from the fate of prize. From the expression on the king's face, his interest in her was decidedly personal. The petite lass was young enough to be his daughter—younger, mayhap—but the look he gave her was unmistakably not fatherly.

The monarch was known for his indiscretions. Rumors abounded that several of those indiscretions may have occurred with men, but the queen's gambit suggested she saw fit to eliminate some of her competition, albeit female in nature. Since Her Majesty's ploy had failed, she now sat with a pout as petulant as her daughter's.

The whole scene made Kallum want to exit the king's court and never return. When the king finally brought forth another lass of his kind and stood her next to the pale-skinned woman with the chestnut hair, Kallum began to turn away. Inan's firm hand on the wrist that rested at his side stopped him.

He glanced at his future laird and saw the warning in his eyes: *Do not do anything to put me at odds with the king.* Inan's earlier request—*order*—still resonated, and this silent renewal made Kallum chafe all the more.

Thoroughly reminded, Kallum stood his ground.

"Well, warrior, which is your choice?" The king waved a hand over the females.

Kallum took another look at his cousin, and a petulant impulse came upon him. Still looking at Inan, he replied, "Both."

The shocked look on Inan's face soothed some of Kallum's irritation.

The king laughed and gave a staccato double clap. "Indeed!"

The smirk on the king's face conveyed the naughty turn his thoughts had taken at Kallum's request to have two women. At once. But Kallum did not care.

"Why, both it is." The king gestured to the next guard on hand and whispered instructions.

Kallum spun to exit the arena.

Inan grabbed his arm. "Both?" The quizzical expression on his cousin's face was almost comical. "How did you go from 'the last thing I need is a maiden' to 'both'? What are you going to do with *two* women?"

Kallum gave a wicked grin. "They are not for me, cousin. They are yours. All yours."

"What!" Inan began to sputter. "Y-you are out of your mind!"

"No, but I *am* out of here. Make sure the ladies get back to MacNeill land safely. I have something to take care of. I'll meet you back at the keep in a few days." He stormed away, ignoring Inan calling his name.

He had been given instructions not to do anything to anger the king while the MacNeills were on castle grounds. He had fulfilled that mandate so far, and he would wait until all his kinsmen left this eve to make his next move. But he would be back.

What he had planned would undoubtedly push the king way past anger and possibly land Kallum with a price on his head, but he couldn't ignore his calling any longer. He had spent the last five years secretly liberating enslaved people across the land. After what he'd just witnessed of the treatment of the enslaved at Stirling Castle, he could no longer justify exempting the king's holdings from his late-night campaigns.

If not for the reaction of a bold lass with a face that used to look like a goddess's, he would now lay dead or dying on the arena floor. He took one last look over his shoulder at the bruised yet proud descendant of African queens. She stood stoically behind the princess, who was now placated because her personal attendant had been spared. Kallum silently admired the lass's bravado and poise. Somehow in her eyes, he was a pariah who had been part of her public humiliation. The disapproval did not sit well with him.

The woman had saved his life. Though she may not think highly of him at the moment, he'd be damned if he let her spend the rest of hers enslaved.

He continued his exit from the arena, a singular thought foremost on his mind: this eve would be the last she served the royals against her will. That is, as long as the last-minute operation he had in mind went according to plan.

• • •

Kallum stood beneath a dark sky and adjusted the black face covering he'd pulled over his head to make sure only his eyes showed through the large opening in the front. He pulled his dark, hooded cloak tighter around his face and shoulders to shield further his visage from the glimmer of moonlight that trickled across the castle grounds. The face covering and hood served to mask his identity.

He hunched into the shrouded corners of the outer castle walls and stood outside the back door, counting the runaways he was to shepherd to the exchange point a little over a day's travel outside Stirling. There, he'd transfer them to an escort who would convey them to freedom across the border into England. He counted ten captives in total, eight men and two women. The bruised maiden from the dais this morn was not amongst those he counted. He surveyed the group and took another count.

He looked to the man who had put himself forth as the leader of this flock. "Where is the other lass?"

The man, known by the name Jeremiah, merely stared at him with a puzzled look.

"The one who stood behind the princess in the arena this morn?" Kallum glanced about.

Was she just slow, or had she gotten intercepted?

A look of dawning comprehension spread across Jeremiah's face. "That one is not one of us."

The response startled Kallum. "What do you mean she is not one of you? She is a captive, is she not?"

"Aye, but she is kept separate even from those of us who worked inside the castle walls."

Kallum considered these words with a creased brow. "And for that, you'd leave her behind? Are you a man of such low worth?" A harsh sound, half frustration half anger, escaped Kallum's throat afore he could consciously quiet himself.

Jeremiah bristled at the insult but did not speak.

A petite lass whose words were still thick with the continent of her birth stepped forward to diffuse the tension brewing between the two men. "Warrior, she would not have come wit' us. I tried on many times to talk wit' her 'bout the notion of escape, but she made clear her plans require her stay put."

"'Tis foolishness." Kallum could not fathom such folly.

He had encountered captives in the past whose fear of the unknown kept them from seeking their freedom, but the lass had been sorely abused recently. She was daft if she'd rather suffer such rough treatment than flee to a life where she could be her own person. Kallum spun, intent on heading inside the castle, when he spied the lass in question slip out a side door.

Relieved she had come to her senses and decided to join them, Kallum took a step in her direction. When she headed the wrong way, he cursed under his breath. This lass was not only going to delay their departure but also get them caught. Tournament champion or not, he had no doubt his head would be separated from his neck once the king discovered he'd been the one to relieve His Majesty of eleven members of his human collection.

Kallum motioned to the other captives to stay put and stay quiet, then took off with silent feet to intercept the female straggler. On edge that this excursion was not going according to the necessarily tight schedule that resulted from his last-minute planning, Kallum made sure not to remove his eyes from his target lest she slip into a shadow and he lose sight of her permanently.

To her credit, the lass stayed in the darkest portions of the courtyard. Suddenly, she paused and quickly glanced in both directions. As if she sensed his presence, she stared for several heartbeats toward the spot where Kallum stood. If the lass could see him, she had the eyes of an owl, but he opted to step into the glow of the partial moon to make sure she could make out his presence.

Anticipating relief that she'd found the guide for their covert caravan, Kallum could not believe his eyes when she bolted in the opposite direction again. If she reached the back of the castle wherein the remaining clans were in the process of departing, the success of this operation was doomed. His frustration turned into anger. Was the bloody female trying to get them captured…and killed?

"Sweet Jesu!" Kallum bit off the words, making them a curse rather than a prayer, and sprinted after the lass.

He overtook her easily, grabbed her around the waist with one arm, and lifted her off her feet. She struggled, twisting desperately in his grasp and kicking her feet wildly. The pressure on his injured shoulder made him almost lose hold. He adjusted until he held her more securely. Soft sounds of frustration emanated from her. Kallum feared she'd get louder, so he clasped a hand over her mouth.

She didn't appreciate the move and took a bite of his hand to prove it. Her teeth sank in deep and held. Kallum clenched his own teeth to contain the bellow that nearly emerged. He squeezed her rib cage and exerted as much pressure as his straining shoulder would allow. He felt her weaken slightly as she fought to breathe, but she didn't release his hand.

Her feet continued to kick, and she wiggled constantly. Her efforts made it harder and harder for Kallum to maintain his grasp one-handed. He felt like he'd captured a wild boar and all he had to defend himself with were his bare hands. Of course, he was armed, but he'd never use a bladed weapon against a lass.

He yanked his hand roughly, but her teeth chewed deeper. Desperate to end the stalemate afore they were discovered, Kallum slid his other hand up to pry her teeth from the meal of its matching appendage. His travelling hand inadvertently caught her breast, and she yelped. His teeth-dented palm came free, but her still-kicking feet landed a strong blow to his shin. He dropped her to her feet.

Without turning, the lass shifted her hips and swung her fist backward with all her might. Right into his cods. A million piercing blades of pain shot through his groin. Grasping his package and gasping for air, Kallum sank to one knee.

The lass didn't wait around to admire her handiwork. She bolted.

Gimpy but by no means completely incapacitated, an angry Kallum staggered to his feet and used his longer stride to bear down on the uncooperative lass. She glanced back as he reached for her. Accelerating, she dodged his grasp.

The end of the castle wall was only a few paces ahead. Her body pivoted toward the corner's edge, but Kallum had no intention of letting her get away. If she reached that corner afore he reached her, the entire escape would be jeopardized. Plus, he now had an extremely personal score to settle with his mystery woman in addition to making her pay for putting all the other captives at risk.

Skewed after her battle with him, her cloak hung

lopsided off her shoulder and billowed loosely behind her on the breeze of her momentum. When she was but a hair's breadth from clearing the corner, Kallum snatched her waving cloak and yanked her up short. The twit lost her balance. Kallum caught her afore she tumbled to the ground, but the small bundle that had been draped over her shoulder went flying.

Having learned his lesson about her teeth and his hands, he clutched up a corner of her cloak and stuffed it into her mouth. He placed a hand firmly over the cloth crammed into her dangerous orifice and pushed her back against the wall. His chest heaved with exertion, and his cock throbbed as it swelled in a manner he was not particularly fond of.

He gritted his teeth and counted to ten—nay, twenty—afore he scolded her hide as best he could with only a deep-throated whisper at his disposal. "You currish, half-witted flax-wench! Are you trying to get us killed?"

CHAPTER SIX

Ailsa glared into the black hole covered by a dark hood. She grunted beneath his hand, and her head moved back and forth. She had a few choice words of her own to hurl at the mammoth varlet, if she could speak. He pushed more firmly against the wad of fabric in her mouth to make clear he had no intention of letting that happen.

Anger laced with a bit of desperation simmered within her, and she tried to kick him. It had worked once afore to get her free. No sense abandoning a working strategy, at least not yet. She refused to let the captain—or whichever one of the royal guards this was—assault her here behind the castle like some wild bitch. It was bad enough the man had delayed her reunion with her clan. To have to suffer the humiliation of his hands on her, with worse likely to come, was not something she could let stand.

She was going home this day whatever it took, or he was going to have to put her dead, lifeless body in a hole in the ground.

Surrender wasn't an option.

"Stop your squirming." Her tormentor's voice remained at a whisper. "I aim not to hurt you."

Ailsa scoffed behind her gag. *Yeah, right.* And she was the rightful heir to the throne of Scotland.

"Hmm. Hmm. Hmm!" She tried to raise her voice beneath the wad of cloak in her mouth, but only a few muffled grunts came out.

He pressed himself more firmly against her. Her back scrubbed against the stone wall behind her and, even through her cloak, she could feel the coldness of the cobbled rocks. When his legs bracketed hers, her panic increased. She could no longer move. Both her legs and one of her arms were held immobile. She tried to shove him with her other arm but found herself completely at his mercy.

He leaned in farther, and she turned her head to avoid his advance.

His voice dropped directly into her ear. "Quiet. I mean only to take you toward the caravan. You were going the wrong way."

Caravan? What caravan? The only people she was interested in meeting were in the direction she had been going, and this brutish knave was going to make her miss their departure.

Was this some sort of new torture?

She had tried to run away twice during her first year of captivity. The first time they recovered her, she'd been severely admonished, isolated, and made to go without food for days. The second time, she had made it farther and stayed free longer, but they had found her eventually. After her second transgression, she had been savagely flogged in the grand hall to make an example of her to the other captives.

Did they aim to send her away from the castle this time? To some fate worse than starvation or flogging or serving the princess bratling?

What fate could be worse than a lifetime of ownership by and servitude to a princess with a finely crafted, shrewdly implemented cruel streak as pure as her royal blood?

Ailsa briefly closed her eyes. It took less than a heartbeat for a more horrific fate, especially for a female with no known family ties, to cross her mind: a life forced to serve men on her back. A shudder of repulsion overtook her, and a gossamer thought of death returned.

She shook it off. She was too close to emancipation to give up now. She must endure and find a way free afore the Connery clan departed the front gates.

Think, Ailsa. Think!

She stopped moving and turned her face back toward the black hole. She peered into the bleakness, looking for any sign of who might be beneath the hood. If this was the captain, he had grown uncharacteristic patience in a quick span of time, or he was taking a new approach to his intended punishment.

With her stillness, her unknown assailant slowly let up his hand. It hovered at the ready above her mouth. In case she decided to scream or some such, she suspected. She pushed the fabric of her cloak from her mouth with her tongue. Causing a fracas would not serve her purpose. She did not want to rouse the rest of the guard. They would simply take her back into the castle, and her efforts would be for naught.

She straightened to as much height as his surrounding body would allow. "I will not let you abuse me again." She kept her voice low, but she wanted no misunderstanding of her intent. "You will have to kill me this time."

"Again?" The genuine surprise in his response led to the abandonment of his whisper. Though his voice remained low, its resonance and cadence were clear. "I think you have me confused with another."

Shock reverberated through Ailsa. 'Twas not the voice she had been expecting, but 'twas a voice she knew. That rich, honeyed voice was not one she would likely soon—or ever—forget.

Recognition sent an odd mix of anxiety and hyper-awareness flooding her body. She'd dreamed of that voice, and the man that went with it, last eve. The sultry, haunting dream had overtaken her slumber to such extent she had been unable to remain under the stifling bed linens for more than a short while. Even now, a full-on flush lit her body in a slow rise from the tips of her toes up through female body parts inconveniently perky at such a dire moment.

Goodness. It was the MacNeill champion. He had come for her.

Had he changed his mind about the state of her face and decided he'd take her anyway?

Two women weren't enough for this man? Did he need a bevy of wenches at his beck and call?

His rugged virility might turn a wanton lass's head, but she could not forget that within his strength he contained a ferocity that made the art of swordplay as facile as a skilled lady's prowess with a sewing needle. She'd seen him kill a man today in a battle that broiled fierce even afore treachery added death play to the contest. Common sense dictated she proceed cautiously, though no less committedly, with her plan of separation from this unexpected impediment to her best opportunity to return home.

She opened her mouth to speak, but the sound of steps upon gravel startled them both into immobility. He recovered first and quickly shuffled her into a corner space where two walls met at the edge of the castle.

One wall jutted out slightly. The door of a back servant's entrance stood only a few feet away.

"Shush," he whispered after he had tucked her into the darkened alcove. "Our lives depend upon your silence."

The MacNeill shielded her from view with his massive body. All anyone would see, if they could see anything at all, was a large, looming figure covered by a hooded cloak.

The steps came closer, and two male voices could be heard. "I'm glad to be rid of those Highland rogues. They have the manners of woodland wildlife," one said.

His comrade chuckled. "You're just afraid one of them might decide to take a piece of your hide."

"Pfft. That's no idle fear. Did you see the size of those beasts? What the hell do they eat over in those northwest lands?"

"I don't know, but I'd like a little of whatever it is."

More laughter followed the comment, and the sound of slapping hands drifted to Ailsa. She could visualize the congratulatory high hand slap one comrade had given the other for his quip.

"Well, whatever it is, that champion blackamoor is gonna be needing plenty of it, lucky bastard."

More chuckles ensued afore the second man asked, "You think that Highlander is planning to have a go in turns with the wenches he was awarded or take them both at once?"

"Does it matter?" Laughter exploded. "Like I said, one lucky bastard."

The MacNeill tensed at the comment. He apparently did not like being the subject of their speculation any more than she liked the thought of being added to his twosome. Or would it now be his threesome? Surely not even a strapping warrior such as he could…would want to…

She closed her eyes—physically and mentally—against the impure images flooding her thoughts.

At a different time, she suspected those men would pay dearly for their inane commentary. As it were, the MacNeill stood stoically while the guards' loud guffaws drifted farther away along with the fading sound of the gravel that crunched beneath their feet.

When the men were out of hearing distance, the MacNeill shifted. "We must go quickly."

He reached for her hand.

She snatched it away. "No." Her emphatic whisper was clipped and short. "I am not going anywhere with you."

Too quick for her to avoid his grasp, he grabbed her wrist and began to walk.

She pulled in the direction of the clan camps. "Let me go. I must meet my people."

"Your people are this way." He continued to pull her in the opposite direction.

She tried to plant her feet, but his superior strength dragged her along behind him.

Frustrated at her resistance, he stopped. "Listen, we do not have time for you to be difficult. We must leave afore they notice how many are missing."

"You don't need me. You have plenty of women to keep you occupied. Leave me be."

The Highlander frowned, as if he could not fathom how the other two women could possibly keep him occupied. "The other women await your arrival. If you continue to be difficult, you will put them at risk as well as yourself. Is that what you want?"

Ailsa took a step back at the confirmation he did indeed intend for her to join his other two female prizes. Albeit she did not get far, since he still held her wrist. The notion that this man expected her to meekly submit to being his property, nothing more than a doxy, defied comprehension. He behaved as if such happenings were normal practice in his world.

Well, for all she knew, they were.

She, however, cared not how the MacNeills lived their lives. Her life was with the Connerys, and she was headed back to Connery land to recapture her freedom. "You are beyond daft if you think I'm going to join your caravan. My people are the other way. Take your women and go. I will be fine on my own."

"Look, I know it can be scary to start over in another place, but I have people who will help you get settled and build a new life."

"I don't need your help."

He paused pensively afore he said, "Your face says otherwise."

She flinched. The callous reference to her bruised face caught her by surprise. Any outraged reply she could have managed shut down behind a shocked gasp. Her fist balled automatically. If she were a man, she would swing on the foul brute. His odious words hurt as much as they angered.

He had shown his disdain for her damaged visage during the tournament awards. So why, then, had he come?

"If my face is such a problem, why on earth would you want me?" She slapped at his hand. "Let me go."

He didn't release her.

She pulled once again in the direction of the clan camps, most likely now dismantled. This time, she leaned with all her body weight and reached out with one hand for leverage. "I still have time to catch them. You must leave me be!"

● ● ●

Catch them? Kallum pondered the odd utterance.

Or had she said, *Catch him?*

Did the lass have some paramour she planned to meet secretly? Surely, she had not swayed some young warrior in just the few days the clans had been on castle grounds for the tournament. He glanced over her in the moonlight. Then again, mayhap she had. She had many wiles at her disposal despite the bruises that left her face discolored but detracted little from the loveliness beneath.

If she had bewitched some young sap and planned to meet up with him under cover of the clan departures, she had most likely already missed him and her opportunity. There was no way Kallum could let her go to find out. 'Twas too risky. He could not chance her revealing information about his presence or the captives who dared flee this night, minimal though that information might be. He must protect the other runaways from discovery. He'd wasted enough time with her antics.

Whatever folly she had been about—simply sneaking around the castle or meeting up with some lad for an illicit tup—it was time to put an end to the nonsense. She would find a new man when she got where she was going.

He pulled against her straining person. When she continued to resist, he gave a hard yank. She bounced against his chest, and he stilled her attempt to disconnect with a firm hand to her back.

"I've had enough of you," he said between clenched teeth and stared into her eyes. "I cannot tell if you're too stubborn for your own good or just plain simple-minded."

Her eyes narrowed at the insult.

"You cannot go that way, and I cannot leave you here." He gripped both of her shoulders and set her abruptly away from his chest but did not let go.

He leaned forward. "I do not know why you'd want to risk staying here, but that is no longer an option. By now, it will have been noticed that you and some of the others are not where you are supposed to be. If you go back, everyone's life is at risk. I cannot allow that." He shook her slightly to gain her attention when she refused to meet his eyes. "Do you understand?"

When she didn't respond, he frowned, then gave her another gentle shake to rouse her from her stupor. "Do you *understand*?"

She returned her gaze to his and trembled slightly despite her best efforts to remain impassive. He was sorry for it. Instilling fear had not been his intent, but she was too headstrong to accept a simple appeal to logic. Just like a woman. He had never met one who wasn't more trouble than she was worth, and clearly this lass was no different.

Her mouth opened, but no words came out.

Oh no. Not this time. He shoved her cloak back into her mouth afore she could speak.

"Not. Another. Word. Not another sound." He

returned to the satisfying position of his hand pressed against the silencing gift of her cloak. "Simply nod your head if you understand. But don't you *dare* make another sound. If you do, those soldiers will be the least of your worries."

She nodded. Slowly at first. Her light-colored eyes glowed loathingly at him in the moon-tinted halo of night. He still couldn't quite make out their color, but an odd sense of uneasiness crept along his spine as he stared into their depths. His entanglement with this woman had taken an odd and unforeseeable turn. He'd sought simply to set her free, but freedom did not seem where this was headed.

Had he led himself into a night venture that would finally cost him his own liberty?

Had he wandered into that one complication that would ultimately lead to his arrest and sure execution?

He had known such a day and venture would come; he had not anticipated 'twould come this soon.

A sense of foreboding wrapped around him, and he was tempted to release the balcony hellion and leave her to her own artifices. She would be his undoing. That certainty was as clear to him as his own name.

Hell and damnation. He had sensed it from the moment he looked into those witchy eyes of hers yonder morn. A lure to destruction. The gateway to a heap of trouble.

He had thought 'twould be of the lustful kind, not the kind that would lead to the end of his secret raids and his head severed from his neck. But here he stood.

He should have said no to Inan from the start and held firm. Or he should have thrown one of the preliminary contests and avoided the championship bout.

Then he would never have been in a position that allowed providence to require this woman's intervention to save his life.

He shook his head to clear the creeping fog of doubt from his brain.

Now that he had started down this path, he could not very well turn back. He could not leave her behind. Premonition be damned. He would not leave a woman to fend for herself in these most dangerous of circumstances. Her perishment would be on his conscience for the remainder of his days, however few those might be.

She would have to come with him whether she wanted to or not. There was no helping what he had to do next.

He grabbed her bag from the ground and shoved it into her hands. "Hold on to this. If it drops, 'tis gone forever. I'll not stop to retrieve it."

He dipped, wrapped an arm around her knees, and tossed her over his shoulder.

She gave a muffled squeak.

"Shh. Remember what I said," he admonished.

Even with the stuffing in her mouth, the outrage in her grumbled utterances was clear. She kicked her feet.

"Hush." He gave her buttocks a hard swat, then jumped when she gave a hard pound to his lower back in retaliation.

He nearly released a startled chuckle at the act. The woman had spirit; he'd give her that. But he was bigger and meaner, and this day, his will was stronger.

"Behave or you will earn another."

An indignant grunt was his only response.

Pity. His hand would not have minded another swat of those well-rounded buttocks. She was a hardy lass, of good stature and possessing the lush curves of a mature woman. Even so, she still weighed next to naught and required little effort to carry. Her kicking legs, though, presented a problem.

He clasped one forearm across her lower legs to keep them still and his other arm across the backs of her thighs to hold her firm and secure. She stopped her struggle, and he quickened his pace.

The reality of the situation rooted around the edges of his pride, then held. He had gone from a rescuer to a kidnapper in less than a breath. The greatest warrior of Clan MacNeill reduced to an abductor of women. How could this once seemingly innocuous trek to court and back possibly get any worse?

CHAPTER SEVEN

Ailsa bounced on the MacNeill's shoulder. With the wadded cloak still stuffed in her mouth, she had to concentrate on taking in air through her nose. The combination of the pressure on her rib cage from his shoulder and her upside-down position threatened to make her light-headed.

She willed herself not to pass out. She could not pass out. Just the thought of her fight to retain consciousness made her angry. She squeezed her eyes shut and fought to hold on to that feeling. The anger. It helped. It helped a lot. The fantasies of what she wanted to do to the brute beneath her when he finally put her down helped calm her breathing. Helped calm her mind.

Earlier, she had considered whether she could appeal to his sense of decency—if he had one—and somehow convince him to let her go. He'd not given her a chance, so hell-bent was he on shutting her up with her own cloak. For the second time!

She dangled from his shoulder, at a loss for how to set things in her favor. Her throat was dry. She maneuvered her hands to remove the fabric of her cloak from its position against her tongue but nearly dropped her satchel. He had said he would not stop to retrieve it, and she believed him. She stopped her efforts. Everything she owned was in this satchel. It wasn't much, but what there was signified all she had left of herself and her connection to the Connery clan.

On the verge of despair, she tried to swallow. The effort was useless.

She racked her brain for an effort, any effort, that might free her or give her some hope of escape. The knowledge that irretrievable time passed while she was carried off like some felled deer and her kinsmen made their departure made her want to cry. She wouldn't. No matter the frustration. No matter the fear. This man would not hear her cry.

She had barely stifled her scream when he grabbed her and tossed her over his shoulder. Her humiliation was only surpassed by her confusion and anxiety. This was not the way this night was supposed to unfold. To have freedom within her grasp only to have it snatched away. To trade one form of captivity for another. To have hope only to be brought down to the vestiges of despair. That felt close to defeat. But he hadn't won yet.

She clutched her satchel and sent up a silent plea. *Please, Mother Yemoja, show me a way out of this.*

She had not paid homage to the gods of her grandparents' native land in years, but today she felt the need for the added protection. Her Christian God had allowed her this trial, whatever his purpose. The mother protector of her West African ancestors would see her safely home. In that she must believe.

Once the MacNeill set her back on solid ground, she'd make sure he rued the day he decided to take her prisoner. She didn't know if it was her divine invocation or the sudden return of three years' worth of abandoned faith that brought about this new clearheadedness, but a plan began to form in her mind.

Unexpectedly, the warrior plopped her down in a cart lined with woolen bed cloths. A grunt escaped her upon her bottom's clash with the hard boards of the wooden contraption, and she scampered to a sitting position. She grabbed at the wad of cloak in her mouth, but the warrior made a preemptive grasp of her wrist.

He leaned in close. Softly, he said, "Do not yell out or bring attention of any kind to yourself. We will follow behind the next clan to depart, subtly and without chaos. Whatever you planned to do afore, you must set it aside and follow along with us. Do not put these people in danger."

She glanced around, noticing the others for the first time. She recognized many of them from service inside the castle. He had mentioned others, others like her he intended to whisk away to places unknown.

He was right. Any action she took to free herself would invariably draw attention to the entire group, especially since the Highlander had no intention of letting her go her own way. Her shoulders slumped, and she nodded her assent. He released her wrist.

Pulling the edge of her cloak from her mouth, she coughed due to her dry throat. His gaze sharpened, and he gave her a suspicious glare. She rubbed lightly at her throat but dared not cough again. The look he gave her promised severe retribution if she made even the slightest of sounds. She tried to swallow and clear her throat as quietly as she could.

After a moment of hesitation, the MacNeill reached under his cloak and removed a small leather vessel that had been secured to his belt with a plaited cord. He removed its small stopper afore he handed her the container. She took it instinctively but paused afore checking its contents. His head made an amused tilt at her hesitancy, and then he reached to reclaim his offer.

She snatched it to her chest, and a satisfied glint entered his eyes that silently suggested an *I-thought-so*. If the man had a sense of humor, he would probably have laughed at her. But he seemed to be missing that, along with his manners.

Ailsa glanced inside the vessel. The opening was too small for her to see into, so she took a delicate sniff. No odor of any kind, other than the scent of leather, came to her nose. She took a small sip. Her eyes closed in blissful gratitude at the taste of water, and she took a longer drink. When she opened her eyes, his fixated stare blazed with an odd mix of heat and curiosity, though the imposing look on his face had not dissipated. In fact, it had deepened. His brow peaked in question at her continued stare afore he held out his hand in silent request for the return of his water carrier.

Mayhap she'd drank a little more than he had expected. With a flush of embarrassment, she slowly handed him the vessel.

Trapped once again by those deep, enthralling sable eyes, she felt a momentary loss of conscious perspective. Everything and everyone slipped away. The inexplicable connection she had felt the first time she'd seen him seared through her, and she momentarily forgot her simmering vexation. She became enveloped in the familiar draw that had made her sleepless last eve and then roused an uncharacteristic inclination to bring attention to herself by trying to warn him of the Donnelly's sneak attack during the championship bout.

Surely, she was losing her rational mind. This man had kidnapped her. He could serve no purpose other than enemy and obstacle. She had to keep her wits about her and not get snared by an innate virility that pulled at the long-suppressed femininity she had intentionally leashed for survival. She suspected plenty of women tripped over themselves to catch his eye and share his bed. She would *not* be one of them.

His hand brushed hers when he accepted the return of his water carrier. The sensation wafted over her skin, and he paused momentarily with his hand still touching hers. Something curious flashed in the depths of his eyes afore he shuttered it and pulled away his hand.

He replaced the water carrier to his belt, his gaze still intent on her. After a breath, he spoke. "I must lead this caravan safely through the castle gates." His voice was so low only she was likely able to hear him. "I need your word that you will behave. If you do, I give you *my* word that I will see to your safety and allow no harm to come to you."

Exacting such a promise seemed a simplistic approach to ensuring her cooperation. She knew not from whence came the impetus to challenge his request, but she could not contain her peevish response. "If I give you my word, how do you know I will honor it?"

He gripped either side of the cart and leaned till his nose nearly touched hers. "I do not." A cold, promissory glint entered his eyes, and his voice dropped to a flat, matter-of-fact tone. "But if you do not, you will force me to kill my first woman."

Her eyes nearly widened. She barely suppressed the startled reaction. An edge of panic threatened to return. This man was not one with which to trifle. A surge of danger vibrated from every pore of his deep-brown skin, and the look in his eyes assured her he meant every word he said.

He motioned toward the others with his chin. "'Tis

all of them. Or you." He stared her straight in the eyes. "Which choice would you make if you were me?"

She stared back at him quietly for two breaths afore surveying the others. She understood his stance. If he was set on helping the others escape, how could he live with himself if he allowed one to cost him the ten? How could *she*? She could not earn her freedom at the cost of others losing theirs or mayhap their lives. She would have to cooperate. At least until they cleared Stirling Castle grounds and had the shelter of the woods around them.

Her gaze returned to his. He still watched her.

She nodded.

He squinted, and his head canted to one side, sizing up her sincerity. Satisfied with what he saw, he gave an abrupt nod, then headed to the front of the caravan.

Wherever he intended to take the others, she had a different destination in mind. She would allow him to lead her out with the rest, but after that, she had a plan—and path—of her own to follow.

• • •

Kallum brought up the rear of the traveling caravan. They had separated from the other clans that had departed Stirling Castle at the same time, and two of the freed male captives drove the horse-drawn cart he had secured to allow the women to travel with less exertion.

The cart was only large enough to fit eight in the back comfortably. With twelve travelers counting him, that left ten people to ride in the back of the cart. So the men took turns walking when they tired of being cramped. Kallum had driven for a long stretch upon getting the group off castle grounds, but presently he felt the need to watch the surroundings from an ambulatory position.

The two mares he had cheaply purchased inside the town of Stirling and harnessed to the front of the cart walked at a steady pace. He'd had to leave his stallion in the other direction from whence they traveled, stashed along the route home. He could not chance that someone would recognize the steed. With his size and solid black coloring, Ogun was memorable.

The group needed to make good time. For this reason, they had made few stops since their departure. Daybreak fast approached, and by now, the king's men were looking for the runaways. The longer the group stayed together, the more attention they were likely to draw. Even more important, the escapees needed to reach the next stop on their journey to freedom by sunrise of the following day. If they did not, the escort who agreed to guide this crew through the next leg of their trip to the English border would depart without them. To make the rendezvous, they would likely need to push on past sunrise.

Kallum could not risk having to lead this crew across the border himself. Once daylight broke on the second morn, continuing to travel in a face covering and hood would not be reasonable. The act would draw suspicion, especially once they got closer to the next burgh, but he could not risk removal of the identity-masking shroud in public. His identity must remain a secret. Otherwise, the risk to his kinsmen was great. As long as no one knew who he was, the king would not be able to locate and arrest him for his night raids nor enact punishment or revenge upon the MacNeill clan.

Concerned with the progress of his entourage, Kallum checked the position of the moon. The night had progressed faster than he liked. They were behind schedule. He had burned unnecessary time vacating castle grounds because of his unanticipated side excursion to rein in the hellion with the shrewish temper.

More troubling, her touch had sent a vibrant awakening pulse from his hand to his groin—impaired though it still was—when he retrieved his water vessel from her prior to the start of their journey. The reaction had thrown him off-center. He'd never had such a strong, instant, physical reaction to a woman.

Lust wasn't unfamiliar to him, but this intense pull went deeper than a standard need for a quick tup with a bonnie female. He'd wanted in that moment to sink into her until his cods were cradled against her buttocks and ride her into screaming pleasure until neither of them had the strength to breathe or the ability to move.

The sound she'd unknowingly made upon savoring a simple drink of water closely mimicked the sounds he suspected she made upon enjoying pleasures of the flesh. He closed his eyes against the torturing image. He needed to stop thinking such thoughts. She was not meant for him, and she already had a man she fancied enough to risk an illicit tryst on castle grounds despite those grounds being monitored by a royal guard with a reputation for unrelenting tyranny.

She puzzled him. She spoke English too well to be a new or fairly recent arrival to the country. No foreigner's accent laced her words. She had obviously been in Scotland from the time she was a child or at least early youth. How had someone raised most of her life in captivity managed to develop such a feisty and prideful bearing?

Had he guessed right the first time he saw her? Was she an illegitimate offspring of the king?

Then why had she been sneaking off into the night? He would think she had certain perks and privileges that provided benefits worth staying put for.

The memory of her bruised face crossed his mind. Such perks should have protected her from abuse as well. Surely even a cad such as King James would not allow his own offspring to be treated such, even if she be of mixed blood. Would he?

Mayhap he would. Yet, while a man with an ego as massive as the king's might find certain amusement in having his unclaimed by-blow serve as an enslaved domestic, Kallum surmised he'd find none in having her serve as a man's proxy for fisticuffs. So, royal progeny she must not be.

As if his thoughts had conjured her up, the woman of his musings approached. Surprised by her unexpected appearance, he glanced ahead to the cart she should have been riding on to find she'd given the king's elderly groom her spot in the cart.

"You should not have given that man your seat. The men were to walk. The cart was so the women could stay rested and we could travel farther longer."

"He is my elder," came her simple reply.

"He is a man, and he is not that old. He should have been the one to walk." His voice was gruffer than he meant it to be.

Kallum wasn't sure whether he really cared that she'd given her seat to the older gentleman or whether he was more bothered that she had chosen to come pester him during her mobility. Her presence was not one he welcomed, especially with the randy thoughts he'd been having.

"He was tired. I am not."

"He is a man. 'Tis his duty to—"

"I am not so weak I cannot walk for a bit. And he is my *elder*." She stopped as she said this last.

Reflexively, he stopped with her.

She gave him a frustrated stare. "Let it go."

He wanted to strangle her. The woman clearly did not know her place. Every conversation they'd had since the beginning of this excursion had been a battle of wills.

Without a word, he started walking again. His annoyance caused him to double his stride.

She scrambled to catch up to him. "Where are we going?"

He did not respond nor slow his pace.

Nearly jogging to keep up with him now, she continued her questioning. "Don't you think we ought to know where you are taking us?"

"Nay. You will find out when you get there."

"Really?" Her foot caught on a surface root, and her footing stuttered afore she regained her poise. Unfortunately, the interruption did not stop her mouthy chatter. "That does not seem reasonable to me."

"I care not whether you think it reasonable. You will go along quietly—" He gave her mouth a quick perusal. "Well, mayhap not quietly."

His teeth clenched, and he looked away from those full lips that made him think of something particular he'd like to see them filled with other than words.

Without looking at her, he continued, "But you will do so orderly and without commotion."

"Will I?" she mumbled under her breath.

He grabbed her arm abruptly and pulled her closer. "Aye, you will," he whispered emphatically.

Her eyes became large orbs, and what he saw there was not fear. At least, not immediately. What he saw was the same odd surprise he'd felt when their hands had touched afore. What he saw was a momentarily undisguised sensual curiosity she covered with a puzzled frown.

"I—um…" Her chest rose in an erratic pattern, and her lips remained parted in a subconscious temptation.

His gaze dropped to those enticing lips, and whatever she saw in his eyes finally brought on the fear.

She tried to pull away, but his hold was too tight. She glanced around to see what the others were doing. They had stopped to watch the interaction between the two of them.

She blushed and pulled against his hold again. "Let me go. *Please*." Her voice was whispered but steady. Only the look in her eyes gave away that there was an edge of desperation to her need to be let go.

He had not meant to scare her. Her mumbled challenge had galled his already edgy disposition, and he had simply meant to challenge back. Her constant disagreeableness irked him, and his temper had spiked. He had never encountered such a headstrong female in his life. He made grown men shiver with a look, and this bit of a woman acted as if he were no more than an irritating uncle.

'Twas insulting and oddly alluring at the same time, and she had read his miffed desire on his face. He had no doubt that discernment was what had shifted her into unease.

His grip softened. He would never force himself on a woman nor harm one in any way, despite what he had threatened when he first dumped her in the cart. An urge to assure her of such surfaced, which irritated him further. He did not explain himself to anyone.

To salvage his peace of mind, he needed to get rid of her as soon as possible.

The woman wanted to know where they were going. Fine. He'd get her there with all due rapidity.

He completely released his hold on her. "If you are so hell-bent on knowing where we are going, how 'bout we get you there as quickly as possible? Let's go tell your comrades you need them to get moving and pick up their pace."

A horrified look crossed her face, but he ignored it and headed toward the stationary cart where the freed men and women waited.

"Nay!" She grasped at his sleeve. "You cannot."

With an exasperated sigh, he stopped and asked with impatience, "And why, pray tell, can I not?"

CHAPTER EIGHT

Ailsa grasped tighter to the Highlander's sleeve. He could not tell those people she had insisted they move faster to their destination. They would vilify her. They already did not like her. Even now, the one named Jeremiah watched her with contempt in his eyes.

He had seen her on many occasions at the castle with the captain. The king's man had acted inappropriately familiar with her whenever he could and took improper liberties. He cared not who watched, especially if those watching were his soldiers or simply other enslaved people. In fact, he seemed to have enjoyed making her taunting a public spectacle. Those who did not know her well assumed she was a wanton who gave the favors willingly. Nothing could be more untrue, but perception oft trumped the truth.

These people were tired. The MacNeill had pushed them unceasingly to move with haste. She'd overheard the younger of the two other women mention that the entourage had left Stirling Castle later than planned because the warrior had gone in search of Ailsa. Ailsa had been surprised these were not the same two women the MacNeill had been awarded at the tournament. Clearly, he had other plans for this group. Plans she had somehow been pulled into and interrupted, so the group already blamed her for the grueling pace set to make up for that delay. If the MacNeill told them she was the reason they must continue to push on without rest, their full hatred would be assured.

She had come to walk with the Highlander specifically to ask him if they could slow down or even stop until twilight. If they did not take a break shortly, several of the escapees would collapse.

"The men are tired. They need a break from taking turns driving the cart, and the women could use a chance to stretch their legs. Surely, we could stop for a while. Mayhap till daylight arrives?"

He was unmoved by her plea. "We cannot. We must keep moving. Our destination must be reached by the following sunrise, or you will miss your opportunity to cross the border."

Ailsa perked up at his unintentional provision of information. "Which border?"

He sighed. "Must you ask so many questions?" The annoyance in his tone was clear.

This was a man not used to being questioned, but she had a right to know what he planned to do with them.

"Yes, because I'm here against my will, and you deign to keep me in the dark about your plans for me. Remember, I am here by your whim, not by choice. I deserve an answer." She waved a hand in the direction of the others. "They deserve an answer."

With two fingers, Kallum deliberately removed her grasp from his sleeve and took a deep breath. Though she could not see his face inside the hood, she heard his inhalation. He was silent for a long moment. She began to fear he would refuse to respond or that he mentally busied himself designing creative stratagems to relieve himself of her presence, like leaving her behind in the woods. Mayhap tied to a tree so predators would feed off her live carcass and leave no trace she'd ever existed save her gnawed-clean bones. The morbid thought made her glance at the nearest tree and repress a shudder.

The MacNeill, puzzled, turned his head in the direction of her glance afore he finally spoke, his voice clipped and tight. "I am taking you to meet a ferryman in the resistance who will shuttle you to the next location. At that stop, you will transfer to another escort who will take you the final way into England. Once there, someone will meet with you and help each of you find honorable occupations in different boroughs." His huge fists slammed against his waist. The action pushed back his cloak and displayed the massiveness of his thighs in his black-and-gray trews. "Does that satisfy Your Highness's curiosity?"

She cared not to be thought of with the same title as the bratchet princess she'd recently abandoned, but she ignored his dig at her personality. Pressing matters awaited negotiation. The reminder of his enormous size and the peek at the handle of not one but two swords hiding beneath his cloak against his back should have been a deterrent to any further inquiry. Yet, all she could think of was that she could not end up in England. She'd be farther away from her clan than she had been in Stirling and more alone than ever.

She began shaking her head without conscious thought. "England? You are taking me the wrong way. I am not bound for England."

"You are now." He began to walk away.

"Nay, warrior." She reached for his arm again and glommed on with a tight grip. "You must take me the other way."

He looked down at her hand. With nothing to be

seen but the edges of the dark hood shifting lightly around his hidden face on the faint breeze and the night-dyed cloak draped around the man-shaped equivalent of a giant specter, the Highlander gave the impression of Death come visit from the Underworld. Ailsa snatched back her hand.

His arm disappeared beneath the cloak. "That way is not safe. 'Twill be the first place they look for you. With many of the Highland clans having recently departed Stirling, the king's soldiers will expect you all to be hiding amongst them. After a few days, when they find you not, they will consider you may have crossed into England or fled to Ireland, but by then you will be long gone and separated such that it will be hard to trace your whereabouts."

She knew from experience the king's men could be persistent in their pursuit of runaways, but if she split from the group, she stood a better chance of staying free this time. They would be looking for a group, not one lone woman.

"I am only one captive. They will not search specifically for me alone."

"You are not alone, lass." He motioned toward the others. "Nor could you find your path the other way without assistance. I cannot let you try on your own. You must meet the ferryman with the others."

Ailsa's mind raced with the possibilities of how to make this work. She had to get home, back to the Highlands. "You call him a ferryman. Will he take us toward the sea, then?"

"Nay. 'Tis only a moniker we use to identify some of the attendants who secret our enslaved people to freedom via a liberation trek. We all consider ourselves mutineers, so we use not our real names, and no one person knows the full route of those freed. 'Tis the best way to reduce the risk of detection or capture."

"But if I could get escort to the sea, I could secure passage to the Hebrides islands." Connery land bordered the coastline to the west of the Inner Hebrides. Travel by sea could expedite her journey and serve double duty of throwing off any of the king's guard who might be in pursuit.

"Why the Hebrides? Once there, what do you hope to find?" The intrigued edge to his voice made her wary.

She hesitated to reveal her ultimate destination. The Highland clans were not all united in their stance over the king's current politics. King James had continued to call for pledges of allegiance from the Highland lairds, but over the years, most chiefs had taken his royal demands as a precursor to a likely plan to strip them of their lands and authority.

Many clans had formed allyships to assemble stronger fighting forces should they have to defend their autonomy. Others, alas, found themselves at war with each other over a difference in approach to maintaining independence from the crown. Talk of the distrust brewing amongst the clans was so rampant it had reached even as far as the servant ranks of Stirling.

Ailsa knew not in which camp the MacNeills and the Connerys fell. Were they allies or foes?

If the MacNeill was an enemy of her kin, then her reliance on him to see her safely to Connery land would be greatly misplaced.

"Well, lass? What say you?" His cloak tented sideways with a point that suggested one of his massive hands had once again found way to his side.

Patience was clearly not amongst the man's virtues.

Ailsa scrambled for a reasonable explanation that would not give away too much. "I know 'tis a port through which many of our kind enter the continent and many lucky ones sometimes find passage out. From there, I will be able to find the safety I seek."

"A lass alone without escort will find much, but safety is not amongst them. I suggest you put that plan out of your mind." He took hold of her upper arm and steered her toward the cart. "Come. Enough of this chatter. We must get moving."

She could not abandon her plan to get home. Change it, mayhap. But abandon it? *Nay!*

Somehow, she had to get the MacNeill to see reason. She felt like an outcast even amongst these runaways who had been enslaved at the castle, then freed like herself. If she could at least garner the group a bit of rest, mayhap Jeremiah would stop looking at her as if he wanted to turn her in to the king's guard himself. Somewhere along this journey, she must earn some goodwill amongst these travelers. She sensed her personal safety depended upon it, especially if her destiny risked being tied to theirs for a while.

"At least let us rest a bit. Surely, we will make better time in the end after a respite." She planted her feet enough to yank him up short.

His grip tightened on her arm. "Woman, you try my patience."

"What I say is reasonable. If you would simply stop to think." This time she could not keep the frustration from her voice.

His head canted to the side, and it dawned on her

she had just implied he was not too nimble of intellect. She swallowed. The lump in her throat moved not, and all her air got trapped in her lungs.

To her surprise, the Highlander released her as abruptly as he'd taken hold.

"All right," he said with the same exasperated tone one would use to placate a small, annoying child. "I will give you a moment to rest, but we cannot tarry long or we risk having soldiers sneak up our rear position."

She started breathing again.

He glanced behind them. "I will take some time to scout the area and make sure we are not followed. Tell the others that when I return, we must move again."

"How long will you be gone?" She wanted time to rest, but she did not want to be left alone with this crowd.

"Long enough to do what must be done." He started to leave, but something in her expression must have revealed her unease. He paused. "Now what troubles you, lass? No sense holding your tongue at this point." The exasperation was back in his voice. "Speak."

"You should not leave us women here unchaperoned with those men."

Her comment seemed to surprise him. "Why not? You will be safe enough with them."

"You cannot be sure of that. They do not want me here. I am not theirs to protect."

He waved away her comment. "It matters not if they want you here. Their obligation is to *me*." He took a step forward. His voice dropped, and its baritone took on an edge. "Did you forget the promise I made you?"

"Promise? What prom—" His words at the cart

afore they departed returned to her. "I-I did not." She caught the side of her lower lip with her teeth to squelch her uncharacteristic stammer.

He loomed closer. His demeanor suggested he took insult that she had not taken him at his word when he assured her safety upon her promise of cooperation. She'd meant no insult. Self-preservation was her only motivator.

The current situation had not been of her making. She intuited the others were no happier to have her joined to their trek than she had been to be abducted by the MacNeill. She knew not whom to trust, but she sensed this warrior offered the greatest protection… when he was present. His self-confidence bred confidence in him from others. Still, 'twas a simple matter of numbers. They were not on his side.

She glanced around, then lowered her voice. "There is one of you and eight of them."

He glanced around as well. "Your point?"

"You cannot guarantee the other men will not misbehave," she continued in a whisper.

"I can."

"You cannot control what the other men will do."

"Aye, I can," he said with no hesitation, no doubt, and a bit of steel that conveyed his absolute certainty in the band of his control.

Her doubtful look did not dissuade his conviction. He stood still and silently waited for her to make a better point or desist.

"How is that, exactly?" Now, she was the one to take on a placating tone. "Especially if you are not here?"

With two quick fingers to the top of his hood, he snatched the covering back enough for her to see his eyes through the opening in his face shroud. He eyed her with a glare that suggested she toyed with him. "I have given the men very strict instructions. Their acceptance of my rules was their only fare for passage to freedom. They know not to cross me."

"And if they do cross you?"

"Simple. I will kill any man who transgresses, and they know it."

Seriously? she thought but dared not say aloud. A search of those dark eyes of his confirmed he was indeed serious.

"Is that your answer for everything?"

"What mean you?" Confusion laced his voice.

"Simply kill them? Or him? Or me?" She pushed out a breath, and her arms crossed over her bosom. "Kill whomever annoys or bothers you?"

He shrugged. "Why not? It solves the problem of ever having to deal with the mal behavior again." Without further commentary, he turned and strode off into the trees.

Mouth agape at his rude departure, Ailsa stood, arms now akimbo, and stared after him. That her fate was inexorably linked to this man's whims went beyond frustrating to worrisome. There appeared to be no reasoning with him. If she could not reason her way to his aid in guiding her back to the Highlands, what hope did she have to get home? Staying with this crew and crossing into England was not an option.

Ailsa headed back to the people in question to deliver the Highlander's message. It was not well received by everyone.

"So, now yer the one passing out orders?" Jeremiah stepped forward. Considered the senior man, though not the oldest, due to his extensive experience, he had been born into slavery and raised all his life to serve royalty. He took seriously his role as the leader of the escapees, which showed in his authoritative tone and demeanor.

Ailsa stood her ground, refusing to be put on the defensive. "Not orders. I was simply asked to deliver a message."

"Aye. That we can see, lassie." He looked around to the others as if addressing his next comment to them. "What I dinnae ken is how ye came to be so close to the Shepherd in so short a time."

A few murmurs of agreement came from the other men. As she suspected, she was not considered part of their pack. Several of the men nodded in endorsement of Jeremiah's comment. A few others gave her a look that suggested they knew exactly how she had gotten into the imaginary good graces of the MacNeill...with indecorous behavior inappropriate for a wholesome lass.

Whatever animosity Jeremiah harbored for her back at the castle now spilled over into her relationships here. His distrust had transferred to many of the others. She glanced at the two women. Neither of them spoke. She could not tell whose side they were on or whether she could align herself with them for any benefit.

Rather than puzzle the question overlong, she grasped onto something Jeremiah had said. "The Shepherd?"

"Aye. That's what they call him. He leads the mutineers in their quest to free as many of the enslaved as possible." He scoffed. "As if ye knew not."

So, the stories about the Shepherd were true. The tales of a larger-than-life warrior said to emancipate Blacks in bondage had reached even as far as the castle. Ailsa stood momentarily stunned to realize stories she considered myths fashioned by enslaved minds desperate to hope for freedom were based in truth, and the Highlander was this mythical leader — or not so mythical — of the secret network of liberty mutineers.

Something else also came to mind. If this be truth, if Kallum MacNeill were indeed the Shepherd, then the warrior saved as many people as he killed...if not more.

Could he truly be as vicious as he led everyone to believe?

Surely, such a man was her best hope to get home to her kin.

Traveling on with the manner of men who stood before her held little hope or appeal. Their current demeanor left little doubt of their small-minded opinions of her. The thought of being left for ravenous predators recurred to her. This time, it was Jeremiah who tied the bindings, while his band of lemmings held her prone. Once the Highlander handed them off to the ferryman, would these men even allow her to continue on with the group?

'Twas one thing for them to be held in check when the Highlander was present. 'Twas another to expect that obedience to continue when he was no longer around to issue reprisals for noncompliance.

"It seems ya have the same knack for bewitching the Shepherd as ya did with the king's captain," one of the men said.

A chorus of "ayes" rang out.

Ailsa silently bristled at the charge. She had no

more wanted the Highlander's attention than she had wanted the captain's. She had been forced to endure the attentions of one and kidnapped by the other. Why were women always blamed for what men did to them when men enforced their will through abuse of strength or power?

"Ye never wanted to associate with us belowstairs minions afore. Ye join our escape only to ruin the timing of our getaway," Jeremiah said. "When did ye have the time to convince him to bring ye along in the first place?"

"I did not convince anyone. He simply assumed I was part of the group. He remembered me from the king's dais at the festival championship bout." She didn't know why she was explaining herself. No matter what she said, this group was unlikely to change their opinions.

"Aye." Jeremiah chuckled. "When he turned you down because of that pounded-upon face of yours."

The elder to whom she'd given her seat slid her a pitying look, and both the women glanced away, unable to meet her eyes.

"Even we lowly belowstairs lackeys heard about that, we did," someone added, and the other men joined in the razzing to laugh along with Jeremiah.

'Twas bad enough to have suffered abuse and ridicule from those who'd held her against her will. To suffer such ridicule from her own kind rankled more than she cared to admit to herself. If she had not already had misgivings about whether or not she belonged with this entourage of escapees, people who thought she had considered herself above them while they'd been enslaved at the castle, she would certainly have them now.

These were not her people, other than by color of their skin. She had to make her own way. This she had always known, but their actions and callous words served as a fresh reminder that she could count on no one but herself. Her way to liberation was the Highlands, and her safe passage there rested with Kallum MacNeill.

When the man returned, Ailsa would make sure he did not leave her again until he'd seen her safely within a day's walk of Connery land.

Or...

She looked in the direction he had departed. *Mayhap I should follow him now?*

The Highlander would not like an uninvited shadow, but with many of the other freed captives not fond of her presence, either, her chance of suffering hostility stood in equal parts whether she stayed put or followed after.

She glanced at the two women who had made clear they would offer no defense of her, then sized up Jeremiah and the men who had been most vocal in their support of him. Despite Kallum's bravado, she did not like the odds of eight against one if it came to that.

All right, mayhap only seven, since the groom had lived into his gray-hair season and the MacNeill would make short work of him. Nevertheless, she felt uneasy being left behind with this bunch. In the time the Highlander was gone, what might they do to her? How far would they dare take any action against her in view of the MacNeill's warning?

She did not want to find out.

She'd rather take her chances stirring the wrath of

the warrior. He was already exasperated with her. Thus, any ill treatment he administered might mercifully be swift.

She turned without preamble, not caring what the others would think, and followed the path the *Shepherd* had taken into the trees. The escapees already thought poorly of her. A few more indecent thoughts would matter little. They would think what they wanted in any event.

The reaction that most mattered was that of the MacNeill, the man who thought his identity was unknown. She'd best keep her knowledge of his name to herself. 'Twould likely be of value at some point, but presently, she was in self-preservation mode. Self-preservation dictated she keep the man's secret for now. She dared not think about the possible backlash should he learn she knew who he was or what he would do when he caught her following him. Doing so might cause her to lose the nerve to continue.

Instead, she took a deep breath and hastened her steps, mentally girding herself for the warrior's most certain ire.

CHAPTER NINE

Away from the waiting escapees, Kallum pressed a hand against a tree and pulled his swollen member from his trews. He had a desperate need to relieve himself, but the chatty wench's well-placed fist to his groin earlier had left him in a delicate situation. His aching and abused cock turned what should have been an easy, thoughtless act into a monumental challenge.

Deep in concentration, he moaned with relief when nature's subtle din finally arrived in uncomfortable staccato spurts. Head back, he thought about his charges at the waiting cart. They could not afford to dally overlong. The hellion had been right, though, he admitted grudgingly to himself. Giving the captives time to rest would allow for a faster pace moving forward.

He closed his eyes and took in the sounds of the woodlands amongst his occasional squirt against a fallen leaf. His eyes popped open at the unexpected sound of approaching footfalls. The steps were light but not quiet enough. Whoever the interloper was, he was a clod at stealth, but it might matter not.

Here he stood indisposed, and the ever-loving spurts that had taken forever to start now would not stop. He could tuck back into his trews and sprinkle himself or stand and fight fisting his manhood. Neither option held appeal.

The footfalls came closer, and Kallum willed himself to stop piddling.

Cessation occurred not.

Ah, fuck! He was going to die taking a leak against a tree. Not the honorable death in battle he had foreseen, and the thought made him angry beyond measure.

If whoever approached was one of the king's search party, the monarch needed to improve his guards' training. Were he not otherwise occupied, Kallum would have already circled behind the stalker and swiftly ended his life. If 'twas merely some ne'er-do-well set on mischief or thievery, the man need seek another occupation. If he lived beyond this eventide.

Kallum slipped his unoccupied hand to one of the two daggers concealed beneath his armpit. His throw would need be swift, and his aim true. If he missed, his attacker would most likely run him through with a sword.

A branch cracked to his left. He whirled and released the dagger with a swift underhanded flick just as the woman known as Anne stepped from the trees. He managed to adjust the throw at the last moment so he'd not throw a death blow, but the thought of impaling a woman startled him such that he forgot about his prior bodily misfunction and released himself to dangle free.

Anne screeched and, much to his surprise, managed to deftly dodge the flying *sgian-dubh* and land indecorously on the ground. The dagger wedged with a *thud* in the tree behind where her head had vacated only instants afore.

She rolled to face him. Pushing up to a sitting position, she braced her hands behind her hips and stared up at him with wide eyes and mouth agape. She blinked twice, sucked in a deep breath, and sputtered, "You... you—"

Her voice cut off when her gaze adjusted, and her eyes grew impossibly wider when she realized she sat staring directly into his naked *tadger*.

"*Wretched*—!" He took himself back in hand and, with a quick swivel, directed his member toward the foliage he'd sprinkled previously. Not happy to have a female audience for his malfunctioning pisser, Kallum made an irritated glance over his shoulder. "Forsooth, woman! What in the name of all God's angels could you possibly have…"

His voice stalled. The troublesome female continued to stare toward his midsection. His back faced her, so she could see or hear nothing intimate. The capricious expulsion he'd managed before her arrival had stopped. Instead, his appendage perked enthusiastically with his realization that her surprise over receiving an up-close view of his package had transformed not into horror but curiosity.

Kallum gritted his teeth against the discomfort of his body's unwanted and untimely hardening over her apparent interest. Even if he fancied a go and she'd been willing, he was in no condition to perform.

Vexed further by that awareness, he growled facetiously between clenched teeth, "Would you like another look?"

"Wh-what?" Her eyes met his.

His brows rose, and he gave a flippant motion with his head toward the matter he had in hand. "I could turn back around if you want."

"Nay!" A deep blush spread beneath her bruised, bronzed-brown complexion, and she whipped around in the dirt to face the other direction.

Ah, there was the horror he had expected.

Perchance, she had simply been in extended shock at the encounter. He himself was still a bit shaken at how close he had come to ending her life. He had never harmed a female. To have gone from tournament champion to abductor and, finally, maiden killer in one pass of the sun would have been more than his conscience could handle.

He leaned his forehead against the bark of the tree and released a low, drawn-out sigh. The complications of the day kept evolving. The thought returned to him that he should have left this hellion to her own devices when she first voiced opposition to his aid back at the castle.

What foolishness that. As if his conscience could have handled that dishonorable act, either.

None the matter. She was here now, and he would have to deal with her until he could pass her to the next escort along the liberation trek.

Holding on to the pleasant notion that his time with her was temporary, he tried to relax and finish his business. Along with the lingering discomfort, the presence of the hellion made his effort impossible.

Noticing his distress, she inquired with hesitant consternation, "Are you not well?"

"I am fine," he gritted out. "No thanks to you."

"Me!" She scrambled to her feet. "What do I have to do with anything? I was simply minding my own affairs when you threw a dagger at my head!"

After a few heartbeats, he abandoned his attempt and properly adjusted himself. He took a deep, calming breath, then turned to face his unexpected visitor. "Nay, you were minding *my* affairs, and your fisted assault earlier this eve has everything to do with my current…"

He swallowed what he was about to say. No way was he discussing with her the workings—or current failure to work—of his manly organ.

It took a moment afore knowledge entered her expression. "Oh," she said slowly, then covered her mouth. "Oh!"

He studied her with narrowed eyes. Was she laughing at him?

Mayhap 'twould be all right after all to assassinate a female. At the least, his current emotions suggested the act would *feel* immensely satisfying.

She coughed suspiciously.

He stalked toward her with a demeanor that communicated "mock me at your peril" without him having to say a word.

She startled and jumped hastily out of his way. He continued past her with a satisfied smirk at her show of alarm. He was relieved to discern she was not wholly immune after all to the element of intimidation for which he was known.

He jerked his *sgian-dubh* from the tall oak he'd speared and replaced it in the hidden sheath beneath his cape. Crossing his arms, he leaned a shoulder against the tree. "You want to explain why you had a sudden wish for death and came sneaking behind me?"

She slapped at the ground covering on her garment. "I was not *sneaking*." Her chin rose a notch. "I simply came to speak with you."

"Speak with me? And this could not wait until I returned?"

"Nay." She averted her gaze. "I thought it best to do this out of the hearing of the others." With head down, she began to pick absently at the remaining debris on her gray overdress.

By her demeanor, he surmised something had happened between her and the other escapees, but he waited without question or response.

Understanding he did not intend to speak, she looked up. Her shoulders lifted with a deep sigh, and then she said in a rush, "I need you to take me to the Outer Hebrides."

Her request surprised him, but he showed no emotion. She had mentioned the Hebrides during their prior talk. He wondered again what pursuit she sought there. She had hesitated earlier when he asked her about her interest in passage to the Hebrides. She'd covered her gaffe quickly. He knew not whether that was a credit to her intelligence or a testament to a dishonest nature. Either way, he sensed she had been less than forthcoming with him.

He wondered what she was hiding. She had wanted to follow a particular Highland clan from the castle grounds. He had guessed she intended to meet up with a paramour. Was she so determined to meet this warrior, whoever he was, that she would risk traveling for days with an unknown male or sailing the sea as a lone traveler to get to him?

"Well?" she asked. Her eyes searched his expectantly.

He studied her. He had no intention of guiding her to the Highlands, but his curiosity regarding her request sought appeasement. "Why?"

In truth, 'twas of no import why she chose that destination. 'Twould not be proper for him to make the several days' journey with her alone, irrespective of her reasoning. Her reputation would be ruined, and she'd have no opportunity to make a suitable marriage match as a result.

Even if he dropped her at her destination with no one aware of the improper circumstances surrounding their travel, what possible motive could be worth putting herself at such risk? She knew not whether he was a man of honor or an abuser of women. If he were the latter, she would be at his mercy with no one around to protect her from him.

Was her unknown man of such importance to her?

He felt a twinge of unease at the thought of her commitment to this meeting or reunion. Why the thought of her loyalty to some unknown lad bothered him, he could not fathom. Yet, the thought of her traveling—foolishly—to meet such a man did indeed bother him. What manner of man could this *walloper* be if he himself had not sought her out but left her to navigate the rendezvous on her own? A man who, in truth, could not be worthy of a strong-willed beauty such as she.

She eyed him suspiciously. "What difference does that make? You were content to abduct me from Stirling Castle and drop me with some ferryman for passage into England. What matter is it to you whether I end up in England or the Highlands?"

Her light-colored eyes flashed. In the full moonlight, he could see the mix of colors that made a unique pattern of brown and green striated with a subtle yellow. No wonder he'd had difficulty discerning her eye color from afar. He'd first noticed the stunning hazel when he'd dumped her in the cart. The color was rare. He'd only met a few people during his lifetime with eyes the odd color. Hers were alluring and reinforced his impression of her as siren, mysteriously beautiful and dangerous at the same time.

And that accounted only for her looks.

Add her contrariness, and she sparked with a fierceness that gave her a magnificent feral glow even her facial injuries could not diminish. Her eyes currently flashed with the intenseness of a wildcat on the hunt. The warrior in him admired her internal fire. And his powers of observation, honed by years of battle and strategy, noticed something else of intrigue. In her pique, her English had acquired a tinge of accent that sounded suspiciously like the intonations that rolled off the tongues of native Gaelic speakers when they dabbled with the king's preferred language.

Despite the distraction of her handsomeness, his soldier's intuition sensed something afoul. He was struck once again by how her regal comportment contradicted her status as an enslaved person. Something about this woman did not make sense. Her circumstances, her demeanor, and now her speech. Not one to appreciate unveiled mystery, his focus narrowed on her.

Whatever the intrigue behind her person, he meant to find out the details. Whether he need find them out by intimidation or by subterfuge, he would discover the truth of it—of her—and the game to get beneath her secrets would start now.

He pushed off the tree.

• • •

The look in the warrior's eyes took on a decidedly ominous gleam. Since all but his eyes were still completely covered by his dark cloak and face shroud,

Ailsa had the awful impression of conversing with *Auld Clootie*, the Devil himself. Unnerved by the ghastly thought and the noticeable change in his demeanor, Ailsa took a huge step backward.

He shifted, deceptively casual with the languid movement. "You seek a boon from me. But you feel no need to explain why a lass such as yourself wants to take several days' travel, alone and unchaperoned, with an unfamiliar male you claim abducted you?" He shrugged. "Very well. If that is your choice, my choice is to say you nay."

He started walking back the way they had come.

"Claim?" Her voice rose. "There is no *claim*. Did you not bodily remove me from castle grounds?" she said to his back.

He spun. "I did not abduct you! I freed you from enslavement. I would think you'd be grateful for my aid."

She harrumphed at the forcefulness of his tone. "That was not aid. That was *interference*. I did not need your assistance."

A movement of his head betrayed his intent to respond.

Her hand shot up palm out. "Don't you dare say it again." She remembered his earlier counter about the state of her face. She need not hear him repeat the demeaning comment.

She glared at him and was taken aback when the edges of his eyes crinkled as if he hid a grin beneath the face covering. The man had never done anything in her presence but project a demeanor of scowl and brood. She had been certain he was incapable of anything as human as mirth.

The memory of his entry into the Stirling Castle courtyard played through her mind. The rustle of muscle beneath his rich brown skin, the air of command as he sat his stallion, and the deep timbre of his voice when he'd challenged her thoughtless and embarrassingly lascivious utterance. Sized for dominance in war, he was a stunning—and impressive—specimen in his broods. From what she had recently observed, his impressive size held consistent through all parts of his anatomy. A hot flush seared through her at the recall of the wickedly indecent image.

To imagine him with a slow, seductive grin—for it could only be slow and seductive with this one—edged with his unique air of satanic danger sent an unexpected pull of wanton awareness through her. The feelings were new for her. She had no experience with wantonness; she knew not even how to flirt.

Why the physical of this man awakened everything feminine in her, she could not understand. He'd done naught but aggravate her from the beginning. When her mother taught her about interactions between males and females, she had inconveniently left out the lesson on how attraction's spark required not a favorable regard.

All thanks, mamaidh, she glibly offered in silent rebuke to her mother's spirit.

In this realm, she mentally shook out her distracted thoughts. She had to make him understand his role in her current predicament, and that could not be done with her mind engaged in indecorous suppositions or biological hypotheses. Surely, once he understood he had ruined her personal strategy, he would feel duty bound to remedy his blunder.

"I had my own plan for independence. Your interference prevented me from carrying out that plan."

"Which was?" he challenged.

She hesitated. She had not yet determined how much she could safely reveal to the warrior. Until she knew whether their clans were allies, foes, or indifferent to each other, she risked much by divulging her ties to the Connerys. She knew not whether she would set herself up for possible abuse or ransom.

At one point during her captivity, she had considered ransom a possible reason for her enslavement. That some royal soldier in want of additional coin had opted to hide her amongst the king's enslaved captives until such time as he could barter her to her kin. The more time that passed without word or attempt at exchange, the less likely this supposition had become.

Here she stood with the MacNeill. He appeared honorable. After all, he devoted himself to service as the Shepherd. He regularly risked his life to free hundreds of people, or more, from enslavement. If the tales surrounding the legend of the Shepherd were even half to be believed, a man such as this could not be a man who would also torment a woman in need. He was a protector by nature. This much she intuited without doubt.

She would need to trust him to offer his protection and escort to her. Even so, she was not ready to trust him with the true knowledge of who she was. Like him, the secret of her identity might be all that kept her safe...or alive. But she sensed if she did not give him some semblance of the truth, he might continue his opposition to assisting her.

"I had intended to insert myself with one of the

clans and travel amongst them to my destination."

"Which clan?"

"We need not labor over the specifics. 'Tis enough that you know my journey would have taken me to the Outer Hebrides."

That was only partly true. Connery land was not in the Outer Hebrides, but it was not far from there. Thus, it was true enough without disclosing to which clan she was kin.

"'Tis it truly a place you seek, mistress, or a person?" Skepticism and condescension laced his voice.

"My pardon?"

"This scheme of yours to insert yourself with a clan. You could not carry it out without detection unless you had the protection of someone in the clan. Who is he?"

"I—I do not know of what you speak." She watched doubt enter his eyes. She wished she could see his entire face. Having this conversation into the shadowed void made it hard to determine whether she moved him in any small way. "I had the protection of no one."

"Lass, if you will not tell me true, why should I trust you? I do not travel alone with those I do not trust. Try again." His voice brooked no disobedience.

Instinctively, Ailsa ran a hand down the length of her single braid, which had fallen over her shoulder, and squeezed. Uncertainty and desperation warred in equal parts in her. He was her only hope to get home.

If he sent her to England, 'twould be several seasons, if not longer, afore she could earn enough coin to return to Scotland. She knew not how those of African heritage fared in England, but she suspected their lots were not fortunate. Add the double censure of being a Highlander, and the English would never accept her without prejudice. Her most likely employ would be as servant or mayhap another lady's maid. Though she'd offer those services this time as a free woman entitled to compensation, neither profession brought a body prosperity. At best, she'd earn only enough coin to subsist. She wasn't interested in merely subsisting, and certainly not half a country away from her homeland.

She wanted to thrive. She was entitled to thrive. She was entitled to return to the Highlands. She had suffered enough; she deserved to go home.

Right now, all that stood between her and home was Kallum MacNeill. What did he want from her? What were the magic words that would make him see reason?

"I know not what you ask of me. My plan depended not on a man. I meant to appeal to the mercy of the lead warrior for—"

He shook his head at her response. His cloak flared when he spun and made determined steps away from her.

Releasing her braid, she took a frantic step forward. "Wait!"

He stopped not.

"I implore you. Wait!"

When his steps continued, Ailsa understood her time had run out. Yet again in her life, she would be cast aside, dismissed as unimportant and insignificant. Never quite accepted amongst her own clan, even by her own father, she had understood the distance inspired by her illegitimate, mixed blood. But here, it rankled that even amongst this band of fugitives she was considered an outsider despite their shared experiences. As she stared at the MacNeill's back, the hollow of familiar isolation and loneliness reared up and threatened to consume her. She could not let this man walk away from her.

Discarding all sense of pride, she dropped her attempt at reason and lowered herself to beg. "*Please*. I need your help."

Unmoved, the MacNeill slowed not his departure.

Knowing not what else to do, Ailsa rushed forward and told the truth no one had believed in three comings and goings of the summer sun. "I am not a slave! I was freeborn in the Highlands."

CHAPTER TEN

Kallum made a slow turn and stared at the lass in stunned silence. As he intended, by walking away, he had given her the impression she had lost any chance to win his assistance. The tactic was designed to move her to stop her dissembling and tell him the truth. Alas, he had underestimated the lass's talent for subterfuge. Of all the shenanigans for which he had prepared himself, this particular absurdity had not made his possible considerations.

'Twas a dangerous game to play. She had to know him capable of ferreting out the falsehood in such a ploy. He prepared himself to call her on the nonsense when his look into her eyes revealed a startling genuineness. No guile hid behind those hazel orbs, but he could not have understood her correctly.

"How say you?" The request for clarity was automatic and borne of shock. He had heard her well the first time.

"Please. You must believe me. My home is in the Highlands. You cannot send me off to England. I will find no peace there." Her voice held much of the vulnerability he saw in her eyes but no longer the hint of accent he had detected afore.

"How can this be?" he asked in Gaelic. He needed to know if his intuition—his ear—had been right.

Her chest rose and fell with a deep breath. "Three summers ago, I came with my laird to the allegiance trials set by the king. During the noonday festivities, I became separated from my clansmen. One of the king's men nabbed me and put me in with a group of captives newly arrived at the castle. I tried to explain the mistake, but I could get no one to listen."

She had responded in English, but it was clear she had understood his question, though posed in a different language. The last vestiges of his disbelief—that somehow he had suspected from the outset was unwarranted—evaporated.

He tried to make sense of her tale, and because his first question had been a simple one, he asked for additional clarification again in the principal language of his people. "What of your kin? Did no one vouch for you?"

It seemed simple enough to correct such a mistake in identity.

"I know not. I never saw any of them again," she responded in fluent, unaccented Gaelic. "The captives were separated from the guests. I kept waiting for someone to come for me, but no one did. Eventually, I tried to escape the horrid life on my own. Twice. I was captured and returned to the castle both times." Her eyes held his with a look that suggested she knew he had been testing her with the switch in language. A challenge lit her eyes as she silently dared him to continue his disbelief of her word.

Kallum shook his head, floored by what she had imparted. A Highland lass abducted from her clan. How could no kin have searched for her? Surely, someone missed her presence.

"What of your parents?" he asked in English. "Your menfolk by blood? How is it that your father or brother never came looking for you?"

If Caitrin, Inan's sister and the sister of his heart, had disappeared, he would have moved mountains and destroyed entire villages until she had been returned. 'Twas the way of the MacNeills. They stood loyal and true, one for the other. He'd suffered taunts and slights as a lad, but he'd never doubted his place amongst the laird's family or the clan. Despite any personal qualms some might have with him or his lineage, each would fight to the death afore allowing an outsider to rise against him or any other member of the clan.

"I have no father. I am my mother's only child. Hence, no brother, either. I lost my mother nigh on two fortnights afore the journey. There was no one to miss me save the group I came to Stirling with, and for some reason, they left without me and never looked back." Hurt filled her eyes and voice as she revealed being, all told, abandoned by the entourage who should have seen fit to protect and shelter her.

Kallum tried to wrap his brain around all she had revealed. He remembered the allegiance trials. Laird MacNeill had been required to attend as well. The chief rode out with the might of his army, led by Kallum himself, lest he face an ambush on the road or even at the castle. King James had hardly proven himself a friend of the Highland chiefs back then. Who he would ultimately be to those of Highland birth still remained to be seen.

But if the monster could steal Highland lasses from their clans and enslave them… *Nay!*

Kallum had never heard of such.

Season after season, he slipped into the night and led the enslaved to lives of independence. That such independence once won could be snatched away had been understood. Enslavers paid well for the capture and return of escapees. 'Tis why he oft arranged passage across foreign borders. But to learn of those taken who had known no life but free left a bitter pall in his gut.

That the king himself had allowed, or at the least had overlooked, such an atrocity under his royal roof meant solemn tidings for the cessation of slave trading in Scotland and Scottish enterprises on Caribbean isles. Those of Black lineage could never truly have freedom until the crown saw fit to denounce in full the sale and use of enslaved laborers. The king would rather pretend it was solely a pestilence of the Portuguese or the Dutch over which the monarchy had no control nor received nary a benefit. But benefit the king did. He savored his sweets flavored with sugar from cane harvested by enslaved souls on Caribbean plantations, ran his household with enslaved servants, and clearly had gifted his daughter a stolen Highland lass of *dubh* heritage.

The Highlands hoped to continue a sovereign government with the king's blessing. How could a monarch who allowed such a grievous injustice to thrive in Stirling Castle and the Scotland beyond ever be trusted to do right by all people of the land, especially clanspeople the crown had been publicly known to denigrate as inferior in education and manners? Wasn't that a similar rationale for why those held enslaved deserved not autonomy or freedom? The treatment of stolen Africans made clear the peerage's and royalty's standard of tolerance of those considered inferior in breeding, intelligence, and supposed morality.

It had been appalling to know the king passed

around maidens as if they were baubles fashioned by a village vendor. To know the king may have stolen one such maiden from her birthright without regard for her freeborn status renewed Kallum's desire to have the king feel the thrust of a sword through his royal gut.

Kallum studied the lass. Questions abounded. Uppermost in his mind were her plans should she return to the Highlands.

"You say you have no kin by blood. Then what intend you to do upon return to your clan? You are a maiden alone. So alone, you had no one to seek you out after disappearance. What can there possibly still be for you in your home lands? Would you even have a place to live?"

A flicker of doubt crossed her face. These were not new questions to her. She had considered these issues on her own. Yet, beneath the doubt, a strong spark of determination shone. This was a lass who had no intention of giving up until she got what — where — she wanted.

"I know not. I suspect my cottage is gone, and I'll have to rely on the hospitality of friends at the beginning. I am a healer. I have supported myself afore with my skills. I shall be able to do so again." She gathered herself and looked him once again in the eyes with a poise any queen would envy. "You need not worry about my arrangements. I ask no lasting obligation of you except you guide me back. Once I am to the Outer Hebrides, I can make my final way on my own."

What she asked was not that simple. His hand rose and fell absently, and he paced to one side, then the other. "Lass, you have not pondered this well. You know not what manner of man I am." He stopped and faced her. "You cannot hand yourself into my control not knowing whether I would do you harm."

"Control?" Her eyes rolled. "You overstate the arrangement, sir. I am not putting myself into your *control*. I shall be controlled by no man." She placed her arms akimbo and donned a fierce expression that displayed undeniable grit. "And I have considered the risk that you might be of low character and take advantage of my circumstances, but I am confident you are not the manner of man who enjoys the harm of those weaker than himself. You live your life as the Shepherd. That tells me all I need know at the moment."

She had the right of it; he would never harm or abuse her, but he had hoped to make her nervous enough to reconsider her request.

He scrubbed his hands down his face, adrift in contemplation.

Sensing his loss for words, she added, "You would not go out of your way to free me to then abuse me yourself."

His hood and shroud were becoming hot. He wanted to throw them off and be done with this conversation and his portion of the liberation trek. He glanced up at the constellations and took note of the position of the moon. He needed to get back to the others and get them moving. This exchange had taken much time. He wanted to give this woman hope, but what she wanted was not feasible.

"'Twould not be proper for me to take you with me. If you are known to have travelled alone with me, your reputation would be ruined. You would have no opportunity for a suitable marriage. You would leave yourself without protection. Healing might offer you a chance at coin, but without the protection of a husband, you would be fair game for any male opportunist. Many of whom would be content to use then discard you."

She started shaking her head in disagreement afore he stopped speaking. "I do not intend to marry, so my reputation is of no import. As for the other, I will make a way for myself and find the protection you mention, without the need to barter control of my body and my life in exchange for marriage simply because tradition dictates I am not a proper and respectable woman without a husband."

Kallum found it interesting she used words similar to Inan's about marriage requiring bartering away a piece of yourself. To this he had no reply. While he himself had no intent to marry, he'd known few women of the same mind. The few with whom he'd made acquaintance did so mainly because they lived a more prosperous life sharing themselves with more than one man. He frowned at the thought of her leading such a lifestyle.

But nay, she had plans to use her healing skills to make her own way. She was a brave lass, and surely a strong one to have endured captivity all this time and retained even a small portion of the spirit she displayed, but there was still the matter of him. He did not see how he could keep his identity a secret through several days of travel with her. Once he removed the hood, she would recognize him.

He knew not who her kin were, and it was clear she wanted him not to know.

His identity could not be revealed to the daughter of a clan who might be amongst the MacNeills' fiercest enemies. She would have the power to bring them low. And for all her shown respect for what he did as the Shepherd, were she recaptured, she would have a great advantage with which to bargain for her ultimate emancipation. The Shepherd was highly wanted for crimes against property. The property was humans who should never have been held like possessions, but this mattered not to those who contributed to the bounty for his capture.

He saw no way but to disappoint her. "'Tis best you go with the others into England, lass. There will be more for you there, and you will have assistance to build the life you want, even if you choose to do so without a husband."

His gut twisted at the look of defeat that crossed her face, but there was no avoidance for it. This was the best way, even if she did not understand so currently.

"The risk of you staying in the Highlands when you are a fugitive from slavery and the crown is too dangerous. Many pursue the bounties offered for escapees from enslavement. The king's bounty is likely to be high. You'd put yourself and your reunited clan at much peril by not putting another country's borders between you and the castle you fled." He reached for her. "Come. We must reunite with the others and move to the next trek point."

With a firm yank, she disengaged from his hold and walked away from him.

She had regained her composure. The look of defeat was gone, but what had replaced it gave Kallum pause. He had the distinct impression the lass was not yet finished with him.

. . .

Ailsa strode from the trees into a bevy of knowing glances and suggestive smirks. She knew what each expression meant, especially with the ground debris that lingered on her garments. Her fellow escapees had decided her following the Shepherd into the woods had led to bartering of a physical nature.

She had not thought of such, and under normal circumstances, she would never have considered such base behavior. Mayhap she should. The warrior may have been more amenable to her request had she allowed him to seek his pleasure with her flesh. 'Twas not as if she were saving her innocence for a betrothed.

Nay. She was desperate but not at the point of desperation that she had to debase herself.

The warrior had not said aye, but on thought, he had not said nay. He'd made reference to the impropriety of their unavoidable, unchaperoned proximity during travel and expressed concern that no life likely remained for her back with her clan. He sought to rid himself of her, but he was not unsympathetic to her plight.

Thus, she must not give up. She must find a way to convince the MacNeill to take her with him after he relinquished the other escaped captives to the ferryman.

She glanced his way. He took charge of those gathered and got the group moving again.

He thought the matter settled.

Not yet, warrior. She knew exactly what she had to do.

Ailsa followed along quietly at the back of the caravan. The MacNeill once again took charge of driving the cart. Periodically, he turned to search her out. She repressed a grin. Was he worried she would scurry off into the night on her own? Or, mayhap, he was checking to see what mischief she might cause in petulance over his refusal of her request.

'Twas clear he found her behavior perplexing. He was a man used to being obeyed without question. She was a woman used to going her own way. She suspected that tendency had much to do with growing up without a father. Without a man in the cottage, she and her mother were accountable to no one save themselves and each other. She'd never had a man direct her actions or control her future like the other lasses whose cottages bordered hers. Such independence was not easily relinquished.

Lest, all told, you be stolen into slavery. She brushed the disheartening thought aside. She must stay vigilant during their trek. As much as the MacNeill watched her, she watched him. She could ill afford to miss the moment he relinquished the reins in preparation to take his leave from their ensemble.

The group made good time. Afore daybreak the next day, they approached a quiet cove with a stream. The MacNeill unharnessed the horses and led them to the water to drink. A short while later, a figure advanced out of the shadows. Like the Shepherd, he was hooded and shrouded so his face could not be seen.

The two conversed out of the hearing of the escapees. After a moment, Kallum nodded and offered the man his forearm. The man Ailsa presumed was the ferryman responded in kind. They gripped near each other's elbows and executed a warrior's shake.

Kallum returned one horse to the cart and led the other aside. After he introduced the escapees to their new escort, the entourage prepared to resume the grueling journey.

The Shepherd stopped in front of her. Their eyes connected, but he spoke not. His right hand lifted toward her face, but he caught himself, startled by what he'd been about to do.

Ailsa sensed regret in him, but she held no sympathy. "Do not look at me that way. As much as it may pain you to send a Highland maiden far from her home, how much more anguish must I feel to be condemned to such a fate?"

"Lass, we have had this talk. There is no better way."

"Aye, there is. 'Tis my future and my reputation at stake. Thus, 'tis I who should have final word on this decision."

A warrior such as he could not fear the reprisal of others. His worry for her had to be his primary reason for turning her away. She was not such a coddling that she did not understand, in part, he was also sending her away for his own self-preservation. He had to have figured out that once they were alone together on the path toward home, he would eventually have to reveal his face, and she would recognize him.

He'd chosen himself over her.

She understood it, but she did not have to like it.

Leaning forward, she muttered, "You need only grab hold of those massive cods of yours, embrace your own risk, and let the opinions of others be damned."

She heard a loud gasp behind her from one of the other female escapees. Apparently, Ailsa had not said the last soft enough.

The MacNeill's eyes narrowed at her, and after a moment, his head gave a subtle shake. Whether in regret or annoyance, she knew not. Without warning, his hands grasped her waist and he lifted her effortlessly into a seated position on the back of the cart, her legs dangling from the back. He motioned the ferryman to proceed, then stood back to silently watch the caravan pull away.

From her Shepherd-designated seat on the edge of the cart, Ailsa watched his silhouette slowly fade into the distance. He stood motionless until the caravan reached the copse of trees that led out the opposite side of the cove from where they'd entered. When the cart turned to leave his sight, he picked up a branch covered in foliage and began to sweep away signs of their respite.

Now that he was no longer watching, Ailsa jumped from the cart and grabbed her belongings.

"What are you doing?" the young lady who had been sitting next to her asked with alarm.

"I need to walk for a bit."

The girl stared at her, confused. The newest leg of their journey had barely started, and the girl's expression indicated she did not understand this untimely need for Ailsa to stretch her legs.

Ignoring the lass, Ailsa slowed her pace and allowed herself to separate slightly from the caravan. Her cart companion glanced her way several times, the last time waving insistently for Ailsa to speed up.

Ailsa nodded but continued to create a straggling distance behind the group. She had no intention of letting the MacNeill send her away, and she did not have much time. Once he finished clearing signs of their stop, he'd mount his horse and she'd be loath to catch him.

Careful to make sure everyone's attention was averted, Ailsa slipped away and wound her way through the trees back toward the cove. She scoped out her fellow Highlander's shadowed figure. He broke his branch into three separate chunks and shucked them into the stream.

When he turned to stride toward his horse, Ailsa shoved her arm and head through the handle of her bag, so it lay crossways against her back, and began to run. She could not let him mount that horse afore he noticed her presence. Branches and foliage gripped at her face and garments, but she batted them away without slowing. Hoping the departing caravan was far enough away they could not hear her voice, she prepared to call after the warrior.

He had taken careful pains to ensure no one saw his face. The travelers had all simply referred to him as "the Shepherd," if they called him by any name at all. She was certain his identity had been carefully guarded throughout his late-night assignations. 'Twas a secret she needed to use to her advantage now, but she had no desire to put him at risk by allowing others to hear her revelation.

'Twas all she had to bargain with. She had no lofty notions that she could make her way back to the border of the Highlands alone or traverse its woods to make it safely to Connery territory. If she were not set upon by scragglers of nefarious intent, she might become feast for some woodland beast. She needed the warrior to serve as her guide and, she hated to admit, her protector.

The MacNeill looked up when she crashed through the trees. Utterly dismissing her presence, he had the audacity to storm at a quickened pace toward his mount. He grabbed hold of the horse's mane and swung up onto the blanket rested across the mare's back. He sat facing Ailsa, but he did not speak. He stared silently, as if waiting for her to explain herself.

She slowed to a walk. She had only taken a few steps when he swung the horse in the opposite direction and encouraged it into a gallop.

Not one to be dismissed so easily, Ailsa hastened to the large rocks that formed a low wall in an arc around the cove. She scrambled up onto the boulders. Frustration, despair, and a bit of murderous rage warred through her system all at once. If he chose to leave her behind, he'd do so knowing he left behind not some mere wisp of a stranded lass but a woman fit to rival him in ability to put forth a fatal threat.

'Twas a dangerous game of one-upmanship she commenced with her next play, but it was the only play she had left.

With a deep breath, she took her life into her hands and yelled, "Kallum MacNeill!"

CHAPTER ELEVEN

So surprised was he to hear his name, Kallum yanked the mare to a stop. Startled by his rough treatment, the mare reared onto her hindquarters and kicked fiercely with her front legs. Kallum leaned forward to keep his seat and soothed the mare with a calming voice.

When the mare's front hooves returned to the ground, he gave her a gentle rub on the neck. "Sorry, lass," he said quietly to the steed. "'Twas an unexpected shock I received myself."

Still rubbing gently along the horse's neck, he turned his face toward the woman he thought he'd seen the last of and quietly considered the predicament he found himself in.

Did she truly know 'twas him, or had she made a lucky guess?

Did that even matter?

If she revealed to anyone she had even a suspicion he was the Shepherd, he'd be hunted, arrested, and executed simply as a matter of caution.

He directed the horse into a slow walk toward her. She stood stoic, seemingly aware of the crossroads at which she had put them.

"If you are wrong, you do this Kallum MacNeill a disservice," he said with a slow, even tone.

"I am not wrong," she replied without hesitation. Surety lent steel to her words, and her chin thrust upward as if she dared him to take a chance on her error.

He nodded. Respect filled him for her ability to

back her offensive move without show of weakness. "If you are right, then you leave me with a difficult choice."

"Aye." She nodded in return. "You must either kill me or take me with you to protect the secret of your name." Her words were matter-of-fact and deceptively without emotion.

She could not be that calm about the options she had laid forth.

"Or…" He relaxed his hold on the mare's reins and fisted a hand high on his right thigh. "I could leave you here to whatever fate shall befall you."

She shrugged. "Which shall amount, in time, to the same as killing me. At least, such would be your hope."

He sighed deeply. "Lass, I do not desire you dead. Of that, I thought you were aware. And I highly doubt you would die if I left you. You are smart enough to make your way back to the caravan. They have not been gone overly long."

And he was prepared to circle back to make sure she managed to rejoin the caravan afore he made his final departure toward home.

"So, you would have me return to the ferryman and trade him or some other in England the secret of your identity in exchange for travel back to the Highlands?"

He shoved off his hood in anger. "'Tis a dangerous game you play, lass. Mind yourself." His free hand went automatically to the hilt of his sword.

Her eyes tracked his hand movement, and her expression revealed she understood the seriousness of the ultimatum she had just made. To her credit, she did not cower away from his snarl of retribution or cringe upon his touching of his sword.

He had faced men with less fortitude than this lass,

and again, he wondered from what clan she bade. She said she was a healer, but she had the hardihood of a lass born and bred in a laird's manor or raised by a warrior of worth. 'Twas possible she had not told him true about being a healer, but mayhap she had high-born status and had learned the ways of healing.

'Twould be but a small untruth or, more so, an incomplete truth. He knew she worried over her fate should he know of her kin. Since she knew his clan name, mayhap she knew their clans were enemies. Were she of high rank in her clan and her clan a MacNeill enemy, he'd have much leeway to secure concessions from her kin for her return.

But were she such a lass, it made no sense that no one had rescued her from Stirling Castle. Or mayhap they had tried and been inept at the task. 'Twas atrocious. Were she a lass of his clan, her ordeal would never have happened. His soldiers would never have left Stirling without her.

She was a Highland jewel. Not just her fairness of face and feminine curves made her so. Her nature and disposition revealed a rarity of woman the likes of which he had never met up till now.

He had wanted to keep her. By the cart afore she left with the ferryman, she had pulled at him in a way he could not explain. He had reached out to draw her close and had barely suppressed a desire to kiss her farewell. The feeling had not dissipated despite her lewd insult about him needing to take his manhood in hand.

He had dismissed the near miss as his "massive cods" doing the thinking and not his brain. Now, he was not so sure his cods—or, more accurately, his cock—were to blame. Though, all told, each would be gloriously happy to have her as well.

'Twas an odd feeling to have the impulse to strangle a woman war so viciously with the longing to slide into her nude body and pleasure her until neither of them could move or breathe. 'Twas certainly not a conundrum he had ever faced.

His hand released the hilt of his sword and crossed over the other at rest at the base of the mare's neck. Intently, he stared into the veiled hazel eyes of his impertinent tormentor. He knew not what thoughts transpired behind those orbs, but 'twas clear she was determined not to be sent away with the others.

He knew not how this would work. The worry over her discovering his identity no longer existed. Somehow, she had already figured that out. But 'twould take him longer to reach the Highlands with her in tow, which would make discovery or capture more possible by any slave hunters who might be about.

Not to be overlooked was also the matter of his inexplicable attraction to the irritating woman. He was not one to coerce a lass. Opportunities for consensual couplings had always abounded where he was concerned, and such appalling behavior was inappropriate for any man of honorable nature. 'Twas not to say that, on occasion, he had not wooed a maiden or two in response to coy games initiated by those wanting to avoid the impression they gave their favors too easily.

In this brazen lass's case, coy games or even gentlemanly wooing were not uppermost on his mind. What he wanted was a soft place to lay her down and drill her until her woman's pleasure exploded within her too many times to count. If her fierceness translated into even half the passion he sensed hidden within her complicated layers, something told him she'd not only enjoy a good romp but would give back as good as she received.

His groin, slightly improved from its abused condition, twitched at the lurid picture that formed in his mind. He was glad he had not removed his face shroud. If the lass could see his face, he had no doubt she'd be able to read his racy thoughts from his expression, and her stoicism would evaporate. What his eyes alone showed, he was not certain, but whatever the lass did see made her squint at him.

Dismissing or unconcerned by whatever she saw, she adjusted the satchel slung over her back so it now rested at her side. "Sending me back is not an option. I will not stay gone. So, MacNeill, you must decide whether my life ends here or I ride with you."

When time passed and he responded not, she lifted both her arms toward him in a pick-me-up gesture. "Well?"

Her boldness knew no bounds, and his *stauner* grew harder at the thought. A scowl formed beneath his face covering. He allowed it full rein, since she could not see it and take it as further misindication that he meant her harm. His irritation at her failure to obey his mandate had not dissipated, but he was entertained by her antics nonetheless.

He had to give the lass credit for spunk. *"Well," indeed.*

With a head shake of amazement, he glanced up at the treetops and counted slowly to ten to give his ardor—and his frustration—time to stand down.

Once he was certain she would not feel the lust she

had inspired, he heeled the mare into motion, swung past the rocks, and lifted the lass off in a fluid motion that obviated his need to stop.

As he settled her before him on the moving horse, the resentment he expected to feel over having his hand forced failed to materialize. Instead, an odd contentment came over him. Deep down, he knew he had made the right choice. Taking the lass back to the Highlands was the right thing to do. Whether she be kin of ally or foe, such a Highland treasure belonged not amongst the English cads.

She belonged with him.

Nay. He shut down that ridiculous, wayward thought. But she did have a right to return home, such as it may be.

Something bothered him about the manner in which she had come to be a captive and the nonsensical nature of why she had stayed one for three long years. Whoever she was, he sensed more to her story of abandonment and enslavement than even she knew.

In truth, 'twas nary his business. He would return her to the Highlands, and hopefully, on the way home, neither she, her sketchy kin, nor the king's slave hunters would come kill him in his sleep.

• • •

Ailsa sat across the MacNeill's lap, both legs dangling over one side of the horse, and briefly closed her eyes. Relief washed over her that he had chosen to take her with him and not leave her stranded in the cove. She had given him a brave face, but, in truth, she had been shaking within.

What if she had been wrong about him? The thought had occurred to her when he'd placed his hand on his sword in anger.

To poke at him with a threat of bartering his identity had been sheer foolishness. Necessary foolishness if she was to get home, but foolish and life-threatening all the same. Her prior deductions about his honorableness and dedication to the protection of others had been self-serving and possibly self-delusion. She might have been wrong.

She still might be wrong.

Turning her head, she looked up at him. He still wore the face shroud, a symbol of his role as the Shepherd. What he did was a great service to the enslaved. She would never jeopardize the future chance of others to obtain their freedom, so she would never have revealed his identity to anyone, but he did not know that.

"I—"

"Shhh," he interrupted afore she could get out what she wanted to say.

She flinched at his abrupt interruption but tried again. "I just—"

"Lass, trust me. Now is *nary* the time to speak with me," he said curtly. "We can converse when we get to our resting place."

Ah, he was still miffed at her. *Fine.*

She shifted to find a more comfortable position. If she could not speak, then she had no way of knowing how far he intended to ride afore he took a break. If she had to ride thus for a long time, she could at least be comfortable.

Her new position put her satchel in an awkward

spot, so she shifted and moved it more forward.

"For Christendom's sake, would you please be still." His deep voice came out gruff and almost pained.

That resonant timbre did odd things to her each time she heard it. Now was no different despite his near growl. A molten tremor skittered through her, and her nipples tightened into hard buds. Luckily, her cape draped in a manner that hid the embarrassing state from the MacNeill's eyes.

Her proximity to him prompted a wave of edginess. She fidgeted with the bag again. "I-I'm just trying to find a more comfortable position for my bag."

He huffed out a breath, then grabbed the bag by the handle and whipped it over her head. With a quick twist of his hand, he attached the satchel to the saddle pouch already fastened to the strings of the horse's blanket.

"Now, please settle yourself, or we will both be uncomfortable for most of this ride."

She looked at him questioningly. He stared back with those sable eyes that hid so much but revealed an unsettling intensity. Breathlessness overtook her, and her lips parted. He glanced at her mouth then slowly lifted his gaze back to hers. A stirring in his lap got her attention, and her mouth dropped open.

Startled and a mite embarrassed, Ailsa hastened to move forward and away from the budding evidence that the pulsing attraction she felt was not a battle she fought alone.

He shot a solid forearm around her waist and held her still with an inescapable grip. "Nay, lass. Stay put, for all that is holy." He reined the horse to a stop, tilted his head back, and squeezed his eyes shut. When he finally opened his eyes to look at her, he said, "If you do not move your bottom again, 'twill all settle and neither of us need be ill at ease."

Slightly nervous, she took a big swallow and gave him a hesitant nod.

"Lean back against me and just rest."

She simply blinked at him, not quite sure that was the wisest move under the circumstances.

"I promise 'tis not a strategy to take liberties. I mean you no disrespect. If you can relax against me, you are less likely to shift on my lap."

Taking him at his word, Ailsa leaned against him. She held herself rigid at first, which made his solid chest an uncomfortable resting place. Eventually, she managed to settle and let the languid motion of the horse's steps lull her into calm. She had no idea how long they rode thus, for sleep overtook her. When she opened her slumberous eyes, they had stopped by a small stream. The sun hung high in the sky. The bright, cloudless blanket of azure suggested they had reached or recently passed midday, and so did her grumbling stomach.

They stopped only long enough to eat and attend their needs, which made Ailsa wonder if the MacNeill had heard her complaining gut as they rode. 'Twas an embarrassing thought, but she opted not to query him about the timing of their break. She ate the fruit and nuts he shared with her and kept her own counsel. His disposition had not changed much, and she decided now was still not the time to start conversation.

His eyes watched her steadily while she ate. He'd opted not to remove his face covering despite her knowledge of his identity. 'Twas a strange feeling being

observed silently from behind the mask with such seriousness. She wondered what he contemplated. What
answers did he seek with that quiet authority that felt
as if he searched inside her for secrets untold and had
the power to actually pull them out? His scrutiny
nearly broke her silence, but she managed to hold it in
the face of his.

When they remounted, her success at holding her
tongue bolstered her confidence in her ability to
weather this unorthodox, temporary alliance, and she
felt more capable of handling the disconcerting need to
ride positioned in front of him. More capable but not
immune, so she made a point to focus on the foliage
and occasional deer or rabbit that skirted their trail
rather than the man who sat behind her. Thankfully, no
additional physical incidents occurred—on his part or
hers—and she found a small blessing in their silence,
for it allowed them to travel for long periods without
any additional clashes.

They rode thus—in quiet truce—for the rest of the
day, taking only small breaks now and again. Ailsa suspected the respites were more for her benefit than his,
and she appreciated the consideration given his continued display of obvious displeasure to have her along.

As darkness fell, the MacNeill walked their mount
into a small clearing with trees all around and reined
the mare to a stop. A hazy orange glow backed the
clouds that showed through the tops of the trees. Ailsa
could hear the flow of water, but she could not see the
source from their current position.

Kallum dismounted from behind her, then reached
up and assisted her from the horse. The ease with which
he lifted her each time made her feel tiny, though she

did not consider herself a petite lass. She usually stood almost a head taller than most lasses in her clan. Still, compared to him, she weighed naught and taxed his strength not in the least.

When her toes found the ground, she looked up into his face and her breath caught. During their ride, he had removed the face covering without her noticing. His handsomeness at close range temporarily dulled her ability to think clearly. Those dark eyes set in a face of gorgeous brown and topped by full brows would turn any lass's head.

This close up, she noticed a small slash through one brow, as if he had suffered a cut there during some prior skirmish. His full lips were surrounded by that low-cut beard that rested along his jaw but left the regalness of his cheekbones on full display. 'Twas more than a lass should be expected to handle upon such short notice.

His hands continued to span her waist, and his attention fell to her mouth like afore. Those sable eyes shifted, and she recognized emotions he had managed to hold in check astride the horse. The raw desire openly displayed in those eyes suggested he was a hungry predator and she the feast he had in mind. More startling than the virile view or the intensity of the awareness growing between them was the realization she had no desire to run from this particular predator nor fear of her status as prey.

Clearly, she had lost her sense of self-preservation back when she had threatened the MacNeill in the cove, and it had yet to return from the point on the rocks where she'd left it. She needed to gather herself. Her current enthralled immobility could be thought an invitation, and she was not prepared to suffer a man's lust this eve. Even a man as striking as the MacNeill.

"You can release me now," she managed to whisper.

His brow furrowed. Seemingly confused by the need for her comment, he looked down and noticed his grip still spanned her waist inside the folds of her cloak, which waved faintly in the light breeze. His fingers flexed, and his thumbs brushed gently upward against the fabric of her dress. A shiver ran through her at his caress, and then he released her and took a huge step backward.

Air filled her previously inactive lungs, and their eyes locked. The loaded silence pulsed with a bevy of unspoken what-ifs. Ailsa lost all sense of time. They stood thus for several minutes or mayhap longer afore one large hand swiped down his face, breaking the intensity of the moment.

When he looked at her again, his eyes had returned to their normal placid shield, and he broke their silent standoff by thrusting them back to the practical. "I'll set up camp. We are far enough away from any burgh that we should be safe to light a fire tonight. It may not always be so. You should prepare yourself that this journey home may be a challenge for you. The evenings can be quite cool once the sun goes down."

She waved off his comment. "I shall be fine. I have survived much these past three years. I am strong enough to handle discomforting weather."

"Good." He nodded approvingly. "I will return momentarily. If you need see to your needs, wait until I return so I know in which direction you go." Rather than leave, he stood motionless before her.

She realized he was waiting for her to acknowledge

his request.

Or was it a command?

In any event, she saw no harm in agreeing. 'Twas a reasonable directive. "Aye. I understand."

Without removing his cloak or swords, he walked into the trees. Ailsa assumed he went to handle his own needs and briefly wondered, with a grin, if all had returned to working order. Not that she wanted him to be in pain, but 'twas nice to know she had meted out some small modicum of the distress he had caused her.

Her amusement morphed into mild relief that they would not spend the rest of the eve without speaking to each other. Such was the relief that she could overlook that his first words to her since early dawn were to underestimate her hardiness and issue terse orders. She had come to expect this to be his customary manner of interaction, broody warrior that he was.

While he was gone, she busied herself gathering sticks and branches. Not many, for she did not want to leave the clearing after committing to stay put until the MacNeill's return. After she gathered enough to start the makings of a fire, she collected some stones to place in a circle for a pit. When the MacNeill returned, she was in the process of arranging the sticks in a pattern that would allow them to catch fire most quickly.

By his expression, he was surprised by her industriousness.

"What? Have you never seen a woman make a fire?"

His hands rose to the base of his throat to undo the ties of his cape. With one hand, he whirled the garment off his back with an easy flare and draped it over the branch of a tree.

"In a preset hearth, aye. But never outside where she had to scavenge the makings on her own."

Ailsa leaned back on her haunches and tilted her head. "Are the MacNeill women so soft, then?"

He walked toward her, showing no emotion at her attempted slight. "Nay, lass. 'Tis simply MacNeill men shelter and protect our women such that they need not fend for themselves in this manner."

His reply served as a veiled reference to a lacking he saw in her clansmen for their failure to keep her safe from abduction and enslavement. 'Twas a point well made in this instance but a reminder of her recent captivity that she needed not. If this was an example of the conversations they would have for the rest of the journey, mayhap her earlier relief had been misplaced. All told, 'twould seem physical comfort…and how to temper the sensual volatility he had awakened in her… would not be the only challenges she faced between here and home.

She glared at him. "Well, when you have no men in your household, you learn to carry out such simple tasks by yourself lest you freeze or starve. I guess on MacNeill land women never know their men to leave or die."

He stopped across from her. "Aye. But on MacNeill land women have others to rely on within the clan. Why did you not?"

Her chest rose and fell, and she rubbed her hands against her thighs twice in a distracted manner while she briefly considered his question. Coming up with no easy answer, she said, "'Tis a long story."

"'Twould seem we have time aplenty." The brow with the nude slash peaked in glib query. "Unless you have somewhere else to be this eve?"

Ailsa thought she saw the corner of his mouth lift. But if it had, he suppressed the quirk almost immediately. His expression fell somewhere between taunt and sensuous goading. 'Twas an expression designed to make most women gleefully toss bare all their secrets. Ailsa would bet many had done so for this man. Though, what he asked of her was no great secret. 'Twas a story well known in her village, so she could see no harm in recounting the tale to him.

"'Twould seem not," she said, then rose and brushed the dust from her garments.

Her hands landed on her hips, and she studied him for a bit. Having made her decision, she added with a pert nod, "Aye, then, Kallum of the Clan MacNeill, why don't you show me the benefits of having a MacNeill man to cater to my care?" She waved her hand at the near-completed firepit. "I'll tell you most all you want to know upon my return."

Not to be outdone, with a completely earnest expression, he made a leg over which he gave a flourish of hand in an elegant bow fit for a queen. "As you wish, milady."

With a roll of her eyes and a shake of her head, Ailsa presented her back to him and stalked into the woods without a backward glance. *Mocking jackanapes.*

Careful to scope out a spot she thought sufficiently out of view—and hearing—of the MacNeill, she took care of her needs. She adjusted her layers of clothing back into place, grateful she had finished her monthly courses prior to her escape. Otherwise, this trip would have been a challenge of a whole other sort.

Finished with her personal toilette, she took a

moment to stand still and simply breathe in the crisp, fresh air. Unbidden, a shout of unadulterated joy rang loudly in her head. *Free!*

She would have shouted aloud if she did not think the MacNeill would think her more eccentric than he already did. Or, more likely, come running ready to impale someone on his sword.

That did not mean she could not bask in the joy here, all alone, beneath a boundless sky with no walls to hold her prisoner. Arms wide, she spun in a circle thrice. A joyous laugh bubbled up from within, and she let it escape.

Free!

She was finally free. Free of enslavement. Free of the princess bratling. And free of the overbearing watch of the king's guard. She stopped spinning, and so as not to insult the divine for the providence of the last two days, she sent up a silent prayer of thanks to the gods of her West African ancestors for bringing her thus far. She had yet to come to terms with the divinity of her oppressors, the God of Abraham.

Unfazed by the disjuncture of faith, she headed back toward the camp. All that remained was to make it home to the Highlands safely. She hoped the MacNeill was up to the task.

CHAPTER TWELVE

Kallum had the fire lit and blazing by the time Ailsa returned from the trees. He had also laid out his sleeping roll for her to use. Since his guest had been unplanned, he did not have a spare blanket roll.

His back against a tree would serve him just as well this eve. 'Twas naught he hadn't done afore. He'd not likely sleep this night anyway. With the lass traveling with him, he would need to keep vigilant watch at night. Should they encounter bandits or other stragglers, the lass would be a tempting prize. And there was still the matter of slave hunters.

The rewards for those escaped from slavery were oft substantial. He could well imagine what price the king had placed for her capture and return. Though the monarch had only days ago offered her as prize, to have her taken from him would be a strike to his ego the king would not let slide.

With a wave of his hand, he directed her attention to the food he had laid out. "'Tis not much left. I expected to be traveling alone. But you are welcome to what you want. We have enough for a day or two, but I will have to hunt afore we reach the Highlands."

She took a seat on a rock near the fire. "Thank you for the offer. 'Tis not necessary this eve. I did bring some food of my own from the castle, not knowing whether the others would have aught to spare. I still have a few portions left that I did not finish when we traveled with the other escapees."

He took a seat beneath a tree several paces away from her rock and placed a forearm across a knee bent toward the sky. "These others… You mean the soldiers of your clan?"

"Aye." She pulled out a tied cloth from which she broke off a wedge of bread and a hunk of cheese.

She extended him a share.

He shook his head in casual decline of the offer and watched her resettle her bundle on her lap. "To what clan are you kin, lass?"

Her hands stopped moving, and she glanced at him. "That is not the tale I promised to tell you."

He gave her an acknowledging bob of the head. "Nay, but I did not say I would not ask."

She shrugged.

He found the stoic gesture well played. He admired her ability to hold her tongue. 'Twas not a quality many women possessed, in his experience. They oft felt the need to fill silence or ramble on about matters of minor consequence. He sometimes suspected they did so simply to hear themselves speak. This particular lass understood the art of saying less to get more. So he'd humor her and ask for a different story.

"Then tell me what happened to your face."

She gave him an evil look.

"I mean no insult. 'Tis but honest, and I would think understandable, curiosity. 'Twas off-putting to see such a change in you on the final day of the tournament."

Again, she shrugged, then glanced back at the contents of her lap. "Someone took issue with my unapproved use of the princess's balcony and dousing of one of His Majesty's honored guests."

Kallum remembered the guard who had watched

her from the courtyard. She'd disappeared immediately after the man had noticed her. "Seems a mite overkill for such a small transgression."

Her head shook, but she did not look up. "Not when you are considered naught but a slave and you are not trusted because you have made several attempts to escape. 'Tis a reminder of your place and inspiration to follow orders strictly."

Ailsa had mentioned her attempts to escape afore. He was not surprised she had been caught. 'Twas not an easy task for a lass alone. His mother had been a fugitive from enslavement. A secret she'd shared with no one save Kallum, and one she'd sworn him to never reveal. She'd fled into the woodlands alone and been set upon by ruffians who used and abused her, then left her for dead. Had not a MacNeill hunting party come across her broken body, she would have died in solitude. Though she had recovered from her injuries, she'd never been the same. A pronounced limp served as a constant reminder of her attack, along with a forever weakened constitution that had plagued her until she'd succumbed to the fever that took her life.

The risks and challenges runaways faced were daunting. Unfamiliar geography, terrain, and sometimes creatures—of the animal and human kind—made the task formidable. A successful escape took careful planning and impeccable strategy. Those who didn't die in the attempt were oft recaptured.

"After the times you were caught, what happened?" he asked, thinking, as he ofttimes did, about how many more captives might reach emancipation if they simply had assistance.

"I was punished."

"Punished how?"

"'Tis not worth thinking on. 'Tis in the past, and I am escaped now. I just need to stay escaped this time." She looked up at him. The look of muted hope and fierce determination nearly did him in.

"What manner of brute would do such harm to a lass's face?" His hand over his knee fisted as he finished the question.

Her eyes caught the movement. She looked him in the eyes when she replied, "'Tis no longer of consequence. I'll not see the brute again, for I have no intention of ever returning to Stirling Castle or even Stirling."

He understood the sentiment, but he would have a name. Should he ever return to Stirling, the brute would learn what it felt like to have one's face abused. Her expression suggested she knew of what he thought and she preferred he not meddle. Too bad. Highlanders took care of their own. At least this Highlander did.

Her kin had let her down. He had set her free.

Presently, he guided her home.

He had a strong sense that she was now his responsibility, and no man abused what was his without retribution. In due time, he'd find out to whom he owed such retribution. This day, he'd allow the lass to hold her knowledge, for they had more pressing matters with which to deal.

"I am still mightily perplexed as to how you came to be a captive. You said you were the laird's healer. I would think someone would notice if the clan's healer went missing."

"I do not know that I was not missed. I know only no one ever found me at the castle. Besides, I was not the laird's healer. I was one of several village healers. The laird's healer became ill the day prior to the scheduled departure for Stirling. One of the clan soldiers sought me out to replace him. Mayhap, 'twas thought no great loss. Upon return home, the laird still had his primary healer."

Though her face was stoic, her voice gave away the hurt she harbored with the thought of being considered so insignificant no one raised a fuss to find her.

"What about during the tournament festivities just past? Did no one of your clan recognize you? Surely some of the soldiers who came to compete had also been a part of the army that rode with your laird back then."

"I saw a few familiar faces, aye. But if they recognized me, they showed no signs."

"Hmm." He found that hard to believe.

She was not a woman easily forgotten. So why did her clansmen ignore what they saw? Either the men present were so low of wit and concern that they saw naught amiss with her being found enslaved at the castle, or they were content—mayhap even desirous—to have her gone. 'Twas the latter that gave him pause.

She looked up suspiciously. "Hmm? What mean you by this 'hmm'?"

He shook his head and rose to attend to the horse for the night. "Nothing, lass. 'Tis just curious is all."

"Curious how?"

He did not want to concern her with suspicions that had no real foundation. He needed to ponder the matter more afore he discussed, but he offered her something to think about. "'Tis simply curious that not one of your kinsmen recognized you or questioned your presence here in Stirling, not even directly to you. Have you ever considered that you were left behind apurpose? Does anyone have reason to not want you on clan lands?"

Her mouth opened, but no sound came out. He sensed she wanted to dispute his comment, but she struggled with some information that made her wonder. He waited for her to share it.

"I... I am not certain, but I can think of no one. I'll admit, I had thought at one time that 'twas part of some ransom scheme. But the reality of that did not come to pass, and with thought, it made little sense. I have no great standing with my clan. I have no wealth. All I possessed was the cottage I lived in with my *mamaidh* and the meager belongings we shared. Though my mother was not well-liked by some, even feared"— she chuckled—"I can think of no reason for them to do acts against me."

He stopped what he was doing. Perplexed, he asked, "Why was your mother feared?"

A warm smile crossed her face. The love she felt for her mother became evident even afore she spoke. "She, too, was a healer. All my knowledge comes from her. She was known in the village for her potions and tonics, many of which were derived from recipes of my grandmother, who lived by the ways of the Vodun of the old country. Many thought my mother a witch."

"Do you have her eyes?" The question escaped afore he realized what he was saying.

"Nay. Why ask you that?"

"'Tis naught. Just a question." He turned back to his ministrations to the horse, uncomfortable to have revealed he'd taken particular notice of the minx's eyes.

"You speak not the truth, Kallum MacNeill. Why did you ask about my mother's eyes?"

'Twas not her mother's eyes he was interested in. 'Twere hers. If she had inherited those enthralling, expressively large hazel eyes from her mother, he could understand why many in her village thought the woman a witch. Truth be told, it had been one of his thoughts upon first noticing the beguiling light eyes of the hellion before him.

The lass had great powers of observation. He did not want her to surmise his fascination with her eyes. She had already experienced evidence of his physical attraction to her. No need to provide her with an additional weapon to use against him. Women wreaked much havoc with the bat of an eye or glance from under the lashes. He had no intention of falling into this lass's thrall.

He gathered himself afore he turned back to face her and put much effort into presenting an air of nonchalance. "'Tis only they are an odd color. Not one I have oft seen."

"Ah." She grinned to herself and began to pack away her leftover food.

Her response puzzled him. "Ah? Just 'ah'?" Now, it was his turn to ask, "What mean you by this 'ah'?"

She smiled at him. "Calm yourself. 'Tis nothing sinister. Simply that I am oft given a second curious glance due to this lovely eye shade I inherited from my dear *da*."

Whatever her feelings for her *da*, "dear" was not what he had been to her. Her snide tone was unmistakable.

Yester eve, she indicated her mother had died.

When she referred to her father, she made quite clear she "had no father," not that he had died, which was a definite distinction.

"You said afore you had no father. How came this to be?"

"Simple. I never knew my father. He left my mother prior to my birth."

"Were they not wed?"

"Nay. I am a bastard."

His eyes widened. Her bald, matter-of-fact acknowledgment of her status surprised him, as did her use of the word "bastard." 'Twas not a word he oft heard from the mouth of a lass nor one he appreciated. The brash moniker had been used against him oft enough as a weapon of ridicule during his childhood.

"I shock you." She moved to put away her bundle of leftover bread and cheese. "No way to be ladylike about being a daughter by-blow. I see no need to pretend."

She sat back down on her rock and pulled her knees up to her chest. Wrapping her arms around her knees, she looked off into the distance. "My father was a white Scotsman, rumored to be quite a handsome and braw soldier. Many believed my mother enchanted him to get him to fall in love with her. But, apparently, her 'weird African magic' wore off. Or he fought it off, some say. And eventually, he ran away to marry another woman." She looked straight at Kallum then. "A woman who looked like him."

Her expression gave away much of how she felt about that particular turn of events.

"So, he betrayed your mother."

"Not according to her. She always claimed he had

good reason to leave. That she even encouraged him to go. Some grand family crisis arose, and he lived within the inner walls of the keep. He did not know she was with child when he left. To tell you true, she said she did not know herself at the time. She told me she realized her condition only after he became betrothed and the wedding was imminent."

She dropped her chin to her knees, and her gaze once again lost focus. "Even without that, I'm not sure it can qualify as betrayal. As I said, they were not wed, so he had no obligation to stay."

"He had every reason to stay if 'twere a coupling spurred by love."

"'Twas for my mother. In fact, I believe she loved that man till the day she died. 'Tis not something I can understand. My mother was strong-willed and bright. She made a way for us through her own enterprises when other women alone struggled or had to make coin on their backs. Life was oftimes hard, especially in the early years. Still, she gave up what she needed from him, even became the object of ridicule for being with child out of wedlock and let him go live his grand life free of the child he left behind."

She lifted her eyes to his without removing her chin from its palliative perch on her knees. "'Tis said he was from an important family. He had obligations to meet that required him to put aside his personal feelings and do what was best for his kin. According to the stories my mother told me, she encouraged him to go when the time came. She did not want to be the source of discord between him and his kin, and she did not see a way for them to have a future together in any event. She was the dark-skinned daughter of parents formerly enslaved. She lived a simple life in the village, the subject of gossip, heinous speculation, and eerie myths.

"When she found out she was with child, she did go to the keep to tell him, but that was when she learned he was on the cusp of marriage to another, at which point she decided he need never know. She believed 'twould do naught but bring hardship to him and ultimately to me, his unborn child."

"You do not sound as if you agree with her choice."

"I think 'tis too easy to say he did not know. They had intimate relations. He had to have known the possibilities such trysts could create. Had he not an obligation to at least check that he had not sired a child afore he moved on with his life? Unless, of course, it did not matter because from the outset he had no intent to claim any brown-skinned offspring."

"He laid with your mother, got her to fall in love with him, yet you think him concerned with the hue of her skin?"

She *pfft* at him. "Many men lay with women like me but have no intent to marry us. We are but a curiosity. To some, an exotic commodity, even. Something to try afore they settle down with the right and proper woman."

"Those are but arrangements of the flesh. You said 'twas a love match."

"Not for him."

"Not for him?" He turned from the horse, a skeptical narrowing of his eyes accompanying the dubious tone of his voice. "If you never knew him, how know you this?"

"What I know is he never came back. If he had loved my mother, he would have returned to her at some point. Searched her out. What I know is that my mother remained in love with him for the rest of her life. She never said as much, but I could tell. She never married or took up with another man. She did not speak of him often, but when she did, she defended him, and you could hear the affection in her voice. I never understood how she could speak of him taking up with another woman with such acceptance." She looked him straight in the eyes then. "Love?"

He nodded for her to continue.

"'Tis a worthless emotion. It makes weaklings of otherwise strong, intelligent women. It takes more than it gives. 'Tis something I can live without. I will never give a man that kind of power over me. The power to leave me broken when he walks away."

Finished attending the mare, Kallum reclaimed his position beneath the same tree he had leaned on previously. "From what you conveyed of your mother, she was not broken. She was a strong, capable mother and provider. And she was at peace with whatever had transpired between her and your *da*."

"Not my *da*, my sire. 'Tis a difference."

"Aye, then. Your sire." He adjusted to a more comfortable position. "Mayhap, you should focus less on what your *sire* did not give you and honor your mother's life and the legacy she did give you by accepting she did what she thought was right for herself and you, though you disagree with her choices."

She frowned but did not comment.

So he'd been right about her mixed heritage, simply wrong about the sire. He suspected she was much better off that her *da* was not the king. Though 'twould seem her father was cut from a similar cloth of dishonor as His Majesty. It explained much about her views on marriage, her intent to live an independent life, and her opinion on the reliability of the Highland male that left much to be desired.

All the same, she had put her trust in him to get her home safely. 'Twas a task Kallum did not take lightly and, after hearing her story, a task he felt compelled not to fail.

He motioned her to the pallet he had arranged close to the fire. Amazingly, she put up no argument about using his sleeping gear. A look into her eyes revealed a solemn mien. Talking about her parents had taken much out of her and left her with a melancholy spirit.

She climbed beneath the blankets and laid facing his position opposite the fire. Silently, she watched the flames for a while afore she closed her eyes. They had traveled far and long this day, so she needed rest.

He was loath to disturb her, but he'd been gnawing on a question since the early dawn. "Lass?"

Her eyes slowly opened, and she focused on him.

"How did you know?"

CHAPTER THIRTEEN

Ailsa had no doubt as to what the warrior asked. He wanted to know how she had known his true identity.

"'Twas your voice."

"My...*voice*..." A complete look of puzzlement overtook him.

His expression made her want to laugh. He was so serious all the time and filled with quiet introspection. 'Twas enough to put people off.

Ah, but that voice of his was as appealing as the sweetest honey stolen straight from the hive. Surely, someone—some woman—had told him this afore.

"Aye, that voice of yours is quite distinctive. Deep. Rich. Melodious." She fought to keep her eyes open, feeling herself drift in a half-awake state. "It wraps around a lass and lingers."

Hmm...mayhap I should not have admitted that last, she thought drowsily.

Squeezing her eyes tightly, she fought to clear her head so she could tell him what he wanted to know without giving away embarrassing details, like her infatuation with his voice.

"From the moment you spoke to me on the balcony, the sound of your voice was forever imprinted on my ears. When you corrected me outside the castle and told me I had you confused with another, I knew immediately who you were." She adjusted the top blanket, snuggled deeper, and blinked at him through droopy lids. "My first thought?"

"Aye?" He gave his rapt attention, his curiosity mixed with a bit of noticeable apprehension at what she might say next.

"That you had changed your mind about the king's offer and had come to add me to your bevy of lemans."

He blinked sharply, and his brows creased.

Mayhap Ailsa had insulted him with the accusation, but 'twas an honest misperception. "I was terrified that I had escaped one horror only to be thrust into another as your whore. Now, I know 'twas not a personal undertaking but a venture of a more gallant nature that put you in my path."

His lips pressed tightly together. He had the most horrified look on his face. Ailsa knew not whether it was her earlier description of his voice that appalled him or her classification of him as gallant. Either way, she loved that she had unnerved him.

She chuckled to herself and thought to ask a question of her own. "Why carry you two swords?" Ailsa had never known a man to carry two swords at once.

"Because I know how to use them," was his blunt response.

'Twas a simple and annoying answer.

She blinked at him. "Are you prone to losing your belongings and thus need a spare?"

The look he gave her suggested he thought her completely simpleminded. "I do *not* lose swords. They are to be respected with the utmost care. A warrior does not let the blade of his sword go blunt, allow the tip of his weapon to touch the ground lest he be on his way to death, and he most certainly does not misplace one."

In her fatigue, the gruffness of his response grated

not as it usually would. Instead, she focused on the lull of his deep, comforting voice and allowed her eyes to drift closed. She knew not how long she slept. All she knew was she was awakened from a sound, dreamless sleep when a hand pressed firmly over her mouth.

Her eyes flew open, and were it not for the hand, her terrified scream would have awakened every beast in the woods. Her eyes quickly focused on the face above her. Even with the still-dark sky, she easily recognized the shadowed face of the MacNeill. He placed a single finger over his lips to warn her to silence, then listened intently to the predawn. With limited movement and no sound, he slid a long-bladed dagger from the belt at his waist.

Motioning her to remain silent, he whispered, "We have company."

Ailsa was instantly awake.

Slowly, the MacNeill removed his hand from her lips. He acted out the need for her to rise stealthily and move to the bushes behind the large rock she had used as a seat for her repast.

'Twas only after she stashed herself behind the bushes that she heard the faint sound of rustling leaves. The MacNeill made his way back to his swords and removed one silently from its sheath. The other, he slid without sound beneath the ground cover of a nearby shrub. With a dagger in one hand and a sword in the other, he crept around the tree he had used as his resting place. Back pressed against the bark, he waited in the shadows cast by the dying fire.

Three armed men eased from the brush and tipped into the camp. They came in three different sizes. The largest had a gut that pushed out the front layers of his kilt. One of his mates was a full head shorter and was so willowy he likely weighed no more than Ailsa herself. The medium-sized one stepped into the clearing and took a healthy drink from a waterskin. The loud belch he emitted afore a self-appreciative chuckle suggested he drank something stronger than water from the vessel.

They looked around the clearing, perplexed to find signs of occupation but no one about. The smaller of the three walked over to Ailsa's pallet and kicked the rumpled blankets as if to make sure someone was not hiding beneath. She nearly grunted at the absurdity of the act. He must have been expecting the world's smallest person to think those folds could hide a body.

When one of them began to rummage through the contents of their bags, Kallum stepped from behind the tree, his sword at his side angled toward the ground. "Looking for something, lads?" he asked in an offhand manner that gave the impression he merely addressed a few old friends.

They all whipped toward the sound of his voice. The biggest one glanced at his comrades and then grinned, content that the odds were three to one. Ailsa was no expert in the matters of combat, but a battle strategist she need not be to notice these three looked no match for one strapping MacNeill.

"Well, hullo there, laddie. Travelin' alone, are ye?" the inebriated interloper asked with a hiccup.

"What's it to ye?" Kallum replied, embracing the dialect in which he was addressed.

"Ah, now don't be like that, mate." The big one took a step in Kallum's direction. "We just thought we'd stop over and warm ourselves a mite by yer fire and mayhap share a little grub." He glanced around the firepit. "Ye do have grub, don't ye?"

"Nay," Kallum responded with fake regret, carefully watching the other two men, who had begun to creep into flanking positions. "Alas, I finished the last of my rations for supper. Ye'll have to hunt up yer own grub."

The big one glanced at his mates. "Ye hear that, fellas? He has no grub." He looked back at Kallum. "What do ye have? A wee bit of coin, mayhap? Or shall we just divest ye of that there mare?"

The three men spread out around Kallum, and he took that moment to deliberately show them his sword.

"Whoa ho! Lookie what we have here, mates. The lad wants to scuffle. Methinks he doesn't want to share." Showing himself to be the leader of this motley group, the big man shook his head and unsheathed his own sword with much fanfare. "Tsk, tsk. 'Tis not nice to not want to share, laddie."

Kallum shook his head in return. "Nay, mate, what's not nice is to take what does not belong to ye."

The MacNeill twirled his sword with a flick of his wrist as Ailsa had seen him do at the tournament. She wondered how he managed to do such without cutting himself off at the knees. Only the littlest of their intruders seemed impressed with the move, though. The runt's eyes went wide, and he searched out those of his mates, clearly pondering that mayhap they should rethink this challenge.

Kallum winked at him. "Aye now, mate, 'tis been a few days since I've had a good sparring, so I'm willing to have a go if we must. But I'm not sure these odds are fair."

The two other men began to laugh arrogantly, not

yet realizing the warrior meant the odds favored him.

"So, because I'm feeling generous this morn, I'll give ye the chance to leave off with all yer limbs intact. Ye go back the way ye came, with only what ye had when ye came, and we can forget this encounter ever happened. Or…" Kallum glanced at each of them in turn, deliberately making eye contact. He'd had enough of the verbal sparring, and his return to his normal speech pattern and harsh tone made clear his change in mood. "I can leave your dead carcasses here for the creatures to break their fast."

Finally understanding the intentional insult in the MacNeill's words, the big man lunged at Kallum with a fierce cry and swing of his sword. The runt hesitated. He had a look about him that suggested he did not want to jump into the fray. His medium-sized buddy, no doubt bolstered by the spirits coursing through his blood, had no such qualms. With two against one, Kallum yielded his sword with grace and dexterity, moving swiftly to the side to dodge a thrust and fend off a parry with the long-bladed dagger in his left hand.

After taking the time he needed to find his courage, the little guy eventually joined the fight. He jumped on Kallum's back, and 'twould seem the three were about to overpower the MacNeill.

Ailsa placed a hand over her mouth to keep from making a sound. She did not want to distract the warrior or give away her location. She needed to find a way to assist or at least distract one of the combatants to give the MacNeill a chance. Looking around her position, she saw only a hand-sized rock at her disposal. 'Twas not much. She'd most likely make no more impression than an insect, but she reached for the stone all the same.

Her concern was misplaced. With a great shove, Kallum tossed off two of his attackers and thrust his dagger into the gut of the drunkard. The man gave a great wail and grabbed at his middle. He looked up at Kallum in surprise. Kallum looked on without sympathy. He made short work of finishing the man, the dagger left protruding from the man's limp frame.

Kallum turned his attention to the two remaining tasks. The sun had begun to rise. The budding dawn made Kallum's harsh expression more visible, but the assailants weren't smart enough to read the fatal danger on his face. Instead, they opted to rush him at once.

He threw the runt aside and engaged the other in sword play. The flying assailant crashed into the bush hiding Ailsa. With a small squeak, she scrambled to get out of the way of the propelled human afore he crushed her. All three men looked her way.

Surprise, excitement, and unmistakable lust flashed across the faces of their uninvited guests. Not necessarily in the same order, but the emotions were there for Ailsa to read without fault. The big guy looked at Kallum like he'd been betrayed by his best mate. Hiding a lass amongst the foliage was apparently an unforgivable act. Ailsa had no doubt the interlopers were no longer interested in the horse or what might be in the two pouches.

What they wanted was her.

The fallen man pushed to his knees and grabbed for the edge of Ailsa's dress. She kicked at his hands. When he grasped one of her ankles, she reached for the rock she had dropped in her scuttle and heaved it at his head. The stone cracked him on the temple, and he howled in anguish. Blood began to trickle into his eye. Ailsa did not wait for him to recover from the shock; she scrambled to her feet and ran.

Her tormentor jumped up in pursuit. Heart racing, Ailsa could hear the renewed clash of swords, which meant Kallum was too occupied to assist. She was not even sure he could see her behind the bushes and trees that covered this part of the clearing. Her chance at escape rested with *her*. What she wouldn't give for a bow at the moment. She was out of practice, having not used one in three years. But at this distance, even someone as out of practice as her could not miss.

Remembering the extra sword Kallum had stashed under the shrubs, Ailsa pivoted back toward the clearing. She was not sure she could lift the heavy metal, but she had to try.

She rounded a boulder, hope for a weapon high, when the man snagged her around the waist from behind and lifted her off her feet. She kicked viciously and scratched at his hands, making it difficult for him to hold on.

He dropped her to her feet and whipped her around to face him. The lurid, gap-toothed grin he gave her made her want to puke. He yanked her close. His pungent body odor and foul-smelling breath assaulted her nose, making the reflex to regurgitate stronger. When he slammed a wet, repugnant kiss against her lips, severe anger exploded past her fear and frustration at being caught. She yanked away and slapped him as hard as she could across the face, but he merely laughed at her antics.

"A feisty one, hey?" He chuckled again. "I likes 'em feisty. Come on, lassie, gives us another kiss."

• • •

Kallum heard Anne scuffle with the tiny bandit, but his focus remained on the oversize cretin he fought. The man wasn't completely inept with a sword, but he relied more on brute strength than technique or finesse. The lass would have to hold her own long enough for him to dispatch the overfed lout.

His combatant grunted when Kallum made a flurry of swings and advanced aggressively to push him back. Lack of fitness caused the man to struggle with his breathing. Clearly, it had been a while since he'd had to use his sword with any urgency or length.

"Hey, Angaidh, quit goofing off with that walloper and come see what I done found. She's a pretty one. Well, 'cepting for this blackened eye." He chuckled, then addressed his catch. "But that's okay, my sweet. It's not yer eye I aim to be looking at." He leaned in for another wet-sounding kiss.

The brazen lass slapped him again.

This time, he slapped her back, then gripped her jaw and squeezed. "I see why yer bloke done already given you a good face-whopping."

She made a yelp of pain.

Out of the corner of his eye, Kallum took note of the exchange, careful not to let the big lout get the better of him.

Anne found the dagger at the man's waist and pulled it free. She struck with an overhand jab, but the monger easily caught her wrist and shook the dagger free. The neutralized weapon went flying into the shrubs.

The two continued to tussle until Tiny wrenched the lass close and exclaimed, "Lo ho! Wait a bloomin' minute. I know ye. Ye're the king's wench, aye. The one who serves the princess." His voice took on an excited tone. "Hey, Angaidh, we won't be needing that 'orse. This here lassie is worth more than ten of dem 'orses."

Tiny directed his words back to Anne: "There's a boon out for ye, lassie. But I don't think the king would mind much if I took a little taste first. Time to stop wasting my time, ye little bitch." He ripped the front of her dress.

The sound of rending fabric made everything in Kallum jump to a murderous rage, and the little hellion was apparently right there with him.

Her knee found Tiny's crotch, and she let out a bellow of rage worthy of any warrior. "I'm not your bitch, you foul-smelling skelpie-monger!"

With a horrific squeal, Tiny bent at the waist, one hand firmly cradling his attacked cods. Not wholly disabled, he reached for the uncooperative hellcat with his other hand and caught the back of her dress afore she could get out of his way.

The disgruntled sounds of the lass's unsuccessful attempts to free herself grew louder.

"Come on, lassie," Tiny panted. "Ye're just putting off the unescapable. Don't be so stingy with yer favors."

Holding the front of her dress together, Anne twisted and turned to free herself from the man's grasp. He used the fabric of her dress to pull himself upward. His weight buckled her to the ground, and he dropped down on top of her. The lass screeched in outrage when the man's hand slid inside her torn bodice.

The sound pushed Kallum's temper past its limit.

He'd had enough of this horseplay.

With three parries and a roundabout swing, he unbalanced his opponent, then imbedded his sword in the man's middle. The man dropped his own sword and took hold of the iron in his gut. Kallum raised a booted foot, planted the sole against the man's lower abdomen, and dislodged the cretin from his blade with a shove of his heel.

Raging, he kicked away the man's fallen sword and left him to bleed against the dirt. Then with long, furious strides, he strode over to the lusty runt on top of Anne. The runt had his hands full trying to capture the lass's flailing fists and keep his precarious perch on her bucking torso. Kallum grabbed him by the scruff with one hand and, with a mighty roar, tossed him with all his might against the trunk of the nearest tree.

A crack echoed through the clearing, and the man dropped immobile into an unnatural position, back broken from the collision against the sturdy oak. Kallum watched to see if he would rise, but life had vacated his empty, permanently open eyes.

Kallum looked down at the feisty and courageous lass. She gripped the front of her dress closed and laid there, chest heaving. She looked straight up toward the dawn sky, staring at the few white clouds overhead and the frantic, circling birds that had been disturbed awake by the heated scuffle. The rapid flaps of the birds' wings and their unhappy caws began to quiet, but his travel companion did not blink or move.

He lowered to one knee beside her and touched a hand to the side of her face. Gently, he slid his fingers behind the base of her head. With his thumb against her lower jaw, he turned her face toward him, wanting her to be okay but waiting for the inevitable tears. He hated a woman's tears. They made him feel inept and useless, but he would not abandon her in this moment if she needed to release with weeping the intense emotions coursing through her.

She turned her gaze to his and closed her eyes when his thumb brushed lightly over her cheek.

"All right?" he asked in a voice barely above a whisper.

She nodded but did not open her eyes immediately. When she did, no tears showed—only a mix of relief, some anger, and something else he could not read. "Aye," she replied softly.

He fully cupped the back of her neck and eased her to a sitting position. He had to fight the need to pull her against him and hold her. She must have sensed his urge to comfort her, because she slid her hand into his, which still rested at her neck, and clasped her thumb around his. With a strong grip, she used his strength to leverage herself to her feet, then moved away from him, that invisible mantle of independence she wore wrapped firmly around her.

With a steady step, she walked over to the runt lying lifeless and stared silently. She glanced about the clearing. The man with Kallum's dagger in his gut also laid immobile, but the man Kallum had run through with his sword was missing. In the commotion, he had managed to slink off into the woods. He was injured badly, so Kallum had no doubt he could track him down and finish the job, but he was loath to leave the lass alone.

Their eyes met. There was no need to speak. Kallum could see her make the calculations he had already made and waited for her to come to a decision. He would allow her to direct his actions. If her peace of mind preferred the vanished lout tracked down and slain, he would do so.

"Border reivers?" she asked.

They were a little farther north than the areas in which the border reivers usually implemented their thievery and pillaging. The outlaws tended to stay within a day's ride or so of the border between Scotland and England. Ever since King James combined the crowns and took actions to suppress the lawlessness along the borders, few dared continue the criminal practices of the reivers.

Kallum suspected these three made their primary gains by hiring themselves out as mercenaries, but that did not mean they had not once acted as border reivers. "Most likely."

"Which means we cannot stay here for long." Her comment was half question but more statement.

He nodded, relieved she understood they needed to move on without delay. If they packed up quickly, their missing guest should be of little concern.

A slight bob of her head conveyed her resolve. "I need only change my dress, and I will be ready to go. See to the camp and horse." She grabbed her bag and walked toward a set of trees.

A wave of anxiety ripped through him at the thought of her wandering out of sight. He jumped to his feet. "Anne!"

She turned at the concern in his voice but gave him an odd look. "Worry not. I'll step only on the other side of this tree. No farther."

Of course, she needed privacy. That he understood, and his anxiousness dissipated knowing she was only a few steps away. Kallum doubted the injured oaf would return, but he knew not whether the man had other mates nearby. They needed to get moving afore they had a party of guests upon them that he could not handle alone.

The trio of interlopers had confirmed what Kallum already suspected. The king had offered a bounty for the return of his escapees. Should they encounter any other travelers, the lass's facial injuries made her suspect if the king had included such details in his writ for capture. While most of her bruises had begun to fade and were barely noticeable, her left eye still held a strong circle of black. With Tiny's additional facial abuse, her bruises would linger for a bit longer.

Kallum had easily dispatched this ragtag band of outlaws, but they had no real skills at combat. He did not want to face dedicated fugitive hunters or members of the king's own guard with the lass still with him. Such opponents would have more skill and a more ruthless drive. 'Twould be a skirmish not fit for a lass's eyes, and her presence would put him at a disadvantage. She could be used to compel his compliance or his surrender should she be taken hostage.

She stepped from the trees, shoving her torn dress into her satchel. She had replaced it with a simple smock she most likely wore for cleaning or household tasks. She came over and awaited him to assist her onto the back of the mare.

He took one last tour around the clearing to make sure he left no signs that would identify who had been there. He turned toward the stabbed assailant to retrieve his dirk, only to notice that the blade was missing. It had been imbedded in the man afore the lass changed attire.

Kallum glanced her way. She busied herself making sure her bundle was secure to the horse.

Only she could have taken it. He would let the matter slide while they made their way to the Highlands. If the lass needed the dagger to feel safe, he'd allow her to keep it for the time being. The blade was special to him, so he would have its eventual return, but for now, he'd make sure not to anger the lass enough that she'd use his own weapon against him. He had no doubt she'd do so without hesitation if incensed. She fought with the fierceness of a born soldier. If she were a man, Kallum had no doubt that with training she'd become a warrior of the highest order.

Focusing back on his task, Kallum gathered a fallen branch and used the leaves to wipe away signs of the camp and the recent skirmish. He would leave the bodies of the thieves. He did not have the time to bury them, nor did they deserve his consideration. The creatures of the woods would dispose of the bodies soon enough.

He needed to expedite this departure and quicken the pace at which he and the lass travelled. He had already spent two more days to return to his own mount than he had planned. Ogun was well-trained and would not wander off on his own—not yet. But the longer this took, the higher the chances that someone would come across the stallion and try to capture him.

They would ride hard today and not stop until they had collected his war horse. With two horses, they could make better time. He just hoped Ogun was where he had left him.

He surveyed the landscape, looking for other signs

that might give away they had been present here and making sure to eliminate all he found. Then he returned to the lass and lifted her onto the horse. An unexpected twinge at his side made him grimace.

Of course, she noticed.

"Are you all right?"

"Fine. 'Tis naught. I'll attend to it after we have progressed many kilometers from here." He looked down and pressed a hand to a cut on his side. His palm came away dotted with his own blood.

She frowned at his hand afore raising her gaze to his. "Help me down."

"Nay, lass. Later." He grabbed the reins and went to mount the horse behind her.

She shoved him off afore he got a good leg up.

The horse danced sideways, and Kallum flared his arms while he teetered unbalanced, but he managed to keep his feet.

He glared at her. "*Woman…*"

They didn't have time for these games. He needed to get the lass home as quickly as possible.

"Don't be difficult, MacNeill. We can ill afford for that to become infected and you to take with fever. 'Tis not as if I'll be able to lift *you* onto the horse in such event." She glared back with stewing impatience.

When he made no move to assist her, she turned completely sideways on the mare and slid off. He automatically caught her around the waist.

"Thank you," she said, her lips lifting slightly as she stepped back and began to examine his side.

The little vixen knew he'd catch her. That urge to strangle her resurfaced.

CHAPTER FOURTEEN

Ailsa looked away from the angry annoyance on the MacNeill's face. She'd gotten the upper hand in this matter. Primarily because she knew his sense of honor would not allow him to let her fall when dismounting the horse. That sense of honor did not mean he was not upset with her. Mayhap, it made him more so. She sensed he hated that she had figured out how to use his personal code against him.

All truth, she was surprised by how much she enjoyed vexing him. Something about this man brought out the contrariness in her. The tension between them as he tried to control her and she fought not to be controlled evoked some of the headiest emotions she had ever felt. Not that she had never faced off against a dominant male, but something about Kallum MacNeill was different.

Something about the way she felt around him was different.

She spread the cut in his tunic wide enough to glance inside at the wound. The slash across his skin was long but did not appear deep from this angle. To be sure, she needed a closer look.

"Remove your tunic for me." She glanced up into his eyes, and the intensity that met hers sent an unfamiliar frolic of emotions through her.

He eyed her without movement, but 'twas not merely obstinance that held him immobile. Her request, though innocent, suggested other possibilities.

Ignoring the charged moment, Ailsa directed him to focus on the task at hand. "I need a closer look, MacNeill. The wound looks not deep enough to need stitching, but to be certain, I must view it without your garment in place."

The MacNeill understood her request for what it was. His piercing sable eyes nonetheless displayed an awareness of the more forward implications of her request. After the briefest hesitation, his voice rasped with an edge borne of aught other than annoyance. "We do not have time for this."

Her healer's mien of authority took over, and her hands went to her hips. "Then stop wasting daylight and do what I ask."

His eyes tracked the placement of her hands, and something flickered in their dark depths afore he pulled off his tunic with a barely visible grimace she was meant not to see. She decided not to mention the grimace and ignore what looked suspiciously like amusement at her expense.

Instead, she touched her hand lightly to his side. His abdomen flinched inward at her touch, but he made no sound.

"Aye, 'tis not deep, but I would clean and wrap it afore we ride on." She glanced at his face again.

All irritation had left his gaze and been replaced by something more visceral. He glanced at her hand, which still rested on his side, and swallowed noticeably. A new tension arose, something that had very little to do with vexation. And there it was again, that shiver of emotion that left her unbalanced and vulnerably raw in a manner she'd never experienced in all her seasons of life. Through all the conflict and verbal sparring and

hostility that pinged between them simmered a temptation, a heated draw, that made everything female in her
want to surface and be bold.

Her gaze remained imprisoned by his, and without
conscious thought, her fingers traced down the path of
grooves outlining his defined abdomen. The feel was
totally different from the bony angles and soft middle
of the runt who had groped her earlier. The planes of
Kallum's skin were ridged with several raised scars, a
testament to his many battles.

'Twas enticing to be this close to such strength,
strength she had counted on with unfailing confidence
to untangle her assailant from her afore he did more
than grope at her breasts. She had survived such grop-
ing on more than one occasion. 'Twas nothing she had
not prepared herself to endure whilst living as a captive, and 'twas nothing she could not handle, though the
callous treatment never ceased to anger her.

When her hand reached the trio of muscles that
made a horizontal line beneath the MacNeill's navel,
she looked down to watch her hand as it slid along the
ridged path and paused to trace a pucker that suggested he'd been stabbed in the stomach sometime past.

His abdomen went concave as he hissed in a breath
and caught her hand. "Anne."

Her eyes flicked to his. He had called her that earlier. It had hit her odd to hear him call her by name for
the first time and use the wrong one. The mistake made
sense, for that was what he had heard her called by the
king. It had never occurred to her that he knew her
only by that name. Her enslaved name. A name she
never wanted to hear again.

"'Tis not my name," her voice near purred with a

breathiness she'd never heard from herself.

His hand tightened minutely around hers at the seductive tone of her revelation, and then his head tilted in confusion.

"'Tis what they decided to call me after my capture. My given name, my true name, is Ailsa."

He reached up with his other hand and pushed his fingers into the base of her loose braid, messy and barely still plaited after all she had been through in the past days. "Aye. Makes sense."

Her eyes questioned his meaning.

"Anne did not suit you." With a gentle tug, he pulled her closer. "Ailsa. 'Tis a strong name. One more fitting a brave Highland lass such as yourself."

Warmth spread through her, and she stared at him in amazement. He thought her brave? The longing, the reverence, in his eyes made her feel desired and significant in a way she'd never known. They stood so close the heat of his skin seeped to her, through her, and his intent to kiss her showed clearly on his face.

Oh, how she wanted his kiss.

He thought her brave! She near trembled at the thrill that a warrior such as he thought her worthy of his admiration, not just his lust.

This morn had come with challenges she could ill imagine facing—or surviving—on this trek without the MacNeill at her side. The urge to lean into his strength and allow him to replace every bad kiss she'd ever received with one that would make her feel like a woman and not like a possession near overwhelmed her. 'Twere not proper, these feelings. Nor was this the right timing or place for them to give in to this pull she had felt between them from the moment she'd laid eyes on him. They needed to be mindful of their surroundings and leave this place as soon as possible. So when his head eased lower, she broke eye contact and looked down to avoid a meeting of lips she was unsure she could survive unscathed.

Her forehead landed temporarily against his bare chest, and her breath stuttered uneasily from her lungs.

Kallum's hand disengaged from the hair at her nape, brushed lightly over her head, then dropped gently to her back. He drew small circles against the fabric of her dress in a reassuring caress and waited in silence while she gathered herself. Her hand quivered against his warm, scar-adorned skin a breath—or ten— then she fisted her hand at her side and pulled away, happy that her head had blocked his view of the prior trembling of her fingers.

"I need to attend your wound," she finally said.

"Aye." No censure or annoyance entered his tone.

Surprised, she looked up. She had expected him to be upset with her avoidance of his advance. She had been the one, this time, to slip them over the edge of propriety.

His lips forged a wry tilt on one side, but his eyes stayed fervent and consuming. "You may want to keep your hands from wandering past the area of the wound, then," he said, his deep voice laced with dark innuendo.

She dipped her head, fighting back the blush she could feel rising. "I'll need to clean the wound, then wrap it. 'Twill not take long."

She grabbed his waterskin from the horse, cleaned the wound, then ripped a few strips from the torn dress she'd changed out of to wrap around his midsection. Once that was done, he replaced his sliced tunic, put her back on the mare, and mounted behind her.

They rode without speaking. Their almost kiss left a quiet tension between them that lent nervous anticipation to Ailsa's journey. He wanted to kiss her. He *would* kiss her one day. 'Twas not a matter of if. More like a matter of when. And the more she thought about that impending kiss, the more she struggled between the lure of a maiden's burgeoning desires and the urge to run and hide.

She'd unknowingly awakened a sultry beast, and she knew not how to handle such an animal.

Hold her own in a battle of wits? Aye.

Fell a rabbit with a shot from a bow? Aye. Well, once she was back in practice.

But illicit encounters between a man and a woman? She had no skill at that.

She had no experience with consensual carnality between a male and female, and propriety mandated that, as an unmarried lass, she should not think on such unseemly affairs.

Marriage factored not into her plans. Accordingly, the social rules that applied to her intended station in life dictated she stay a chaste, singlewoman or enter an abbey or some such. She certainly had no intention of entering an abbey. She had a hard enough time embracing the teachings of a church that ignored—even justified—the enslavement of an entire people. No need to be that much of a hypocrite.

Did that mean she would never know the passion between a man and a woman?

Many females decried the act as painful and not worth the trouble. Those who believed in love matches oft told a different tale. She knew not which ones to believe.

And, if she indulged, whether the experience be pleasing or horrid, would that make her naught but a whore?

Her mother told her much about what went where and why when a man sought his pleasure, but she never mentioned repeated pain or unappealing couplings. Ailsa got the sense that her mother's memories of times with Ailsa's sire were anything but unpleasant. In fact, those very memorable liaisons caused many to label her mother a whore. 'Twas not what Ailsa had thought or believed of her mother. 'Twas not a designation her mother had accepted or allowed to shame her or make her cower from public life.

If Ailsa were to live her life on her own terms as her mother had, she must be prepared to leave off the opinions others might have of her. In which case, if she were to consider testing the boundaries of mating, 'twas mayhap best to engage in such matters of the flesh with a man she did not find amiable—a man like the MacNeill—so that amorous emotions were not at risk.

Liar. Her brain called foul on her classification of her feelings for the MacNeill as uncongenial, but she shut it down. Whatever feelings of amity she thought she lacked for the warrior, she could not deny he was easily the most virile man she'd ever met—tall, braw, and strong.

And foul tempered.

She glanced over her shoulder to check his expression. He stared back at her, that sliced brow peaked in curiosity, lips tilted at one edge in arrogant tease.

Except when he wasn't. And when he wasn't, he was devastating to her senses.

That lazy smirk sent a tingle through her, and the

feel of his muscled arms surrounding her as they rode made her feel not only safe but heated from her center down through the tips of her toes.

She was not so simple as to believe that the act of loving equated to the emotion love. She need not succumb to the latter to indulge in the first. The question was whether she wanted to indulge in the first, and if she did, was the MacNeill the man with whom she dared indulge?

The dilemma perplexed her through most of their ride for the day until she finally dozed off in his arms.

• • •

Kallum nudged Ailsa to wake her. She snuggled deeper into his arms, not wanting to be roused. She made a contented sound and rubbed the side of her face against his beard. He went immobile at her nuzzle, shock and desire coursing through him.

While he held himself taut, she did it again, bunting against him like a contented feline. Visions flooded him of what it might be like to have her nuzzle against him this way when they were both fully nude and stretched out on a bed, skin to skin. His hold on her tightened.

'Twas his tightening embrace that finally made her eyes flutter open. She looked up at him. Her cheek still rested against him in such a way that her skin brushed the edge of his chin when her head moved. She hummed lightly, seemingly enjoying the feel of his facial hair against her soft skin. Her lips lifted, and then she was the one to go immobile. The reality of what she had done flitted across her face along with a wash of embarrassment.

The embarrassment did not last. The look in her eyes shifted, and a pulsing curiosity took its place. He'd seen the same curiosity in her expression when she'd traced the scars on his stomach this morn. Daringly, she lifted her hand and rubbed her palm against the opposite side of his face. He did not move, waiting to see what she would do next.

Her hand traced his beard to the base of his ear and slowly came back the other way to feel the hair along his chin and upper lip. Her fingers brushed his lips in the process, and for a brief instant, she left her fingers against his closed mouth with a pensive expression on her face. He suppressed the craving to touch his tongue to her fingertips, not wanting to startle her so much that she'd stop her tactile exploration.

Finally, she dropped her hand to the edge of his mouth and pressed his face close to hers while she rubbed her cheek deliberately and with quiet relish against the other side of his beard. When she dropped her hand, she looked directly into his eyes unrepentantly.

"*Why…*" He cleared his throat to alleviate the noticeable strain in his voice, but the gruffness lingered. "Why did you do that?"

She held his gaze and admitted, "I was curious." A blush lit her skin afore she added, "I've been wondering what that would feel like, and I wasn't sure I'd get another chance to find out."

He stared down into those light eyes he found so mesmerizing, then ran his thumb across her pouty lips. She'd been curious about the feel of his beard against her skin. He was curious about the feel of her lips against his. Pushing one hand into the hair at the base of her skull, he held her gaze and allowed her to see all the raw emotions she inspired in him. The desire. The need. The growing hunger. He wanted her to have no doubt of his intention: put an end to this burning, desperate yearning to kiss her.

Slowly, deliberately, he leaned in, his lips less than a hair's breadth from hers. He paused and held, giving her enough time to stop him if this was not what she wanted. He had made the mistake earlier of making a move based solely upon his own urges. This time, he would take his lead from her.

When she made no move to stop him or pull away, he dropped his lips to the fullness of hers. The softness of first contact made him moan deep in his throat. He ran his tongue along her lower lip, then pressed it lightly against the seam of her lips to gain entry. She opened to him without resistance. The taste of her exploded against his tongue, and his world reduced to only the feel of her in his arms, the brush of her lips against his, and her soft whimper as she tasted him back.

The briefness that was supposed to be this kiss dissolved. He wanted more.

He wanted much more.

He wanted it all.

He wanted all of her.

His hunger deepened, his control shattered, and he let loose the desire he'd held in check for days.

• • •

Ailsa's world tilted a little. A pit of desire opened low in her belly, and the feel of the MacNeill's tongue against hers made it burn in a hot flame that spread from her center outward. The softness of his initial press of lips deepened. When his tongue danced against hers, she pressed back gently at first. This was new for her, but it felt right.

She sank into the kiss, letting the gentle tug of his teeth against her lower lip spark a thrill that led her hand back to his face. The soft tickle of his beard against her palm and the stroke of his tongue as it dueled with hers made her pulse leap.

Her skin got hot. The sun had begun to set, but she felt as if its rays burned at their hottest point directly onto her skin. A mewl of pleasure escaped her, and an urgency rose within the MacNeill. His attack on her senses intensified, and he spread the heat of his insistent ardor to her through the teasing of his lips, the stroke of his tongue, and the touch of the giant hand that trailed down her side to rest at her lower back.

He pulled her closer, disengaging his lips to trail kisses along her jawline. His tongue snaked out to lick at a corner below her ear, and she shivered. He hummed in his throat at her reaction and did it again. And yet again, when she nearly unseated herself from his lap as she writhed in ecstasy.

He tightened his hold on her and nibbled and sucked as if he never intended to stop. The flames he'd lit in her flicked higher, near to consuming her. Ailsa's head tilted back of its own accord, and Kallum took the exposed neckline as an invitation to extend his press of lips down the frontline of her throat.

His tongue dipped inside the top edge of her dress, where the loose ties revealed her collarbone. He licked along the hard line, then stopped to suck on one of the center knobs that bordered the hollow of her throat. A flash of need shot straight to that private center between her legs, and she began to squirm. Pressure built deep in her woman's place. Something intense bloomed just out of reach, and it was making her edgy.

"Kallum," she breathed as she wriggled on his lap, needing something more but not sure more of what.

He lifted his mouth from her throat and captured her lips again. He stroked in with his tongue, and she allowed herself to mimic his every thrust and tangle. Soon, they were both making sounds that rumbled noisily from deep in their throats and flushed the birds from the branches above their heads.

Ailsa's breasts felt heavy, and her nipples budded in approval of the feast he was making of her. His manhood pressed against her hip, a rigid rod that should have made her nervous, but her heart pounded so fiercely she could focus on nothing save the thought that it might burst.

With one last squeeze, Kallum nipped at her bottom lip and backed down the kiss to soft presses and licks. When his head finally lifted, his chest rose and fell in heavy pants and his dark eyes were glazed and dilated.

She, too, struggled to catch her breath, so it took her a few moments to be able to speak. Even then, she did so with difficulty. "Why…did *you*…do *that*?"

He rubbed his thumb across her kiss-swollen lips. "I was curious," he breathed. "And I wasn't sure *I'd* get another chance to know how 'twould feel to taste you."

CHAPTER FIFTEEN

The way Kallum stared at her made something flip in Ailsa's stomach. He smiled, just a little at the edges of his lips, his eyes suggesting he knew a secret worth sharing but withheld it to use against her at a later time. 'Twas strange to see him smile, really smile, not that wicked grin thing he did when he was about to kill someone.

The pressure at her core slowly started to recede, but she still felt unbalanced, flushed, and uncannily like she'd lost out on something life-altering. A warm haze surrounded her, and she felt a slight euphoria from the lingering effects of that kiss—his kiss. 'Twas a memory she'd pack away to pull out on future nights when her life as a singlewoman of independence got daunting.

Kallum ran his thumb across her bottom lip again. "Aye. Curious indeed."

He finally shifted her so he could dismount, then lifted her down. He dropped the mare's reins to ground-tie her.

Ailsa glanced around their latest campsite while she collected her scattered emotions. The area housed a shallow cave at the base of a rocky hillside fronted by a grove of trees. The cave was wide enough for people to spread out seated or prone but not tall enough for Kallum to stand inside. 'Twas more like a small niche carved naturally into the rock.

The MacNeill removed their belongings from the mare, stashed the items at the mouth of the half cave, then immediately began looking around the tree lines surrounding their secluded pasture.

She stepped up beside him. "What are you looking for?"

Without looking at her, he tucked in his lower lip to cover his bottom teeth and gave a shrill double whistle. The pounding of horse's hooves echoed a few moments afore his big, black stallion came charging out of a grove about a half kilometer to their left. The horse wore no harness or halter.

"Him," he replied.

The beast charged toward Kallum, not looking as if he intended to stop. Ailsa quickly took several steps backward, but Kallum stood his ground. The stallion halted abruptly in front of Kallum and snorted fiercely. The animal shook his head and pawed at the ground with his front right hoof. The stallion was huge. Ailsa could probably walk under him simply by tucking her chin to her chest.

Kallum placed a hand against the horse's forehead and rubbed. "I know. I'm late. But you look no worse for wear."

The horse bobbed his head as if in agreement with Kallum, and Kallum chuckled softly. His adoration for the stallion showed in his expression and constant rubs and touches to the beast's head and torso. From the stallion's reaction to Kallum's touch, the bond between the pair held strong both ways.

After the beast quieted, Ailsa returned to Kallum's side. She raised her hand, palm facing out, toward the animal's muzzle.

"Careful!" Kallum grabbed at her wrist, but afore he could stop her, the stallion's lips began nibbling her palm.

Ailsa giggled. The horse's nibbling tickled her hand.

Kallum stared at her then the stallion with utter amazement. "He...doesn't usually like strangers. He's been known to bite."

"Hmm. He most likely smells your scent on me."

"My scent?"

"Aye. My grandfather was a master with horses. He was the best groom in the village. He taught me that horses are very in tune with humans through our scent. Our fear, our joy, many of our emotions, they sense through our smell. Since we just...um...since you just..."

The horse took several steps forward and sniffed Ailsa around the head and shoulders, saving her from having to finish a description of what she and Kallum had recently done on the back of the mare. She laughed and pushed lightly at the horse's head to get him to stop, but he continued.

Kallum stepped in to shove him away. "Ogun! Stop that! Find your own girl."

The horse headbutted him on the shoulder as if offended by the rebuff, then pivoted and sauntered over to check out the mare.

"Ogun? You named your horse after the African warrior god?"

Kallum's gaze snapped to hers. "Aye. You know the African lore?"

She nodded. "My mother kept the old stories alive. She would oft tell them to me when putting me to bed as a child, as her parents had with her. How come you to know those tales?"

"Same. My mother would tell me tales of the old world when I was a lad. She arrived in Scotland after being kidnapped from the old country shortly afore reaching marriageable age. Even after she learned to speak English well, her voice retained the sound and cadence of Mother Africa. I loved most to hear her tell the stories of Ogun coming down to Earth and clearing a pathway for the other gods." His eyes lost focus. "Sometimes, I still miss the sound of her voice."

Ailsa could feel his loss across the space separating them. The loss of a mother was something they shared, mothers who both told them tales of the old country. She'd never had that connection with another person. Although the Connery clan had a noticeable population of Blacks, their small numbers were spread across the village. Plus, with her mother's notoriety and Ailsa's status as a bastard of mixed heritage, friends had not been a common experience for her.

She thought back on the tales she remembered of Ogun. Kallum's choice of name for his steed was fitting. Besides being a warrior, Ogun was also known in Yoruba culture as the god of justice, his wrath swift to mete out consequences for those who transgressed. The black stallion together with the Black Highlander made quite a pair. A warrior riding a warrior. She imagined seeing the steed bearing down on them with Kallum MacNeill on his back would make many a man shiver with trepidation.

She glanced at the MacNeill. He observed her with the oddest expression on his face.

All of a sudden, he whipped around, grabbed the short bow he had retrieved with his other belongings, and, without a word, headed for the trees.

"Where are you going?" she called after him.

"To hunt," he said without turning around. He took

another two steps, then stopped. He turned to look at her, his expression now blank and his sable eyes shielded. "Do not move from this spot."

He departed without waiting for an answer.

Ailsa stared at his retreating back. The mercurial, standoffish Shepherd had returned, barking orders and treating her like a lackey to tremble at and blindly follow every command. The lingering glow from her first real kiss evaporated like mist sucked into the burning rays of a rising sun.

She had no clue what she'd done to upset him this time.

• • •

Kallum stomped into the bushes without a thought for the game he needed to hunt. Foremost on his mind in this moment was escaping the woman who had disrupted his life. First, she'd inserted herself into his journey home. Second, she'd ignited his ardor to the point he acted like some randy lad not yet weaned from premature releases. And now, she'd started crawling inside his head to tinker with his memories and his emotions.

That comment about her mother telling her stories from the old country at night. If he did not know for certain she could not have learned such information about him from another, he'd have thought she played games of a nature to manufacture commonalities between them.

It had been a long time since he had thought of his mother, and of all women, for it to be this brazen troublemaker who brought her to mind was as disconcerting as it was unsettling.

Hell, even his horse liked her. *Traitor!*

What manner of scourge—or sorcery—had overtaken the world when you couldn't count on your ornery stallion to act ornery?

Kallum had been right from the first. The lass had the powers of a witch. She'd even jested she'd descended from a witch. 'Twas no jest to him. He felt the lass's spell luring him in, and he needed to extricate himself. She still held his secret, but he knew not hers. 'Twas a dangerous situation to be in, and he needed to pay heed that the lust in his cods did not cost him his neck.

A hare jumped across his path, and Kallum missed the opportunity to shoot it. He swore under his breath, then nocked an arrow so he'd be at the ready for the next bounder. Once he focused, he made short work of collecting two brown hares for supper and headed back to the campsite.

He glanced around but saw no sign of Ailsa. At first, he thought she'd simply wandered off despite his order to stay put. The dratted female never did what she was told. He dropped the hares by the firepit she had set up afore she disappeared to wherever she'd gone and walked around the fringes of the brush bordering their site. He moved slowly but noisily, to give her time to make herself known if she were perchance in the middle of handling some private need.

When he found no trace of her, his residual anger from their earlier encounter fled, and his heart thudded as momentary fear gripped him. Had she been taken?

He did a quick visual recheck of the camp but saw no signs of a struggle. Mayhap another band of miscreants came upon her with the element of surprise and took her, but the little hellion would have put up a fight to free herself. There would have been signs. At least, that's the story he told himself.

Still, he'd have no comfort until he was sure she was all right.

Not daring to call out in case he was wrong about the circumstances of her capture, Kallum unsheathed a sword and made his way slowly through the trees. Mindful to watch the ground for any signs of disturbance, he soon picked up a trail of footprints. They appeared to be small impressions like those that would be made by a woman. Ailsa.

From what he could tell, she'd been alone when she'd walked this way. He prayed she'd stayed that way.

Being careful to make no sound, he approached a small clearing from whence he could hear the sound of rushing water. The sound suggested a waterfall flowed not too far ahead. He cleared the trees, and the sight that greeted him nearly felled him to his knees.

Ailsa stood knee-deep in the water, wet from the neck down. She had removed her smock but still wore a linen chemise, mayhap out of caution should she be discovered during her bath. The lightweight material was soaked clean through and clung to every curve and angle of her plump backside. The material had gone gossamer and allowed the nudeness of her ravishing brown complexion to glow through as if not covered at all. She looked like some ancient goddess of the forest bathing amongst the foliage of her kingdom.

"Sweet Jesu," he uttered without conscious thought.

The roar of the waterfall should have covered the soft utterance, but the din of his sword tip carelessly scraping the rock at his foot reverberated over the pond's surface. He glanced down in shock at the treacherous hand that had allowed such sacrilege to occur, and Ailsa dropped low in the water upon seeing she was no longer alone. Her wide eyes found him on the bank while her long braid bobbed behind her on the surface of the water.

The dark tips of her breasts hovered just above the water line and showed visibly through the drenched material of her chemise. The russet brown of her nipples, beaded from the kiss of cold water, beckoned him with a silent song more powerful than any siren who'd ever beckoned a sailor. Kallum could not shake off the thought that the entreaty would also prove just as deadly.

He took an unconscious step forward. Ailsa's mouth dropped open, an anxious look in her eyes, and she threw up a dripping hand to warn him back. The movement of her arm made her wet chemise slide across her right breast, and Kallum's eyes were once more drawn to her bosom. He took no more steps. His hand clenched tightly around the hilt of his sword, and the ardor he'd only recently leashed began to rise in his loins yet again.

Ailsa finally noticed his stare focused not on her hand or her face but on her bosom. She glanced down and realized all she unwittingly displayed. Her opposite arm crossed protectively against her chest, blocking Kallum's view of the lovely jewels he longed to take in his mouth and suckle until she began to whimper as she had done while squirming in his lap during their kiss.

Kallum shook his head to clear it. 'Twas not

honorable to invade the lass's privacy such. He whirled around to present his back to her.

"When I did not find you at the camp, I became concerned. I did not mean to intrude on your privacy. I shall meet you back at the cave." He walked away without looking at her again. If he glanced back, he was not sure he would be able to stop himself from walking into that stream and taking a taste of those luscious, budded *cìochan*.

When he reached the firepit, he dropped to dress the hares for roasting. Focusing on the task of supper prep would help prevent his mind from replaying the alluring sight of Ailsa standing wet in the pond. He hoped.

She was not his to lust after nor his to keep.

His fingers clenched on the hilt of his blade, and he focused on cutting away the skin of the second hare to push away that annoying, recurring thought of keeping her. He was not a man who longed to mate with a woman for a lifetime. He'd never considered the option appealing. Women were beautiful and tempting and luscious places to dabble when he needed a release. To keep one for longer than that invited nagging and responsibilities and the frustrations of constant vigilance to countermand their betrayals or their manipulations or their weaknesses.

Except there was nothing weak about the brazen lass bathing in the pond.

He stood, annoyed by all the ways in which the lass impressed him. 'Twould be easier if she were just a bonnie face.

'Twould be easier if you knew to whom the lass was kin.

And therein lied his biggest frustration. How could he trust a woman whose background remained shielded in secret? To be kin to a clan who took so little care in their women they had allowed her to be enslaved without attempt to free her—how could she continue to defend such people?

Those were ties to which he preferred not to bind himself. If he were in fact to ever bind himself to a female, that is.

Get a grip on yourself, Kallum. 'Tis merely lust. If you were to have the lass, all would pass.

He looked up when he heard her step into the clearing. The relief that flooded him at her return flushed out the mad he'd been trying to work up.

Her hair was unbound. It spread in thick, wavy curls about her shoulders. The intimate sight of her loose hair renewed the stirring in his loins, and her beauty tugged at him more fiercely than ever. The thought of bedding her rose, but even more strongly returned the thought of keeping her. He had no need for the household oversight that a wife could provide. More important, he had no need for the constant distraction a lass such as this one would create. He wanted her anyway.

He was a warrior. He lived a warrior's life, a life fraught with danger and unavoidable combat. As he stared at the goddess before him, for the first time in his life, he got the sense he was about to fight a battle—a very personal battle—he could not win.

• • •

Ailsa felt speared by the look in the MacNeill's eyes. His gaze roamed over her, and she sensed he saw not what she currently wore but all he had inadvertently seen at the water site. The air crackled between them, a charge as potent as a leftover lightning strike.

The fine chisel of muscle hidden beneath his tunic flitted through her mind. 'Twas a vision seared into her memory. Now that she'd not only seen but felt those ridges and planes, the sensory recall of her fingertips wreaked havoc with feelings she wasn't sure she had words to describe. If his remembrance of her wet body caused half the agitation she currently felt, they were at a dangerous crossroads.

Heat swamped her insides and gave her a yearning she was afraid he'd see in her eyes, so she looked away and went to pack her things without speaking. He was gallant enough not to comment on what he had come upon at the pond, but the unspoken consideration did little to reduce the pulsing physical awareness between them.

An anxious disquietude disturbed Ailsa for the rest of the evening. After she had supped on the fresh meat brought back by the MacNeill, she refashioned the braid she had untangled in the short time the broody man had given her privacy at the water to wash up or bathe as best she could. No matter the effort to distract herself, her mind continued to race. Yet, she could find no clear answers to the questions that had plagued her since the start of the day.

By the time she had returned from bathing, the MacNeill had not only set hares to roast but also had set out his blanket roll for her to use. When they retired for the night, he motioned her inside the partial cave and laid himself in front of her across the mouth.

He had said few words to her while or after they

supped. He'd been irritable and standoffish. She knew not what she had done to annoy him, but he had said enough words to explain they would not keep a fire this eve, since they were close to the borders of clans without amicable ties to the MacNeills.

To assist with warmth, he had tied his cape to branches anchored into the ground and tented it open across the entrance to the cave. The setup would help block the wind, as would his body. Wrapped in the great plaid he had retrieved from a satchel that had been stashed deep in a thicket of bushes, the MacNeill settled in for sleep positioned with his back to her.

Despite the warrior's sullen disposition, Ailsa laid behind him, wondering what 'twould feel like to fall asleep with his arms wrapped securely around her the way he did when they rode together. This day may have been the last time she felt those arms encircle her. On the morrow, she would ride separately from him. She now had her own mount. Given the unwavering temptation to engage in naughty acts with the man, she should consider such change of circumstance a blessing. Yet, a part of her felt regret. There were times that being with him gave her a sense of security she hadn't felt in over three years.

She did not want to keep him, but a part of her wondered what 'twould be like to hold on to him for just a little while. To pretend that mayhap, just possibly, she could have a small portion of normal. Be a normal woman, not the woman who was always the outsider. The woman who always had to be strong for herself because no one else would be strong for her. She knew how to take care of herself. She'd been doing so all her life, but sometimes being the one to take care of yourself made living hard and lonely.

Ailsa never wanted to give up her independence. She'd learned the hard way, though, that independence could be fleeting and taken away in ways other than the bondage of marriage. Didn't she owe it to herself to seize what little bit of life she could?

She and the warrior laid less than an arm's length apart. If she reached out for him, what would he do?

Would he roll over and take her in his arms?

Would he offer another one of those kisses that would make her feel as if she were about to tumble off the edge of the world?

She'd seen the look in his eyes when he'd found her bathing. He'd wanted her. He might find her irritating, but he wanted her the way a man desires a woman.

She knew not how to initiate loving. She had no experience with what to do or what to say.

Or even what not to do to mess things up. She silently laughed at herself.

The MacNeill would know such things, though. If she had the guts to test his awakeness with a touch, she had little doubt he'd take control and teach her the rest.

She now understood why courting couples were mandated never to be alone without a chaperone. An inexperienced maiden was no match for controlling the raging temptations of the flesh in the face of a mature male who knew his way around a lady's wares. A cranky, disapproving elder was the perfect remedy to douse the catching flames of a maiden's desires.

No matter. Ailsa would never have a proper suitor offer her courtship. Thus, mayhap she need not worry about caving in to the callings of the flesh.

She rolled toward the MacNeill's back. Tempted to

reach out a hand.

Did she dare?

His response to her caresses of his beard proved he liked her touches, and what he'd offered her in return still left her with a pulsing need deep in the region between her legs. Now that he had awakened her womanly passions, they would not quiet.

She snaked a hand out of the bedroll she had wrapped around her and held on to the blanket where it tucked under her chin. She waited.

She waited for the courage to possibly take something for herself that she wasn't supposed to have but might give her a sense of freedom and power that had been denied her since her captivity.

She waited, but the boldness did not come this night.

She tucked her hand back inside the blanket.

So much for being brave, she chastised herself, then rolled onto her back.

Less than an arm's length away from the MacNeill, she fell asleep with turmoil still blazing inside her.

For the second morn in a row, she awoke with hands on her. This time, large hands painfully gripped both her wrists. She fought hard against her assailant even afore she managed to open her eyes, the need to break free a panic inside her.

"Nay. Nay!" She tussled, but no matter how hard she fought, she could not break free.

CHAPTER SIXTEEN

"Ailsa. Ailsa! Wake up!" With a double grip, Kallum shook the lass for the second time.

Her eyes finally popped open, and she stared up at him with glassy, unseeing eyes. He got the sense she was momentarily somewhere else.

"'Tis I, Kallum. Wake up, lass."

"Nay!" A look of horror lived in her eyes, and she shoved at him. "Get off!"

He released her immediately, and she rolled away and to her knees. Her hands went out to fend him off. They trembled.

Instinctively, he knew 'twas not him she truly fought, but he remained immobile to give her time to come fully awake. "You slept fitfully and were calling out in your sleep."

She looked around the cave, then toward the entrance, afore her gaze centered back on him.

"Reliving your fight with our tiny thief?" he asked softly.

Her hands went down, and she finally focused on him rather than some mysterious demon from her dream. "Nay." Her response was but a whisper.

He sat back on his haunches. "Night terrors?"

"Not so bad as that." She rolled down onto one hip and looked away from him. "Just a bad dream."

A part of him warned his conscious mind not to ask any questions, but another part of him could not manage to be so circumspect. "Bad dreams or bad memories?"

Her solemn eyes lifted. After a moment of contemplation, she said, "Both."

His teeth clenched at her response. If 'twere not the runt she fought off in her dream, then who was it?

Ailsa rose to her knees beside the sleeping pallet and began to roll it up. She remained silent in her work and did not meet his eyes.

Sensing her need for space, he stood and began dismantling the cape tented in front of their shelter. He folded away the cape and stashed it in his satchel, then walked over to a tree facing opposite the cave mouth. He leaned, back against the tree, with arms folded across his chest and one ankle crossed over the other. He did not want to pry into what seemed a harsh memory, but what he suspected was behind her dream troubled him.

"Lass, what were you resisting in your dream?"

Her movement completely stilled. She stared down at the half-rolled blanket, seemingly frozen. Her shoulders finally dropped, and she sat back on her heels. "Something tells me you already know the answer."

"I know naught for certain. Of what I am thinking, I pray I am wrong."

She finally met his eyes, and when she spoke, her voice was so soft he could barely hear her. "You are not wrong."

The anguish on her face tore at his gut. He should dare not ask the next question on his mind. 'Twas intrusive. But once again, he could not stop his tongue. "Did you…succeed?"

Eyes still on him, she nodded. "Aye, but 'twas not by much."

His tolerance for men who abused women set at

naught. He fought off the clenching of his fists.

Ailsa continued her explanation without looking at him. "The second time I ran away, they found me while I slept. I awakened in the grip of a king's soldier who thought he deserved a...a..." She struggled to find the right word. "A boon for having been the one who found me. He managed to overpower me, but he was interrupted from taking what he wanted when the remaining searchers rode up, the captain of the king's guard leading the entourage.

"The captain berated the soldier. Not necessarily because he felt I deserved better treatment but because, I'd always sensed, the captain considered me his—and only his—to torment. I never understood why. He took little interest in any of the other captives, but with me..." She finally looked up, and her gaze found his again. "'Twas almost as if I was as much his as the princess's."

She wrapped her arms around herself, the gesture fraught with self-preservation as well as disquietude. "When we returned to the castle, I expected I'd have a private—and extremely *intimate*—audience with the captain. Instead, he opted to flog me viciously and repeatedly in front of the other enslaved servants. He wanted to make sure my failure served as a warning should any other captives think to seek freedom. And he made sure I knew the fate I'd narrowly escaped upon my capture could come to pass at his hands anytime he chose."

It took all Kallum's strength to control the emotions raging in him and not walk over and wrap her in his arms, to give the comfort she looked so desperately in need of. But she was a proud lass. She had not wanted his comfort after her altercation yester morn, and she would not appreciate today a gesture she would see as an offer of pity.

To think, she had been sorely abused in the past and, like yester morn, had nearly endured the full taking of what a woman should only give freely. A visceral reaction boiled up from his core, one that spoke of protection and possession and *revenge*. Though those were not the only emotions that assailed him.

A strong wave of guilt washed over him. She had been fresh off an assault—that had not been her first—and like a cad, he had tried to kiss her. Though she had seemed fine at the time and had assured him she suffered no lingering harm, she may have simply been having a delayed reaction to her ordeal.

Her encounter with the border reiver had obviously affected her enough to bring on disturbing dreams of a past attack. He should have been the one to know better. The lass was young yet, and she was determined to never show weakness.

Then she had inflamed him with her gentle caresses along his beard. It had been a simple matter of a maiden's curiosity, he was certain, but he had allowed it to tempt him into near deflowering the lass on the back of a horse.

Idiot!

He pushed off the tree, needing to do something with the coil of energy roiling inside him. His first thought was to ready the mounts. Now that he had retrieved Ogun and found his saddle and belongings deep within the thicket where he had hidden them, he and Ailsa had everything they needed to make good time.

A pull toward Ailsa derailed his approach of the horses. He'd fought that pull yester eve. When she'd talked about her *mamaidh* telling her the tales of the old country, he realized 'twas yet another commonality between them. He had barely come down from the arousal inspired by their kiss only to be assaulted by a tenderness that unnerved him. He'd fled to go hunting, but it had not helped to staunch the pounding in his blood that pulsed unfailingly for the lass.

He stopped in front of her and offered her his hand. She placed her small, strong fingers in his, and he helped her rise. For the first time, he noticed her delicate hand held a layer of toughness. Not the callused roughness of his, but a texture that spoke of a working woman's hands, a woman of substance with a backbone of steel.

He couldn't not touch her. He ran his thumb and first finger down the wisps of wavy hair that fluttered at her temple, free of the braid she had freshly replaited last night after her trip to the water. Then, he dropped his wandering fingers to caress her cheek. "See to your needs, lass. Today we do not stop until we reach our destination. I'm taking you home."

Ailsa placed a hand around his raised wrist and squeezed afore she walked calmly into the brush to take care of her early-morn toilette. Her calmness would likely be a limited reprieve once she realized he had not specified to whose home.

Kallum sighed. He would keep that information to himself until they reached the edge of MacNeill lands.

He dismantled the camp and made sure he left nothing behind that could be used to identify them. He gathered his belongings and attached them to Ogun.

Last, he gathered Ailsa's satchel so he could attach it to the mare. The heavy weight of the bag perplexed him until he remembered the lass had snagged his dagger out of the dead thief from yester morn's attack.

"What are you doing?" Ailsa stood at the edge of the clearing. Her face held a look of absolute horror.

She rushed at him and snatched the bag from his hand.

"Packing our mounts for departure." He narrowed his eyes at her, her odd behavior making him suspicious.

She glanced quickly into the satchel, then tightly closed it. "I'll take care of it. Thanks."

She looked away from him, but not afore he saw something close to panic in her eyes.

"What are you hiding, lass?"

She shifted warily away from him and blinked innocently. "What?"

"I think you heard me." Kallum advanced one deliberate step after another. "What's in the bag you want me not to see?"

"'Tis naught!" She took in a slow breath and blew it out, the act clearly designed to steady her nerves. "Naught that would be of interest to you," she said with more composure.

"You speak not the truth." He baldly returned the words she had said to him on the query about her eyes.

When he was but a step away from her, she backed away, nearly tripping over a large rock at her feet. She faltered, unbalanced. The bag dangled at the end of one of her flailing arms, and Kallum took the opportunity to snatch it back.

"Nay!" She regained her balance and lunged for the bag.

He held it aloft, easily out of her reach.

"There's naught in there that belongs to you or is your concern, Kallum MacNeill. Return my belongings posthaste!"

"Ah, *leannan*, that is where you are wrong. I believe you've pilfered my dagger and it lies within."

Her brows rose at his use of the term *sweetheart*, but she twisted her hands anxiously at his accusation. "I did not pilfer it."

A mocking slant of his lips silently denied her claim. "And I'll be needing it back. 'Twas my father's, and 'tis all I have of him."

"I meant only to arm myself in case…in case…" She dropped her hands, fisting one at her side as she was wont to do when angered. "'Tis no matter. Hand me my bag." She held out a hand as if she truly expected him to obey her order.

Kallum ignored the demand. He understood she had wanted the protection of the dagger after they'd been attacked. But 'twas not the pilfered dagger about which she was concerned. Otherwise, she would not be so willing to give it up.

He made to open the bag.

"Nay." She leapt at him. "I'll do it."

Kallum denied her access to the bag. She grappled with him in a continued attempt to retrieve her satchel. He fought her efforts with one hand, holding her off without hurting her. Her ruckus became so chaotic, he accidentally dropped the bag.

The satchel fell open with the hilt of his dagger peeking out amongst the remains of her torn underdress and a cloth item displaying tartan colors.

Kallum bent to retrieve it.

"Don't," she said with almost desperate quietness.

She tried to beat him to the cloth. She failed, and he lifted it, horrified to recognize the colors of the plaid.

He held it out toward her. "What is this?" he demanded.

She snatched the item from his grasp and pressed it to her chest. "Why, 'tis a sash, of course."

"Those are Connery colors."

She notched up her chin. "Aye."

"You're a *Connery*?"

Kallum felt his chest seize. She was a Connery? This beautiful, brave, fierce lass was a *Connery*. 'Twas not possible.

"Aye," she said cautiously, leery of his unflatteringly incredulous tone.

The Connerys were a lot of foul, dishonorable outlaws who committed barbaric acts against other clans in an attempt to usurp as much land and control over the Highlands as they could garner.

"You're kin to those barbarians who helped the MacGregors slaughter the Colquhouns at Glen Fruin?" He stormed away from her, needing space lest he do something to a lass he'd never done afore.

The Colquhouns were MacNeill allies, bound by both marriage and blood. The laird's sister had married a Colquhoun chieftain. Her husband, third in rank in his clan, and their sons were slain by the MacGregors with the assistance of the Connerys in a most foul and deplorable manner.

"'Twas a dishonorable double ambush that amounted to an unjustified slaughter." Kallum began to pace back and forth. "And what of the forty innocents burned by the MacGregors and their allies in the barn?

'Twas abominable."

Her face flushed with anger. "'Tis not as if I was responsible for that skirmish. I have no say in matters of wars or allies. And you act as if the Colquhouns were such innocents. What of the two MacGregor lads they hanged afore the battle occurred, simply because the younguns pinched a mite of food to cease their hunger when stranded away from home for the night?"

"That act was not confirmed!" Kallum shouted.

"Ha! Say you and the Colquhouns. As if they would admit that freely. Are you so dense, then, MacNeill?"

He lurched at her, then stopped himself. "No wonder your people left you behind. They have enough villains in their midst without the need for a foul-mouthed hellion to stir up more trouble."

The hurt that crossed her face caused a pain in his chest, but he could not stop himself from ranting. To think he had thought of bedding her, of keeping her. A *Connery*. The betrayal he felt at this revelation weighed heavily, as did an inexplicable feeling of loss, like boulders pressing down on his sternum and near collapsing his lungs.

"Connerys cannot be trusted. They are vile, deceptive, and they rely on underhanded treachery instead of honorable war tactics. To be allies with the MacGregors, a clan so vicious they were allowed to be hunted by the king, is telling of their nature. The use of the MacGregor name has been banned by the crown. MacGregors who do not abandon the name risk punishment by death, and these are men your clan readily takes in and shelters and allows to adopt the Connery name."

He ran both hands down his face, then back over his

head, removing the leather tie at his nape as he went and letting his twisted locs swing free. He loosened the tie, one of many made for him by Inan's sister, with the beaded loop that adjusted easily so as not to tangle in his hair upon removal. After he slid the leather onto his wrist, he stared at Ailsa, half expecting her to look haggard or shriveled or to have grown horns now that he knew she was a Connery.

But she was still beautiful, and the pull was still there.

"I am a dead man."

His morbid statement shocked her. "What?"

His head started an uncontrollable movement from side to side. "You know my secret. A Connery knows the truth of my misadventures. I should have left you at the cove. I am a dead man. *You* will be the death of me."

"Nay, Kallum." She reached for him. "I would never—"

"Don't touch me." He yanked his arm from her grasp and walked away, needing to gather his wits.

A deep female snarl rent the air a mere breath afore a dagger imbedded in the tree behind him.

He jerked to eye the treed dagger, then the hellion who threw it. "Did you"—he advanced on her, stalking like a wildcat after prey—"just throw…a *dagger* at my head?"

She backed away, her retreating steps in sync with the pace of each of his advances. "Nay." She grinned menacingly at him. "If I had been aiming for your head, you'd have a dirk stuck between your eyes."

He lunged for her. She avoided his grasp and ducked in between the horses. The lass was fast, but she

had nowhere to go but open space. This was one altercation she could not win.

Kallum pulled up short when she stepped from
around Ogun holding his bow with an arrow nocked at
the ready. He gave her a wary consideration. "Know
you how to use that, lass?"

"You willing to risk that I don't?" One eyebrow
lifted, and her lips curved in a saucy smirk.

Damn, if her spunk didn't arouse him. What a
shame she was a Connery.

He examined her stance, the position of her elbows,
and the placement of her drawing hand at the edge of
her mouth. The lass had had training. How accurate she
might be remained to be seen.

He had somewhat of an upper hand in that the bow
had been fashioned with a draw weight set for him. The
lass had not half his strength, so she was unlikely to be
able to make an arrow fly with much momentum. Even
so, he dared not approach her straight on.

He feinted as if grabbing for her. She scrambled
back a few steps.

Ah, she did not really want to shoot him. Good to
know. But he continued to be careful. That she didn't
want to shoot him did not mean she *wouldn't* shoot
him.

He feinted again but this time did not stop. She released an arrow. The arrow flew wide. She reached back
behind her head and pulled out a second arrow she'd
stashed out of sight down the back of her dress. She
had it nocked with lightning-quick speed.

The lass had demonstrated afore that she had quick
reflexes, but his were quicker. He managed to push up
the bow afore she could release a second shot.

He snatched the bow out of her hands and lifted her off her feet, unmindful of the bandaged gash on his side. "What you need is a good spanking."

Her eyes widened. "You wouldn't dare."

"Ah, lass, you forget to whom you speak." He grinned when her large, expressive eyes revealed the instant she remembered they'd been in this situation on the night of her escape.

He dropped the bow, walked her over to the mare, and tossed her over the mare's back like a bag of grain. Her feet kicked in protest, but he grabbed her ankles with one hand and swatted her bottom with the other.

"Stop!" She bucked and tried to free her legs.

Kallum held on and gave her another swat.

"Dammit, MacNeill. Stop! You have no right. I was just defending myself. You deserved it!"

She was right. He did deserve her wrath. The words he'd said to her were horrible. He'd been shocked and angry, but that was no excuse for his behavior. As she had pointed out, she had no political power in her clan to make decisions of war or alliances. Still, he wasn't ready to release her. He was getting too much satisfaction from this spanking.

The headstrong minx had thrown a dagger at him and then shot at him with his own bow. If she'd been a man, she'd be on the ground with that dagger in her gut. Instead, he rubbed a hand over her plump bum afore swatting her solidly two more times.

When he stepped away, she kicked backward, knocking him on his arse. Then she scrambled up to sit astride the mare, grabbed the reins, and heeled the mare into a gallop.

Kallum swore aloud. He should know by now not to

underestimate the lass.

Rising, he retrieved his bow from the ground, then collected his two arrows and pulled his father's dirk from the tree. He was not concerned about the lass getting away. Ogun could run down that mare with a full kilometer head start.

He glanced down at Ailsa's tartan sash and belongings on the ground, tempted to leave them where they laid. But the lass had held on to them through three years of captivity. Clearly, they were of significance to her. He scooped them up, taking a moment to inspect the brooch pinned to the sash. The Connery clan crest sat in the center of the silverish brooch and was surrounded by a circle of interweaving Celtic knots. A flying falcon, the Connery family symbol, looked about to take flight from the crest. The falcon's eyes were made of embedded red glass, most likely to coordinate with the red of the Connery tartan colors.

Another surge of disbelief hit him. He shook it off and stuffed Ailsa's things back into her satchel. After adding her possessions to his on Ogun, he finally took off after the hellion. To his surprise, he did not have to go far. She had pulled up and sat on the mare waiting about a half kilometer away. He walked Ogun up to face her.

"I know not which way to go to avoid trouble," she said when he stopped. "I comprehend you now think I deserve whatever fate befalls me, even death, but I cannot help the clan of my birth, MacNeill. I give you my word—not the word of a Connery, but the word of a captive you helped free—that I will not reveal to anyone that you are the Shepherd. All I want is to go home. Please." She swallowed noticeably. "*Please* do not leave me behind."

Kallum studied her face. What it took for her to toss aside pride and beg for his continued assistance showed on her face. He had no cause to trust a Connery, but for now, he would have to trust that *her* word could be counted on. He could not very well abandon the lass on the border between the Highlands and the Lowlands. He'd never deserted a captive under his watch. To do so now to a lass with no kin to back her would make him no better than the Connerys he had decried.

His mother's plight came to mind, the lone runaway with no aid who had nearly died at the hands of the ruffians who came upon her during her escape. 'Twas not a fate he could allow or accept for the stalwart lass. With a brief nod, he headed Ogun in the correct direction, and the mare followed.

He and the lass rode through the day with few stops and kept going into the night. They were close to MacNeill land, and he wanted to not spend another night with Ailsa forced to sleep out of doors. Although she was a Connery, she was still a woman. She deserved that much consideration.

To her credit, Ailsa made no complaints despite the arduous schedule and kept pace with him on her mount. Several hours afore dawn, she swayed in the saddle. He reached over and grabbed her hands around the reins to steady her. Ogun pressed against the side of the mare, and Kallum looked into Ailsa's fuzzy eyes. She could barely keep them open.

The lass was tired and needed to rest, but Kallum dared not stop. Their attackers from the other day had confirmed there was a bounty for her return. He could not risk that others were out looking for her. He knew not whether *auld* Angaidh had other comrades within the area and might even now be following their trail. Ailsa had suffered night terrors of a past assault, and the longer they stayed out in the open without support, the more risk that she would have to suffer such again.

He needed to get her into the safe confines of MacNeill keep, although he still did not know how he was going to explain her to his kin. 'Twas bad enough she was a fugitive from the king. To also be a Connery added a difficult pall to the mix.

"Lass, I know you are tired, but we cannot stop for sleep this day."

She looked at him and nodded. "Aye, I know it. I shall be fine." She heeled the mare to continue on.

Kallum held firm to the reins and directed the horse to stop.

Once again, Ailsa had amazed him. She was determined to continue on, understanding the dire circumstance she was in, but he was afraid she'd fall from the horse. These last days had been a true ordeal for her. He could not understand how she was not ready to curl into a ball with her knees at her chin and remain thus for a full fortnight.

"Ailsa, look at me."

Her tired, hazel eyes, still ringed with fading bruises, focused on his face.

"You are in no condition to continue to ride on your own. Let me carry you."

She looked at his lap, then back at his eyes. He saw the uncertainty there. He had not been subtle about his lustful interest in her, and this morn, they had fought until he overpowered her and enacted physical retribution. Hence, he understood her hesitation, but right now, he needed her to trust him to mind his manners.

"I give you my word, lass. I'll not take advantage. Trust me," he coaxed.

With a drowsy nod, she reached for him. "Aye, MacNeill. 'Twould seem I have little choice in the matter."

He helped her onto Ogun. The war stallion was massive and would not notice her slight additional weight. They would be able to travel thus, without the need to stop, right to the edge of MacNeill lands.

He settled Ailsa crossways against him, then tied the reins of the mare to Ogun's saddle with enough slack to allow the horses a comfortable separation. With Ailsa nestled safely in his arms, he rode on toward home. The lass quickly fell asleep.

The closer they got to MacNeill lands, the more Kallum realized what a predicament he carried from his lap to the lap of his kin. He had to present the lass to the laird and ask the laird to give her protection, but the clan name he had for the lass tied her to men who had murdered the laird's nephews and brother by marriage.

The wrong kin was not the only concern. She knew Kallum's secret. His own kin did not know he was the Shepherd. He could not allow the lass to go traipsing off unescorted to spread the knowledge of his identity to whomever would listen. 'Twould lead to Kallum's execution, and the MacNeills would likely be stripped of their lands.

She'd given Kallum her word that she would keep his secret, and Kallum believed she had been sincere.

Still, the risks were great.

All told, the lass deserved some concessions. Even Laird MacNeill could not ignore that she was of Highland birth and had been wronged. Regardless of the consequences due Kallum for his outlaw behavior, the lass deserved to stay free, whatever her clan.

At early dawn, they reached the bottom of the rise over which they would find the path into MacNeill lands.

Kallum tilted his head down to whisper in Ailsa's ear. "Lass, we are approaching clan lands. Wake up."

Ailsa blinked herself awake. "What?"

"We are in friendly territory. You may want to return to your own horse afore we reach a point where we can be spotted by the sentry."

She reached up and fingered the loose tendrils of her hair across her cheek, showing self-consciousness about her face for the first time since she'd been with him. 'Twas odd behavior, in his opinion. The bruises had faded much. Even the area around her eye had less of a discolored ring.

He grabbed her wrist. "Do not do that."

"Why not?" She tugged gently against his hold.

"You have nothing to be ashamed of. Those are your battle scars. Warriors wear their battle scars with pride."

She scoffed at him. "I am not a warrior."

"Aye, lass. You are." Unable to help himself, he pressed a light kiss to her lips. "You simply do not realize it yet."

• • •

Ailsa did not feel like a warrior, but she held on to the tingle that zipped through her at Kallum's kiss and put on her warrior face. He helped her shift over to her own mount, and they prepared to head into friendly territory.

Once they reached the top of the rise, the vision that greeted her was extraordinary. A large keep nestled in the curve of a series of hills. A stone skirt encircled a well-kept manor and a maze of cottages and structures that spoke of a well-run clan. From this elevation, she could see the village that spread out beyond the keep proper and the sheep that grazed in the grassy pastures beyond the back gate. A flowing stream curved around the pasture and the hills, and in the distance, she could see a waterfall that poured over a rocky ledge.

Ailsa glanced up and recognized the banner that hung from the sentry tower. 'Twas one she had seen at the tournament, the one that displayed the MacNeill crest. Her gaze whipped to the MacNeill mounted beside her.

"You did not bring me here," she hissed.

He did not even have the decency to look chagrined. "'Twas the proper choice."

"'Twas not what I asked of you, nor was it your choice to make!"

"Aye, 'twas," he countered in a matter-of-fact tone.

"How think you that?" Truly perplexed, Ailsa wondered if the overbearing clod could possibly be as clueless as he was arrogant.

"You know my secret, lass, and now that I know yours, we must be strategic about how you get home."

"I cannot be here." She squeezed the mare's reins

and seriously considered urging the mount into a fast gallop in the other direction.

"Why can you not be here? You will be safe amongst my clansmen. Just do not tell anyone you are a Connery. I must handle that first with the laird." The quiet authority in his voice overlooked the extremely difficult position he had placed her in without so much as a *by your leave* or any advanced warning.

Men could be so simpleminded sometimes.

"Even so, your soldiers will recognize me from the castle. 'Twill be only a matter of time afore the king's guard is summoned so some warrior from your army can collect the bounty for my return."

He gave a dramatic sigh. "I could not very well take you to the isles and leave you there. 'Twas no point in me helping you navigate your way back to the Highlands only to have you accosted or kidnapped or bonded back into slavery.

"Think on it, lass. If you want to get back to your clan, you need the protection of a powerful laird. Laird MacNeill is such a laird. He will not allow a Highland lass to be stolen—again—from her homeland, nor will he allow a MacNeill clansman to be the reason 'tis made so. Nor will I." Kallum shifted in his saddle. "Laird MacNeill is our best hope. He'll offer you sanctuary and protection from those who would attempt to return you to enslavement. I am the commander of his army. No man in this clan will defy his orders or dare defy mine."

Yeah. Yeah. Because you'll kill any man who does, and they know it.

Somehow, the notion—while likely accurate, despite the mocking voice in her head—did not offer her much comfort. She had a sinking feeling she may have traded one form of captivity for another.

"Ailsa," he said gently.

She glanced at him, or more like glared.

"You are safe now. The laird will see you are returned to your kin if that is what you want." He gave her a meaningful look. "Of course, there is much to be sorted out there. You may find 'tis in your best interest to stay put with the MacNeills."

Not bloody well likely. 'Twas not even a consideration for Ailsa, especially not until she was certain she wasn't in more danger at the MacNeills for being a Connery than she was for being a fugitive.

Ready or not, she was about to enter the den of the enemy. Time to find out whether she'd be embraced or cast aside—yet again.

CHAPTER SEVENTEEN

Kallum heeled Ogun into a canter, keeping the mare tethered to the stallion, and led Ailsa down to face the MacNeills. The gate opened for them, and they rode into the middle of the courtyard. Kallum dismounted.

A young, bonnie lass with light brown hair pinned at the nape and flowing down her back came running from the manor.

Without stopping, the lass launched herself at Kallum's chest. "Kallum! You're finally home!"

He caught her and twirled her around with a laugh.

His laughter shocked Ailsa. 'Twas not a sound she would ever have associated with the braw warrior. His face near shined with adoration as he placed the lass onto her feet and planted a kiss on her forehead. Ailsa wondered who she was, and the twinge in her gut at the obvious affection between the two took her by surprise. 'Twas not as if she had or wanted a claim on the MacNeill. Her carnal fantasies aside, Kallum MacNeill was not hers to possess or feel possessive over.

"Caitrin, lass, you must stop tossing yourself around thus. You are no longer a bairn. With the size of you, one day, I'll be unable to catch you and drop you on your arse."

She swatted him on the arm. "Ha. Not funny. I weigh but a pittance. You will be sporting gray in your locs afore you can't lift the likes of me. And you are late."

He gave the twists of his ponytail a jaunty flick and

winked at her afore he asked, "Late? Says who?"

"Says *me*," the lass responded with a pout. "Inan said you'd be along 'shortly.' That was days and days and days ago. We were about to send men out to look for you."

"*We* or you, my little worrier?" He tapped his index finger to her nose.

Caitrin blushed at his comment, then turned her gaze to the mare. Her eyes widened upon finding Ailsa astride the horse.

The girl—woman—Kallum had called Caitrin shifted her gaze from Ailsa to Kallum back to Ailsa and finally to Kallum again with a perplexed look upon her face. "You brought a woman home?" The awe, and mayhap some disapproval, in her voice did not escape Ailsa.

Noticing where the lass's attention focused, Kallum moved Caitrin gently aside with the back of a hand to the front of her shoulder and came to assist Ailsa in dismounting the horse.

He turned back to the lass. "Caitrin, this is Ailsa. Ailsa, this is Caitrin. Inan's sister and my favorite pest."

One of Caitrin's hands went to her hip, and she canted it at a sassy angle. "I am not a pest."

"Aye, you are, and everyone knows it." The wink he gave her took any sting from his words.

"Well, Kallum"—the warrior who had stood with him at the tournament strolled into the courtyard—"how nice of you to finally grace us with your presence."

Kallum acknowledged him solemnly. "Inan."

Inan peered at Ailsa, and it took but a moment for his eyes to widen with a look of disbelief. He covered it quickly. Caitrin noticed it not, but neither Ailsa nor Kallum missed the indication that Inan remembered her from the tournament dais.

Inan stepped up to Kallum and lowered his voice to prevent Caitrin from overhearing. "Are you out of your mind? You did not take the princess's handmaid."

"Nay, I did not."

"Think you I do not recognize her?" Inan hissed.

"Aye, I'm sure you do. She is quite memorable." Gone was the open, joyous Kallum. The hard-edged warrior with the shut-off expression had returned.

Inan shook his head. "Forsooth! Tell me you have not let your cods rule your head. You would bring the king's wrath down upon us for a leman?"

Kallum's hand shot out and grabbed Inan around the neck. "Careful how you refer to the lass. I'll not have her disrespected."

A gasp escaped Caitrin at the physical exchange between the two men. Hearing the sound, both men glanced at the lass with concern, suddenly realizing their disagreement was playing out in the most public of spaces.

"What is the meaning of this?" A distinguished elder man with his hair flowing loose about his shoulders and an air of authority in his manner descended the manor steps. He favored Inan immensely, or more likely Inan favored him. The men were obviously blood kin.

Immediately, Kallum released his hold on Inan and faced the elder. "Sire." He gave a respectful nod.

The man continued his approach and nodded in return. He stopped in front of the two men and addressed Inan. "Your cousin is home but minutes and already you two are at each other's throats. What is the problem this time?"

Cousin? Ailsa gave Kallum and Inan a close inspection and wondered how the two were cousins, as neither looked to be of mixed blood. Of course, her kind came in all hues, and 'twas not uncommon for a mixed bairn of a dark-skinned parent to come out the same shade as that parent. Such did not appear to be the case between the two warriors, though.

Still at odds, they glared at each other, and Inan's eyes suggested he dared Kallum to explain their tiff to the man whom Ailsa had figured out was the MacNeill laird.

Transferring his attention to Laird MacNeill, Kallum explained, "No problem, sire. I simply have a need to discuss of matter of great importance with you." He glanced at Inan, then back at the laird. "In private."

This last seemed to intrigue the laird. While he pondered Kallum's statement, the man finally noticed Ailsa's presence. His gaze wandered over her disheveled attire and lingered on her still-discolored face. His expression showed nothing of his thoughts on what he viewed. The MacNeill men apparently had a clan-wide mastery over stoicism.

"A matter that concerns your lass?" the laird asked.

Kallum's brows puckered. "She is not my lass, sire. But, aye."

The laird grunted at Kallum's denial and returned his gaze to Ailsa. "A concern with which Inan does not agree?"

Inan waved his hand for Kallum to continue the explanations and crossed his arms defiantly against his chest.

"I would continue this conversation inside, sire, if you will allow. 'Tis a matter of much importance and of a sensitive nature."

"Very well." The laird offered Ailsa his arm, his expectation she join them made clear.

Ailsa took a step backward. "Nay, your lairdship. I would not intrude on your council."

"How can you intrude when I suspect the sensitive matter of much importance involves you?" He offered her his arm again. "Come."

Ailsa cringed internally at the thought of being escorted inside the MacNeill manor to be offered to the laird as a Connery intruder, but she dared not insult the man by rejecting his offer a second time, especially in public. She looked condemningly at Kallum but laid her forearm over top of the laird's.

Once they entered the manor, the laird led them past the grand hall toward a room that housed a massive desk, positioned across from the door but at an angle that had a corner behind it. When seated at the desk, the laird would be able to see all parts of the room by simply looking up. He motioned her to take one of two chairs that flanked a round tea table just inside the door to the right. The table sat in front of one panel of a massive, partitioned bookshelf that stretched all the way from the door to the corner of the adjoining wall.

Ailsa shaped her lips into a closemouthed smile, the effort feeling forced and unnatural, but she dared not risk being perceived as someone other than a submissive lass grateful to simply be in the laird's presence. Whatever manner of clan produced a warrior as cold-bloodedly deadly and unflappable as Kallum MacNeill would likely have leadership of a similar disposition. In her experience, the nature of the leader set the tone for an entire family, clan, and even country. She graciously acknowledged his offer of seating but chose to remain standing.

The door shut firmly behind her, and the ominous snick of its catching knob mechanism reverberated throughout the room. With his hand still on the closed portal, Inan gave her another glare. A wave of anxiousness flooded her. She experienced a disconcerting feeling of being trapped with no way out. She swallowed, desperate to settle her nerves and wet a mouth that had gone completely dry.

Kallum made his way to the large fireplace within the wall to the right of the desk.

The laird perched his backside against the desk's front edge and crossed his arms. "So tell me: who is this lass, and why is she here?"

"She is one of the king's slaves, apparently escaped from Stirling Castle," Inan informed the laird.

"She is not a slave."

"I am not a slave."

Kallum and Ailsa countered at the same time. They glanced at each other in surprise.

"*Pfft*, think you I remember you not from the tournament, lass? 'Tis not a face one is likely to forget." Inan's hand made a circle motion in the air in the general direction of her face.

Once again, a MacNeill saw fit to remind her of her bruises. The cad.

"Aye. What you do not know is how I came to be there."

"Does it matter?" Inan replied.

"Aye, it does." The laird stood, apparently tired of watching the antics of his warriors. He approached

Ailsa, stopped in front of her, surveyed the damage to her face, and took note of her bruises along with something else she could not quite decipher. "Tell me."

She recounted the tale of her capture bluntly and without embellishment. She felt the bitter dregs of the memory of that horrid day when she had let her guard down for want of a view of a Black trumpeter.

The laird nodded at the tale, seemingly satisfied with the explanation.

"There's more," Ailsa said.

"Ailsa." Kallum's warning tone was clear.

"*Kallum*," she replied with a similar tone. She would not be corrected or deterred.

The laird and Inan eyed them both curiously at the exchange. Not surprising. She had yet to find a group of males who were used to a woman who spoke her mind. No matter. She'd not have these MacNeills play a game of cat and mouse with her future, the risk of being found out hanging over her head like some sword of Damocles. Kallum had brought her here without consulting her. He'd not control her actions from this point forward.

"I will not have this matter hanging over my head," she said to Kallum. "'Tis best they know the full truth up front."

Kallum stepped toward her. "I told you I would handle this."

Her hand lifted and motioned him to stay put. "Aye, but I did not tell you I would defer to your way of handling it."

His jaw clenched, but Kallum did as she bade.

When she turned to the laird, both his brows perched high in his forehead. She took a furtive glance at Inan to notice a similar expression upon his face.

Great. Now what have I done? She took a deep breath. Kallum's kin thought her a difficult lass already, and they had not yet received her most disturbing news.

She girded herself but blurted out her sure-to-be-unwelcomed revelation. "I am Ailsa Connery. I am told my kin and clan are allies of your onetime enemies the MacGregors." She stood silently, arms at her side, and watched the laird's face closely to glean what she could of his thoughts, but his mien remained unreadable.

"She's a *Connery*." Inan near threw himself across the room to get to Kallum. The look on his face showed a hideous scorn even worse than that of Kallum's when he'd realized her clan name. "You knew she was a Connery as well as an escaped captive of the king, and you still brought her here amongst your kin?"

"I had little choice in the matter." Kallum rubbed a hand down his face, then dropped his head when his hand brushed back up and over his hair. His large fingers stopped at the leather cord securing his locs and removed the tie as if freeing the binding would also loose the words he seemed unable to find. He slid the cord onto his wrist and returned his gaze to her. "Once she defied my attempts to leave her behind or escort her to the English border, I could not very well leave her to fend for herself in the woods."

"Though you wanted to," Ailsa interjected.

"I never said that."

"'Tis not what you said that gave it away."

Kallum scowled at her. With his locs loose and flowing about his face and shoulders, the scowl did little to intimidate her. Like the first time she'd seen him let his hair down, the shock of his handsomeness haloed by twisted strands that called sensuously for the tease of her fingers made her want to melt, preferably right into his arms. 'Twas unfathomable how a man with so much brood also held a virile beauty that could tempt even the most pious of lasses.

Ailsa shook herself mentally. Here she stood in the lair of the enemy, yet she allowed her randy body to usurp her sense. She had to keep her wits about her. This attraction to the MacNeill could not be allowed to divert her from persuading the laird to give her temporary sanctuary.

She returned her attention to the laird, hopeful that her moment of amorous distraction had not been evident. "To be fair, sire, Kallum did not learn of my clan name until yester morn. I refused to reveal it to him. All truth, if he had not discovered it by accident on his own, he would not know it even now."

The laird did not move from his spot in front of her. His head had tilted a little at her name revelation, and, even now, he surveyed her with quiet contemplation, but he spoke not.

"'Tis proof she's as scheming as her kin." With a condemning shake of his head, Inan glowered at Kallum. "Bad enough you burdened me with your female trophies from the tournament, one of whom follows me around as if her mere presence underfoot will tempt me to keep her permanently, and the other who—" He clamped his mouth shut to stifle whatever else he had started to say.

Kallum smirked at him. "The other who what?"

"Never mind." Inan's eyes shuttered afore he continued. "Suffice it to say, you've stirred up enough commotion without adding *this*" — he motioned toward Ailsa — "to the pot."

This? Ailsa bristled at the slight. Now she was a "this," someone — nay, *something* — deserving of less than human consideration.

Inan's eyes sought his father's. "*Da*, she cannot be allowed to stay here. We — "

"Why can she not?" Kallum interrupted, his previous scowl unaltered.

"You know as well as I that we will soon have the whole of the king's army down upon us. Or, worse, her serpent kin sneaking in amongst us to reclaim their harpy."

"Watch yourself, Inan." Kallum's voice dropped low and held that edge of steel Ailsa recognized from afore he had sent two border reivers to their deaths and severely wounded a third.

His cousin simply stared at him, having recognized the challenge in his voice.

"I warned you once," Kallum said to him.

"Aye." Inan stepped to Kallum until they were nose to nose. "And what aim you to do about the matter?"

"*Enough!*" Ailsa said to the feuding cousins, who postured like two stallions fighting for dominance over a herd.

Inan's head snapped her direction. His mouth hung open.

Ailsa emptied her lungs with a slow, drawn-out frustration and fingered the thick, scraggly braid that hung over her shoulder and down the front of her chest. She was clearly making an impression, but she thought 'twas not one that worked in her favor. Nonetheless, she would not have the cousins feuding over her. As much as she wanted the protection of the laird and his help to return home, she could not have Kallum at odds with his kin over the likes of her—an enemy of his clan and an annoyance he'd wanted to rid himself of from the start.

She addressed the man truly in charge of her destiny. "I need not stay long, Laird MacNeill. I need only hospitality for the night and an escort to the border of my clan's lands on the morrow. I can make my way home from there."

"Nay." The firm refusal came from Kallum.

She shot him a look to be quiet.

"Do not give me that look. You know as well as I that you may not be safe even amongst your own kin."

"And why is that?" Inan asked with an insouciant smirk. "Why would a snake not be safe amongst snakes?"

Her hand fisted at her side. For the second time since she'd started this trek to freedom, she wished she were a man so she could put another in his place.

She saw Kallum's gaze track her hand movement and relaxed her fingers afore either of the others noticed.

"'Tis of no import," she said, directing the answer to no one in particular.

"'Tis of great import," Kallum countered, then addressed the other men. "I have doubts that her abandonment at the castle was an accident."

Inan looked from one man to the other. "How is that our issue to remedy?"

"You'd have her—"

The laird put up his hand, cutting off Kallum. He looked to Ailsa. "How came you to be in Clan Connery?"

"I was born there. My grandparents were stolen by sea raiders of the Hebrides from the bowels of a Portuguese slaver. Though they did not know each other prior to capture, my grandparents were from the same tribe and spoke the same language. Unlike many captives, this gave them someone to cling to during the arduous journey, and they stuck together.

"After the pirates docked in Scotland, my grandfather proved himself to be an expert horseman when the Connery laird, who was at port at that time, had his prized destrier spooked and nearly injured by a wall of cargo crates that toppled while being transferred. My grandfather captured and settled the stallion, which was known to have a difficult and unruly nature. The laird was so impressed, he purchased my grandfather on the spot.

"My grandfather, who was in love with my grandmother by then, convinced the laird to purchase my grandmother as well. They were introduced to the stable owner responsible for providing horses to the laird's army, and my grandfather was allowed to work there and buy his and my grandmother's freedom over time. After the stable owner died, my grandfather took over the stables and became the laird's marshal of horses."

Inan gave her a skeptical look, not wanting to believe a duplicitous Connery. "So you and your parents were born in the Highlands?"

"My mother was, aye."

"And your father, lass?" asked the laird.

"I never knew my father, but aye, he was a Scot and a Connery."

"How know we this story to be true?" Inan asked.

"I care not whether you think my story true." Her temper roused, Ailsa switched without conscious thought to her native Gaelic. "You do not want me here, and I wish not to be here. Help me get to the borders of Connery land, and we will both get what we want and never have to see each other again." She nearly snapped the last few words.

"She speaks Gaelic?" The awe in Inan's voice was almost as irritating as the fact that he'd addressed his comment to Kallum instead of her.

Kallum simply looked at the man as if he'd sprouted two heads, since the answer to the question was obvious.

Ailsa wouldn't bother to tell the monger that in addition to Gaelic and English, she also spoke Yoruba and passable French. Her nerves were frayed. She was hungry. And tired. She'd escaped bondage, been nearly abandoned and forced to go to another country, dealt with a surly MacNeill for days, staved off an assault by border reivers, and insulted repeatedly from the moment she'd arrived on MacNeill lands. She'd had enough of these people.

Sensing her near disintegration, Kallum stepped next to her. "The lass is tired. We rode for more than a day without rest, and we have yet to break our fast. I will settle her in a room and return to discuss this matter in more detail."

"A room? Here?" Ailsa gave Inan an apprehensive glance.

The look he gave her in return suggested he was likely to slit her throat while she slept. The last thing she wanted was to stay under the same roof as him.

"'Tis not necessary to house me here, Kallum. I am

content to find a place in the village."

"You'll not stay in the village. You'll stay where I can keep a close eye on you."

"Not here." Inan walked over to the fireplace and leaned his shoulder against the mantel, arms and ankles crossed. "The village sounds like a really good option."

"'Tis not up to you," Kallum snapped. "Remember? You are not yet laird of this clan because you are too much of a *cladhaire* to face your responsibilities."

Kallum looked to the laird for an answer, ignoring the furious pout of his cousin to whom he'd just referred, in essence, as a spineless sluggard. A story lurked behind that insult, and Ailsa wondered about the history between the two. Though they fought, beneath the dispute, she sensed a deep sense of love and loyalty. She'd seen brothers fight with less acrimony and descend into an undeniable hatred.

Again, the need to not be a source of discord between these two rose fiercely within her. Unlike her, Kallum had a place and family that accepted and loved him. She'd not be the reason he became an outsider adrift from his clan and forced to be a loner.

"Lass, why do you not wish to stay here?"

At the laird's query, Ailsa realized he had been watching her closely this whole time. "I…um…simply wish not to impose, sire."

He gave her a look of skepticism. "Now, lass, you have not been shy about speaking your mind this whole time. Speak freely."

She glanced furtively at Inan afore she responded. "I prefer not to be housed in quarters where I am likely to be slaughtered in my sleep. I would rather bed with your sheep in the pasture."

Kallum's head shook with disbelief beside her, but the laird's lips quirked at the edges.

"I am beginning to understand," the laird said.

Ailsa's grip returned to her braid. "Understand what, your lairdship?"

"Why you are truly here, of course." He gave Kallum a speculative look afore he addressed him directly. "Kallum, 'twould seem the lass is not comfortable with hospitality that would place her in close proximity to your cousin. I leave you to work out the details with her, and I will ponder how to deal with the larger issues surrounding the king and the Connerys. We will speak again at supper."

The laird went to sit behind his desk and effectively ignored the trio.

Kallum snapped at Inan, "Fine. I will put her in the cottage."

The incredulity on his cousin's face was almost comical. "Your mother's cottage?"

"Aye." Kallum took Ailsa by the arm and guided her out the door.

Ailsa wondered about the significance of this cottage he planned to take her to and why Inan was so shocked she'd be allowed to use the abode. She had a feeling she'd been handed into the middle of another source of family discord, but she was too tired to ferret out the nature of such affairs.

Kallum was silent the entire time he led her to the cottage. When they arrived, he left the door open to avoid the perception of impropriety and set her satchel, which they had retrieved from the horses, on a dusty chair. Then, he pulled a dusty cover off the bed and replaced it with a fresh blanket from a stack of folded bed linens in a trunk at the foot of the bed. The cottage had obviously not been used in a while.

"I apologize for the stuffiness." He swung the door wider to let in more fresh air. "The cottage has not been inhabited in a bit, but I assure you all is fine beneath the layer of dust. I will have someone bring you something to eat." He glanced at the cold fireplace, then back at her. "Do you need me to build you a fire afore I leave and mayhap haul you some water to make tea?"

His face contained his normal stoicism, but his eyes looked troubled. The fight with his kin had bothered him.

She shook her head. "Nay, MacNeill. I am fine." Placing her hand on his forearm, she added, "I am sorry to cause a rift between you and your cousin. 'Twould have been better if you had taken me to the isles as I asked."

He glanced into her eyes, and the turmoil beneath the sable orbs changed from a lurking sadness to a piercing awareness hot enough to burn. "Nay, 'twould not have been better." He rubbed the back of his first finger down the side of her cheek. "For either of us."

She leaned momentarily into his touch, wanting to raise her hand to finger his locs much as she'd done his beard. She reined in the urge and pulled back.

His eyes crinkled at the edges as if he were privy to and humored by the tactile longing in her most private thoughts.

Dropping his hand, he took two steps toward the door, then stopped. "Inan will come around. He is a fair man. Once he gets past the initial shock, he will recognize our need to offer you protection."

Without further words, Kallum departed. Ailsa wasn't so sure his confidence in his cousin was well placed. 'Twas a confidence she did not have. Her instincts were telling her MacNeill land was not the place to tarry for any time. She needed to leave this place as soon as possible, mayhap even afore sunset.

She slid the wooden beam in place across the door and wondered if she could figure out on her own how to get home from here.

CHAPTER EIGHTEEN

Kallum heard Ailsa slide the wooden beam into place to secure the door. The lass was cautious about her safety, and he blamed her not after that fiasco with Inan. He could throttle the blackguard. To worsen the pot, he'd seen the looks on Laird MacNeill's and Inan's faces when Ailsa had motioned him "stop" in the library and he had stopped.

He'd thought nothing of it at the time. The lass could be contrary. He had simply not wanted an all-out war in front of the laird.

In hindsight, Kallum had never allowed a woman such influence over his behavior. And now, he'd placed her in his mother's cottage. The place was his sanctuary, reserved for those occasional moments when a reminder of being different drove him to solitude to prevent him from committing mass mayhem. His room at the manor was not sufficient isolation at such times.

Glancing over his shoulder, he stared at the closed cottage door. He waited for second thoughts to hit or a moment of regret that he had left Ailsa amongst his mother's things. 'Twas a place no woman save Caitrin had ever been allowed to enter after his mother's death. Despite the wait, no such feelings arose. And that was possibly the greatest tell of all.

He was falling for the lass.

Kallum shook his head at himself. The feel of his locs moving back and forth made him think about Ailsa's expression when he'd let down his hair in the library. The look of longing and desire had been unmistakable. Even just a moment ago, in the cottage, she'd given him that look again. He'd left in a hurry because what the look inspired him to do with her would not be proper.

The thought caused a twitch between his legs. That he'd been in an almost constant state of arousal or semi-arousal since she'd threatened his identity in the cove made him want to curse. He owed her the respect of not making her the leman Inan accused her of being. She was not the kind of lass you stole favors from without honorable intentions, and what he had in mind was not the least bit honorable.

He strode briskly away from the cottage. She and he alone in a space with a bed was not a good idea. Despite her obvious fatigue, she'd been lit with desire. He'd seen that look in a woman's eyes enough to recognize the thoughts that lurked beneath the surface. To see it in Ailsa's eyes was a temptation down a dark path he was not sure he could return from.

Instead, he headed for the stream he and Inan frequently used for bathing. He'd had naught but minimal opportunities to wash as best he could while traveling from Stirling. 'Twould feel good to completely submerge himself in the stream. Plus, the water should still have a bit of chill at this time of morn, which would help take the edge off the budding *stauner* in his trews. If not, he might have to result to a good chugging.

• • •

Ailsa heard a firm knock at the door. The knock was not strong enough to be Kallum, so she supposed it might be someone with her food.

She opened the door to find Caitrin on the other side. The memory of Kallum's reaction to the lass in the courtyard caused a tweak of envy in Ailsa's chest. 'Twas irrational. Caitrin was Inan's sister, so Kallum would think of her as a cousin. Though, a little voice in Ailsa's head taunted a reminder that the kinship was not one by blood. She beat back the voice with a reminder of her own: she'd be leaving soon, and whom the MacNeill had affections for was none of her concern.

"May I enter?" Caitrin asked after being kept waiting at the door. The lass glanced at Ailsa's face, but to her credit, she commented not on the residual bruising and suppressed any reaction that could show on her face.

"*Ach gu dearbh.*" Ailsa stepped aside, letting the lass know that she was of course welcome.

Ailsa felt like a dunderhead for simply gawking at the lass instead of letting her in immediately. Caitrin held a basket in her hand, which she took over to the table that Ailsa had cleaned during her wait. Ailsa might not be staying on MacNeill lands for long, but she knew she'd need to eat and at least gather her strength afore she set out on the final leg of her journey home.

Seeing no need to hole up in dust and dank, she'd cleaned. The cleaning had allowed her time to think. What she needed was a better understanding of where she was. She could tell east from west with the rising and setting of the sun, but she knew not for certain where the MacNeill lands sat in relation to Clan Connery's.

If she could get a glimpse of the surroundings from the hills behind the keep, she might be able to make out landmarks that would aid in her navigation.

Caitrin smiled at her and interrupted her thoughts by opening the cloth covering the basket and allowing the scent of freshly baked bread to fill the room. "Kallum ask me to have someone bring you something to break your fast. Since we had already eaten at the manor, I was afraid they'd not bring you the prime foodstuffs. So, I packed the basket myself."

The purity and lack of guile in the girl's smile made Ailsa feel guilty for her earlier wayward thoughts. Whatever the lass's relationship with Kallum, she had done nothing to Ailsa to deserve anything but a kind and proper greeting.

"Thank you. Would you care to join me?" Ailsa asked.

"Nay. I've eaten my fill and shall easily be stuffed till the noon meal. But I shall sit with you while you dine if 'tis all right?"

Ailsa did not want to sit; what she really wanted was a walk around the grounds. Who better to help her with that than Caitrin?

She slipped an apple into her pocket, then grabbed a chunk of bread and a wedge of cheese. "You know what I'd rather do, Caitrin?"

The lass shook her head.

"I'd rather take a walk. Would you mind showing me around? We could mayhap go up to the hills behind the keep so I can get a clear view of the lands."

Caitrin clapped her hands together at the suggestion. "Aye, a fabulous idea. I'll show you my favorite place to watch clan comings and goings. From this spot, you can see almost the entirety of MacNeill lands, and we will be able to see the soldiers practice their battle maneuvers." She grinned mischievously and linked her arm with Ailsa's. "Kallum will be there."

The obviously intentional additional information made Ailsa give Caitrin an inquiring scrutiny.

"Oh, come on. Kallum has never brought a woman home to the manor, and I see the way he looks at you. Moreover, I see the way you look at him when you think he's not looking."

Ailsa's denial headshake commenced with such alacrity and force her shoulder bumped into Caitrin's. "I think you have a vivid imagination. I look at him no different than any other member of your clan."

"Including my brother?"

Whatever expression Ailsa made to that question made Caitrin laugh.

"I thought not." Caitrin opened the door. "I heard about your audience with my father. Ignore my brother. He can be such a wanker at times."

The way Caitrin rolled her eyes and made much drama out of the put-down of her brother made Ailsa smile. The lass was completely irreverent, which was something they seemed to have in common.

Her smile quickly faltered when she thought about how much the lass might know of her audience before the laird. "Know you all we discussed?"

Caitrin's expression sobered as well. "About your clan?"

Ailsa nodded.

"Aye."

The feeling of unease that crept up Ailsa's spine must have showed on her face, because Caitrin was quick to reassure her.

"Worry not." She squeezed Ailsa's arm closer to her. "'Tis no matter to me to what clan you are kin. I fathom not why the menfolk hold such grudges for years and years. 'Tis not as if you were personally responsible for what happened. Yet..."

"Yet what?"

The lass looked uncomfortable.

"Tell me true, Caitrin. If you have a problem with showing me around, I could ask another."

"Oh, nay. 'Tis not that." She glanced into Ailsa's eyes with a look that was almost ashamed. "'Tis just... well, many of my clan may not understand. I ask you to be careful who you ask for assistance. I know my father, Inan, and Kallum do not plan to tell anyone else who you are, but matters such as these are oft hard to keep a secret."

'Twas sound advice. Ailsa had already sensed her welcome here would be limited. "Then glad I am to have your kindness. And dare I say your friendship?"

"Oh, aye!" Caitrin smiled again. "So as your *friend*, tell me true about you and Kallum. I know something happened between you two on the journey."

"*What!*" Ailsa could not suppress the horror that came over her. She jerked her arm from Caitrin's.

The lass turned bright red. "I did not mean *that*. Holy Mother Mary! I'd not be so crass as to suggest you... I mean..." The red of her face deepened, but she could not say aloud the words she thought. "Well, you know."

Ailsa studied her closely. The lass was truly chagrined for the impression she'd given. She was several years younger than Ailsa, and Ailsa suspected she had been sheltered all her life by the overbearing men Ailsa had dealt with this morn. She decided the slip had been inadvertent.

She needed an ally in Clan MacNeill. She could ill afford to throw away friendship offered due to a misunderstanding over something so trivial. Ailsa had never been one to make quick mates, or mates of any kind, truth be told. That this lass offered easy comradery, seemingly without ulterior scheme, motivated Ailsa to overlook the awkward moment and attempt to make a friend in this land of the enemy.

She slid her arm back into Caitrin's. "I forgive your slip of the tongue. 'Tis of no import. Let's take that walk now."

"Okay. And as for your feelings for Kallum…" Caitrin's eyebrows rose, and she dropped her voice to a conspiratorial whisper. "Your secret's safe with me."

The blush rose despite Ailsa's best efforts not to react to Caitrin's light teasing. Ailsa had never been able to control the wayward emotional display.

"Aha! I knew it." Caitrin began to giggle as she led her out of the cottage. "It's okay; almost every woman in the clan is in love with that one. It can't be helped."

Caitrin's laughter was infectious.

"*Every* woman?" Ailsa asked, beginning to chuckle herself.

"Well, not me, of course. At least not that way. Or at least not since I was a young lass and I asked him to marry me when I was but five summers."

Ailsa jerked her gaze to Caitrin's face. "You did not."

"Aye." The lass gave a self-deprecating shrug. "That's when mother explained that he was like my brother, and brothers and sisters did not marry. Kallum simply smiled and assured me when I grew into a woman, I'd find another I'd like better for a husband than him anyway."

"What did you think of that?"

"I didn't believe him then, and I still don't. Truly, what man can compare?" She looked at Ailsa for confirmation.

Ailsa intentionally gave no reaction. She'd not fall into that trap of self-betrayal. Caitrin had already intuited too much.

At Ailsa's nonresponse, Caitrin grinned and continued her tale. "Since he also said he'd never marry, I always thought 'twas no matter, because I would always be his favorite lass in the whole world."

"Oh…" Ailsa tensed at the revelation. Given Caitrin's supposition about Ailsa and Kallum, that should make Ailsa decidedly not one of Caitrin's favorite people.

The lass bumped shoulders with her. "Stop that. I was *little*. I'm older and wiser now. Still, no man compares to Kallum, but I think of him as my other annoying brother. With Inan, Kallum, and Thane — who's away apprenticing with the MacLachlans — a lone girl can get completely stifled by the overwhelming *man-li-ness* of brothers."

Caitrin rolled her eyes again. An act Ailsa was beginning to understand was a frequent habit.

"Kallum can be an overbearing, heavy-handed brute at times. But that doesn't stop me from loving him. Besides" — the lass grinned wider — "I know how to turn him into a softy."

Both Ailsa's brows rose with that claim. *Kallum a*

softy? Hmm.

She didn't see it, but she ignored the incongruous description of Kallum to pursue the answer to a question she'd had since she first heard a MacNeill refer to him as cousin. "How came he to be a member of your family?"

"Well." Caitrin released Ailsa's arm to keep her balance as they trudged up a hill. "That happened afore I was born, but what I know is his mother used to serve as lady's maid to my aunt. She was originally found by my uncle and a hunting party. She had been badly beaten. Apparently, they thought she would die but still carried her back to be attended by our healer. She recovered, and they soon discovered she was with child."

"Kallum did not know his father? But he carries a dagger he says belonged to his *da*."

Caitrin nodded. "His mother had a few belongings on her person. The dagger was found beneath her. She gave it to Kallum. I'm told she knew who his father was but never revealed his name to anyone or even where she came from—if 'twas from a Highland clan or the Lowlands or she had escaped the household of some peer. Many assumed she was too ashamed to admit the truth. That his father had been part of her attack, which was why she was found lying on his dagger."

They topped the hill adjacent to the sheep pasture, and Caitrin took a seat beneath the shade of a tree. "But I once overheard my aunt say Kallum came too soon for his seed to have been planted during the attack. She believed his mother knew she was pregnant all along and had fought so hard to live so that her child would survive.

"She died of fever when I was little, and my aunt

and uncle chose to raise Kallum as their own. What I remember most about her was how beautiful her voice was. Neither English nor Gaelic was her birth language. She spoke with an accent that seemed almost musical to me. When she would tell me stories, 'twas like slipping into a magical world."

The voice was the same standout memory Kallum had of his mother, a woman who had brought him into the world likely as a bastard like Ailsa herself.

Stirred by the beauty that laid in front of her, Ailsa abandoned the talk of Kallum to gawk at the hillside view. MacNeill lands were indeed gorgeous. She turned slowly to survey the full vista. Her gaze followed the pasture past the waterfall in the distance she had noticed upon their arrival. Where the stream curved out of eyesight, a grouping of trees grew thickly. The tributary that led to the sea, and thus the Inner Hebrides, most likely wound that way.

She took note of the information, then sat beside Caitrin. Her gaze fell on the courtyard below. Over a hundred men in various stages of undress sparred, wrestled, and fought with a wide range of weapons. Amongst the throng, Ailsa noted roughly a dozen or so Black soldiers. Even so, her focused fell on Kallum almost immediately, her eyes drawn to him as if he were the only man on the field.

He exercised bare-chested, wearing nothing but his kilt and boots. He had apparently ditched the wearing of trews upon his homecoming as well as the wrapping she had placed around his wound. The cut could not yet have fully healed. 'Twould serve the hardheaded lout right if it festered. She shook her head at the macho stubbornness but had to admit she liked the wardrobe change. It gave a lass something fine to look upon on a day when she felt naught but isolated and homesick.

The dusting of dark hair covering the center of Kallum's chest and the line it made downward drew Ailsa's attention. When he did a roundabout, the movement of his kilt gave her a thrilling peek at the muscled thighs she remembered well from their first encounter. What was it about a glimpse of a man's knees beneath the hem of his kilt that did crazy things to a Highland lass?

She smiled to herself at the thought, continuing to watch Kallum. He sparred with a much younger soldier. Kallum held a one-handed broadsword in one hand and a parrying dagger in the other. The parrying dagger rested primarily at his side while he brandished the sword with agile ease. He clearly toyed with the youngster, but the activity beneath the high sun still drew a mild sheen of sweat for his exertion. The magnificence of his bare torso covered in manly dampness set Ailsa's heart pounding and stirred a tingle deep in her woman's center.

Ugh! How she hated her uncontrollable reactions to the man. His physical beauty made her want to touch and taste, and the memory of his lips against hers inspired thoughts of what 'twould feel like to have those lips roam other places on her body. The racy speculation prompted a soft gasp to escape her lips, and the man of her lust turned his head and looked right at her.

The act caused an eerie sensation to wash over her. No way he'd heard that almost non-sound. 'Twas as if he'd sensed her thoughts, and an unearthly tug had compelled him to look up. Her mother would say such had not been happenstance.

Her mother had been a romantic. The woman believed in fated souls and love that transcended human will and intention. In invisible threads that wove around destined lovers and pulled them unerringly and consistently toward each other regardless of where they went...or how hard they fought.

Ailsa shivered. She herself had never believed the tales of souls fated to be drawn together by spiritual forces. Though, the more she was around Kallum MacNeill, the more she was starting to believe.

"Uh-oh," Caitrin said beside her. "You've been spotted."

With difficulty, Ailsa pulled her head from its speculative fog and looked at Caitrin. "What?"

Caitrin nodded toward the practicing army below. "You've been spotted. Kallum comes this way."

Ailsa gripped the girl's hand. "Don't leave me," she said softly without looking at the approaching MacNeill.

Caitrin frowned. "You're afraid he would do you harm?" Her tone made clear she was offended on her cousin's behalf.

"Nay, 'tis not harm of which I am concerned. You cannot leave me alone with him."

Young eyes searched her face. It took a moment afore comprehension dawned. "Oh." Caitrin's eyes widened. "Oh! I *seeeee*."

Her singsong tone and mischievous grin made Ailsa want to choke her.

"I think I'll be going now." She pulled her hand from Ailsa's grip and rose.

"I thought you were my friend."

Caitrin leaned in and whispered, "I am your

friend. You can offer me thanks later." The lass glanced up as Kallum topped the rise. "Hi, Kallum! Bye, Kallum," Caitrin crooned as she fled down the hill.

"*Traitor!*" Ailsa yelled, rising to her feet.

The only response was the sound of Caitrin's fading giggles.

Kallum looked between Ailsa and Caitrin, confusion on his face. He had no clue what had just transpired, and Ailsa had no intention of clearing up that confusion.

When he spoke, he asked not for clarification. Instead, he said, "Lass, I would speak with you."

He had put a fresh tunic on.

Thank Olorun, she thought, though the memory of how he'd looked without it lingered fresh in her mind. She swallowed. "Speak about what?"

"This foolish resolve of yours to return to Clan Connery."

The fire of her arousal doused and sparked into instant anger. How dare he continue to try and direct her future? She was not his to command.

"'Tis not foolish, MacNeill. 'Tis my home. What would you have me do? Stay here amongst enemies who wish me dead?"

"No one wishes you dead, lass." He scrubbed a hand across his mouth.

At least he had not bothered to deny she was amongst enemies.

"Nay? Not even Inan?" She placed her hands on her hips and silently dared him to deny it. "Have you spoken with your cousin since this morn?"

"Inan is not the issue. He knows better than to

mess with—" He cut himself off and clamped his lips closed.

"Than to mess with what?"

His eyes sheltered. After a brief pause, he responded, "You."

Somehow, Ailsa did not think that was what he'd been about to say. No matter. Caitrin had admitted there were those in the clan of whom Ailsa should be wary. She'd keep Inan on that list.

"If 'tis enemies with which you are concerned, I'd think you'd not want to go back to a clan that treated you like so much rubbish they had no qualms about abandoning you to a life of enslavement. Connerys are cowards and lowlifes."

"*I* am a Connery."

"Not anymore. Now, you are a fugitive from enslavement."

"How say you thus? You cannot strip me of my birthright."

"The birthright of a bastard among dishonorables? Surely you jest." He stormed a few steps away from her, his irritation starting to peak with hers.

Inevitably, 'twas always thus with them. They seemed to bring out the worst in each other. Understanding the flare of emotions that roused whenever they were together for any significant amount of time, Ailsa ignored the comment about her being a bastard. She had admitted as much to him days ago. She understood he tossed the moniker at her as persuasion, not insult.

But her clan dishonorable?

How could he not understand that every jab at her kin was a jab at her?

She glanced at the dirk sheathed on his belt. His father's dagger.

The dagger she'd thrown at his head.

The dagger she was about to grab and shove deep into his despicable gut.

CHAPTER NINETEEN

Kallum watched Ailsa's hand fist. He'd noticed her do the same thing several times, the first time on the night he'd abducted her. He'd angered her then like he angered her now. He had no doubt that were she a man, she would have already taken a swing at him. Why that amused him, he could not say. But it did.

When she glanced at the dirk on his belt, he moved farther away from her and leaned against a tree. She was unlikely to be able to wrest the dirk from him, but he'd been subject to enough of her maneuvers not to chance it.

He nodded in the direction of her tightened fist. "Are you planning to do something with that? Or just stand there in a threatening stance?"

Ailsa simply glared at him.

He ran a hand over his hair, front to back, and grabbed at the leather hair tie that kept his locs bound at the base of his neck but did not remove it. He'd not be able to maintain this conversation if Ailsa looked at him the way she had the last time he'd let his hair down.

"Lass, I do not understand how you can ignore how you came to be at the castle from which I freed you."

"I did not need you to free me."

"Need I remind you?" He pointed. "The face?"

She recoiled with an embarrassed flush.

A small part of him felt bad for using her misfortune against her, but if she would not listen to reason, mayhap she would listen to her own experience.

The colors of her injuries were changing. Even the darkest of the purplish-black markings had softened to a brownish-yellow. Other spots were pale remnants of their original discoloring. He moved to reach for her chin to get a closer look, but she slapped his hand away.

He sighed. He hated to be the bearer of bad news, but this woman must face the truth. "That was what your kinfolk left you to. Yet, you make haste to return to a clan that allowed you to be enslaved with no second thought?

"In three years, Ailsa; think on it. In three years…" He paused and flicked up a finger to emphasize this to be his first point. "Not one member of your clan came to the castle to look for you? Or for any reason?"

He stepped closer to her, and she moved backward with his every step until she'd unknowingly backed herself against a different tree.

He could feel his hackles rise. Though he was not angry with her, he was indeed angry. What type of leader took his people with him to an audience at court, then did not bother to verify all members of his clan returned with him? Dead or alive.

"Not once did a Connery have business at court?" He flicked up another finger and continued to do so with each point he made. "Not once did your laird get called back before the king to be indoctrinated into the king's rhetoric exhorting the inferiority of the Gaelic language or the barbary of the Highland people? Not once. Not. One. Single *time*"—he inhaled a deep breath to rein in the growing loudness of his voice—"did a Connery soldier, laird, villager, or *sewing woman*, for Christendom's sake, visit Stirling and ask after a kinswoman who had disappeared on a prior trip to the city? That makes no sense."

That a contingent of soldiers had left this woman behind and no one had thought to look for her in over three years was beyond appalling. It spoke of ineptitude, negligence, and a telling statement of how the Connerys felt about people of Ailsa's and his lineage.

"If you had mattered to your kinsmen, they would not have left until they found you or were, in the least, shown your dead body to know that you were unable to return."

"How do we know they did not? Until I return and seek my own answers, I will never know for certain."

"I think you can know. Those soldiers you rushed to meet on the night of our escape. Were they all newly added to the force? Surely at least one of them remembered you. The captain? Were he not the same man? Another of lesser rank? A lieutenant or even one foot soldier. Which one searched you out upon recognizing you at Stirling?"

Her mouth opened then closed without response. The expressive, multicolored hazel of her eyes revealed that she had pondered the question, but her silence gave away her failure to come up with a countering reply.

He placed a hand against the tree above her head. "These men were supposed to be the best warriors of your clan. Why else would they have been selected to accompany your new laird to court? After the recent loss of a leader, no army commander worth the air he breathed would have risked the newest chief by selecting slack-offs and novices. There is no thought but that several of the men at the tournament this past sennight would have been a part of your laird's protection when he traveled to the castle with you in the entourage."

His chest heaved. He looked into those beautiful eyes caught between anger and the budding dampness of tears born of inescapable knowledge, plus something a lot more dangerous to his emotions. Something that pulled at him like nothing he had ever felt.

"How is it that not a single man remembered a lass as bonnie as you?" His voice lowered and deepened. "Not possible."

"As bonnie as I used to be, you mean," she whispered sarcastically.

"Nay. I say what I mean." He leaned in an involuntary inch. "You are beyond beautiful, Ailsa. The fading marks of a man's hurtful hands can do nothing to counter that. And no man who lies with women would soon forget your goddess face."

He looked down and allowed his gaze to roam leisurely over her from head to toe. "Nor any other part of you."

He understood what it was like to be outnumbered amongst people with some members who valued him less than those who looked like them. While it had not been such with the whole of the MacNeills, his presence on occasion made others uncomfortable for no other reason than his hue. He'd not let her near the Connerys again until he deduced why someone had been uncomfortable enough with Ailsa to want her gone.

Though her eyes blazed cinders intended to burn him whole, the lure of her lips tempted enough for Kallum to put his life—and mayhap again his cods—at risk by leaning in for a kiss. His folly at allowing the blood rushing to his loins to make his brain forget with whom he dealt showed itself when she pulled his dirk from his belt.

"How dare you insult me as no more than dishonorable, lowlife spawn, then try to kiss me." She raised her hand with an overhand grip on the dagger hilt.

He caught her wrist easily. "You're doing that wrong, *leannan*. You're too small to come at a taller man with an overhand jab. That's why the border reiver disarmed you so easily. If you're intent on causing harm"—he adjusted her hold—"use an underhanded grip and shove the dagger into the gut."

He pulled the tip of the dagger to his abdomen. "You're a healer. You know the areas on a man to cause utmost damage. For good measure, thrust all the way in, to the hilt, and twist. Mayhap even add a slice across the innards."

Pushing in closer so her back went flush against the tree, he pressed against the point of the blade until it pierced the fabric of his tunic. "You've pulled a dagger on me twice now. Shot at me with a bow. If you really want to maim me, lass, here's your chance." He squeezed her hand around the dagger and pulled it into him. "Go ahead," he taunted in a low, seductive voice. "Shove."

Ailsa's chest heaved up and down with labored breaths. She had that look in her eyes again that rested between anger and frustrated wetness, but she no longer looked as if she aimed to injure him.

"You don't want to hurt me, lass."

"Aye, I do." Her tone was adamant, but her voice wavered with her efforts to hold back the incensed tears that threatened to spill.

He shook his head. "Nay. 'Tis time we faced the truth."

Her brow creased. "What truth?"

"All this animosity between us is not about how much we dislike each other." His gaze dropped to her full, luscious lips that still tempted despite the dirk resting against him in a most dangerous spot. "'Tis about something else entirely."

Hazel eyes searched his warily. "What, exactly?"

"How much we want each other."

Her head motioned in denial.

"Aye, lass. And I can prove it." He dropped his mouth to hers without preamble, relinquished the hand around the dagger pressed against him, and left himself vulnerable to her stab.

If he was wrong about her intent, he cared not. Another taste of her lips offered a blissful slip into Nirvana. He'd accept whatever harmful consequence his daring yielded.

He placed his hands on either side of her face, cradled her cheeks in his palms, and slid his tongue between her lips. She did not immediately engage in the kiss, but she did not pull away. Taking that as reassurance he'd been right, that her passions flared as high as his, he moved a hand to the base of her skull and tilted her head for better access to a mouth he'd wanted to plunder again since her tease of his beard had led him to his first taste.

She groaned softly, and soon her tongue brushed tentatively against his in response to his insistent exploration of her mouth. Like the first time he'd tasted her, his control snapped, and he went from merely kissing to claiming her whole.

The sound of her own pleasured moan broke her spell. She yanked away from the kiss and blinked up at him. Slowly, her focus dropped to the blade in her hand, a blade he no longer gripped at all.

Her face flushed, and she refused to look back at him. "Damn you, Kallum MacNeill," she said, her voice low and tight, afore she stormed off toward the pasture in a huff.

He considered going after her, but then thought better of it. She was madder than a hissing wildcat, and he cared not to tangle with that further this day, especially since she'd made off with his dirk yet again.

He would seek her out later. She was his, and he'd almost slipped and said thus aloud to her when she'd asked about Inan's murderous intent.

Inan knew better than to mess with what was his. That the lout made Ailsa feel unsafe on lands Kallum intended to be her new home was unacceptable. He took off in the opposite direction of Ailsa. 'Twas time Kallum dealt with that bawbag cousin of his.

• • •

Ailsa sat on the hill with the view of MacNeill sheep on one side and a view of MacNeill soldiers in the midst of training on the other. It had been six days since Kallum had kissed her only a few meters from this spot. The memory of the easy way he had turned her into a malleable ball of need with a simple kiss annoyed her. Still.

And made her yearn for him.

Every centimeter of her skin seemed to throb with longing for his touch, and 'twas driving her daft. She must leave this place soon or succumb to his subtle but seemingly inevitable seduction, and the longer she stayed, the more she wanted to succumb.

Though she had seen him every day, she'd avoided being alone with him under any circumstance. Luckily, he had not sought her out at his mother's cottage. She could no longer fathom being alone with him. He'd said their volatility was more about desire than animosity. She was beginning to think him right.

The memory of her cowardice at the mini cave on the journey here kept taunting her. Had she acted then, at least she would have been in control of her passion and no one would have been the wiser. Now that she had waited, she felt like he had all the power and had put down a challenge she couldn't allow herself to lose.

Moreover, how likely was it that no one in this clan would suspect her bodily surrender?

What peculiar notions these. To deny herself what she wanted out of a sense of one-upmanship or concern for others' opinions spoke of a weakness unbecoming the daughter of Helenor Connery. 'Twas not behavior of which her mother would be proud.

Ailsa glanced down at the soldiers, finding Kallum's braw frame easily—as usual—amongst the sparring men. Shaking her head in frustration at her continued fascination with a man she wouldn't allow herself to have, she looked toward the loch and discovered several women of the clan washing linens.

She took note of the easy rapport the lone brown-skinned woman of the group had with the others. Her name was Florie. She had introduced herself to Ailsa several days ago as the wife of one of the Black foot soldiers. Like her, the woman was the descendant of Africans who had been bound for enslavement in the

Caribbean and other territories of the British Crown—
including those of Scotland herself—but were stolen
from Portuguese slavers by pirates. While some of
those ancestors managed to escape after reaching
Scotland's shores, many were sold to the wealthy, like
those with whom Ailsa had been enslaved at Stirling
Castle.

Ailsa had learned that, for generations, Clan
MacNeill had given emancipated or runaway Africans
sanctuary and allowed them to become free and enter-
prising members of the clan. Many of the soldiers of
her lineage she had spotted the other day had been
born into the clan.

The information had shed much light on Laird
Aymer's willingness to enfold Ailsa into his throng
even after learning she was a Connery. Fugitives were
not foreign to the chief. Of course, his love for Kallum
had also played heavily in his decision, but 'twas nice to
know his history of being equitable predated her arrival. The knowledge helped quiet some of her unease
that he would secretly arrange for her return to the
king.

Such a secret arrangement had been on her mind
since the night of her arrival. She had thought to leave
that night but had feared she'd lose her way. She had
not been confident that knowing the direction in which
Connery lands lied would be enough to help her navigate her way safely home.

Another act of cowardice on her part?

The sound of Florie's laugh distracted her from answering the self-imposed question. The woman glanced
up and, seeing Ailsa, waved. Ailsa waved back. She
wondered if such ease of life would ever be possible for

her here. All she'd ever wanted was to live on her own terms and make a respected living for herself as her clan's primary healer. Return to her clan did not seem to be forthcoming with any due haste, and most of the MacNeil women did not speak to her.

Caitrin swore 'twas because they were jealous of Ailsa's connection to Kallum and not for any other reason, but Ailsa had her doubts. She was an unknown, she looked different than the majority of them, and she suspected a few had heard whispers of her possible connection to Clan Connery. None of these were factors upon which to build a lasting friendship.

Even when they or their families had need of healing, they chose to suffer until the lone MacNeill healer could make his way to them rather than allow Ailsa to attend them. 'Twas insulting. 'Twas also a waste of what she had to offer these people.

Would any MacNeill ever willingly accept her as their healer?

Was there even the smallest chance she could live her dream on MacNeill land instead of Connery, or was she lost to having any sense of belonging ever again?

"What are you doing?" The voice of the only person to befriend her so far startled Ailsa out of her reverie.

She had not heard Caitrin approach.

Caitrin sat down beside her.

"Thinking."

"Thinking about what?" Caitrin wrapped her arms around her bent knees and surveyed the entirety of the view. Upon noticing the sparring soldiers below, she grinned at Ailsa and said, "Oh."

Ailsa looked at her, then quickly looked away. The knowing glint in the girl's eyes was too much to deal with at the moment. The lass had asked about what had happened between Ailsa and Kallum after she'd abandoned Ailsa on the hill the other day. Ailsa had denied all.

"I see Kallum is below," Caitrin volunteered.

"Aye."

"Exactly how was it, kissing my cousin?"

Ailsa immediately flushed hot at the unexpected question.

"Aha! I knew it! You did kiss him the other day." Caitrin whirled to face her. "Why did you not tell me true?"

Ailsa jumped to her feet and took off over the hill, toward the falls. She would not have this conversation with Caitrin right now. Her emotions were too raw to face being mocked.

"Ailsa, wait!" Caitrin followed after her. "I'm sorry about the teasing. I did not mean to upset you. Please wait."

Waiting was not in Ailsa's plans today. She wanted to escape. Escape all, including the turmoil in her mind, the cravings wrecking her body, and a hollow loneliness she could no longer pretend did not bother her.

'Twas Kallum's fault all.

He'd turned her into a witless female who knew not her own mind. Moreover, he'd made her doubt her kin.

For three full years, all Ailsa had thought about was getting back to her clan. To hear suspicions that her enslavement had been not an accident but a plot executed apurpose left her adrift between her past and her future. If such be true, then going back to Connery land would not be the homecoming she had envisioned; nor would it be wise, lest she could ferret out the culprit or culprits responsible for the deed.

"Ailsa." Caitrin grabbed her arm from behind and snatched her around. "Forgive me. *Please*. I did not realize my jest would disturb you so. You are the closest friend I've ever had. To finally have another woman to talk to who does not treat me different because I am the laird's daughter is something I've treasured. Almost like having a sister. I've always wanted a sister."

Her hopeful expression pulled at Ailsa. Ailsa understood Caitrin's question had been intended as harmless. The lass had no way of knowing the dark and despairing mood Ailsa was in.

"'Tis all right, Caitrin. I fault you not. I'm simply not in the best of moods this day."

The girl wrapped her arms around Ailsa and squeezed. "Aye. I can see it. Is there aught I can do to help?"

Instinctively, Ailsa's eyes closed, and she leaned into the hug. She, too, had always wanted a sister or even a brother. A sibling of any kind would have been nice. As a child, Ailsa used to search the crowds when she went to market with her mother in the village. Anytime she saw someone with eyes the same color as hers, she would wonder. Could that lad be my brother? That lass my sister? That man my father?

The fantasy that one day her *da* would return for her had lived within her for years and years, until she'd reached womanhood and put away such foolish wishes.

She squeezed Caitrin in return. In Caitrin, Ailsa had found a true friend. Mayhap it was time to stop brooding about what she didn't have and start appreciating the few blessings amongst the storm clouds following her of late.

"What's going on here?" Inan's voice intruded on the moment of bonding between Ailsa and Caitrin.

"*Ugh*," Ailsa groaned quietly over Caitrin's shoulder.

Caitrin giggled, knowing how much Ailsa and Inan despised each other.

Ailsa turned to find Inan sitting on his mount beside a mounted Kallum. *Ugh, ugh, ugh! Not both of them.* Could a lass not get a day of peace?

Ailsa let her voice drop into a singsong cadence and, mimicking the accent of her grandmother, said, "What does it look like I'm doing, Inan MacNeill? I am binding your sister so I can conjure a spell that will put a curse on the progeny of the house of MacNeill."

Inan glared at her.

Caitrin slapped a hand over her mouth to control the laughter threatening to burst free. Ailsa continued her ruse and began to speak in Yoruba, moving her hands around ominously and allowing her voice to take on a creepy edge. She recited nothing but an ancient West African tale, but Inan did not know that. His horrified expression gave her much satisfaction.

Recognizing Ailsa's ploy from the story she'd told him about her mother pretending to put a curse on villagers when she got tired of their antics, Kallum found nothing amusing about Ailsa's performance. "*Ailsa*," he snapped with a warning tone.

Ailsa ignored him. She took a step toward Ogun and, with her hands still waving, continued her otherworldly recitation to include Kallum.

Inan forced his horse to walk backward away from her. "The lass is a sorceress as well as a Connery? Caitrin, step away from her this instant!"

Ignoring Inan's comments, Kallum issued another sharp rebuke. "Ailsa!"

"What!" she snapped back, once again speaking in English. "Go away. Both of you." She issued Inan a glare of her own afore focusing on Kallum. "Can I not get one day of respite from your constant presence? You're driving me daft, MacNeill."

Ailsa wandered closer to the stream's edge and stepped onto a large boulder embedded in the bank. Facing the water, she released a loud, angsty scream. All her frustration poured into the disgruntled squall. The sound echoed across the lazy currents, even over the constant din of the falls nearby.

She turned back to the others in time to see Inan dismount his horse and give Kallum a look of concern afore he took hold of his sister and pulled Caitrin farther away from Ailsa.

Insulted, Ailsa wrapped her fingers around the hilt of the dagger she had belted out of sight under her overdress. She could gift the world with one less MacNeill today.

CHAPTER TWENTY

Hand still on Caitrin, Inan gave Kallum a searching look. "The lass appears not to have all her faculties. You sure you don't want to take and drop her at the edge of Connery lands?"

Inan flinched when Caitrin hit him open-handed on his upper arm hard enough to echo across the inlet.

Kallum dismounted and ran a hand over his head, front to back, trying to rein in his exasperation. "No wonder the lass does not like you. Be still, Inan."

Inan threw up his hands, palms facing out, in a facetious gesture of innocence. Kallum knew him not anywhere close to innocent; nor was he apologetic for his unkind words about Ailsa.

Kallum understood the lass's frustrations. Time had passed, but she was no closer to going home than she had been on the first day of her arrival at MacNeill keep. He had sent one of his best soldiers to scout out what he could about the Connery contingent that had traveled with Ailsa to Stirling Castle and what tales abounded after her supposed disappearance. One name came up repeatedly in the reports he had received: Alastair Connery. The man was the Connery chief's cousin and second-in-command.

By all accounts, Alastair had been in charge of organizing the Connery caravan three years ago. The Connery laird, who was young yet, was reported to take much guidance and advice from his second-in-command. Kallum had much yet to learn about the dynamics of the Connery leadership, but Ailsa was going nowhere until he sorted through all the anecdotes and rumors.

He walked toward the upset lass still standing on a boulder. From her perch, she stood eye to eye with him.

Under his breath, he whispered to her, "Don't you dare."

Those light eyes of hers narrowed on him, and he motioned with his head to the grip she had on his father's dagger hidden within the folds of her dress. He did not think Inan understood what peril he risked by antagonizing the lass, but Kallum did. He'd prefer she not mortally wound the cretin despite the truth that he was acting like an arse.

Her mischievous grin implied she'd not decided to accept Kallum's warning. "I'd be doing your clan and the entirety of the Highlands a favor, and you know it."

A sigh rose from the depths of his soul, and he let it out with a heave of his chest. To have two people he cared about at odds with each other was a struggle for him. At least Caitrin had befriended the lass, which meant there was not a complete schism within the family.

Kallum wanted it all to go away.

"You would not. Put your hand down." He put out his hand. "Better yet, return the dirk to me."

"Nay, Kallum MacNeill. The dirk is now mine to yield and mete out justice." She had reverted to her West African accent. "It calls for the blood of a MacNeill mongrel." She cackled wickedly as she looked over at Inan.

Kallum's jaw clenched. The hellion was going to remain difficult. "Mayhap he'd not be such an arse if you'd not antagonize him so."

Her cackle slid into a normal laugh of disbelief. "Me antagonize him? What of what he does to antagonize me? Have you not given *him* that speech about what will happen if he crosses you?"

"Don't mock me, Ailsa. I've had enough of this. Come down and give me my blade."

She pulled the weapon from its sheath and held it at the ready. "Nay, I think I'll keep it."

Kallum noted she held the dirk with a proper underhand grip the way he'd shown her the other day. The lass was a quick student. She was also a menace, and this day, she needed to be taught she could not take her angst out on others without repercussions.

"Quit coddling the wench. Just take it from her."

Ailsa looked over at Inan as he spoke, and Kallum took the opportunity to swoop in and snatch the dagger from her hand. She fought for it, but Kallum tossed the weapon onto the ground, out of reach, and twisted her off the rock so her back hit his chest. She lifted her legs and kicked until she caught him in the shin. Remembering their first encounter, he dropped her to her feet but protected his cods from any wayward fists.

She stomped on his foot, and he gave a grunt of discomfort.

Enough was enough. He picked her up, stomped her to the water's edge, and tossed her into the stream. She went in with a yelp and a big splash. When she came up flailing, Inan stepped up beside him with Caitrin in tow.

"'Twould be to my advantage to be still, as I was told, and not raise this point. But, um, Kallum?"

Short on patience, Kallum scowled at his cousin.

Inan gave him a speculative look. "Do you know even if the lass can swim?"

Kallum whipped his head toward Ailsa. Nay, he knew not.

Ailsa continued to flounder in the water, and Kallum could not hold back his curse. "Fuck!"

Inan placed his hands over Caitrin's ears and broke into uncontrollable laughter. Caitrin disengaged from her brother's hold and made to run toward the water's edge.

Inan grabbed her back. "Not now, pet."

Her head swiveled to him. "But she needs help."

"Kallum will help her."

Having already dropped his weapons and tunic, Kallum hopped on one foot as he rushed to pull off one boot, then reversed the process to remove the other.

"But he's upset with her," Caitrin whined.

"Yeah, he's something with her all right." Still chuckling, he gathered Caitrin in a sideways embrace. "Your friend will be fine."

Ailsa disappeared beneath the opaque current. Wearing nothing but his kilt, Kallum rushed to the bank and dove in. He swam under the sweeping riffles until he reached Ailsa. Grasping her around the waist, he kicked them up through the stream's surface. She sputtered and shook her head to whisk away the lingering droplets that ran in rivulets down her face.

He searched her visage for signs she'd been harmed or suffered an extreme fright. "You all right?"

The look of betrayal she leveled at him through piercing, brownish-green eyes suggested he'd pay for this transgression for many days to come. With an evil grunt, she slapped the pool's surface and splashed water in his eyes. When he shook it off, she did it again and again.

He grasped at her hand. "Stop that!"

She fought him and continued to shove water in his face with every chance she could.

"Ailsa, stop or I will drop you back in."

Through her struggles and grunts, Kallum was not sure the angry wildcat even heard him. But he'd had enough of whatever had put her in a mood this day, so he let go.

She dipped under once and came up with a huge gasp for air. With a quickness, she latched onto him, grabbing at his shoulders with both hands and wrapping her legs around his waist. He could tell she was still irritated, but beneath the annoyance, he could feel her true fear. She trembled in his arms, and real tears mingled with the glistening water droplets that caressed her cheeks. 'Twas more than Kallum could stand. He swam them both to shore. Rising from the waves, he cradled her against his chest and went to have a seat on her boulder.

Dripping wet, he pushed back the loose tendrils of hair plastered to her face and held her cheeks with both hands. "How is it that a lass who can throw a dirk with accuracy, shoot and re-nock a bow faster than most archers, and speak Gaelic, English, and Yoruba does not know how to swim?"

Her voice was but a whisper. "There was not a tutor for that." She tucked her face into his neck and clutched onto him with a tight grasp.

Without thought, he dropped a kiss to the top of her head and gently rubbed her back. "Mayhap I will have to help you remedy that gap in your learning."

"Really?" Inan said behind him.

Without looking up, Kallum waved his cousin away. He had forgotten Inan and Caitrin stood in observance, but in the moment it mattered not. All that mattered to him was the lass in his arms. The rest of the world could fade into oblivion.

"Come, Cait," Inan said in a disgusted voice. "Let's return to the manor. Trust me, we need not be here for this."

The sound of Inan pulling Caitrin away gave Kallum some comfort. He could not deal with the feuding between his cousin and Ailsa right now *and* deal with the challenge of keeping her safe from outside forces while simultaneously keeping her spirits high.

When the clop of Inan's horse's hooves was far enough away that Kallum knew his words could not travel to his cousins' ears, he lifted Ailsa's face with a cupped hand beneath her chin. "Tell me what's bothering you, lass."

Behind the struggle to keep more tears from falling, she looked at him with sad eyes. "I want to go home, Kallum."

"This is your home now, lass."

"Nay, 'tis not." She curled her legs up into his lap and snuggled closer under his chin. "I have been on my own for a long time, but here at MacNeill keep is the first time in my life I have truly felt lonely. I may not be totally accepted at Clan Connery, but I am not the enemy I am here. I can face being an outsider amongst my own things, in my own cottage, with my own people. At the least, I will have a chance to earn my acceptance, to earn the protection of the laird and the consideration due a respected healer. Can you not understand that?"

He pulled her back against his chest and buried his nose in her damp hair, content to hold her and breathe her in. An ache filled his chest that she felt so alone and displaced. He understood her desire to go home, but he worried home was not all she expected.

He still had not come to grips with the way she'd been left behind in Stirling. Something was not right with that. His gut told him there was more to her story, and mayhap Alastair Connery held the key.

"Aye, lass, I understand you are homesick. But you should not have to *earn* protection from your own clan." He once more gripped her face between his palms. "Who you are should have been enough for them. You deserve their regard and protection simply because you were born a Connery. Having to earn the love of your own kin when you've done nothing to violate clan law or the moral standards of your people is the highest betrayal of the Highlander way of life.

"That you became the strong, fierce lass you are despite their disgraceful treatment is a testament to the woman you are. Trust that you are enough not because of what you do but because of who you are in here." With two fingers, he gently tapped her chest twice over her heart. "You are a treasure. A treasure I want to be safe and protected. I cannot protect you if you are not with me. Can *you* not understand that?"

"Is it my protection you seek?" She paused, searching his face for the answer she sought. "Or my favors?"

He pushed out a breath and closed his eyes. 'Twas a fair question.

Upon opening his eyes, he admitted, "I deserved

that. And if I were to speak true, 'tis both I want. But I can live without your favors if you choose not to share them. I could not, all told, live with your harm. Were I to hand you over to your clansmen and you were hurt or sent back to captivity, I would be unable to live with myself." He caressed one of her cheeks with a bent finger. "Can you not give me a little more time to know you will be okay?"

She lifted her own hand and caressed the right side of his beard with an open palm. "Aye, Kallum MacNeill, I will wait if I must, but know I will not wait forever."

He acknowledged her stipulation with a nod, then dropped his lips to hers. She opened to him without resistance and touched her tongue to his. The sweetness of the offered kiss seeped into him, and he lingered over her mouth as if he sipped the sweetest of nectars. It was a slow, intimate, all-consuming kiss. When he finally pulled away, he dared not believe the look he saw in her eyes. A look many a man would kill to have a woman he wanted level on him. A look that said of all the men in the world, *he* was her one man.

His heart squeezed at the foolish thought. The lass wanted to kill him as oft as kiss him. Their passions ran high for each other. Neither could deny the strong attraction between them, but his destiny was here with the MacNeills, and Ailsa's goal was to return to land Connery. When she did, he'd make sure she had no enemies amongst the jackals left alive to do her harm.

He lifted her from his lap and put his boots and tunic back on. Grabbing her hand and his father's dagger off the ground, he escorted her back to his mother's cottage with Ogun walking unguided behind them. She would need to gather herself and re-dress for the evening meal. She had been summoned to the laird's table this eve. The laird had news to share that involved her. Kallum had been on edge since he learned of the required audience. It was why he and Inan had come looking for the lass. Well, that, and he had something for her.

At the door to the cottage, Kallum shared the summons with Ailsa, which was not well received. She abhorred gatherings amidst large numbers of MacNeills. He escorted her inside but stayed standing within the open doorway.

To take her mind off her nerves, he gathered the pouch he had stashed amongst his weapons. "This is for you."

She took the pouch from his hand, and her gaze jerked up to his. She recognized the pouch immediately. "'Tis the dagger presented to you by the king."

"Aye."

She offered the pouch back to him without opening it. "I cannot take this."

He pushed it back at her. "You can."

"But this is very valuable."

"It is not worth more than my life. And that, I owe to you."

"I do not understand," she said, finally accepting the pouch.

"If you had not warned me of the Donnelly's approach, I would have died that day with his sword in my back."

Her brows lowered, and she stared at the pouch reflectively. "You could not possibly have heard my warning over the noise of the crowd."

"Ah, goddess, the look in your eyes told me everything I needed to know."

She frowned with incomprehension. Her eyes were so expressive. She apparently did not realize how much of her thoughts they and her countenance oft revealed.

He placed his hands over hers and slid the bejeweled dagger from its pouch. "I did not have to hear your voice to hear your message. And for that, I owe you my life." He folded her fingers closed around the blade's handle. "Keep the dagger. Then mayhap you need not continue to steal mine."

Her lips tilted up at his playful jab.

Good.

Happy to see some of the sadness leave her eyes, he winked at her, then closed the cottage door behind him as he left her to rest until this eve.

He needed to find the laird. He could no longer take the suspense. 'Twas time the laird revealed exactly what was about to transpire, and Kallum intended not to leave the sire's presence until he had *all* the answers he sought.

• • •

Shortly after the evening meal had commenced, Kallum stormed toward the cottage he had loaned to Ailsa. The obstinate woman had been summoned to the manor for supper but had not bothered to heed the summons. Her audacity had reached a point he could no longer tolerate. His disposition had already been surly. The laird had not cooperated with Kallum's attempt to get the pending news from him at an early audience. The chief had insisted on waiting to reveal the information with Ailsa present, since 'twould affect her future.

Now, the lass had gone and insulted the laird by being late to her audience or mayhap not intending to show at all.

He shoved open the door without knocking.

Ailsa whirled at the sound of his entry. Eyes wide with fright, she clutched at the tatters of her clothing. A smattering of relief entered her eyes upon recognizing him.

"Kallum, know you not how to knock?" She made a great show at bravado, but her voice held not its usual bite when chastising him.

The sight his eyes fell upon doused all the furious fire from his veins and replaced it with icy dread. She stood holding the remnants of the top of her dress together. The garment was rife with dirt and leaves as if she had rolled around on the ground. The impression of a man's hands circled the column of her throat, and half her hair had come loose from the bundle atop her head she must have piled it in after her dousing in the stream.

"What happened?"

She spun away from him. "Naught."

"'Tis not the truth. Tell me what happened." He took a step forward.

She whirled back around at the sound of his footfall.

His teeth clenched at her obvious skittishness. He held his ground, but with effort, and intentionally softened his voice. Yet, he was no less adamant with his interrogation. "Who did this?"

"Kallum, let it go." It was a common demand of hers where he was concerned, but today, it was accompanied by a near pleading look in her eyes, not her usual fire.

She hesitated a moment afore she turned away from him again. "Please leave so I may make myself presentable. The laird expects me at the keep. I am already late." Despite her best effort, her voice broke on her last sentence.

She reached for a clean dress laid out on the bed. 'Twas one of Caitrin's. Caitrin had loaned a few items from her wardrobe to Ailsa until Ailsa could have new ones of her own made. The lasses were close to the same size, though Ailsa's figure tended toward more womanly curves.

With the caution he would use to approach a frightened mare, Kallum edged toward Ailsa. He kept his voice low despite his urge to rail and scream. Someone had assaulted her. He'd have a name, or he'd attack every man in the keep and village until he found the culprit, who would soon learn what it felt like to be handled so brutally.

When he reached her, he gently moved the loose hair from her neck. She flinched at his touch but did not pull away. He surveyed the large handprints visible on the bronze-brown of her skin, and the hand at his side fisted.

"Ailsa," he snapped.

She jumped at his harsh tone.

He took a deep breath to stifle the hard edge to his voice. 'Twas not her he was mad at. He tried again with more control. "Tell me who did this to you."

She pulled the top of what remained of her dress around her throat and tried to move away from him. With a gentle but firm grasp, he placed a hand against her far cheek to turn her face toward him. She winched at his touch. With a creased brow, he lifted his hand and gazed at the faint redness across her cheekbone. The mongrel had hit her.

Nay, the man would not get a beating. He would find his death this day.

"You will tell me who did this."

She pulled away. "I will not. I have handled the matter. He did not succeed in his ultimate goal, which was to terrorize me until I shivered with fear in front of him. I have faced greater tyrants than him. I am fine. Now leave so I may dress properly."

Her face held the familiar obstinance he had come to expect. She had made her decision and would not be swayed. Unfortunately for her, neither would he. He was tired of her need to face tyrants, as she herself ought to be.

He glanced down at her belt. Her new dagger rested snuggly in its sheath. If she had her dagger with her during the encounter, Kallum had no doubt she had fought back, and a fight from her would be no trifling matter. Afore she could anticipate the move, he grasped her right hand—the hand he'd seen her fist numerous times with the desire to punch him over some callous remark or thoughtless action. He turned the hand, delicate yet strong, so her knuckles were revealed to him. As he expected, they were bruised and beginning to swell.

He had guessed right. She had fought back, and the heathen who attacked her would have the markings to prove it.

He whirled and stormed out the door.

"Kallum!" Ailsa rushed to the doorway and called

anxiously after him, "Where are you going?"

Hands clenched and burning with the need to pound someone into dust, Kallum did not look back or slow. "To teach someone some manners."

CHAPTER TWENTY-ONE

When Kallum reached the manor, he took the stone outer steps two at a time. Inside, the men sat at supper. The hall was full and loud with the sounds of manly banter and raucousness. He glanced around, looking for a man with a blackened eye or other noticeable sign of a recent tussle. He suspected his target may also have a dagger wound somewhere on his person.

One table of soldiers was louder than the others. A man who served as a second lieutenant to the foot soldiers guffawed loudly. The second lieutenant's friends joined in his laughter. The smarmy look on the soldier's face and the bawdy nature of the table's conversation made clear they were an irreverent, raunchy bunch. When the man scratched at his forearm covered by the long sleeves of his heavy tunic, a prescient tickle rose up Kallum's spine. The garment was an odd choice for this time of day during the sunny season. The man should have been overly warm.

With an instinct that had served him well in battle throughout the years, Kallum stalked to the soldier's table. Deliberate purpose guided his steps. The man had his back to him and had not yet noticed his approach, but those who sat opposite the second lieutenant suddenly looked up. No doubt they sensed the impending retribution.

Whatever look they saw on Kallum's face made them all launch to their feet almost as one. Arms flailed as several struggled to keep their balance, and the bench on which they sat toppled with a loud crash. The noise and startled looks on the wary faces of his comrades warned Kallum's target of the predator at his back, and the soldier turned his head with a curious stare.

Once he faced Kallum, Kallum got a good look at the bruise beginning to form beneath the man's left eye. Bristling, Kallum yanked up the man's forearm, nearly unseating him. A quick yank lifted the man's sleeve to reveal a soiled bandage. Unceremoniously, Kallum snatched off the bound cloth.

The man cursed with pain and outrage, but Kallum cared not. The fresh cut he revealed made him roar like a rabid wolf entangled in a snare. Throwing both hands against the front of the soldier's tunic, Kallum wrenched him from his seat as if he weighed no more than a newly born bairn and heaved him halfway across the room. The man landed with an indecorous *thud* and slid into a wall. The hall erupted in chaos.

Inan leapt from his seat. "Kallum! What in God's name are you doing?"

Kallum ignored the question. The authority and command in Inan's voice could not temper the rage he felt. Not this day. Not this time. Naught was going to stop him from beating this wretch of a soldier until his life force spilled onto the ground and completely left his body.

He followed after the heap of arms and legs slumped half against the wall and dragged the man to his feet with one hand. His other fist bashed into the cretin's jaw thrice in quick succession. He opened his hold on the third blow, letting the man slam face-first back onto the floor. The stunned soldier quickly righted himself and scrambled backward with the speed of a beached crab fleeing the beak of a herring gull.

Eyes wide, he threw up a hand when Kallum reached for him again. "Wait!"

Kallum did not stop. Two brave but misguided foot soldiers, mayhap two of the second lieutenant's regiment, dared to step between Kallum and the floored mongrel.

Without hesitation, Kallum pulled his sword, lamenting that he carried only one this eve. "Interrupt me only if you are prepared to die."

. . .

"Oh, *no*." Ailsa stood in the doorway of the keep's grand hall. She had arrived in time to see Kallum toss her attacker across the room. Now that he'd pulled his sword, the situation was worse than she expected. The man was set to kill someone, and everyone would blame her.

How could he?

In a clan where she was already treated like an unwanted interloper, this incident would make her even more an outsider.

"Kallum! Stand down this instant and tell me what the fucking hell is going on." Inan jumped down from the raised dais on which the laird's head table sat. "What has this man done that you treat him thus?"

Kallum did not take his eyes off the two foolhardy blokes blocking the source of his rage. "He abused a woman."

Inan looked over at Ailsa. From the look in his

eyes, he knew immediately to which woman Kallum referred.

All remaining eyes in the room followed Inan's gaze and settled on her. She wanted the floor to swallow her whole and lightning to strike a certain MacNeill who had a knack for butting in where he didn't belong.

Hendrik MacNeill struggled to his feet. "I do not know what the sow told you, but I did not lay a hand on her."

Kallum growled low in his throat at the word *sow*. Had not Inan been there to grab his sword hand, which raised in tandem with his throaty growl, he would have sliced through the side-by-side human blockade and run Hendrik through with his sword.

"You lie." Kallum's unhesitating words left no doubt that Kallum believed not her attacker's words. "The *lass* said naught. 'Tis you who have just revealed the deed."

Hendrik glanced at her with a venom in his eyes that suggested he thought she'd played a part in some trickery to set him up to confess. Ailsa cared little about his upset; she was too taken aback by Kallum's surety. Little had been said to him about the circumstances surrounding the incident, but here he stood certain she held no fault in the matter. For a man who seemed to think the worst of those born Connery, his confidence brought upon an unexpected warmth.

"You're going to believe a *Connery* over me?" The man well-nigh spit upon saying the Connery name.

The entire hall erupted into one giant gasp of horror.

"She doesn't belong here! Time she goes back where she belongs," he added with an evil look in

Ailsa's direction.

Ailsa stood transfixed at the realization Hendrik had known all along who she was, and now every soldier, every MacNeill in the hall knew her for certain to be from an enemy clan. The contempt on Hendrik's face explained much about his behavior earlier when he'd come upon her pacing behind the keep's back wall. She'd been trying to work up the nerve to attend supper with a hall full of MacNeill soldiers. The man had called her an unwanted, Moor *fud*.

Nothing like being insulted by a male who reduced you to the vulgar tag for a female's most private part. Clearly, in his mind, the only thing worse than a Connery was a brown-skinned Connery.

"So you admit being with her earlier?" Inan asked with a firm hold still on Kallum. He ignored the growing buzz resulting from Hendrik's announcement of her surname.

"I admit naught," Hendrik replied, too arrogant to sense the danger he faced.

"You already did, you vile excuse for a man." Kallum shook off Inan's hold.

Not to be outdone, Inan wrested the sword from Kallum's grasp. Kallum did not resist. In fact, he was deceptively accommodating of Inan's pilfering of his weapon. The act was misleading because Ailsa knew, as did Inan, that all Kallum needed to kill the man was his bare hands.

Hendrik in his stupidity continued not to have a clue. Ignorantly more confident facing a swordless Kallum, the man puffed out his chest. "This is ridiculous. How could you think I would even lay hands on a woman like her? She's just a—"

He caught himself afore he finished his statement, suddenly remembering to whom he was speaking.

"She's just a what?" One side of Kallum's mouth tilted up in a not quite grin, nor full smirk.

Ailsa had seen that look on his face twice afore. Each time had been just afore he killed someone.

Understanding the unspoken message behind Kallum's grim-reaper grin, Inan stepped in front of Kallum to block his access to Hendrik.

Facing the accused, Inan said emphatically, "I suggest you not answer that if you want to live."

Inan handed Kallum's sword to one of the wall men, then waved them both away. He returned his attention to Kallum but continued to block Kallum's direct line to Hendrik. "What know you of this matter?"

"In truth, she said naught to me of her assailant. I know only what I saw upon entering her dwelling."

Horrified, Ailsa stepped forward. He would not tell these people how he had found her earlier. "Kallum, do not—"

Inan held up a hand to silence her. "You will not speak unless spoken to. Do not interrupt this matter."

She glanced around the room, once again aware of all the eyes focused on her. She glanced at Kallum, then Inan. If they were set to make a spectacle of this matter, they would do so without her. She turned to leave.

"You are not dismissed." Inan's voice promised reprisals for disobedience. "Do not take your leave until you are given permission."

Ailsa's feet stopped moving, but she allowed her conscious mind to displace. She spun to face the hall once more, but her mind transferred to a place where she seemed to observe the embarrassing happenings from outside herself.

Inan continued his questioning of Kallum. "What saw you?"

"Her garments were torn and soiled with leaves and dirt. She has the impression of a man's hands bruised onto her throat."

The nature of the murmuring changed to a dull lull of speculation. Ailsa closed her eyes, certain she could hear the pity behind the morphed sound.

"Ailsa."

She opened her eyes at the sound of Inan's voice saying her name.

"Show us your neck."

She refused him with a shake of her head.

"Lass, 'twill be revealed voluntarily or involuntarily," he promised. "Choose."

Her overall hatred of Inan doubled upon his high-handed order, but she did as he demanded. Untying the high neck of the dress she had donned, she pulled it wide so the marks on her neck became visible.

A hush fell over the hall, and the eyes of every man in the room glanced toward Hendrik.

"He dies," Kallum stated emphatically.

"No!" Despite her mandate of silence, Ailsa could stay quiet no longer. She'd not be the reason this man was put to death. She would not be able to walk about the holdings ever again.

"He dies," Kallum repeated. "I'll not have such a man under my command. Nor should he be allowed to live so he can abuse another woman on another day. Any man dishonorable enough to do that to a woman,

especially one who gets away with it, will attack another. Justice demands he be punished. I say his
punishment be death."

Hendrik sputtered afore finding his voice. "That is
not your decision to make, Commander. I am entitled
to an audience before the council."

Inan looked to his father, who had remained silent
up to this point.

The laird stood. "Kallum, such punishment is
harsh."

"Would you consider it harsh were it Caitrin he had
assaulted?"

Laird Aymer's expression hardened at Kallum's
query. The look on his face made clear that had the
man put hands on his daughter, Hendrik would already
be dead.

Ailsa rushed to stand in front of the laird. "Laird
MacNeill, death is too harsh. I prevented him from doing any real harm. I'll not be the reason for his death."

"The reason for his death would be his own heinous
actions," Kallum interjected.

Ailsa ignored Kallum and continued her plea to the
laird. "Sire, I implore you." She tried not to panic as the
laird studied her silently.

His expression suggested he wanted to give her
some deference in the matter, but now that Caitrin had
been added as a comparison, his inclination to side
with Kallum was strong.

The laird switched his gaze to Hendrik. "Tell me
true, Hendrik. Are those your marks on the lass's
neck?"

A tick commenced in Hendrik's jaw. He had been
put on the spot. Ailsa held her breath as she wondered

whether he would have the hubris to present a falsehood to the chief. When he nodded an affirmative answer, she breathed again.

"Then there is no need for a council proceeding unless your comrades deem it necessary." The laird raised and spread both his arms to encompass the entire hall. "Is there any man here who stands with Hendrik in his request for a hearing before the council?"

Ailsa glanced around the hall, expecting to see the majority of the men side with Hendrik. To her surprise, only the two soldiers who had attempted to shield him from Kallum raised their hands.

The laird shifted his gaze from the mostly stoic crowd to his adopted nephew. "Kallum?"

'Twas a one-word question, but all it entailed was clear. He'd leave the decision of Hendrik's punishment up to the meddling cretin.

Ailsa's shoulders dropped. This could end only one way. Kallum had always made clear severe transgressions warranted no mercy.

When she looked at him, he was watching her. A lot was said between them with no words at all. She implored him with her eyes to understand what a death sentence for Hendrik would mean for her continued stay at Clan MacNeill, however long that might be. She held little hope he'd be swayed by the silent plea.

He inhaled a deep breath and let it out, all the while keeping his gaze trained on her. The entire hall watched the two of them watching each other. She felt like a spectacle put on by a court jester, but she held her ground and waited for the MacNeill to give his decision.

"He is banished."

She started to protest even that, but Kallum held up his hand and gave a look that made clear he'd have no opposition in this.

"He is banished, lass, or he dies. This is the only concession I can offer you. No middle ground exists. I'll not have him on the same land as you. Do you understand? He must leave MacNeill keep and the villages beyond this very eve or I shall send him to Hell."

The mandate was better than she had expected but still not without potential repercussions for her. She nodded at Kallum nonetheless. 'Twas a major concession he offered, this divergence from his personal code. She understood that he offered the leniency against his better judgment in deference to her constant nagging that his answer for everything did not have to be *kill and kill yet again*.

She tried to appreciate the gesture and not think about the family and friends of the man now banished because of her. By morn, every member of this clan would know of the outcome, and they'd also all know her ties to Clan Connery.

Whatever temporary sanctuary her stay here had been meant to be, that safe harbor had ended. And mayhap that had been Hendrik's intent all along.

She took a step back and started to leave.

Inan stopped her. "Stay where you are, lass. We still have a need to meet with you."

Inan motioned to a soldier, who was given instructions to escort Hendrik from MacNeill lands. While Inan discussed the final outcome with Kallum and Kallum went to retrieve his sword, Ailsa slipped away.

She'd had enough of MacNeill lands herself. 'Twas time she found a way home.

CHAPTER TWENTY-TWO

Kallum retrieved his sword and looked over to find Ailsa gone. The discovery did not surprise him. The lass was likely upset with him.

He could not help his outrage at finding her shaken and bruised and soiled. He'd tried to compromise by letting live the man who dared touch her. He knew her thoughts about his penchant to exact justice at the end of a blade and sought a different tactic this time. But 'twould seem it had not been enough.

He sighed.

Inan walked up beside him and glanced around for the missing Ailsa. "Does that woman ever do what's she's told?" he asked.

Kallum stared at the empty doorway afore responding. "Nay." His tone revealed his slight amusement at the notion.

Inan looked over at him with a raised brow. "That amuses you?"

Kallum merely shrugged.

In a lowered voice meant only for Kallum, Inan snarled, "You need to follow that lass and retrieve your cods. She's leading you around by your wee *dobber*. If you need to bed the Connery whelp to get it out of your system, then have at it so—"

Kallum's fist to Inan's mouth cut off whatever else Inan had intended to say. His unsuspecting cousin stumbled a step afore he wiped at a trickle from his lip and glanced at the blood on his fingers. He responded with a rapid counterpunch that caught Kallum on the chin.

Revved and itching for a fight, Kallum charged, and they devolved into fisticuffs in the middle of the grand hall. Neither gave an inch, each steadfast in keeping his feet. The men remaining in the hall began to cheer and chant and take sides.

Kallum and Inan traded blow for blow until the sound of the laird's fist slamming against the grand table boomed throughout the room.

"Enough!" The laird walked in between Kallum and Inan. "I've not seen such a ridiculous ruckus out of you two since you were lads."

Inan wiped at his bleeding lip with the back of his hand. "'Tis not my fault he's allowed himself to be bewitched by a daughter of our enemy. The sap."

"'Tis not hard to understand," Laird Aymer said. "She has the similar fire of a woman we once knew."

Surprised by the revelation, Inan asked, "Who?"

The laird grinned in Kallum's direction. "His mother." He shook his head in mock commiseration, then laughed. "The lad had not a chance."

Kallum frowned at the comment. What on earth did his mother have to do with the situation?

"You think not?" Inan studied his father's face, intrigued by the comment. "I think 'tis just the matter of lust after a bonnie face and even bonnier form."

Kallum was tempted to take another swing at the monger for the comment, but he settled for a warning glower, since the laird stood between him and Inan.

Ignoring Kallum's look and the warning that went with it, Inan continued his derogatory speculation. "Care to place a wager, *da*? Kallum does not form female attachments. As soon as she is out of his sight, she will be out of his mind."

A shake of the head met Inan's offer. "Son, 'tis a fool's bet. All told, if you are set on handing over your coin, I'm happy to take it."

Kallum grunted. "I am standing right here, ye ken?"

"Aye, we know it. But 'tis no matter." The amusement had not left the laird's face. "You can never get back what the lass has already taken from you."

Kallum tensed, not sure he wanted to know the answer to that riddle of a comment.

Inan had no such hesitancy. "Which is?"

The man who had served as his second father patted Kallum on the back, then glanced at Inan. The playfulness was gone. He said with all sincerity, "His heart, son. The lass has already captured it, and she walks around with it in her pocket, tied up with a lovely ribbon. The only question is whether that ribbon be of our tartan colors or that of her kin."

Inan took one look at Kallum's appalled face and guffawed.

"Ah, you see, Inan? Our Kallum does nothing without a fight—not even fall in love." Laird MacNeill placed a hand on Kallum's shoulder. "You were a son to my brother in every way that mattered, and he loved you more than even if you had been of his own seed. So let me stand in his stead and give you a piece of fatherly advice.

"Despite your warrior's strength, 'tis futile to continue to fight what you can never defeat. 'Twill hurt less and cause you less frustration, our Kallum, if you simply surrender." With that, the laird strode away without a second glance.

Staring after the laird's retreating form, Kallum groused to Inan. "Your *da* has clearly lost his mental faculties. 'Tis past time you agree to accept the lairdship."

With a vehement shake of his head, Inan scowled and defended himself. "Don't turn this on me 'cause you want not face the truth. Everyone can see you have feelings for the lass but you." A slight bob of his head toward the entryway through which Ailsa had disappeared indicated Inan's slight reconsideration. "Well, and mayhap the lass."

Taking a step closer, Inan made sure Kallum looked him in the eyes. "I'd not have called it love, but I have no experience with the sodden emotion. Thank God." He audibly pushed out a relieved breath. "But if *da* is right and 'tis more than lust between you, then you seem not to realize what you fight more than each other is the stubbornness with which you both try to hold on to grim notions about the burdens of relationships on one's independence. None need apply to you.

"'Tis your choice to accept or nay that you have finally met a lass of a will perfectly suited to yours. And if you have, I apologize for my slanders of the lass. I am concerned only for your welfare. If she holds true to her kin, I do not see how you can trust her. But if you are willing to overlook that flaw, I'll try harder to overlook her ties to the Connerys."

Stunned by the notion that Aymer believed he had fallen irreversibly for the lass, Kallum simply stared at his friend by choice, cousin by adoption, and brother by affection. To hear the brother of his heart speak similar nonsense sent him reeling. Kallum himself had considered the soft spot he felt for Ailsa. The feelings arose at the most inconvenient times and oft made him feel like a man who had lost all common sense.

But love?

Nay. 'Tis not possible. He was not built for such emotions.

Even if he were, he could not be saddled with a mate. He had a mission to achieve, a calling he could not abandon to build hearth and home. His voluntary nighttime forays led him into frequent danger and made him an outlaw. How could he condemn a woman to tie herself to that? What woman would knowingly want to risk all and live with the constant threats that came with harboring a criminal?

Inan raised a hand to his shoulder. "The lass has an unmistakable independent nature and is hell set to hold on to it. Should be of no consequence to you, who are strong enough not to need her to be less of who she is for you to feel like a man. So if she is what you want, then 'tis time you let the lass—and everyone else— know so I do not have to prevent another execution because some poor lout has overstepped his bounds with the woman."

Inan's expression relaxed. "Besides, if I am wrong and you do not want her, young Dougal is more than willing to offer for the lass."

A deep growl rumbled low in Kallum's throat at the mention of the awkward foot soldier who mooned at the lass every time she passed by him. That he was smitten with her was obvious for all to see. He lived only because he had not been foolish enough to act on his amorous feelings.

Inan guffawed again. "Aye. 'Tis as I thought." He patted Kallum on the shoulder much like the sire had done, then gave him a good-natured shove. "Come. We need see to the men afore the results of what happened here seep into their morale. A few battle maneuvers should take their minds off the drama and get them back on their responsibilities."

Battle maneuvers sounded right good. Kallum fell into step beside Inan, all that had transpired between them forgotten, but he had a need to work off some steam. 'Twould remain to be seen whether any member of the regiment had the guts to spar with him. He smirked as a thought brought a lift to his mood.

Inan took one look at him and began to shake his head. They knew each other well enough that Inan could guess what was on his mind. Kallum waggled his brows at his cousin, who snorted at his antics.

'Twas time to have a little fun, for Kallum was of a mind to start the sparring with the asshat mates of Ailsa's attacker. Defense of such vermin deserved a good arse beating, and an arse beating they would get.

• • •

Ailsa sat in the middle of Caitrin's bed upstairs in the manor later that night. She had been hiding out ever since she ran into Caitrin shortly after the debacle with Hendrik in the grand hall. She had not wanted to return to the cottage because she knew that would be the first place Kallum would come looking for her. She had not been ready to face him.

After hearing the tale of all that had happened, Caitrin had disappeared for a while. Ailsa had been afraid she would reveal her whereabouts, but Caitrin surprised her. The lass returned with a light repast for

Ailsa and two women, Gavina and Libby, Ailsa recognized from the group who did the wash with Florie. Florie also accompanied the women, which helped Ailsa feel more comfortable with the small gathering but not completely at ease.

Caitrin's guests each carried several garments slung over their arms.

Florie walked to the bed and dumped her armload on the coverlet. "Caitrin told us what happened. Don't worry about Hendrik," she said to Ailsa. "The man was a wanker. He deserved his punishment."

"More, even," added Gavina in her husky alto. She was the widow of one of Kallum's archers and maybe a score in years older than the rest of them. "You were too nice, lassie. You should have let Kallum do him in."

Gavina stepped over to the bed and dropped all but one of the dresses she carried. "You'll be needing a few more things to have any sense of womanhood. What with heathens daring to accost a woman right here within the clan proper. 'Tis a disgrace." She held up a lovely green frock with tight sleeves to the elbow and flared, wide sleeves to the wrist. "Come on, lass, stand and try this one on."

Rising from the bed, Ailsa stared at the dress, wide-eyed. The garment was beautiful, with braided gold ribbon stitched along the sleeves and bodice. She felt overwhelmed. Tonight's incidents had shaken her. First the attack by Hendrik, then Kallum's strong reaction to it. 'Twas an unusual thing for her to have a champion, and to find a champion in a man with whom she had exchanged more arguments than pleasantries was twice the surprise. Now, here she stood with women who offered clothing of their own to replace the dress destroyed during her altercation with Hendrik and add a few extra garments to her meager wardrobe.

"Oh, Gavina, 'tis much too pretty." Ailsa put her hand to her chest and took a step backward. "I could not possibly accept this from you."

"Why, I thank you for the compliment, as I made the dress myself. But don't be foolish. I have plenty of dresses. You need it more than I. Besides, if I have need of another, I'll make me another." She stepped forward and started attacking the fastenings of Ailsa's dress. "So, let's get this done."

Swatting Gavina's hands away, Ailsa laughed. "All right. All right. I get it. You're not going to take a 'no' for answer."

Florie, Caitrin, and Libby all laughed, too.

Placing a hand to a hip, Florie said to Ailsa, "See what we have to deal with down at the loch?"

Gavina waved a dismissive hand at their affable chiding and helped Ailsa into the green masterpiece. It fit her well, and Ailsa nearly cried upon catching the stunned reactions of her new friends. And it was the thought of *new friends* that moved her even more than the dress. After the recent days she'd had, knowing she didn't have to be isolated save for Caitrin and Kallum made the lingering ache in her soul lessen.

"The dress suits you," Libby said in awe.

"Aye. I think you're right, Libby," Gavina agreed. "I dare say it looks better on her than it ever did on me. 'Tis the lass's coloring. The dress just suits."

Ailsa ran a hand down her abdomen and the frock's skirt and allowed herself an unrestrained smile. Having more than one friend could be fun. Mayhap she need not rush to leave after all. The dangers of lone travel were no less great this day than they'd been on that first. If she had the companionship of these women, might she be content until Kallum could ferret out the truth of her abduction?

She decided she wanted to try.

The ladies and she got busy trying on and evaluating all the dresses. Florie's were too loose on Ailsa, but Libby's worked as well as Gavina's. When they were through, Florie, Gavina, and Libby departed, and Ailsa had an overpowering urge to speak with Kallum.

She couldn't stop thinking about what had happened earlier in the grand hall. She had known Kallum wanted her physically, but this eve she'd seen something else in his eyes when he looked at her, something more than lust. Then he'd offered her a boon by retracting his death sentence for Hendrik and agreeing to have the man banished instead. 'Twas no small give for Kallum MacNeill to alter his position, and she could not get the act out of her mind.

Now that she had gotten over her initial anger at his meddling, she understood 'twas not meddling he'd been about. He'd promised her earlier all he wanted was to protect her. Whether or not she agreed with his tactics in handling the matter, she understood his bravado emanated from a protector's spirit.

The man was a natural guardian of those unable to stand for themselves. His secret life as the Shepherd proved so much about what was truly in his heart, in his soul. That he would fight one of his own clan over her said much about what had not actually been said between them. She needed to find him.

She creeped down the hallway belowstairs toward the back entrance. Though the men had finished sparring some time ago, she dared not chance that some might linger in the courtyard. She wanted not to encounter anyone but Kallum at this time. After Caitrin checked Kallum's room to make sure he had not returned inside, she had shared he oft went to the falls after evening maneuvers to be alone or sometimes to think. She suggested Ailsa look for him where he had thrown her in the water.

The sky had darkened. Ailsa stood outside the back door and allowed her eyes to adjust to the contrast of the dimness after the candlelight of the manor hallways. She had initially been concerned to travel to the inlet this late, but Caitrin had assured her that, by now, the entire keep had heard what had transpired at supper and understood Kallum to be her champion. To Caitrin's thinking, only a foolish man with a death wish would dare even approach Ailsa from this day forward. She hoped Caitrin was right.

With the aid of the rising moon, she could see well enough to find her way to the inlet where the small falls fell. She walked that way, slightly apprehensive about whether Kallum still harbored irritation over her uncooperative behavior earlier and would find her intrusion on his solitude insufferable. When she cleared the trees that led to the boulder upon which she had her screaming fit, she stopped in awe. The sight that greeted her made her flame from the soles of her feet to the heated blush of her cheeks.

Kallum stood beneath the waterfall, the ledge a short height above his head. The water fell from the overhead stream in a steady, middling flow, its rush not having been fed recently due to the dearth of rain. The gentle flow left the water clear as it trickled down over

Kallum's head and allowed her to see him fully and completely. He stood with his back to her, his tall, sinewed form completely naked from head to toe.

His hair was down. He stood with arms spread wide and palms pressed flat against the wall of rocks that backed the falls, one of his beaded hair cords secured around his wrist. His head was bowed in silent contemplation. The cascade of water poured over his hair and skin, dampening his locs and spilling over his broad shoulders.

She watched, tantalized by the liquid dripping over the muscles of his back, past the delectable dimples above the sculpted curves of his buttocks to rush down the backs of his thighs. He shimmered in moonlit wetness like a mystical being come to life, a nude god emerged from nature's richness. Her hands itched to touch all that water-kissed virility, to stroke over where his backside swelled into thick thighs and solid calves. To allow her fingers to glide over every centimeter of damp skin and muscular goodness would be her greatest living fantasy.

Her breathing quickened, and the feel of her underdress against her roused nipples became almost unbearable. She longed to shed the cloth barriers to the cool night air she desperately needed against her skin to counter the hot longing that made her breasts heavy and her womanhood throb.

While she stood there silently committing to memory the beautiful sight made by a naked Kallum, his fingers against the rocks suddenly bunched. A tenseness invaded his shoulders, and slowly, he lifted his head. She watched the excess water flow through his soaked locs and weave a jagged path down the blades between his shoulders, then over and through the planes of the firmly rounded globes of his arse.

A tremor rushed through her. She had not moved nor made a sound, but she was certain he'd sensed her presence.

CHAPTER TWENTY-THREE

Ailsa's heart began to pound. Propriety dictated she flee and not be caught ogling a man's nakedness, but a want paralyzed her. She stood immobile, unable to breathe, barely able to think.

With an unhurried turn of his head, Kallum glanced over his shoulder. His gaze locked unerringly on hers. No hesitation. No searching required. He'd known right where she stood.

From this distance, she felt, more than saw, the intensity of his gaze. Everything in her responded to the silent hunger that pulsed between them. Propriety, properness, even self-preservation dissipated into nothingness.

She took a step toward him, and he dropped one hand from the wall. He half turned, his front knee bent in a manner that flaunted a bold, masculine stance. With his body only half facing her, his manhood hid behind a solid thigh. Hit instantaneously with a consuming desire, Ailsa wanted nothing more in life than the full view, the full Kallum.

She took another step and pulled at the crisscrossed laces of her overdress. Each step she took became more deliberate, but she rushed not. The ties loosened, and she slipped her arms from the dress's sleeves. She let the garment fall to the ground and stepped out of the abandoned folds. Next came the belt that attached to her hips the dagger he had gifted her. With no thought as to the value of the blade, she allowed the prize to drop to her feet and kept walking.

When her hands went to the lone tie at the neck of her loose, white underdress, Kallum's eyes tracked their promissory movement. She stopped and pulled the loosened top from her shoulders. Removing her arms, she pressed the front to her breasts and let the rest pool languidly around her hips and buttocks.

She was close to him now. No more than a few meters away. This angle brought a glimpse of the semi-stiffened arousal between his legs and the shallow, panted breaths that made his chest rise and fall with near as much labor as hers.

Her feet stopped moving; nervousness threatened.

He turned fully, disengaged his other hand from the wall of the falls, and offered her a complete view of all that made him male. Ailsa slowly took in the strong jaw, the low beard, the full lips that promised pleasure beyond a kiss. She allowed her eyes to roam lower, across the damp hair on his chest, down the planed ridges of his abdomen, and lower still.

His manhood stood at full arousal now. Thick, long, and curved toward the sky, his staff jutted from a dark thatch of hair growing between his thighs. The thought of what he would do with that once she offered herself to him made her shiver. 'Twas a shiver more of anticipation than fear, but a bit of the looming trepidation factored in.

Kallum did not move. He stood, half out of the falls with water pouring down his back, and watched her with hooded eyes. His gaze slipped once more to the hands she had clasped tightly to the fabric hiding her breasts, then lifted back to hers. His sable eyes called to her, though he said not a word. Within those eyes, she found courage; she found strength.

With a deep inhalation, she released the dress and let it fall in a billowed cloud around her ankles. Bare to his gaze, she could not bring herself to advance. Her breath stopped coming. Her inexperience made her uncertain. She knew Kallum would not hurt her intentionally, but the sheer size of him seemed to make what she knew of loving a mite challenging.

He must have sensed the misgivings rising within her, for he raised his hand palm up to bid her come to him. The simple gesture broke her hesitancy, shattered whatever doubts she had. If she never laid with a man again, she would have the memory of this one moonlit interlude with the MacNeill, and she could not allow herself to not be brave this time where her desires for him were concerned.

She stepped out of her slippers and forward from the pile around her feet, then lifted her hand to place it in his. His fingers grasped her fingertips, and he lifted them to place an extended kiss on her knuckles. He eased backward into the full flow of the falls and pulled her beneath the water's cascade.

As the water drenched her face and poured over her head down the loose braid at her back, both his hands rose until his thumbs bracketed her ears. His big hands wrapped around the back of her neck, and he tilted her face up, brushing away the damp tendrils that plastered over her eyes and temples. The awe in his eyes made her feel like the most treasured lass in all of Scotland.

"Ailsa," he breathed. "You are beyond beautiful. And you are mine forever." His deep voice caressed her woman's vanity as well as her ears, and then he dropped his lips to hers.

The sensation of the water flowing over her skin and the dance of his tongue inside her mouth lulled Ailsa into a hazy state of wonder that made her hum aloud. His mouth still dominating hers, his hands roamed down her shoulders, glided on wetness down her arms, and found her wrists. He wrapped his hands around each and raised her arms to place her hands flat against his chest, allowing her palms to feel the tickle of the soaked curly, dark hair that covered the center. When he released her wrists, his hands returned to her drenched body.

He traced the sides of her waist through the water droplets down to the curves of her hips, then slid them over her wet skin to the mounds of her buttocks. He caressed them gently at first until the act seemed to undermine his control. With a groan Ailsa wasn't quite sure was of pleasure or frustration, Kallum pulled her hips flush against him, his full arousal hard against her belly.

The hands at her butt kneaded and stroked. With each massage of his fingers, her belly rubbed against his firm manhood, and a tingle started deep in the apex of her thighs. Pleasure assaulted Ailsa from the front and the back.

Kallum trailed fingers up her spine, gently tracing the knobs on the ascent. The gentle caress made her bow under his touch and caused her nipples to graze against the dusting of hair on his chest. The sensation rocked her and unleashed a feral desire to feel more of him. Her curious hands explored up to his shoulders. The glide of her palms on hard muscles and the liquid-induced silkiness of his skin pulled a whimper from some deep chasm of longing she'd not known existed within her.

In tune with her growing desire, Kallum brought his hand around her front to a breast, and his thumb flicked over its peaked, hair-sensitized bud. Ailsa trembled. This time, the tremble was all pleasure. Kallum noticed her reaction and flicked her tight bud again. Her hands flew to his biceps and grasped tightly. She felt dangerously close to collapsing at his feet. The intensity of the sensation that shot from her nipple to her woman's center near undid her. She called out in sensuous surprise, something wonderful and unnerving just out of her reach.

"Ah, lass," he breathed in that rich, deep voice she loved. "Are you that close? And here I thought 'twas only I who would enter into this without control." He ran his hand down her stomach and caressed over the spring of curls that narrowed down to a vee at her center.

"Spread your legs for me, *leannan*." His enthralling, honey-covered gravel of a voice floated over her and added to the headiness of the illicit words he uttered.

Ailsa looked questioningly into his eyes, feeling scandalous and needy at the same time.

"Let me take you over, lass. If you reach your woman's pleasure soon after I enter you, I will not last long enough for either of us to experience the true wonder of our coupling."

Not quite certain what he meant by take her over, Ailsa spread her legs nonetheless, completely understanding what he meant by her woman's pleasure. The naughty girls in the village talked about the intense pleasure a woman could feel when a man was talented at the loving act. She'd always been intrigued but had not had the audacity to touch herself, as others had, to try and find out about this mysterious sensation.

Here, with Kallum, was her opportunity to finally experience the mystery firsthand.

"Aye, lass, just like that." He slid his middle finger through her curls, damp without from the flow of the falls and within from her spiraling passions.

Her mouth opened on a keening cry when he circled her central nub, and he took advantage to tongue deep into her mouth while simultaneously sliding his finger inside her. Ailsa nearly shattered from the intense pleasure that pulsed from her center into her shivering thighs. Something mystical and looming hovered beyond the tendrils of pleasure shooting deep inside her. Kallum's finger ministrations brought the elusive sensation closer and closer.

"*Kallum…*"

"I'm here, lass. Tell me what you need."

"I know not. It feels…it feels…like I'm about to burst apart."

"Then let yourself burst, my goddess. 'Twill feel unlike any pleasure you've ever known."

He slid a second finger inside her and adjusted her sideways so he could shelter one of her legs between his thighs and spread her other wider with the outside of his foot against the inside of hers. He pressed deep and twisted his fingers wickedly inside her and again on the way out.

Her head fell back, and water splashed against her breasts as she cried out. He kept her from collapsing with a strong arm tight across her back and repeated the finger play. He watched her face closely the entire time. She closed her eyes, feeling exposed and vulnerable and foolishly like the novice she was.

His fingers stilled inside her. "Open your eyes, *leannan*. Don't hide from me. Let me see the pleasure I give you."

Her teeth gripped her bottom lip, and she opened her eyes.

"Keep your eyes on me the entire time, lass. I'll not lead you astray."

He pulled her side tighter into him and slowly began to handstroke her again. He added his thumb to the sensuous torture by finding her central nub again and rubbing with the flat of it. Ailsa's insides began to quiver. Her hips took on movement of their own accord, seeking his fingers when they would retreat and adding a swivel when his thumb hit that glorious spot that made her want to scream in ecstasy.

"That's it, my sweet. Move thus until what's coming can't be held back anymore."

When the rapture hit, Ailsa felt as if her body had been thrown without warning off a high cliff and shattered into tiny pieces during the fall. She no longer had to wonder what Kallum had meant by take her over. She trembled against him, her inner core pulsing against the fingers he moved gently inside her to allow her to recover from *la petite mort*, as the poets sometimes referred to it. And she did indeed feel as if she'd just died a little, in the most wonderous way.

When she returned to herself, Kallum extracted his fingers and dropped his lips to her dripping neck. He tasted and licked, all the while pressing her abdomen tight enough against him to rub his manhood in minute strokes against her damp skin. The constant flow of the water that poured down on them, his touch, the stroke of his arousal all combined into a sensory overload that made Ailsa want to melt into this man and never emerge.

"I can wait no longer, my sweet. I need to be inside you. Tell me you are sure you want to give yourself fully to me." He lifted his head and gave her a seductive tilt of his lips. "I'll not have you come after me in the morn with the dagger I gifted you."

She smiled at his jest and lifted her hand to his jaw. She rubbed, thrilled by the difference in feel caused by the beard's dampness. "I am yours to do with as you wish, warrior. Promise me just one thing."

"Anything, my goddess." He planted a kiss on the palm at his jaw.

She sighed, the gesture near melting her heart, and said softly, "You cannot spill your seed inside me."

* * *

Kallum lifted his head and searched Ailsa's face for uncertainty. Was this her veiled way of telling him she did not want to fully consummate their liaison? Her eyes were glazed and half-lidded but, from what he saw, held no doubts. She wanted him as much as he her. She was asking only that he take precaution.

He understood the why behind the request. *No bastards.*

They had both lived the lives that such travails and stigma entailed, and neither wanted to flaunt the risk of passing on such a way of life.

"Aye, my sweet, I understand." For the honor of experiencing her carnal pleasures, agreeing to be careful with his seed was no hardship.

The smile she gave him was glorious.

Humbled that she trusted him enough to voice her wish and even more so that she had no doubt he would comply, his heart cracked open, and he allowed himself to feel all the laird had warned him he could not fight. Though he could not express in words the unfamiliar sentiments budding inside him, he could show her with his hands, with his mouth, and with the pleasure he'd unleash in her once he was embedded deep inside her warm center.

He fused their lips once more, licking along the outer edges of hers afore sliding his tongue in for another taste. He lingered, bemused to realize kissing her was more satisfying than a full tup with any other woman. Remembering the luscious breasts that were so sensitive to his touch she near found her woman's pleasure from his caress alone, he abandoned her mouth to take one dewy nipple into his mouth.

He suckled her, pulling on the bead with his lips and tongue until she whimpered in ecstasy. He replaced his mouth with a hand and slid his lips across the valley between her plump *cìochan* until he reached the other peaked bud. Sucking deep, he swirled his tongue until she pebbled and her passion-induced mewls rippled from her mouth down through his aching loins.

The intense urge to lay her down pulled at him, but he could not here on the uncomfortable rocks, and she would get covered in mud should they return wet to the embankment. Lifting his head, he burrowed kisses into her neck while his mind searched the area for another alternative.

"Turn around, lass." Despite the confused look on

her face, he turned her. "Trust me."

He shifted her to the falls' edge, where the shallower water and elevated ridge allowed her to stand several meters taller, convenient for how he aimed to take her. Several large boulders laid stacked at the corner where the bank ended and the falls' flow began. He pressed himself against her back and reached for her wrists again. Tilting her over with the press of his own torso, Kallum placed her hands against the soaked rocks that rose as high as her waist. Her body canted forward, and he nestled his stiffened length against the line of her buttocks and rubbed.

The urge to slide immediately within her tempting heat was strong, but he held off. Instead, he placed a hand against her belly. His other hand cupped beneath her chin where it joined with her neck, and he placed his lips close to her ear.

In a throaty whisper, he let her know, "I aim to take you from behind, lass. Tell me now if this unnerves you."

She shook her head, her braid swishing in the flow of water down her back, and reached behind her to rub along the front of his thigh. The sensuous caress made his cods throb, and he could wait no longer. Moving the hand against her belly lower until his last two fingers rested against her nest of tight curls, he kissed beneath her ear and placed himself against the entrance hidden between her thighs.

He fought himself for control and patience. He'd seen the concerned look in her eyes upon viewing his full endowment. He knew she would expand to accommodate him, but carelessness or haste on his part could cause her much discomfort in the process.

Her first release had left her nearly ready for him, but he moved his little finger back to the centralized point of pleasure beneath her woman's curls and teased the swollen nub until Ailsa began to writhe hungrily in search of satisfaction. He added a second finger to his external ministrations and simultaneously pressed the tip of him inside her moist sheath. Her inner walls pulsed in search of their second release, and the half moan, half growl that escaped him at the feel of that intimate, tugging grip likely scared the nocturnal beasts wandering about the wooded inlet. But suppress it he could not.

Not since he was a lad with his first woman had Kallum felt the urge to spill so soon upon entering a female, and he was not yet fully seated. The falls continued to douse them, the petite hand against his thigh flexed, and control began to slip away. When Ailsa released a moan of her own, the sound caused his cods to tighten and a tension to settle in his lower back.

A sense of urgency overtook him. He adjusted his hand between her thighs to make shallow circles and pulled out slightly only to stroke back inside by the same amount. His hips pumped in a slow and gentle but persistent undulation that deepened each stroke by measured amounts. All the while, he nibbled along her neck. The sweet tang of the seed oil she used on her hair mixed with the enthralling scent of her unadorned, damp skin to entice him beyond the moment to another plane of awareness. A plane in which only the two of them existed.

Ailsa cried out as her second completion gripped her. Additional wetness flooded his partially embedded tumescence, and Kallum bent his knees to ease fully inside. The deep stroke made his buttocks tighten and Ailsa release a startled gasp of part shock and possibly part rapture. The exquisite clasp of her fluttering tightness around his *stauner* forced Kallum to fight against the onrush of a disastrous early completion. He took several slow, deep breaths. Once he'd beaten back the near rapid end to the greatest eve of his life, he covered her completely, one arm circled beneath her breasts and the other low across her abdomen.

Not sure whether her emoting had been of pain or pleasure, Kallum asked against her ear, "Okay, my sweet?"

She nodded silently.

"Ailsa, I'll not move until you tell me you are all right."

"Move," she ordered in the faintest whisper.

Unsure of the directive, Kallum squeezed her tightly. "What? Are you—"

"*Move*," she said more forcefully. "Kallum, please, I need you to move."

A shiver ran through him at her plea. The longing, the lust in her voice washed away all hesitancy, and he began to move. He pumped with controlled ease but steadily increasing force. The more sounds she made, the more his hips worked and the more his cods threatened to spill, but he fought off the traitorous untimely release for the second time.

The rush of the falls echoed around them, and beneath the splash of the water, Ailsa caught his rhythm and pushed back with his every drive forward. He levered up, both hands grasped firmly to her waist, and added his strength to each of her backward presses. Their syncopation quickly blended and made them each frantic with overwhelming need. Ailsa's sounds of enjoyment grew louder, and Kallum clamped a hand over her mouth, pulling her slightly upright.

Sound carried over water. Unsure whether the din of the falls was enough to cover the sound, he dared not allow her cries full rein. Though 'twas late and no one should be about, he wanted not to rouse any possible interlopers. To squelch his own emoting, he buried his face in her neck and prayed for her to find her woman's pleasure again soon. Her passionate responses and active hip movements made it near impossible for him to hold back any longer, but he'd not let go afore he'd gotten her to another shattering of her own.

Once again, he slid his smallest finger lower to caress her budded nub and began to rub in tandem with his deep strokes. In her ear, he crooned naughty words of encouragement until he felt her insides seize around him. He rode the rapture of her squeezing flesh until he could resist no more and pulled himself from her with a tight grip at the base of his rigid rod. His seed shot in forceful bursts along her lower back, and he clenched his teeth to hold back a mighty roar. He let the spattering of the falls rinse away the evidence of his ecstasy, while he held fast to Ailsa to prevent her from collapsing against the drenched rocks.

Once the grip of release loosened, he kissed Ailsa reverently on the side of her neck and hugged her tightly from behind. Her head lolled back to rest beneath his shoulder. They stood thus, bathed by the continued spill of the falls. Neither spoke. Kallum was not sure he could. What he had experienced was unlike any coupling he'd ever had, and the extent of his release was unnerving in its intensity.

He could not believe he had ever been so foolish as to think all women were the same. Ailsa was nothing like any woman he'd ever met. Weakness did not define her. No constant drama of a damsel needing rescue or set on coy manipulations were part of who she was. That she stood her ground in disagreements with him and did not hold back with her opinions had vexed him to no end upon first meeting her. Now, all her blare and bravado filled him with an insatiable need to claim her fierceness for himself. And after what they'd just experienced together, he did not see how he could ever want to be free of her.

He would never be able to let her go. He understood that now.

The search to unearth the Connery villainy that led to her demise at the castle was convenient for his current purpose: keep her with him as long as possible. Yet, once the mystery was solved, even that would not be enough for him to willingly accept a surrender of the lass to her home clan.

He lifted Ailsa and sat upon the rock he'd used to brace her while he covered her. He adjusted so they were out of the path of the water, and she snuggled into his chest. He could feel her begin to shiver now that they no longer made their own heat with their active coupling. He needed to retrieve the lass a covering, but first he wanted a closer look at raised impressions he'd felt along her back but had been too preoccupied to focus on.

She flinched when he ran his fingertips over a raised scar on her back, pulling away from him with a look that revealed she'd forgotten about the marks she bore when consumed by her passions.

He tried to keep her close, but she stood and faced him so he could not see her back.

"Ailsa, turn back around."

"Nay, Kallum. 'Tis naught."

"Good. Then should be naught to show me." He waited, but she did not comply.

He reached out and took both her hands in his, pulling her to stand between his spread thighs. He could see pebbles of chill form along her arms, so he stretched to retrieve the great plaid he had abandoned afore he began to rinse himself in the falls. He shook it out, wrapped it around her, then regathered her hands in his.

"So, my scars disgust you?"

Her head jerked back. "Of course not."

"But I have many. You touched but a few of them that day in the clearing." His slashed brow rose. "Were those touches steeped in aversion? For 'twas not dislike I remember on your face."

"That is different."

"Different how?"

"I am a woman. 'Tis different for a warrior. A woman should not have scars."

He chuckled. "And what if that warrior is a woman?"

"What?" She moved to reclaim her hands.

He held tight.

"Do not jest with me, Kallum MacNeill."

He grinned, only now realizing how much he loved to hear her say his name. "There are some, you know. Mayhap not many, but enough that 'tis not a foolish consideration. And what of the Irish pirate queen who raids ships along the coast of Ireland and Scotland to liberate their cargo, setting many of our people free in the process without want of payment or reward?"

Ailsa had heard tales of the pirate queen, but she'd never have the audacity to compare herself with the woman's impressive escapades.

"Do you remember what I said to you upon our first reaching MacNeill keep?"

She made a twisted face. "Um…don't tell anyone I am a Connery?"

He swatted the side of her buttocks for the smart comment. "Nay. When I told you that you are a warrior. You just do not realize it yet."

He placed his hands on her waist and turned her. Pushing down his plaid, he traced a finger down several raised scars that looked to be the result of a flogging.

"Your punishment?"

She nodded.

He said nothing in response. His words would be but empty salves to an atrocity he could not undo. "You are all the more beautiful to me because of your battle scars. Never be ashamed of them. They helped make you the fierce lass that you are and…" His voice trailed off, and he became quiet.

She looked over her shoulder to search his face. "And what?"

He looked down, pondering whether to speak true. Finally, he glanced up and pulled her close enough to press a soft kiss to her lips. "And were it not for all you went through to be burdened with them, I would never have known you."

Her eyes watered.

"Don't cry, lass. I know you would rather have not had to endure the enslavement, the failed escapes, the floggings, the cocky Shepherd who interrupted your reunion with your kin."

She chuckled softly at his reference to himself, tracing her hand lightly through the hair on his chest. "I'm not so sure that is true."

Their eyes met. What he saw in hers, he dared not hope mirrored what he felt.

"I, too, can no longer imagine never having met you, Kallum." She curved her hand to his jaw with a reverent look. "All I thought about for three years, three endlessly long years, was leaving my horrid lot at Stirling Castle. But it brought me here to you, and I am beginning to wonder why."

He tensed at the reminder her words sparked. Their tribal ancestors did not believe in coincidence. Destiny got its way, with or without your cooperation. He could not help but feel that fate was fast closing in on them.

CHAPTER TWENTY-FOUR

In the early morn, Kallum laid in bed with Ailsa in his arms. He had escorted her back to the cottage and could not resist another chance to pleasure them both. He'd shown her what it felt like to have the rough of the beard she liked so much rub against the insides of her thighs and his kiss deep in her woman's center. The sounds of her ecstatic cries still played in his ears.

He smiled. She was rather vocal in her pleasure, and he found he liked it.

He'd been careful not to spill his seed inside her each time they coupled, which amounted to three more times throughout the moon's glow. The lass was completely worn out. Even for him, his appetite through the night had been insatiable. But dawn approached, which made him restless. He still needed to take Ailsa to an audience with the laird. Whatever announcement the man had for the lass had yet to be made.

His fingers played lightly over her arms as he watched her sleep. He needed to find a way to leave the cottage discreetly. He should probably rise even now and leave afore the dawn broke, but he was loath to slink away into the dark morn. He preferred to awake—or for her to awaken—in his arms. He would address the matter with her after sunrise. For now, he was too tempted to watch and to touch.

The loose hairs at her temples had blossomed into bushy curls as they dried. The look was adorable on her. He tweaked one, letting the springy curl accordion back into place.

She shifted in his arms, then snuggled closer. Lying with her like this every night would be any man's dream life. His hands continued to play in her hair while he contemplated what it meant that he wanted her to stay and she wanted but to leave.

When next he looked down at her, her eyes were open. She watched his face but said naught.

He dropped a kiss to her forehead. "Hullo, *leannan*."

"Hullo." She stretched her arms over her head and elongated her legs to stretch through her feet. Snuggling back against him, she said, "You seem troubled. Is aught amiss?"

"No troubles, my sweet. I'm just contemplating that I should have left afore dawn arose." He glanced toward the light seeping under the window coverings. "I have put you in an indiscreet situation."

To his surprise, she showed no distress. Her face remained in relaxed contentment, and her hand played lightly in the hair on his chest. "Unlikely. Many think poorly of me as it is. Others already assume we have had a tup or two. Why else would a warrior such as you champion a poor, Moor wench like me?"

The frown he leveled at her made her chuckle.

"Don't look at me thus. Those are not my words. I'm only passing on what others say and whisper. Some not even pretending they want me not to hear."

"Did you have it so much better at Connery keep after your *mamaidh* passed?"

Her head bobbed toward her shoulder, which lifted in a half shrug. "Not so bad as this, nay. Though even in my clan there were those who preferred not to seek my services as a healer."

"Without siblings or other blood family, that must have been lonely at times."

Her hand stopped moving, and she thought about his statement afore she replied. "Aye. I often thought about what life would have been like had I known my father and had a brother or sister or two, but 'twas not to be."

She *hmm*ed a little to herself.

"What?"

She shared with him her habit of searching out people with eyes the same hue as those she had inherited from her father and wondering if they could be related to her. The game had started as a way to entertain herself and eventually changed into a reminder that her father had abandoned her to create another family.

"I eventually stopped looking. The pain became too great." Sadness seeped through her voice.

"Ah, lass, I am sorry." With a fist beneath her chin, he tilted up her head and placed a soft but thorough kiss upon her lips. "I would spare you that pain if I could."

Her hand rose to his face. "But we both know 'tis not possible. I am alone and have but myself to count on." She rubbed gently across his beard afore returning her hand to his chest. "'Tis why I've always aspired to rise to lead clan healer, which would guarantee me quarters within the keep walls and consistent patrons of my services. That way, I could live independently without the innuendo and dangers a young single-woman would otherwise face."

"You have never wanted to be matched for marriage?"

"So that everything I own would fall under the control of my husband, and I would be subject to censor if I failed to follow his every order?" She gave him a look of mock horror. "Nay, I can do without that kind of life. Again."

"Again?"

"Aye. I just escaped an existence that required I follow the orders of others and have no free will or possessions of my own. Though marriage is not the same, 'tis close enough."

He frowned, not liking the comparison. "Not all men would treat a woman as naught but property or not allow her to control coin of her own." He heard himself say the words but could not believe he was defending a way of life he had always avoided.

She laughed mirthlessly. "Why are you so quick to defend potential husbands? Caitrin told me of your commitment to never marry. So why your concern that I would do the same?"

"'Tis not concern that you make such a choice. 'Tis simply I would think a man who met a woman as fierce and willful as you would be loath to change her. 'Twould be a tragedy."

He was not used to women who were not either afraid of him or completely infatuated with him or mayhap a bit of both. Getting to know Ailsa had been a unique—and challenging—experience for him.

"Careful, MacNeill, or I might think you are offering for my hand." As she climbed atop him, her eyes sparkled with a familiar mischief that gave away her jest. She straddled him. Only the tangled bed linen separated her bottom and his lap. "And how foolish would that be?"

She grinned down at him. The smile and the glorious view of her lush breasts made his semi-erect staff twitch beneath her.

Her eyes widened. "You cannot possibly want to go again." Shaking her head playfully, she gave him a wistful look. "I don't think my body can take any more, MacNeill."

He placed his hands in the crux where her legs met her torso and slid her backward onto his thighs, moving the bed cloth with her. "Aye, but you can handle me in other ways."

Her curious expression made his cock twitch again. This time, her eyes watched its movement. Her gaze on him increased his arousal and caused most of his blood to rush to his loins, which made his staff fully rise and stiffen.

"Ailsa," he said in a gruff voice, "put your hands on me."

She glanced at his face, and whatever she saw there caused a naughty glint to enter her eyes. She reached forward and stacked one hand over the other around his now full *stauner*.

Just the touch of her hands nearly sent him over. His eyes closed, and a groan of bliss escaped him. Her hands squeezed with curious exploration. Without having to be told, she moved her hands up and down when his hips began to pump. The pleasure took him quickly to a place beyond control.

He grasped her hands beneath his to slow her movements.

"Not right?"

"Too right," he growled between gritted teeth. "But I want not to release yet. Slowly, my sweet. Slowly."

He showed her the way of it. Once she got the gist of the pressure and rhythm he liked, he released her hands and allowed himself to revel in the thrill of her touch. When he finally gave over to his release, he grabbed the bed linen and covered himself to catch the spill of his seed, having used all the bath sheets during the night.

Sated and lazy after their play, Kallum gathered Ailsa in his arms, content to be alone in their cozy domain. The morn advanced outside, and he fast felt the world pressing in on them. They would have to leave the cottage soon and face the laird.

For now, he held his goddess close and contemplated how he'd get to keep her, and whether he'd have to fight his own clan as well as the Connerys to make it happen.

• • •

After sunrise, Ailsa stood in the manor library, watching a furious Kallum pace before the laird's huge desk. Inan, too, was present, but he remained silent.

The laird focused on his angry nephew. "Kallum, calm yourself."

Kallum whirled to face him. "Calm myself? You have set the lass assuredly back into captivity. How could you have advised the king that she was here? 'Tis a betrayal!"

The laird shook his head. "Nay. Think on it, lad. The lass could not very well spend the remainder of her life wondering each day if 'twould be the one day the king or his regiment came to haul her back to Stirling. 'Tis no way for a person to live."

Ailsa knew the laird was right, but she could not shake the ominous feelings that had risen within her at learning Laird Aymer had sent a missive to the king about her presence at MacNeill keep.

"I have advised the monarch that the lass is Highland born and under my protection. He comes to see for himself."

"He comes with his army, no doubt." Kallum's voice was snide.

The laird sighed. "Aye, I imagine so. But we have faced the king's might in the past over issues important to our kind. We will handle this, too. You must trust me in this, lad. 'Tis a matter of diplomacy that must be played right."

Kallum continued to pace. "The king will not likely be persuaded Ailsa is other than his property to retrieve, and with the might of his army behind him, he need not even pretend to be discerning in this matter."

"His discernment will not matter. In this, he has not the advantage." 'Twas Inan who finally spoke.

Kallum glanced at his cousin. "How figure you that?"

"'Tis simple." Inan's grunt of dismissal was ever confident. "He will face us on our lands this time, not his. Moreover, we will know when he approaches. *Da* has tasked me to ride out to meet his contingent when they are about a day's ride away."

Kallum's cousin pushed off the wall he'd been leaning against and walked over to stand in front of him. "And finally, he will face an army trained by the greatest commander in all the Highlands, a warrior who fights the fiercest battle when faced with protection of his people and matters of honor. I dare think any opposer who faces an army led by a Kallum MacNeill who fights for *more* than even his people or honor" — Inan's gaze flicked briefly to Ailsa, and then he placed a hand on Kallum's shoulder — "shall fight a losing battle. We must see this through. The missive cannot be undone."

Kallum looked at the laird, then at Ailsa, afore his eyes settled back on his cousin's. "Pretty words, Inan. As 'the greatest commander in all the Highlands,' I would think I warranted a consult afore such actions were taken." He shook off Inan's hand. "The missive should never have been sent."

Without another word or a backward glance, Kallum stormed from the library. The anger and feelings of betrayal he felt near seeped from his skin.

Inan shook his head and looked with concern to his father. "He may not forgive you this for a long while."

"Aye, I know it, but the matter could not be helped." The laird turned toward Ailsa. "Know, lass, my thought was only of what's best for both you and Kallum. You cannot look behind you every step of your life, and he cannot stand as your champion against the king alone. We must elevate the matter to more than a lost servant. We —"

"Escaped slave," she interrupted.

The laird frowned at the seeming contradiction from her first day of arrival.

"When it comes to my relationship with the king, I *escaped* from enslavement. Thus, I am considered by him an escaped *slave*, not a 'lost servant.' There is a difference," she clarified.

Laird Aymer set his jaw and nodded, understanding her distinction between the perspective of an enslaver versus those enslaved. He acknowledged gravely, "Aye, you are right, and we must speak the truth rather than coat unpleasantries with honey." He stepped to stand in front of her. "You are a discerning lass. I hope you understand that lest I elevate our stance from a matter of his escaped *slave* to a matter of politics set to impress Highlanders into permanent bondage, we have not a chance to outwit the king's advisors and get the monarch to see this as another attack on the autonomy of the Highland way of life."

She did understand, but that did not mean she had no concerns that the ploy would not work. "I believe you did what you thought best for your people. I cannot fault you that, but you should know that does not take away my worry for what will become of me." Her hand twisted into her skirt. "How soon, then?"

The laird's brows bunched in confusion.

"How long do I have afore the king arrives?"

Laird Aymer retrieved a parchment bearing a broken royal seal from his desk. "This response arrived only yesterday. If he left shortly after it was sent, he should arrive within a few days' time. A sennight at the most."

Her hand rubbed at the creases she'd unwittingly created in her skirt, and she tried to process that she had mayhap five—or at most seven—days until her fate would be decided. "I understand. I will speak with Kallum. I am sure I can make him understand as well."

She moved to exit, but Inan stepped in front of her.

"Now is not a good time for that discussion," he warned. "'Tis best to let Kallum go when he gets like this. He's not fit to be around."

"'Tis best for me to go speak with him. 'Tis me he is

concerned for, so 'tis only me who can put his mind at ease. Step aside, Inan."

When he did not move, she proceeded to go around him.

He gently grabbed her arm. "Not even I face down Kallum when he is thus."

She snatched her arm from his grasp. "Then 'tis fortunate for me I am not you."

She went in search of her angry warrior and found him at their clearing, sword in each hand, fighting unseen demons. The blades crossed and slashed through the air in an elegant flurry that looked more like an exotic dance than the practice of battle moves. He spun and lunged forward, right knee bent, and thrust the two blades in a stabbing motion that made them cross one over the other to form an X that would have speared two men at once had there been any men present to fight.

In his stance, he saw her and straightened. The metallic hiss of steel caressing steel floated to her ears as he separated the swords. He slid them both into the special double sheath on his back, the one he'd worn during their liberation trek. She'd not seen him wear it since they reached his clan's lands.

He gathered in several deep breaths afore speaking in a honey-edged baritone on the cusp of control. "You should not have come. I need time to think."

Ailsa walked to him. "I *should* have come. For what you think on is what will become of me."

She moved to put her arms around him, but he took a step back.

"Not now, Ailsa. I am not fit for your company." The tightness of his tone revealed his lingering anger and the frustration that laced it.

"Aye, now." She followed his continued steps backward. "Be still, warrior, for I will not go away."

His head fell back, and she felt his frustration pulse and rise. Partly due to the situation they faced with the king, and partly, she suspected, because once again she had failed to heed his instructions. She smiled a little at the thought but did not let it fully blossom. She was here to reduce his stress, not antagonize him.

She placed her hands at his waist, her thumbs braced against the sides of his firm abdomen, and pushed him backward until he sat on a huge boulder not far from the edge of the falls. She stepped between his thighs. When she placed her hands on his shoulders, he let his head fall forward until his forehead rested against her bosom.

She held him thus, saying nothing, simply allowing him to feel whatever emotions he battled. Her hands went to his hair, brushing over the top of his head until she reached the gathered strands tied at his nape. She fingered the individual strands, relishing in the ability to freely touch his locs—to touch *him*.

His hands found their way to her waist. He pulled her closer and eventually wrapped his arms around her. She was no longer sure who was holding whom, who comforted whom, but they rested thus in quiet commune. He held on, and she petted tenderly, quieting the tension in him.

Slowly, her hands found their way to the corded tie that bound his twisted locs from her full appreciation. She wanted to remove it but could not fathom how the bead and leather cord worked together to slip on and off as easily as he made it look.

He glanced up, a question in his eyes.

"How do you take this on and off so easily?"

He tilted his head sideways, and slowly, so she could see his movements, he used his thumb and forefinger to slide one side of the leather partly through the bead so the tie loosened from his hair. He slid it off and offered it to her.

She tried to slide it on her wrist, but the circle was too small. "I don't understand. If it fits on your wrist, how does it not fit on mine?"

With a patient upward tilt of his lips, he adjusted the tie wider, slid it on her wrist, and pulled the loose ends of the cord until the whole fit snugly around her wrist. Upon closer inspection, Ailsa noticed that this bead was actually a small shell that rested on an interesting knot that allowed the cord to slide through its hole, one way to tighten and the other way to loosen.

She smiled fully once it was in place.

"What are you planning to do with that?" he asked.

She slid her arms across the tops of his shoulders, pushed her hands in the full fall of hair at the back of his head, and graced his lips with a slow, deep kiss. When she broke off, her voice whispered, "I plan to keep it. When I must leave, I shall have something to remember you always."

His eyes darkened at her mention of leaving. She understood—and felt—the low spirits that came with the thought of their parting, but she would not dwell on them. While they still had time, she would enjoy being with him.

"We still have a week." She hoped. Grabbing his hand, she pulled him up. "Come."

He did not resist. "Where are we going?"

"You are going to give me my first swimming lesson." She flashed him a suggestive grin. "Then we are going back to the cottage."

His lips rose simultaneously with his slashed brow to give him a look of racy skepticism. "You are not yet physically ready for more bed play."

Laughter bubbled up, and she allowed it to come. 'Twas true she had muscle aches and tenderness in places she'd never afore experienced them, but that did not mean she wanted to forego more of the euphoria she'd found in his arms. These pleasurable discomforts kept her mind off the tender bruises remaining on her neck from yesterday's encounter with Hendrik and reminded her that even here in the land of enemies, she had found some joy.

Ailsa skipped away from Kallum. "Ah, but did you not teach me this morn that we can do much together that does not require I take the full of you inside me?" She turned, skipping backward so she could see his face. "Unless, of course, you are not interested in more of my comforts."

With a growl low in his throat, he charged her, and she screeched as she attempted to avoid his grasp. She failed. He swung her off her feet and spun her around. In that moment, Ailsa could well imagine having this joy of being wanted, of belonging, to hold onto forever. Their time together no longer remained within their control. But mayhap within the pleasures of his touch and of her touching him, she could hold at bay the demons of doubt now taunting that her time of liberty may soon come to end.

She would wallow in the memories they would soon make in each other's arms and hold them always in her heart. She had to survive the swimming lesson first, and she felt almost as apprehensive about this spontaneous whim as she did about the king's impending arrival, but she knew Kallum would allow no harm to befall her in the water.

Besides, the fun would truly start after they left the water and headed back to the cottage.

CHAPTER TWENTY-FIVE

Ailsa's lack of proper swimming attire prevented them from doing more than working on her ability to float that first day, which she tried while wearing only her chemise. Given the time of day, Kallum was loath to allow her to swim for long in her undergarment, and the looming promise of more bed play did much to shorten his attention span.

On the second day and again this morn, they moved to a distant pool in a secluded cove. Kallum managed to show her how to tread water and conquer the basics of the swimming stroke, but she swam unclothed at Kallum's encouragement, and the swimming instruction quickly turned into more lessons in the ways in which a man could pleasure a woman...or a woman a man. She had no true complaints in that regard, for Kallum had patiently allowed her to experiment each day and let loose the curiosity inflamed by her un-shackled passions.

She'd been bold enough last night to take the lead in bed. The whole had led to an attempted—and tanta-lizingly successful—romp of loving with her on top. His long, thick shaft filled her so deeply from that position that the specters of his movements tingled within even now as she dozed in his arms.

He'd taken to staying with her until dawn. Stealing these moments with him held off—usually—the anx-iousness building within her as the king's arrival drew ever closer. One day soon, she could be ripped from her warrior's arms. He'd assured her he'd not let her return to enslavement, but against the king, that might not be an assurance he could uphold. So she laid here in his arms, half awake and half asleep, wondering if the morrow or mayhap the day next would bring about her recapture.

A loud booming knock at the door crashed into Ailsa's thoughts. She sat bolt upright, and her heart dropped. *Naaaay! Not yet.*

They could not come for her yet. She was not ready.

Kallum leapt naked from the bed and grabbed a sword.

The booming knock resumed. "Ailsa! Ailsa! Wake up." The voice was Caitrin's.

With a frantic gaze, Ailsa looked at Kallum. Upon hearing his cousin's voice, he'd reached for his kilt and now covered himself.

"Ailsa! Florie needs you. You must come quickly."

Ailsa threw on a chemise and rushed to the door. "Caitrin, what is it?"

"'Tis her son. He burns with fever. He's been thus for nigh on two days and does not improve. The clan healer is with her, but he has not been able to break Alby's fever. He speaks of the worse. Florie is beside herself. He'll not listen to her, and her husband is away, as is Inan. I looked for Kallum but did not find him in his room." Caitrin stepped into the cottage. "I don't know where—" Her eyes cut to the shadows where Kallum stood. "Oh."

With a searching expression, Caitrin glanced between Ailsa and Kallum, then at the rumpled bed linens. "*Oh*," she repeated with a knowing glint in her eyes.

Kallum seemed amused by his cousin's reaction and remained silent. Ailsa opted to ignore the irreverent chit's insinuating utterance, glad the lingering night left the cottage dark enough that the blush she fought was not visible. She rushed into her overdress and slippers, then grabbed a few small pouches from her stash of herbs.

With a hand to Caitrin's arm, she steered the lass out the door. "Come. Show me the way."

When they arrived at Florie's, the sound of arguing could be heard from inside.

"No. You will not." Florie's voice was adamant.

A male voice mumbled something unintelligible afore they heard Gavina's husky voice shout, "Let go of her!"

Kallum stormed passed Ailsa and threw open the door. Upon entrance, they saw the healer with Florie clutched in one hand and a small cup of some potion in the other. Gavina stood ready to wallop the man with an empty kettle as he worked to pull Florie away from the bed on which laid a limp boy of about eight or so years.

"Enough!" Kallum's sharp bark made the man flinch.

He immediately released the mother, and Gavina jerked down the kettle.

Florie ran to Ailsa. "Ailsa. Thank Heaven." She pulled her over to the bed. "He won't awaken. Alby's fever worsens, and whatever he gives"—she glanced at the cup in the healer's hand—"seems to make Alby worse, not better."

"Now, see here," the healer sputtered. "You need to stand aside so I can treat the boy properly."

"What's that you give him?" Ailsa asked.

He looked at her as if she were an insect beneath his foot. "Who are you to question me?"

"I, too, am a healer. Tell me what you give the boy."

Two soldiers appeared at the threshold of Florie's small cottage. They were soldiers who served with her husband. Somehow, news of Florie's troubles must have circulated to them, and they'd come to lend their support. Ailsa used the male healer's moment of distraction at their appearance to wrest the cup from his hand. He made to grab for it, but a quick step forward by Kallum inspired him to snatch back his hand.

Ailsa sniffed the contents of the cup. She recognized the scent of the herb from which he'd made the potion. 'Twas not a bad choice in the case of fever, but whatever the boy suffered needed something stronger.

She set the infused potion on a side table and placed a hand on the boy's forehead. The level of heat shocked her.

"What is it?" Florie's frantic voice let her know she'd failed to guard her expression. "Save him. You must save him!"

Gavina grabbed Florie and held on to keep the woman from throwing herself at the bed.

Ailsa's gaze sought Kallum's.

He stepped to her. "What is it, lass?"

"He burns excessively, Kallum. We must reduce this fever as fast as possible lest he expire afore any potion can take effect."

At the news, a mother's despair poured from Florie in a throaty moan, and her eyes flooded with tears.

The MacNeill healer, unfazed by the mother's keening, defended his handiwork. "We have a cloth bath we've been using to calm the fever. If she'd but let me give the lad his next herbal infusion, he might have a chance."

"No!" Florie struggled to free herself from Gavina's hold. "Ailsa, 'tis the same potion he's been giving Alby for days. Yet, my son worsens. You must do something."

Ailsa dipped two fingers into the bowl being used for the boy's cloth baths. The water was tepid. "This needs to be colder. Much colder." She glanced around the cottage.

Sensing her problem, Kallum said, "I can have the men fetch cold water from the stream."

The two men moved immediately to do as Kallum suggested.

Ailsa shook her head. "'Twill take too long."

The soldiers stopped and glanced at her, then Kallum.

"Tell us what you need, lass," he said.

"With the distance of the stream, there and back will take much-needed time. Plus, the water will warm some during the travel. We must take the boy to the stream."

The MacNeill healer rushed irately to the bed. "That's absurd. The boy is not fit to travel to the stream. You need to step aside and let someone with true experience handle this."

The man was easily two score older than she, but his arrogance was going to kill Florie's child. Ailsa saw doubt enter the eyes of the two soldiers and concern envelop Florie. Florie was the first MacNeill to seek her assistance with healing. Ailsa would not fail her over the posturing of a pompous know-all.

Her voice took on an obstinate edge. "You've been

treating this boy for days. Has he gotten better even in the least?"

The man's lips flattened.

"So 'tis as Florie said. Her son worsens, and you continue with the same efforts that work not. 'Tis my turn now. *You* need to step aside."

Kallum signaled to the two soldiers, who stepped in front of the healer to prevent him from further interference.

Ailsa went to Florie. "We must reduce his fever. Once that is lessened, I have stronger herbs that should make a difference."

The healer's grunt of disbelief echoed in the room.

Gavina's head snapped his direction. She spat a menacing shush in the naysayer's direction and hugged Florie reassuringly.

Ignoring him, Ailsa looked into Florie's eyes. "Do you trust me?"

Florie brushed at her crying eyes but did not hesitate. "Aye."

Not waiting for Ailsa to tell him to act, Kallum scooped up the boy and headed out the door. Gavina stayed behind to change the boy's bed linens. The others, save the healer, followed Kallum.

When they got to the stream, Kallum walked in holding the limp lad secure against his chest. Ailsa made to follow him in, then hesitated.

Florie glanced from a hip-deep Kallum to a non-moving Ailsa. "What's wrong?"

Caitrin brought up the rear and explained to Florie, "She knows not how to swim. Kallum is trying to teach her, but 'tis a challenge in the dresses she has, and the other option… Well, that is not a workable solution."

Florie's eyes grew wide, easily deducing the other option meant swimming unclothed. With a quick look at her son limp in Kallum's arms, she turned anxious eyes back to Ailsa. The look gave Ailsa all the motivation she needed to put aside her own fears to vanquish this mother's turmoil. She placed a foot into the water.

"Ailsa, wait." Florie placed a trembling hand on her forearm. "You needn't go in the water." Her eyes held understanding beneath the worry, and she gave Ailsa's arm a squeeze. "Tell me what to do."

With a deep breath, Ailsa patted the woman's hand. "'Tis all right, Florie. I will tend Alby." With a return squeeze, she added, "All will be well."

• • •

And all had gone well. Ailsa had set aside her fear and entered the cold stream. She'd bathed the boy while Kallum held him. They'd managed to reduce the fever, and with Ailsa's potion, he'd awakened by midday. The boy was still bedridden, but he would recover. Ailsa had left additional herbs with Florie and specific instructions on how to brew the necessary infusion.

Never wanting to be afeared of water again, Ailsa was determined to conquer the swim stroke this day, and she wanted nothing to distract from that goal. Having learned her lesson about Kallum's lack of focus, Ailsa invited Caitrin along this eve to act as a buffer. She would check on Alby later.

For now, she stood by the stream and knotted a light tunic under her breasts. On her bottom, she wore a pair of short trews Florie had loaned her from her son's attire. Alby was big for his age, and Florie had been happy to do so as an act of gratitude for Ailsa's help breaking the lad's fever.

Even with more appropriate attire, Ailsa still floundered in the water as she tried to get the hang of synchronizing leg kicks with arm movements.

Kallum laughed, shirtless beside her in the water with his hand beneath her. "You're trying too hard, lass. Relax and trust the water will hold you up as you make your strokes."

He dropped his hand, and Ailsa began to sink. Having learned not to go out deeper than she could stand with her head above water, she planted her feet and stood.

"Ugh!" She swatted the uncooperative water, diverting her face from its retaliatory, mocking splash.

"Come on, Ailsa. You can do it!" Caitrin yelled from the edge of the water. "Stop thinking so much."

Easy for you to say from the bank of the pond. In her frustration, Ailsa could not help the ungracious thought. If she'd been closer to Caitrin, she'd have pulled the too-chipper lassie into the drink. Instead, she focused on a more relaxed float and practiced her strokes again and again.

Caitrin eventually waded into the pool with her, and the lass's antics relaxed Ailsa enough that, shortly afore dusk, Ailsa found herself swimming with little effort. When the pair finally rose from the water, they celebrated with much jumping and squealing. Satisfied with her progress, Ailsa redonned her newest dress with its stylish leather bodice, and she and Caitrin made plans for how they would celebrate her amazing progress.

Kallum's voice intruded on their revelry. "Now that

you are redressed, *leannan*, we shall have you practice cutting yourself free of the dress while in the water."

"You want me to do what!" She glared at him like he'd grown two heads.

"We've only practiced swimming for enjoyment. If you fall in the water fully clothed or are thrown in due to foul play—"

"You mean like by you?" she interrupted, her hands going straight to her hips.

Caitrin giggled beside her, and Kallum's lips twitched as he gave a one-shouldered shrug at her reminder of how he'd learned she could not swim.

Not put off by Ailsa's interruption, Kallum continued, "The weight of all those layers will pull you down quickly." He motioned to the laced bodice of the dress she'd swapped for the soaked tunic and short trews. "You will not have time to unlace bodices or undo buttons or bows. You must know how to cut away hindering pieces so you can move well enough to swim to shore or survive long enough in the water to be pulled out."

Ailsa revolted. "I like this dress. I'm not jumping in water in it or cutting it up." 'Twas one of the dresses she'd received as a gift from the laundry women. Gavina had fashioned this one special for Ailsa using the ladies' personal stashes of fabrics and ribbons. No one was getting near this dress with a blade.

"I'll have another dress made for you," Kallum said dismissively.

She gave him another obstinate glare. "I do not need you to have another dress made for me. I'm keeping *this* dress whole."

Kallum began to advance on her. She took several

cautious steps back and kept her eyes on him for any sudden movements.

"Ho, what is this?" Inan stepped into the cove, a wide smile of interest on his face. "Time to dunk the Connery into the water again?"

With another giggle, Caitrin informed him, "No. Kallum wants Ailsa to get in wearing her dress, then cut it off."

Inan's brows lifted, and he gave Ailsa a considering look from head to toe. "Well, it seems I have arrived at the right moment to enjoy the show."

Ailsa stared in amazement, mouth agape, at Inan's overtly appreciative gaze.

He leaned a casual shoulder against a nearby tree. "What? While I find your shrewish behavior off-putting," he said to Ailsa, "I *am* a man. As a man, I willingly admit the form wrapped around that temperament is quite appealing to look upon. So if you are interested in revealing yourself to all, I'm more than interested in enjoying the unveiling." Inan crossed his arms and ankles in an attentive stance.

Kallum gave him that throaty growl Ailsa had come to recognize as Kallum's innate, spontaneous warning afore holy hell unleashed, but Inan, the cad, simply grinned at his cousin. Caitrin took it all in while trying, with obvious difficulty, not to descend into hysterical laughter.

"While *you* stand here a lout in both manner *and* appearance," Ailsa countered to the interloper. "Go away, Inan."

He pushed off the tree and advanced toward her. "Nay. I think maybe I'll help things along."

Ailsa began to retreat and reached for her dagger

but found only empty space. She'd not worn it to the stream. Knowing she'd be with Kallum the whole time, she'd decided she'd have need for no other weapon.

Kallum stepped between them afore Inan could get close. "Enough, Inan," he said. "Do not interfere."

"You aim to give me orders, Commander?" Inan replied.

The bald reminder of their differing ranks made Ailsa cringe. 'Twould this lead to more than a light-hearted scuffle between the two?

Kallum's hand went to the hilt of his dagger, but Inan's lips began to twitch as he unsuccessfully tried to suppress a grin.

Laughing, Caitrin stepped sideways between them and spread her arms straight out with raised palms designed to warn back each man. "Okay, you cretins, cut it out. You're unnerving Ailsa. She thinks you're both idiot enough to come to blows over this."

Kallum looked at Ailsa's face and removed his hand from his dagger. He went to gather the rest of their belongings and winked as he passed by her.

Tingles of something warm and fluttery flittered in her stomach.

Inan stepped silently to her side, and the flutters immediately stopped.

He crossed his arms. "You had nothing to fear from me. You do realize he would never allow any man to harm you? Not even me." Staring intensely into her eyes, he searched for some answer he did not seem to find. "I only hope, my little Connery, you'd do the same for him."

Enemy. Ailsa stared at Inan's back as he walked away. He'd always see her as the enemy.

Her gaze shifted to Kallum, who jested lovingly with Caitrin as he strapped on the sword he had removed to give Ailsa her swimming lesson. Whatever she felt for this braw, strong, fierce warrior—she had not yet the courage to give it a name—and as much as she enjoyed the comradeship she'd found with Caitrin, Florie, and the other women, how could she ever stay here, even to extend her time with the MacNeill, when the future laird of his clan saw her as naught but the enemy and an unavoidable source of danger for his kinsman?

Maybe it was time to force the issue of her return to her own clan. Then she'd not be here when the king arrived.

CHAPTER TWENTY-SIX

Late into the evening, Ailsa and Kallum lingered in her bed. She drowsed in his arms. The marks on her face had dissipated, and he enjoyed the opportunity to enjoy unobserved her full beauty. He played with the wisps of hair at her temples. She had shared her concerns with him about staying put at Clan MacNeill with the king set to arrive at any moment. She wanted to leave for Clan Connery on the morrow, but he'd denied her. While he'd not been happy with the laird's missive to the king, he would not now try to outrun the inevitable confrontation.

Ailsa had not been happy with his refusal to help her flee nor his promise to stop her if she tried. She'd covered her disappointment by coaxing him into debauching her so thoroughly she'd not had the energy to stay awake after, let alone to stew over concerns. They had explored each other from head to toe. He understood she'd used his physical pleasuring to temporarily forget her worries. 'Twas a using he had not minded. He'd learned his Ailsa had an adventurous spirit when it came to bed play, but there was one thing they had yet to try that Kallum found hard to expel from his mind.

He wanted to feel her mouth on him.

Kallum swallowed, doubting she'd ever done such and needing to be careful to ask her in a way she knew she could say him nay without judgment.

He nudged her gently with a lift of his shoulder.

"Ailsa, do you remember when I put my mouth between your legs?"

She tilted her face toward his, her blush so deep the coloring went down her neck and part of her chest. He found it endearing that she could still blush after all they had done with each other and to each other. 'Twas a beautiful sight.

He rubbed a bent finger down the heightened color of her chest, then placed a hand to the back of her neck. He pulled her close and kissed her deep. Their tongues played with careless abandon, and Ailsa rubbed her leg against him in her excitement.

When he released her lips, he kept her face close. "'Twill feel as good to me if you put your mouth on me in much the same way."

She gave him a skeptical look. "Kallum, I doubt I can fit the whole of you in my mouth."

"Aye, not all of me. At least not this first time, but however much you fit, if you are willing, will feel glorious."

Her thumb rubbed over his swollen tip. "You leak. Is that from excitement at the thought of what you ask me to do?"

He nodded. He could no longer speak with her thumb engaged in an exquisite torture that belied the gentleness of her touch.

She sat up and placed a hand low around him. She squeezed, then used her other hand to cover his tip with a circling palm. He groaned at the intense pleasure such simple rubbing spurred.

The wicked grin she gave him upon hearing the sound made him wonder if mayhap he should have waited for this request.

"So, you are saying if I replace this hand"—she kept circling her palm—"with my mouth, I will make you shake and moan uncontrollably, as you did me last night?"

He swallowed, and his brows knitted. Why did she sound as if she were about to exact...revenge?

She chuckled at his nonresponse. "This I am curious to see."

Her head dropped slowly, and she kept her eyes on him the entire time until her lips touched the tip of his manhood. She opened the slightest bit and licked at his slit. When his hips jerked at the teasing touch of her tongue, she gave a satisfied hum.

She licked him again and again with an occasional suck at the head of him. The foreplay was nigh on torture. His engorged staff longed for attention of a more thorough sort.

"*Ailsa.*" Her name came out choked in a voice that revealed his distressed state.

Her gaze sought his. Her lips lifted from him, and she asked with an innocent smile, "Aye, Kallum?"

Dear God, is she going to make me beg? The imp!

"Stop teasing. Take me all the way in, lass."

She rubbed her fisted hands up and down his shaft, then enthusiastically sucked him deep into her throat. The effort flooded Kallum with a rapturous tingle through the tips of his toes, but his pleasure was tempered by the sound of a feminine gag.

He grabbed quickly at the sides of Ailsa's face and pulled out to the tip. "Easy, sweet. Take a little less to begin."

Ailsa adjusted and sucked him in again, managing only about half his length, but the suction nearly made him shoot his seed immediately.

With a pant to control his release, Kallum ground a heel into the bed and slowly pumped into her mouth. "Swallow, lass."

Her eyes searched out his questioningly, her mouth still in place.

"Suck me to the back of your throat and swallow. 'Twill make me—" He cut off with a loud curse when her throat worked in a swallow.

His toes cramped, and he could feel tension in his lower back. He was done; naught on earth or in the heavens could stop this building release. When he felt Ailsa's throat work for a second time, he grabbed at her cheeks.

"Ailsa, I'm about to spill my seed." His teeth gritted as he tried to hold back. "This first time, you may not want to let me finish in your mouth."

He tried to pull her head up, but she held on to his shaft with hand and mouth. The curious expression on her face clued him in that she had decided to try the full experience.

Rising onto her knees, she dropped her hands to the front of his thighs, sucked him in as deep as she could, and swallowed. He shot off, thighs trembling and hips lifted into the suction of her mouth. She followed him down when he'd spent all he had. Her hands rubbed gently up and down his thighs to settle him. When he finally lay quiet and semi-limp, she removed her lips from him.

With a wipe of her mouth across the back of her hand, she crawled up his body to lie on his chest. She kissed him on the corner of his mouth, and he placed an arm around her back, keeping her draped over him like a human blanket while he drifted into a sound, dreamless sleep.

The next morn, he rose quietly so as not to wake her. The king would likely reach MacNeill lands by sometime this eve, and Kallum needed to meet with the laird in preparation for the monarch's arrival. He still did not trust the king would be just in this matter, but he understood Laird Aymer's intent in sending the notification that had spurred the king's visit. So he had made peace with the laird.

He donned his kilt and attached his kilt pin. Looking at the markings on his pin made him think of the tartan brooch Ailsa owned. He stepped over to the bed rail where she kept her sash and lifted the cloth for inspection.

This time, he took care to examine the weight of the brooch and walked it to the window to study the red eyes of the falcon in the sunlight. The brooch was true silver, not some metal pounded and buffed to look like silver as he had originally thought, and the falcon's eyes were real jewels. The stones refracted the sunlight in a manner no glass ever could.

Where and how had a village lass, born of an eccentric healer, come upon a brooch of such value?

Studying the crest within the heart of the brooch, Kallum noticed something else that made his insides tighten. He glanced at the sleeping Ailsa. Whatever his personal feelings for the lass, he now knew 'twas of utmost importance she be protected not only from recapture by the king but from return to any Connery save the Connery laird himself.

Kallum replaced the sash to its spot on the rail and stood, momentarily admiring the beauty of the woman with whom he'd spent the last hours enjoying not only pleasures of the body but pleasures of the mind. She was easy to talk with, an unusual experience for a lifelong soldier such as he. He was not long on words with any person but certainly rarely with a woman. He could not remember ever taking the time to talk with a bedmate about matters other than those of the flesh, except mayhap matters of sustenance or laundry.

To think, this day could be their last time together. The thought rested not well with him, but he would face the unavoidable confrontation coming. He would seek out Laird Aymer to prepare their strategy for the audience with the king. Kallum would have to leave the diplomacy to the laird. He was not skilled in such matters. His temper made him poorly suited to sway with words. He preferred the persuasiveness of a well-wielded blade.

He slipped from the cottage and found the laird amongst the two most senior members of the clan council. Inan had already been dispatched to meet the king, whose entourage was reported by MacNeill clan scouts to be about a day's ride away. Kallum joined the meeting so he would know the nuances of the proposed negotiation to prepare for any possible complications. About the time he was ready to depart to prepare the soldiers who had not been dispatched with Inan, a frantic Caitrin ran into the grand hall.

"Kallum! Kallum! She's gone." She raced to him out of breath, having clearly run most, if not all, the way from the cottage.

"Who's gone, pet?"

"Ailsa. I just came from the cottage, and she's not there. She's nowhere to be found."

"She may simply be out for a walk or gathering roots or some such."

After word spread of what she'd done for Alby, more members of the clan had started approaching the lass for healing advice. So Ailsa had taken to gathering more plants and roots to make tisanes and potions. She'd said it also kept her busy so she'd not go daft with the waiting for a resolution to her plight.

"Nay, Kallum. All her things are gone. I checked." Caitrin's face looked frantic. "All her dresses, all her herbs. Everything is gone!"

Kallum could not believe the lass would take off on her own. She had been concerned about facing the king and expressed doubts as to whether the laird could pull off the diplomatic maneuver he had planned, but Kallum had not thought her worried enough to jeopardize her personal safety to flee MacNeill land on her own.

He rushed from the manor to check the cottage for himself. As Caitrin had indicated, the cottage held naught of Ailsa. Even her tartan sash no longer hung from the bed rail, and that was the most telling sign of all.

She left the sash of Connery colors in plain view in the cottage to make her feel less homesick. She did not wear it when walking the keep or the grounds beyond for fear of reprisals from those resentful of a Connery's presence among them. The only reason to take the sash with her would be because she had not planned to return.

Upon taking his leave of the cottage, Kallum stepped on something. He looked down and noticed the leather hair tie Ailsa had him remove for her keeping. So much for her keeping it forever in memory of him. Its significance had apparently not been as great as she had put on.

He squeezed the discarded tie in his fist, anger overtaking him at her fickleness and abandonment without so much as a goodbye. He slipped the tie onto his wrist and returned to the manor.

When he arrived, he found the laird with a missive in his hand and a frown on his face. Caitrin stood close by; her hands fluttered between wringing each other and the folds of her dress.

"'Tis from Inan. The king has decided to detour to Connery keep rather than stop here. His captain and half his regiment have already departed for Connery land."

"Something is amiss," Kallum said.

The laird nodded. "'Tis my way of thinking as well. Think you it has aught to do with your lass?"

"She is not my lass, and I know not. 'Tis no longer our concern. She has made her decision to trust her fate with her kin. She will have to face whatever that gets her."

"Then she *is* gone," the laird said.

"Aye. As Caitrin indicated, there is nothing of her in the cottage."

"And you are sure she left of her own free will?" Caitrin asked.

"Lass, what other option is there?" Kallum asked softly, not wanting to upset her more than she already was. He understood she and Ailsa were friends. It had been thoughtless of Ailsa not to think of the lass afore departing.

Caitrin wrung her hands. "I know not, but I know

she would not leave without saying goodbye to me. Something has happened to her."

"Pet, she has been homesick for a long time. With the king set to arrive at any time, she simply chose not to wait around. She likely had not time to search you out."

Her head shook in disagreement. "Nay, 'tis not the way of it. I know it. I can *feel* it. She is in trouble."

Disquiet rose in Kallum. Despite his anger with the Connery hellion, he could not stomach the thought that she might have met with trouble or foul play.

The laird stepped to his side. "Kallum, are you certain the lass would leave thus? Even without saying goodbye to Caitrin? To you?" He searched Kallum's face. "I realize I know not the lass as well as you, but she does not strike me as the disloyal sort, and I believe she was a true friend to Caitrin."

Kallum began to ponder all the circumstances of the day. Looking at Laird Aymer, he asked, "When did the missive from Inan arrive?"

"Not long afore you arrived back from your search for Ailsa."

"'Tis more than half a day's ride from where Inan would have stopped to rest and send news." Which meant the Connerys had intercepted the king's entourage with a tempting proposition even afore Ailsa could have disappeared. Something had been put in the works mayhap as early as yester morn.

Kallum glanced at the extra tie on his wrist.

"Do you love the lass?"

Kallum glanced up at the laird's question but did not respond immediately. "I...was fond of her, but 'twas not more than that."

The laird scoffed. "Ha. That is your pride talking. Try answering me with your heart."

Unnerved to be put on the spot, Kallum paced a few steps away from the chief, then paced the other way.

"Fine. You do not have to answer that question. I'll ask another." The laird planted himself against the edge of his desk. "Do you think the lass loves you?"

"She has never said the words." This was one response Kallum could quickly give.

"Yet you have given her the words?"

Once again, Kallum was silent.

"I thought not." Laird Aymer made much show of shaking his head. "The stubbornness between you two. 'Tis a wonder you can stand each other's presence." He stood. "Oh, wait. Half the time you cannot."

Kallum glared at his laird.

"Eye me all you want. But you two are like halves of the same person, so stop letting your hurt feelings color that strategic mind of yours. Think, Kallum. Close your eyes and visualize Ailsa the last time you saw her. What did she say? What did her expressions tell you about the truth of her words? Would the lass have left you without a word? A note? Some sign?"

The laird's last words spurred Kallum to glance at his wrist again. The corded tie placed there taunted him. He could hear Ailsa's voice: *I plan to keep it. When I must leave, I shall have something to remember you always.*

Her words had been genuine, of this he was certain, as had what transpired between them after. The lass was in love with him. She had not given him the words. Most likely for the same reason he had not given her the words. They were both too set in their outsider ways to truly trust in someone else to stay.

If she had left of her own accord, she would not have left the leather tie behind. Even if she had fled out of fear the MacNeills could not protect her from the repercussions of the king, she would have fled with his hair cord still around her wrist.

It had been left behind as a sign. A small trinket that whoever took her would have overlooked or thought nothing of. But it had been a sign to him. That she, his Ailsa, had not left him. Not yet.

Which meant she had been taken, and only one type of vermin would sneak onto lands of another and remove a lass under protest. Connery vermin.

And if they were taking her to an audience with the king's captain, the man in charge of the king's captives, then she was in grave danger.

He took off at a dead run.

"Kallum, wait!" The laird chased after him through the library door. "You cannot do this alone. You must wait for Inan to return with the rest of our army."

Kallum kept moving. Ailsa did not have time for him to wait. If he left immediately and traveled fast, he might be able to reach Connery keep about the same time as the king's entourage.

He would not put other men of his clan at risk by being outnumbered, but he, himself, would do whatever it took to free his goddess again, or he would die trying.

CHAPTER TWENTY-SEVEN

Ailsa jerked her hand away from the Connery soldier who shoved her into the Connery manor's grand hall. She scowled at the man's rough handling of her and at the two traitorous MacNeills standing behind him, the two friends of the banished Hendrik. Somehow, they had been persuaded to snatch her from MacNeill lands and turn her over to a small contingent of Connery soldiers.

No one had said two kind words to her since her abduction, which made her wary that this was not intended as a "welcome home" gathering.

She stumbled a few steps afore she noticed four men seated at the grand table. At the head of the table sat Alastair Connery, a man she recognized as the lead chieftain and the Connery laird's second-in-command. It had been Alastair Connery who had sent for her to serve as stand-in healer for the laird during the trek to Stirling Castle three summers ago. Surely, the man would recognize her.

With a sense of relief that this might not be the ordeal she had imagined, Ailsa walked toward the table, then came to a dead stop. Seated amongst the Connerys was Hendrik MacNeill. He had abandoned the MacNeill colors for Connery plaid, so Ailsa had not noticed him at first. The smirk he gave her sent a shiver of dread down her spine.

"Welcome home, Ailsa," Hendrik said with a grin that would put *Auld Clootie*, the Devil himself, to shame.

Ailsa lifted her chin and mentally braced herself but ignored his disingenuous greeting.

Alastair Connery stood. "Greetings, Ailsa Connery. 'Twould seem you have abandoned your kin for illicit relations with a member of one of our enemies. When I was told you had deserted your appointment three years ago, I was surprised a lass such as yourself would be so dismissive of the opportunity you were given. Then to find out you'd done so for an assignation of an improper order—well." He spread his hands and canted his head as if in deep contemplation. "Let's just say my reaction was more than disappointment."

"I did not abandon my post three years ago." Ailsa's reply was forceful, but she fought to remain respectful. This man held her future in his hands. "Your soldiers abandoned me after I was taken against my will by the king's captain for impressment into the king's bevy of enslaved persons."

Alastair's eyes widened. "*Slave?* What fancy is this? You expect me to believe such nonsense? The king's man would not dare take a Connery as a slave or even as a servant without so much as a *by your leave* from the laird."

She took a step forward, and the soldiers posted at each end of the table moved to intercept her. Alastair raised his hand to stop them.

Pulling in a slow breath, Ailsa gathered her aplomb. "I *was* taken, and I have spent the past three years enslaved at Stirling Castle. The king's *man* made sure no one knew that I was a freeborn Highlander and that I either fulfilled my duties or faced dire consequences."

Alastair sat back down and drummed the fingers of his right hand against the table. "That is not the story I was told. And if you were held captive at the castle, how came you to be at MacNeill keep? Are you saying you were also held by the MacNeills against your will?"

I was. At first.

But she could not tell them that without implicating Kallum in her escape from the castle. Since other captives disappeared on the same day as she, such information would lead to a supposition that he might be the Shepherd. Such a supposition could lead to his death, something she could not envision or allow.

"Well?" Alastair gave her a calculating look.

Hendrik leaned back in his chair and grinned from ear to ear.

There was a game afoot here. She knew not the parameters, but she sensed a snare would trap her whether her response be affirmative or negative. At stake seemed to be saving her own reputation and life or jeopardizing the life of Kallum.

"I only came to be at the MacNeill keep recently. Until then, I was retained at the castle."

"How came you to depart the castle?" Alastair asked. "If you were held captive as you suggest, then escape would have been a grand coup. Not one, I would think, you could do alone."

Alastair was on a searching expedition, exploiting a silver tongue to twist at words until he could use hers to his benefit. But how?

Did he suspect Kallum was the Shepherd?

Had Hendrik provided information to be used against them both in retaliation for his banishment? Would he even know information to share? Or had he simply made up tales to ingratiate himself to the Connerys in exchange for acceptance into the clan?

If 'twas a game of mental chess they wanted to play, then she would play her lot. "Your doubt is understandable. I did indeed foul my attempts at escape the first two times I tried, but I learned much. I was much cleverer this third time."

Shock registered on Alastair's face at her admission of prior escape attempts. The look was genuine; he had not expected such a revelation. The reaction suggested the man knew her tale of capture to be true, but he covered his facial slip quickly.

"I see. And where do the MacNeills come in? Hendrik tells me their army commander is particularly fond of you." Alastair's unsubtle smirk made clear the intimate tenor of this fondness of which he spoke.

Ailsa scowled at Hendrik. The man had squandered the mercy she'd given him. 'Twould seem Kallum's philosophy that you killed a serpent when you had a chance lest it slither back to bite you held much merit after all. When next Hendrik faced the MacNeill, the snake would face certain death. Ailsa prayed she'd be alive to witness the affair.

"Hendrik overstates the matter," Ailsa said to Alastair. "The commander came upon me in the woods and helped me find my way back to the Highlands. I became disoriented and unsure of the way. I may have perished without his assistance. As such, the man felt responsible for me. In truth, he did not learn I was a Connery until days later. The laird offered me temporary accommodations until such time as they could negotiate my return to you."

"This all seems a convenient and unlikely story— MacNeills giving quarter to a Connery—but we will settle this matter shortly. The king's captain is on his way here as we speak. If 'tis true you were captured inadvertently, then we will settle the matter when the monarch's guard arrives.

"If I find, on the other hand, that you did indeed abandon your station those years ago, then you will receive no protection as a Connery. In which event, your status as a captive will be restored. You will be returned to the captain and the king's household."

Alastair gestured toward Hendrik. "And Hendrik will be allowed to collect the reward for your return for bringing your presence to our attention."

What! This made no sense. She was a Connery. Alastair knew she was a Connery. No rationale, under any circumstance, existed by which she should be returned to being a captive. Enslavement as punishment for transgressions did not exist under clan law. Even if it did, this sham of a council had no way to gather legitimate proof she had abandoned her obligations at Stirling or committed any other violation, though she sensed they would find a way to prove what they wanted.

She was being set up to go back to the castle.

"You cannot do this! 'Tis not right. I must speak with the laird." Her nerves were shaky, but Ailsa kept her voice calm.

Alastair shook his head. "Our laird has taken ill. He must rest. He has left this matter to me. I have asked two other members of the council to stand with me on the matter. You can be assured we will get to the bottom of this."

Ailsa looked at the other two men seated at the table. They sat quietly, nodding in agreement with Alastair at significant moments in his speech. They were merely Alastair's lemmings. They'd give no independent thought to this matter. Her only hope was to get to the laird. "Surely, I can be granted a small audience with the laird on a matter of such grand importance. I'll not tax his strength. I am a healer. I know the bounds beyond which not to push the ailing. Mayhap I can help the sire."

Alastair made much show of nodding and seeming to be deep in thought. "I do remember that you have healing skills. 'Tis why I sent for you when our clan healer became indisposed those years ago. My man has all under control this time; we need not complicate the laird's care with bizarre or nontraditional methods."

Ailsa took affront at the chieftain's classification of her healing methods, all the while noting he referred to the clan healer as *his* man. That wary feeling along her spine began to tingle again. She thought of Kallum's supposition that her stint at the castle may have been apurpose. In which case her selection to travel with the laird's entourage as healer may have also been strategically maneuvered. What might Alastair and his healer have had to do with the events that had made such selection possible, even necessary?

The Connery laird appeared to have more than one serpent in his kingdom.

"Do not take offense at my words." Alastair laughed, clearly enjoying her reaction to his poorly veiled insult. "Your mother was known for her African Vodun ways. I meant only that we will stick with known Celtic methods of healing in this keep. Nothing personal."

He motioned for one of the soldiers standing in attendance to take hold of her.

"We will board you in one of the unoccupied upper bedchambers until the king's captain arrives on the morrow. You will be summoned when 'tis time for you to face the consequences of your actions."

Snatching her arm from the grip of the soldier who came to escort her, Ailsa gave one final glare at Hendrik, who sat with that smug smile still firmly on his face. "You should have taken my mercy as the gift it was. Relish your momentary reign of mayhem. You'll not have a chance to enjoy whatever riches they have promised you." She took a step forward and lowered her voice menacingly. "Know that he will come for you."

His smirk faltered at the edges, and Ailsa took perverse joy in the knowledge Hendrik knew immediately of whom she spoke.

"Aye, Hendrik, and when he comes, he'll bring your death with him. I look upon a dead man. Death looks becoming on you."

When she repeated her last sentence in majestically accented Yoruba, Hendrik jumped to his feet. "Get her out of here!"

Ailsa began to laugh at Hendrik, and her soldier escort ushered her toward the stairs. If the men watching thought her compliance a sign of her meek acceptance of the fate they had designed for her, they were in for grand disappointment. Alastair claimed he knew of her mother—he should have learned the woman had raised not a cowering damsel.

The door to this chamber they led her to had best be secured and guarded, for she'd not let it hold her otherwise.

• • •

When they brought supper to her chamber prison, Ailsa made a point to glance into the hallway.

Seeing her curiosity, the soldier who'd delivered her meal smirked at her. "Both stairs are guarded below. You'll not escape afore Alastair is ready to hand you over, so do not try anything foolish."

Thanks to his words, Ailsa noted for the first time that a second set of stairs graced the far end of the hall. She noticed also that those stairs not only went down but curved up. The Connery manor had a third level above. They'd not house a prisoner on the same level as the laird they wanted her not to see, so she'd bet her life the laird's chambers were above those stairs.

She ate the full meal they'd brought her, unsure when she'd next have the opportunity to eat. They'd thrown her satchel of belongings into the room afore locking her away. She grabbed it and slipped the straps of the bag over her head and across her chest, with the weight of the satchel against her back. Quietly, she opened the bedchamber door and looked from end to end of the hallway. No soldiers were stationed on this level. They'd made the misguided decision to protect only the lower level, not expecting her to have the audacity to sneak *up* the stairs.

Slipping into the hallway, she stayed in the shadows cast by the flicker of two meager candles amidst a half dozen unlit ones, until she reached the bottom step of the upward-curving stairs. She listened intently, trying to determine whether guards or others might be stationed above in proximity to the laird's chamber.

Upon hearing no sound, she slowly took one step at a time. Her heart pounded. 'Twas foolish daring she engaged in, but she felt she had no other choice. Alastair had voiced that she would "face the consequences" of her actions, and her serving soldier had taken great pleasure in announcing she was trapped until Alastair could hand her over. She had already been adjudged guilty. Her planned audience before a council tribunal was a farce designed only to give the appearance of justice. She was assuredly going back into bondage at Stirling Castle.

She thought of Kallum, and a huge pressure built in her chest. Gripped by the unexpected sensation, she sat abruptly on the second to last step. One hand went automatically to her chest and pushed against the weight that had lodged there. She missed the MacNeill. She had not been prepared for the depth of that emotion.

Her eyes closed. Self-torture made her wonder if he missed her, too.

She glanced down at the empty wrist of the hand at her chest. She'd left behind the hair tie he had given her. She regretted that decision now. Some voice in her head—the voice of a foolish woman who had allowed her emotions to get the better of her—had spurred her to drop it as she was pulled from his mother's cottage. Some sentimental notion had overcome her that he'd see it and understand she would never leave it behind willingly.

A part of her hoped he would come for her, even as another part chastised such wishful thinking. She had fought off that second voice when torturing Hendrik, but now she could not shake the taunting doubt. Kallum knew she wanted to leave MacNeill keep, so he'd most likely see her absence as voluntary flight. Despite the pleasure they had allowed themselves to seek in each other's arms, they had never fully learned to trust each other, and that distrust would cause him to overlook her message.

Now, she no longer had even the smallest of trinkets to remember him by, and the void ratcheted up the pain in her aching heart. She fingered the hilt of the jeweled dirk belted beneath the folds of her dress. She still had the dagger Kallum had given her, because the traitors sent to abduct her had not bothered to search her for weapons. Arrogant men that they were, it had not occurred to them a female would be armed. Though the dagger had been Kallum's, it was truly the king's contraband, so it held not the value of a simple leather tie knotted around a shelled bead. Plus, she would be stripped of the weapon soon enough if she allowed herself to be forced back into enslavement.

You are a warrior. You just don't know it yet.

Kallum's voice filled her head, reminding her she possessed the grit of a warrior, and the battle wasn't over unless she chose to surrender.

She stood.

Surrender she was not ready to do. She still had a chance if she could convince the Connery laird of the truth of her circumstances. First, she needed to find the laird. Second, she would need spin the tale of a Connery lass's abduction. She glanced down at her attire. Nothing about her garments suggested an affiliation with the Connery clan. Anyone who came upon her might have doubts about her presence here. Of course, if those someones be soldiers, her opportunity was lost, but if they be merely household domestics, she might still have a chance.

Pulling around the top of her satchel, she retrieved her tartan sash and pinned it on. Satisfied she'd at least look the part of a Connery, Ailsa took the last step surreptitiously and peeked through the top baluster to determine whether she was alone on the floor. A light shone under a door at the end of the hall, but no persons were visible. She made for the light and listened at the door. When no sound accosted her ears, she eased open the portal to the view of a huge fireplace filled with a roaring fire. The flames threw a strong orange glow around the room and a burst of heat that stifled Ailsa's breathing.

A lone figure laid visible on the bed. He rested on his back, covered by a blanket up to the middle of his bare torso. Between the heat and the blanket, Ailsa could not surmise how the occupant could possibly be comfortable. Intentionally keeping her steps light, she tiptoed to the side of the bed.

The pallor of the bedridden man startled her. It had been a long time since she'd seen him, but she recognized this wilting figure as Laird Coen Connery. He was younger than her by a few turns of the seasons, but he looked as if he was slowly approaching an aged death.

Ailsa's hopes and heart took a dive.

She had half expected Alastair to be lying about the laird's failing health, part of the chieftain's ruse to get away with having her removed from the clan. To take a closer look, she grabbed the looped handle of the metal stand holding a lit candle on a nearby bed table and hovered the light near the laird's face. A grayness tinged his skin. She placed the back of her hand against his forehead. His skin felt extremely warm, but that warmth felt more like the results of the heat of the room rather than an internal fever.

Taking hold of one of his hands, Ailsa saw grayish half moons in the beds beneath his fingernails. She leaned over him and lifted one of his eyelids. He moaned, and his head lolled away, but not afore she saw what she needed to see.

She straightened. As she set aside the candlestick, a personal sense of despair warred with anger on behalf of the young laird. She had seen this pallor and coloring afore. What it signified meant the man was in no condition to come to her aid. The laird's body was fighting an internal plague but losing, and she suspected it was getting some sinister help with that failure.

The chamber door swung open, and Ailsa jumped away from the bed. A young woman entered carrying a tankard of steaming liquid. She startled upon seeing Ailsa, which caused some of the liquid to splash over her hand and onto the floor.

She ignored the scald, and her eyes widened. "Who are you? What are you doing in here?"

Rushing to the side of the bed, the woman placed herself between Ailsa and the laird afore she dropped the steaming tankard dismissively onto the bed table. She desperately searched the laird for any signs of foul play. He had moaned again at the sound of her voice, and she gently quieted him with soft drags of her fingertips against his temples.

"Shh, Coen. I'm here. All is well. Quiet now," the woman crooned.

The laird settled, and the unknown woman leveled an angry stare at Ailsa. "How did you get in here?"

Ailsa blinked at the woman. She did not know who

the woman was or her role in the household. She was not dressed as a servant. Her dress showed worth, and her familiarity with the laird's person suggested they were family or close in other ways.

"Tell me immediately who you are and what you want, or I will summon the laird's guards and have you permanently removed from the manor." She made to move toward the door.

Ailsa gripped her arm. "Wait! Don't." Intuiting the woman's concern was foremost for the ailing laird, Ailsa added, "I mean him no harm."

The lass's gaze skirted back to the laird's bed, and beneath the look of worry, Ailsa saw a flicker of something stronger.

Looking back at Ailsa, she asked, "Who are you? I have not seen you afore in the manor. Are you newly appointed to the household?"

"Nay, I am from the village. My name is Ailsa. I had hoped for the laird's assistance in a matter of importance. When Alastair told me he was ailing, I doubted his word but thought I might be able to help if by chance 'twere true."

"Well, you were smart not to trust the laird's cousin. He is content to have Coen abed. 'Tis the lairdship he wants, and with Coen ailing so, Alastair wields that position—"

"And power."

"Aye." She gave a discerning nod to Ailsa. "And power, in Coen's stead." She went back to the laird's bedside. She dipped her hand into a water-filled basin, retrieved a cut cloth, and folded it into thirds. "I am Mairi. Tell me, Ailsa, how thought you to be able to help?"

"I have skills at healing."

Mairi's gaze whipped toward Ailsa. "Truly?"

Ailsa nodded.

"No wonder Alastair did not want you to see Coen. He's allowed no one but the old clan healer to attend Coen, and I swear that man has no urgency about the matter. He does naught but give Coen a tisane for the pain laced with a sleeping draught. I swear they are content to let Coen sleep himself to a slow death." Mairi draped the folded cloth in her hands over the laird's forehead.

He moaned at her touch.

"His last tisane is wearing off. He has much pain without it." She reached for the abandoned tankard.

Ailsa grabbed her wrist.

Mairi tried to shake free of the grasp. "What's wrong with you? Let go!"

A slight tug-of-war ensued for Ailsa released her not.

"What is that you give him?" Ailsa asked.

"'Tis the tisane prescribed by the healer."

Ailsa forcibly took the tankard from Mairi's hand and sniffed. "Are you the one who mixes the tisane?"

"Aye. I trust no one else to administer the potion at the proper times. The last time I did, I arrived here to Coen shivering with the chills and writhing in pain."

Ailsa gave her a solemn look. "Then you are the one who is killing him."

CHAPTER TWENTY-EIGHT

"*What?*" The response was more a breath than a word. "Never. I would never do such a thing. Coen and I grew up together. He is my oldest and dearest friend." Her trembling hand rose to press against the center of her chest. "Why would you say such?"

"I believe the tisane is laced with a root that is poisonous upon human consumption."

"And you can tell that from the smell?"

Ailsa nodded. "It has a bitter aroma. I cannot be sure simply from the drink you brewed. Several legitimate herbs for mixing pain potions have a similar smell—and taste—but I suspect that is why your healer made sure to give you the pain potion and the sleeping draught mixed together."

"He's not my healer," Mairi snapped. "No friend of Alastair's can be trusted, but Coen sees not his cousin's faults. 'Tis Coen's nature to try and see the good in all. Alastair mocks that trait whenever he can, making others think Coen may not have the disposition of a leader when nothing can be further from the truth. A man need not be an ogre to be a strong and fair laird. With Coen's continuing sickness, though, it may not matter."

Ailsa moved forward and placed a hand on the shoulder of the distraught lass. "Do you have the packet of herbs the healer gave you to mix the laird's tisane?"

Mairi reached into a pocket hidden within the side folds of her dress and pulled out a small muslin pouch tightly closed by a drawstring.

Opening the pouch, Ailsa took a short whiff of the crushed herbal concoction. The bitter smell was stronger. She stuck in her thumb and forefinger and took a pinch of the herbs. After rubbing them gently between her fingers, she glanced down at the faint gray stain left behind on her fingertips. The tinted fingertips tingled with a slight numbness.

She looked up at Mairi. "I am fairly certain this potion is poisonous."

Coen stirred restlessly behind them.

"He begins to feel the pain now that the sleeping draught wears off," Mairi said.

Ailsa stepped to Coen and placed the back of her hand over his forehead again. His skin was damp with perspiration.

"I am not sure pain is the source of his discomfort." She glanced at the roaring fire, then the blanket covering the man's chest. "He is too warm. Why is the room kept so hot?"

"After Coen got the chills, the healer instructed us to keep the room heated."

Ailsa lifted a skeptical brow. "The healer you said you did not trust?"

Mairi stared at her, a sense of comprehension crossing her face.

"The chills indicate something specific is going on in the body. Once that is remedied, no need exists to keep the person heated." Ailsa pulled the blanket from the laird's half-clothed body. "Except mayhap the warmer blood will help the poison spread throughout the body faster and more efficiently."

"Damn them." Mairi sprang to her feet and went to

douse the fire. When she looked back up, she noticed Ailsa's surprised amusement. "What, you've never heard a lass swear?"

Ailsa laughed. "Only if you count the lass standing in front of you."

Mairi's lips quirked. "Then you and I are destined to be friends, Ailsa Connery." One of her hands went to a hip. "So, tell me, *friend*, what else must we do to save Coen?"

Taking Mairi's muslin pouch to the corner of the room, Ailsa dumped the contents into the chamber pot. "I do not have much time. They will come looking for me soon." A quick glance out the window portal indicated that the night progressed. "If they do not look for me until the morn, I think we can get the laird awake and lucid. Since it has been a while since his last tisane, the effects of the poison should begin to wane if we do not continue to administer the other healer's concoction. Tell me all of what has ailed the laird."

Understanding much from Mairi's description of Laird Connery's discomforts and ailments of the last few days, Ailsa dug through her own bag. Luckily, she had begun to collect and store many of her own herbs. She wanted to give the laird a potion designed to help him stay awake, but she had only a little of the necessary ingredients, and she decided to save them until he'd had more time off the poisoned root. Instead, she gathered two small packets. She took three pale brown leaves from one and a small nourishing root from another.

She turned to Mairi. "I need you to prepare another draught. Can you do so without raising suspicion?"

Mairi nodded. "I believe so. I've been at Coen's side

for the last five days. No one questions me when I come and go."

"Good." Ailsa handed the leaves and root to the woman. "Crush the leaves as fine as you can, then shave in a little of the root. Stir it all well into a hot draught and return as fast as you can. This will help him regain his strength. Also bring back something for him to eat if you can. We must get sustenance in him if his body is to heal itself."

After Mairi left to attend to the necessary potion and search out some food, Ailsa stepped back to the laird's bedside. He perspired still, so she removed the cloth from his forehead and wet it again in the water in the basin nearby. She wiped his bare chest and shoulders and hoped the wetness would give him some comfort.

When she leaned over him to wipe his opposite shoulder again, his eyes popped open. Ailsa flinched but did not pull away. She waited, wondering if he would reject her ministrations.

Hazel eyes not much unlike hers stared back at her. His gaze dropped to her tartan brooch, then back to her eyes. Squinting, he reached a hand toward her brooch, but the effort was too much for him. His hand fell.

"Grandmother," he whispered afore he succumbed once again to his drowsiness.

"Oh no. Delirium has set in." A returning Mairi stood transfixed and worried in the doorway.

Ailsa rushed to close the door, not wanting to chance that someone would walk by and see her in the room. "Nothing you described of his symptoms indicated that he should have delirium, especially without a fever."

"Then why did he think you were his grand-mother?"

"I don't think it was me he was talking about." Ailsa fingered the tartan brooch that was the only possession of value she owned. "He was reaching for my brooch."

Mairi set aside the trencher of sweet meats, bread, and cheese she'd brought up from the kitchen and stabilized into one hand the tankard she carried. She approached Ailsa and eyed the brooch closely, and then her widened eyes searched Ailsa's. "Where did you get that?"

The look of awe in Mairi's eyes made a trickle of apprehension run through Ailsa. She took a step back. "My mother gave it to me. She said it belonged to my grandmother."

"Which grandmother?" a weak, male voice asked from the bed. Coen leaned up on one elbow, watching Ailsa closely.

Mairi rushed to his side. "Coen, be careful. You must not overtax yourself. We think you may have been given poison." She placed the tankard on the bedside table and moved to lower him to the bed.

He refused her efforts. "Aye, I could hear you two talking about the sleeping draught and the poison root, though 'twas hard to open my eyes, but I am tired of being prone." Though he spoke to Mairi, he kept his eyes intently on Ailsa.

The room suddenly felt stifling again. Ailsa found it difficult to breathe. She took another step back, a need to flee rising fiercely inside her. She could not explain her apprehension, but a prescient intuition told her what was about to happen might be as life-shattering as her enslavement. She glanced toward the door.

"Don't leave." The urgency in the laird's voice kept her in place. His hand was lifted, but he let it drop into his lap. His breath labored, as if that little bit of effort had cost him much. "Mare, don't let her leave. She mustn't leave," he said to Mairi afore his eyes drifted closed.

Mairi tried to push him back onto the bed, but he continued to resist her.

His eyes fluttered open. "Nay. Help me sit up."

Adjusting pillows behind him so he could rest upright, Mairi looked at Ailsa. "Please. You must stay. You do not know his determination. If you go, he will try to follow you, and that he cannot handle as of yet."

Ailsa's instinct urged her to care not how much the laird could handle. Her time was limited, and she'd offered what help she could. Important now was that she save herself. She glanced at the door again.

Mairi tried to get Coen to drink the new draught she had prepared, but he rejected it. With a frustrated sigh, she scolded, "'Tis not the sleeping draught, you foolish man. I know you want to stay awake to speak with Ailsa. 'Tis something to make you stronger. Ailsa has skill at healing, and 'tis her potion I have prepared."

When he still did not take the drink, Mairi sat on the edge of the bed beside Coen and spoke to Ailsa. "You said you needed Coen's help with a matter of importance. 'Twould seem you have a chance for the audience you wanted. Is fleeing now truly your best—or wisest—course?"

Ailsa held her ground and squeezed her grandmother's brooch so tightly it pricked her palm. The laird's question rang in her ears. *Which grandmother?*

"I knew only one of my grandmothers," Ailsa said softly as she stared into the dying embers in the fireplace. "I have always assumed the brooch belonged to her." She grabbed for a hardbacked chair beside a small table to the back side of the door and sat abruptly.

Somehow, Ailsa knew without them saying a word that her African grandmother had not been the woman who owned this brooch.

She finally gathered her nerves and looked directly at Coen Connery. "This brooch was not hers, was it?"

"'Tis doubtful. That brooch shows the Connery family crest." Coen eyed her carefully.

"Aye, that I know."

Whatever reaction the laird had been looking for in her face, he must not have found. "Nay, Ailsa, I don't think you understand. The crest with the falcon taking flight in the manner depicted in your brooch is a special crest reserved only for those Connerys who are direct blood descendants of the Connery lairds."

Her head began to shake in denial even afore he finished. "'Tis not possible. My *mamaidh* would have told me."

"That, too, is doubtful. If she cared for your safety." His hand slid across the bed until he captured Mairi's. He looked at her and swallowed noticeably.

"You noticed her eyes?" she asked him softly.

He nodded at her, then looked back toward Ailsa. "There is only one way your mother could have gotten that brooch. I think you have much to share with us about how you came to be here." He took the tankard from Mairi with his other hand and took a long drink. "Talk to me."

Understanding his willingness to drink of a potion prepared at her direction as his offer of trust, Ailsa returned the gesture by recounting the tale of her childhood. He ate while she spoke, asking a few clarifying questions periodically. When Ailsa recounted her tale of enslavement, she could tell Coen now remembered her from that trip. Tension built in him when he realized the life she had been forced into and learned of Alastair's plans to return her on the morrow to the king's captain.

He looked at Mairi. "Alastair knows. 'Tis no other reason for him to try to get rid of the lass in such a way that guarantees she'll not return."

"Knows what?" Ailsa asked, her gaze bouncing between the two. Suspicion and Mairi's comment about her eyes—which no longer seemed merely coincidentally the same color as Coen's—gave her a good idea of the answer, but she needed to hear him say it first.

"Something a curious lad found out years ago when he made the mistake of sneaking into his father's hidden journal." He paused, and Mairi placed her other hand atop his in encouragement. "That my father loved another woman afore he married my mother, and after that woman sent him away so he'd do his duty by the clan, she bore him a daughter without telling him. A daughter he later became aware of but could not claim publicly without scandal to her or her mother, but whom he found ways privately—much to the consternation of her mother—to nurture from afar."

"Me?" Tears filled Ailsa's eyes.

Coen nodded.

"The tutors? My bow?"

He nodded again.

"And most likely many other ways of which I was not aware." She wiped at her eyes. She'd never thought much on those times her mother's resources seemed more than what could be purchased with the earnings from her healing. Now, Ailsa suspected, though her mother had sent him away, her father had never abandoned her in full. "But why did he never come meet me, talk to me, even once?"

"I cannot say for sure what was in his mind. I do know that, like me, he searched you out. Unlike me, he found you, and from entries in his journal, I do believe he actually talked to you on more than one occasion. He could not help himself. Out of respect for the wishes of your mother, and probably because he understood her concerns for your safety were valid, he simply did not tell you who he was."

Ailsa thought about all the times she had looked for her father in the crowds of the village. One of those times, she had likely found him but not known it. She shook her head, part in amazement and part in sadness. "What does all this have to do with Alastair's plans for me?"

Coen glanced at the window. Dawn would break soon, and the king's regiment would be arriving.

Returning his gaze to Ailsa, he explained, "He is the son of my father's only sister. She wed a MacGregor, so Alastair was not raised a Connery. He came to the clan only after the king's ban of their surname. Since we have the same Connery great-grandfather, should I die, he would have the rightful claim to the Connery lairdship. That is, unless it became known my father's true firstborn child lives. In which case, my sister"—a weak smile graced his lips as he called her sibling for the first time—"you would rightfully be laird, and your sons or daughters after you."

With mouth agape, Ailsa sat stunned. "I don't want to be laird," she whispered.

Mairi took in Ailsa's expression and chuckled.

Of all Ailsa had wanted for her life, being laird of Clan Connery, or any clan, had never been part of her considerations. What she truly wanted, she realized, was a certain MacNeill commander, a man who would never leave his clan to stand beside the laird of a clan he hated.

Coen shrugged at Ailsa's confession. "Duty rarely comes packaged in what we want. Your blood speaks for itself."

Still in shock, Ailsa stood. "My mixed blood."

"That matters not." Her brother reconsidered. "Well, 'tis true 'twas convenient for Alastair's purposes. For he used it to get rid of you in a way that did not warrant he have the blood of your death on his hands. But for all other matters, it makes no difference."

"Are you sure the Connery people will agree with you?" Ailsa challenged.

"They have no choice." His look was fierce. "Considering my cousin—*our* cousin—was in the process of slowly killing me, you are the only true family I have left. No one best dare disrespect that or you."

Family? Ailsa let that sink in, then sank back into the chair. She once again had family. A brother. For the first time since her ordeal with the Connerys had started, she felt hope.

She smiled at him, her brother. "And you are the

only family I have left."

"While I hate to break up this moment of bond-ing…" Mairi rose from her perch on the side of Coen's bed. "Dawn will break soon. If we don't get Ailsa out of here afore the king's men arrive, Alastair may still get his way. You are in no condition to stand as her cham-pion, Coen. Not without support."

"Aye. And given all Ailsa has told us, I cannot be sure how many of my men now stand with Alastair." He swung his legs over the side of the bed. "Ailsa, bolt the door."

Ailsa locked the chamber door, then went to aid Coen.

"Mairi, you must take her out through the hidden passageway. Find your brother. I know I can count on him to stand with me. Have him bring whatever men he knows to be trustworthy and loyal. I must fully dress and be belowstairs by the time the king's men arrive."

"Coen, you cannot. You have not the strength." Mairi came round to Coen's other side.

He wrapped her in a half hug. "Stop worrying, Mare. I will find the strength. I must face Alastair and the king's men, or we risk a coup. You said yourself, I cannot stand without support. My friend, there is only one man I can know for sure would never betray me. That man is your brother. You will find him and send him to me, and all will be well."

The sound of footfalls in the hallway drew their at-tention.

"The house awakens. You must hurry." Coen shoved Mairi in the direction of a bookshelf that covered an entire wall.

She placed her finger atop a single text and tilted it

out without removing it. The panel on which the book sat slid outward, and Ailsa stared in surprise. Not wasting time, Mairi grabbed a lit candle and motioned Ailsa to follow her. They stepped into the portal, and Mairi triggered a mechanism that closed the disguised doorway. The click of the bookshelf resetting sounded immediately prior to a knock at the laird's bedchamber door.

Time was truly up.

Ailsa crept behind Mairi down the stone steps leading from the laird's chamber. They reached the bottom of the stairs, and Mairi doused the candle. She pushed open the portal, took a peek outside, and then motioned the all clear. With daylight dawning and a roused household, their getting out of the secret passageway and safely past the back wall would be no easy venture. As she followed Mairi into the orangish-red tinted air of early morn, Ailsa held her breath and prayed they would remain undetected and succeed in finding Mairi's brother with all due haste.

CHAPTER TWENTY-NINE

Kallum slunk from the trees at the top of the hill that overlooked the courtyard of Connery keep. The dawn sun had not fully risen, but he had little time afore its rays would eliminate his semi-dark cover.

Surveying the gathering below, he noted the king's captain and the soldiers under his command standing in front of the stone steps of the manor. Many Connery men littered the courtyard, but he saw no women. They must be holding Ailsa inside. With the king's captain still in attendance, Kallum was certain Ailsa was alive and still here. He had no doubt her recapture was the captain's complete motivation for making this journey.

The men on the raised porch were agitated, all except a pale figure who stood stoically by the door. The king's captain argued with a tall Connery who looked to be in charge of the gathering—most likely Alastair, from what Kallum knew of the man.

Something was wrong.

The irritated voice of the captain rose to Kallum's ears, but Kallum could not clearly make out the words spoken. Given the captain's unhappy demeanor, Kallum suspected his hellion was causing problems or was not where they expected her to be. He certainly hoped it was the latter.

Surveying the layout of the Connery manor and surrounding structures, Kallum calculated his odds for a direct approach. He may have been able to handle the dozen or so Connery warriors alone if not for the presence of the hordes of men in the king's uniform. Kallum did not know if the king's soldiers would intervene in a private clan dispute, but with the captain's personal interest in recapturing his Connery fugitive, intervention was not outside the realm of possible.

Stealth would be his best option. If only he knew where they were holding Ailsa.

He did not have long to wonder.

An agitated feminine voice broke through the muffled male murmurings. "Let go of me!"

Ailsa.

She snatched her arm from the grasp of a Connery soldier as he pulled her from around the side of the manor. Another soldier labored behind her to bring along a second struggling woman. The pale Connery took an agitated step forward at the sight of the women only to be blocked by Alastair. The men exchanged heated words afore the pale one reached for the hilt of his sword. The man looked not strong enough to wield the weapon with any effectiveness, but Alastair backed off. The deference told Kallum much about the status of the proceedings below.

Alastair would only defer to one man. The pale figure could only be the Connery laird, young Coen Connery, and Coen appeared not to be in sync with whatever plans Alastair had negotiated with the captain. For that reason, the chief might get to live.

The soldier escorting the second woman pushed her up the stone steps and shoved her dismissively onto the platform. She stumbled, and Coen caught her. She whispered something to him. Whatever it was, from his face, the news was not good.

Kallum needed to get closer so he could hear what

was being said.

He discreetly picked his way closer to the keep gate, which had been left open after the passing of the king's regiment. Remaining on the elevated rise, he planted himself behind a tree but within hearing distance of the assembly below.

"Ah, cousin, I see you are feeling better," Alastair said to Coen.

"No thanks to you," came the young laird's tart reply.

Alastair chuckled. "I have no idea what you mean, but I am glad you are able to join us this day. 'Twill make these proceedings so much simpler if we can handle the escaped wench and clan rule all at once."

Coen pushed the unknown maiden behind him and stepped in front of Alastair. "Watch yourself, *cousin*. Your disrespect of the lass will not go unpunished."

"Ha! You think to punish me? Surely you jest." Alastair moved till he was nearly nose to nose with the laird. "I've been running this clan since you were a sniveling lad still crying over the loss of your father. Even after you came of an age to no longer need a regent, who do you think the clan leadership truly looked to? You think to challenge me? And over your father's bastard daughter?"

A collective gasp rolled across the courtyard, and a feral snarl escaped Kallum at the vicious slur.

"I think not." Alastair motioned to three men standing off to the side. "Restrain her."

A Connery man grabbed Ailsa from behind by both her biceps. Two MacNeill soldiers stepped to either side of him. 'Twas the two cretin friends of the banished Hendrik, causing Kallum to do a double take. 'Twas no

Connery who restrained Ailsa; 'twas the banished Hendrik himself done up in sheep's clothing.

Kallum strangled the murderous rage that tempted him to rush recklessly into the Connery courtyard and run Hendrik through with his sword. He could not afford to do something rash. Ailsa needed him, and he needed her too much to fail.

'Twould seem he'd been right about her brooch being a symbol of the blood kin of the old laird. 'Twould also seem Alastair had known all along. The man had purposely tried to vanish the lass. The second-in-command had sinister plans afoot.

"I'm sure your maiden friend informed you that your reinforcements are not coming." Alastair glanced at the woman behind Coen. "We intercepted the women afore they could alert your childhood mate of your need for his assistance. Most of the soldiers you see here"—Alastair waved his hand over the courtyard—"stand with me, and I've decided to take a stand for what is rightfully mine: the Connery lairdship. I exert my right of challenge."

Another, though smaller, collective gasp rose from the fringes of the courtyard. What few loyalists the laird still had apparently rimmed the edges of the crowd.

Alastair gave Coen a cocky grin. "Given your recent ailments and your current appearance, you're in no condition to fight. Thus, if you simply concede, then I shall let you live." The man strutted a few paces away, posturing for the crowd like an actor putting on one of William Shakespeare's plays. "You'll have to leave the clan, of course. But I'm sure you'll adjust to having to change your surname." His grin turned wicked. "I did."

"You cannot do this!" Ailsa shouted. "'Twas your poison that laid him low. He must be given time to recover."

"Au contraire, my dear cousin," Alastair replied. "'Tis more than fair. If your newly found brother is not fit to the task, he may have a champion. Of course, the best warriors in this crowd stand with me. *I* am the force to be reckoned with here. I have the backing of the best men of the Connery army, the support of the king's guard, and I've even turned the loyalty of three members of our fierce enemies, the MacNeills." He whirled dramatically to face Coen. "Who, young Coen, do you have to back you?"

Kallum detached the bow he had brought with him and grinned as his plan of action became clear. Alastair Connery had unknowingly given him the entrée he needed to rescue Ailsa, and that was his cue.

. . .

Ailsa flinched when the pop of an arrow pierced the chest of the man to her right, followed swiftly by the duplicative pop of a projectile into the chest of the man to her left. Hendrik's mates each made a loud *thud* when their dead weight dropped, one after the other, to the stone floor. Hendrik whipped Ailsa in the direction from whence the arrows had come and hid behind her. Her face rose to the hill outside the front gate, and her heart thumped in quick, successive beats that made it difficult to catch her breath.

The sight that greeted her was the most glorious sight she'd ever seen. Kallum, foot perched on a boulder, stood with lowered bow in hand, the light breeze teasing his loose locs.

Alastair's archers whipped around and raised their bows in the direction of the attacker, but Alastair stayed them with a hand. "Hold!"

Appalled, his head archer stared at him. "But we are under attack."

"Nay. He's attacked naught but two MacNeills, and two traitor MacNeills at that. We cannot retaliate without the act being seen as an open act of war against the MacNeill clan."

"'Tis their commander," Hendrik offered. "He has come for the lass."

"Let him come," Alastair replied. "He'll not get her."

The king's captain, who had remained quiet and detached until this moment, stepped forward. "The lass is mine," he stated emphatically.

Alastair gave him a sardonic stare, one brow perched in amusement at the soldier's bold statement.

The captain cleared his throat. "To return to the king, of course."

Alastair's lips quirked at the late correction, but he responded only to Hendrik. "Nothing has changed. You will be rewarded for your capture of the lass, and now"—he glanced down at the dead MacNeills—"it appears you will not have to share the bounty." He chuckled at the crude obviousness of his statement.

"You do not know this man, Alastair. Do not play games with him," Hendrik warned. "He'll not stop until he gets what he wants."

With a flick of his hand, an unconcerned Alastair signaled the Connery archers to stand down. They lowered their bows, and Kallum strode into the courtyard, his bold swagger belying his status as a lone warrior entering a den filled with a score of vipers.

Kallum stopped at the bottom of the stairs of the manor and planted a foot on the lowest step. "I have come for the lass who was taken from MacNeill land against her will."

"The lass is a Connery," Alastair replied. "Her presence here is not your affair, Commander."

"You made it my affair, Alastair, when you convinced two traitorous MacNeills to steal the daughter of your former laird from my protection, and even now allow her to be handled by a vile mongrel who assaulted her when he lived as a MacNeill."

The look of disgust Alastair gave Hendrik suggested that even in his villainy, certain acts were beyond the chieftain's condonement. Despite his reaction, Alastair commented not on Kallum's revelation about Hendrik but rather questioned her warrior with faux innocence. "Protection? A Connery under the protection of a MacNeill. Protection from what?"

"Why, you, of course." Kallum took the steps one at a time, casually mounting the porch as if he were an invited guest instead of an interloper from an enemy clan. "The story of her *accidental* enslavement never made sense to me. It took me a while to figure out the why of it."

Kallum's gaze diverted to Hendrik, who still held Ailsa in front of him. "The lass is not large enough to make a sufficient shield. If I had wanted you dead, an arrow would already grace your neck and you would be sprawled on the ground with your friends. You live only because you currently wear Connery colors." A deep, guttural growl entered his voice. "Unhand the lass if you want to stay that way."

The tightness of Hendrik's grip increased on her arms. Ailsa could feel his rising tension and his growing fear. He glanced momentarily at Alastair, who offered him no direction or sympathy. Hendrik's gaze moved to the king's captain.

"Your bounty is contingent upon the escaped captive being delivered to me, not the MacNeill. Decide wisely, Hendrik." The captain's tone made clear he considered there to be no real choice to make.

Anger rising, Coen stepped forward to address the captain. "Did you not hear the part where the lass is my *sister*, not some captive?"

The captain shrugged. "A convenient story, but one that cannot be verified. The king tasked me with retrieving the Moor bitch, and retrieve her I shall."

Ailsa bristled and lurched at the captain. Her movement caught Hendrik off guard, and he nearly lost his hold of her.

"I'll show you who's a bitch, you sorry excuse for a soldier." She spat the words in the captain's direction. "You'll not control me ever again." Tired of being handled like a piece of livestock, Ailsa whirled and shoved an elbow in Hendrik's face. He stumbled back a step, and she grabbed his shoulders, positioning him for the hard knee to the groin that followed.

He doubled over, cursing her loudly. He tried to reach for her retreating figure with the hand that wasn't wrapped around his abused cods, and Kallum's hand went to the long-bladed dagger in his belt.

Coen's sword found Hendrik's throat first. "Touch her again, and you die, irrespective of those Connery colors you wear. I don't know what arrangement you have with Alastair, but I'm still the laird here regardless of his challenge."

Ailsa ran into Kallum's arms. "You came," she whispered, touching her hand to his chest.

"For you," he crooned into her ear, "always." He squeezed her tightly with one arm, bow still gripped in his opposite hand. Slowly, he slid his hand up her spine to cup the back of her neck and pressed his lips tenderly to her temple.

In that moment, nothing else mattered to Ailsa except the feel of his beating heart beneath her palm, his familiar sun-and-wind scent rising to comfort her, and the feel of his hand at the base of her skull. The strength of his hold suggested he'd never let her go, and that was quite all right with her.

"I'm sorry," she said against his throat.

"For what, my goddess?"

She looked up at him. "For interfering with your punishment of Hendrik. If I hadn't, we wouldn't be here."

"Nay, lass, you do not know that." His thumb and first finger squeezed beneath her hair. "Alastair is a blackguard of the most determined kind. He would have found another to do his bidding. Besides, 'tis never wrong to offer mercy. Hendrik simply was not deserving of your lenience. That is his failing, not yours."

Without releasing her, Kallum looked to the king's captain. "I wonder," Kallum said, "does the king know you were paid to hold a Highland lass enslaved in his castle?"

The captain's face faltered for a moment afore he gathered himself. Ailsa wondered how Kallum knew such or if he'd just guessed. If he *had* guessed, the captain had displayed a guilty countenance suggestive of his complicity in the plot.

"You speak absurdities, MacNeill. 'Tis not a matter of your concern in any event. Once the issue of Connery leadership is settled, I will handle the matter with the new laird." The captain glanced at Alastair. The look said all about whom he expected to prevail in the challenge yet to be resolved.

"There's just one problem with Alastair's challenge." Coen sheathed his sword. "'Twas not issued to the proper Connery."

Alastair's brows slanted downward. "What nonsense is this?"

Coen held out his hand to Ailsa. Perplexed, she looked briefly at Kallum, then stepped hesitantly forward to take her new brother's hand.

He addressed the crowd. "This is my sister, Ailsa Connery. Firstborn child of my father and rightful heir to the Connery chief mantle. Any challenge for leadership issued must be made to her for, as of this moment, I renounce my false claim as laird of Clan Connery."

Confused murmurs arose from those watching.

Ailsa whispered to Coen, "But I told you afore, I don't want to be laird."

His eyes softened. "And I told you afore, that duty rarely comes wrapped in what we want." A solemness filled his expression. "As you have indicated, I am ill fit to meet Alastair's challenge. His challenge loses credibility if I am not laird."

Alastair guffawed. "You jest."

His men laughed with him.

"You cede to *her*? Ha. She is a bastard."

"You know well, Alastair," Coen responded, "under clan law, when it comes to succession, it matters not whether an offspring is born out of wedlock or deemed legitimate."

With his hand cockily on the hilt of the sword in the scabbard at his side, Alastair said, "Don't be foolish, Coen. Think you this trickery will stop me from my claim?" He stared regretfully at Ailsa. "I wish not to kill a lass, let alone one kin by blood. But know, cousin, that I withdraw not my claim. Think seriously on this matter afore you let Coen use you as a pawn in a battle you cannot win."

Coen released her hand and stepped forward. "Then you acknowledge Ailsa's birthright as my older sister and your blood cousin?"

"Aye, and she should have stayed at the palace where I placed her. At least then she would have her life."

A horrified rumble flowed through the crowd.

"So, 'tis true?" Ailsa stepped up beside Coen. "You admit that you are the reason I was impressed into slavery? Three years. Three long years you left me to be owned like an animal, humiliated, nearly violated." She reached for the dagger still belted undetected beneath the folds of her dress.

Understanding her purpose, Alastair responded in kind with a hand to his dirk belted in plain view.

Kallum grabbed Ailsa's wrist and stayed her from pulling the dagger clear. "No, my sweet. The right to kill him shall be mine. And only mine."

Alastair laughed coldly. "Nice thought, MacNeill. But once I defeat your wench and take my place as chief, she'll be returned to the palace as the runaway slave she is." He grinned. "And as my first decree, I will sentence you to die for interfering in Clan Connery politics."

"How could you do something so vile?" Ailsa still could not fathom that anyone, especially a supposed family member, would hate her so much as to arrange her enslavement.

"Ah, Ailsa, I meant you no true harm. I paid well to make sure you served in the king's palace in a superior position. You were lady's maid to a princess, after all. A cushy life for a lass such as yourself with no known blood family. What life would you truly have had on your own? You were not oft sought out as a healer. Regardless of your grit, soon you would have had to make a living on your back like all other village wenches without male protectors. I saved you from that."

"Whom did you pay to protect me from castle occupants who oft threatened to use me on my back or set to beat me so severely that permanent scars grace that back?"

Alastair startled, truly surprised by her comment. He glanced at the king's captain, who stood stoically under his gaze, but 'twas clear Alastair understood her meaning and the culprit.

Through clenched teeth, Alastair said, still looking at the captain, "'Twas not the agreement I reached." He turned back to Ailsa. "If I had wanted you abused, I need not have sent you off to Stirling to accomplish such. I simply needed you out of the way, where no one would find you. But now that you are here, the challenge stands."

Kallum stepped up beside Ailsa. "Then your challenge will be met by me."

The uproar that rose from the crowd devolved into near chaos. First, they learned their old laird had fathered a daughter of mixed lineage out of wedlock, then their young laird renounced his lairdship, and now an enemy MacNeill stood to champion the putative new chief. The scandal of it all had begun to spread throughout the clan, for the crowd expanded, and the number of additional Connerys in the courtyard made Ailsa nervous. She knew not who was friend or foe. If all, or even most, of those present stood with Alastair, then Kallum stood no chance of getting out of this debacle with his life.

"You cannot," she said to the MacNeill.

He ran a hand down the side of her face. "But I must."

Ailsa leaned into his touch. "You cannot trust Alastair and his men to fight fair. This is a trap. I feel it. You must feel it, too." When he didn't respond, she looked at Coen. "You mustn't allow this."

"Ailsa," Coen said, "it is you, the MacNeill, or me." He gave a self-deprecating wave down his person, honestly noting his condition did not bode well for a battle. "Of the three of us, sister, who do you think is most suited?"

She looked again at Kallum. "You mustn't do this. 'Tis sheer folly."

"Ailsa, on this, I am firm. You will not dissuade me." His sable eyes bored into hers, and she experienced an instant of panic.

She knew that set of his jaw, that look in his eyes. Nothing would make him back down now that he had accepted the challenge. "But why? Why would you do something so foolhardy?"

He returned his bow to his back and grabbed her face with both hands. "Because watching you die is not an option."

Dispirited, she let her head loll forward. She could not help thinking, though she was unable to voice the words aloud: *Yet you would condemn me to watch* you *die.*

His lips found her forehead, and they stood thus for several intense moments.

Unimpressed with the display, Alastair called an end to the interlude. "Enough!" He surveyed the three of them. "This is all such a lovely spectacle, but the MacNeill warrior can*not* serve as Ailsa's champion. He is not a Connery."

Her brother dismissed Alastair's statement. "He need not be a Connery to serve as champion. Clan law provides that he—or she—who is challenged may only *appoint* a champion who is a Connery, but a *volunteer* to serve as champion may be of any clan."

"True." Alastair smiled. "But, cousin, you and I both know that clan law specifically requires that such volunteer be at least kin to a member of the house of Connery through blood or marriage, which the MacNeill is not."

Coen studied Ailsa. She stood in the circle of Kallum's arms. He glanced at the MacNeill, who watched him closely. Their eyes held in silent communication, and then Kallum gave her brother a subtle nod, which Coen returned.

"What?" Ailsa looked between her newfound sibling and the man she had come to love. Something had transpired between the two. She knew instinctively that it had to do with her, but she could not think straight enough to figure out the what of it. "What's going on?"

"'Twould be nice for you, Alastair, if you were able to stake your claim by besting a lass or a man you'd striven to incapacitate via foul means. Unfortunately, there is a slight flaw in your plan." Kallum's lips quirked, and for a change, the pleasure Kallum took in issuing a taunt reached all the way to his eyes. "*Cousin*."

Alastair's brow furrowed. "Cousin? Of what blasphemy speak you now, MacNeill?"

"Simple. You will have to go through me after all." Kallum released his hold on Ailsa.

Afore he set her to his side, he removed one of two hair ties from his wrist and placed it on one of hers. 'Twas the shelled tie he had given her at their falls.

He whispered for her hearing only, "Remember, always, why I came. Because I got your message, and protecting you meant—and always will mean—more than my life."

CHAPTER THIRTY

Grabbing the hand Kallum had just released, Coen inspected the leather tie Kallum had placed on Ailsa's wrist. He glanced at the similar tie remaining on Kallum's wrist, and the tension in his shoulders released. Whatever he understood of Kallum's and Ailsa's exchange from their shared trinkets made the young Connery's breathing relax along with his shoulders.

Though he'd made a silent pledge with Kallum to save his clan, evidently the brother had been concerned as to whether he was about to do right by Ailsa. 'Twas a good sign. His hesitation evidenced the man's genuine affection for Ailsa, though they had only recently met. Kallum might have to find room in his inner circle to add another liked Connery. Who'd have thought such was ever possible?

"Ailsa," Coen said to his sister, "give me your sash."

Still appearing confused, Ailsa removed her tartan sash and handed it to Coen with trembling fingers.

"People of Clan Connery," he began, "may I introduce you to Kallum MacNeill, Army Commander of Clan MacNeill, our new allies, and future husband to your newest chief." Coen grabbed her hand and placed it over Kallum's.

More Connerys pushed into the crowd, and those along the outer edges cheered at the announcement. An unhappy Alastair bristled with a rage-distorted face, and a stunned Ailsa looked between Coen and Kallum.

Finally regaining her staggered senses, Ailsa jerked her hand from Kallum's and shouted at Coen. "You cannot! You have no right to make such a decision for me."

"To the contrary, my sister, as your brother and the oldest living male in your household, I am your guardian despite being the younger of the two of us. I alone have not only the right but the obligation to secure an appropriate marriage match for you."

"But not to him." She stepped away from Kallum. "He does not want to marry me."

Coen took an amused peek at Kallum. "On that, you would seem to be mistaken."

Kallum stood, arms crossed against his chest, and glared at her. "You find me not a suitable mate?"

"'Tis not that, you hardheaded cretin." She stepped to him, fierceness in her eyes. "You have made it perfectly clear that you intend never to marry. I'll not be foisted off as some pity bride." She pointed at Alastair. "Not even to defeat him."

"Ailsa, this has naught to do with pity." He gave her a chastising look.

"But you…you…you said…" Her foot stomped in frustration as words failed her. "What changed?"

"I met you."

"That is not an answer, MacNeill."

"Aye, 'tis. You're just too angry to accept it."

Her hands found her hips, as they were wont to do when she got upset and was shifting into hellion mode. "Answer my question in truth. What has changed?"

Grabbing her by the back of the neck with one hand, Kallum drew her solidly against him and fused their mouths together. She pushed against him, but he did not release her. He delved into her sweetness, not caring who watched. The fire that always lit when they dared tempt Cupid's kiss burned fast and fresh until its sensual nature became improper for public display.

Catcalls rose from the men and giggles from the females in attendance.

"You try to distract me, MacNeill." Her voice softened as she became pliant in his arms. "Answer my question."

"I am. You're just not paying attention." He grinned, a slashed brow raised in quiet challenge.

She stared deep into his eyes, ready to continue the protest. Then something shifted, and her eyes widened. She had finally seen all he felt but had never said.

It was time he gave her the words. "Aye, lass. You are the only woman I have ever found worth marrying because you are the only woman I have ever loved." He placed a soft peck against her lips. "I love you, Ailsa Connery. And you *will* marry me because I will never allow any other man near you. Any man who tries will die by my hand." He smiled at the last, knowing how she would take it, and only half jesting.

"Of course," she replied with an exasperated shake of her head. "Because that is your answer for everything, MacNeill."

Though inappropriate for their current situation, Kallum chuckled at her comment. She leaned into him and momentarily rested her head against his chest. He took her hand and offered their joined grip to Coen, who wrapped the whole with her sash.

When she looked up, Kallum said, "'Tis only a handfasting, lass. If you prefer your independence and choose not to consummate the promise, I will not hold you to the marriage."

Knowing she'd be no more capable of foregoing their intimate pastimes than he, Kallum was confident that would never transpire. She frowned at his confident expression. The churning of her brain showed behind her eyes. If she could find a way to back out of this later, she might, but Kallum had no intention of making that easy on her.

A manic growl sounded behind them. "I'll not be robbed of my rights by this trickery. Vow of marriage or not, MacNeill, I recognize not your status. And for your hubris, I sentence you to die now. I'll take by force what is mine." Alastair drew his sword. Glancing toward the courtyard, he yelled, "To arms!"

Kallum shoved Ailsa behind him and met Alastair's advance with his own sword. He thought to stash the ladies inside the manor, but men loyal to Alastair blocked the doorway as they battled with a few Connery soldiers still loyal to Coen. Changing plans, Kallum went on the offensive and drove Alastair back toward the stairway.

The two men dueled, but Alastair was no match for Kallum's righteous rage. The chieftain could not hold his ground, and Kallum drove him down the stone steps and into the midst of the fray. On the ground, Kallum took stock of those around him. Coen's men were outnumbered and no match for Alastair's forces.

The few Connery loyalists were falling in fast numbers. Alastair's bragging about having control of the best of the Connery army apparently had been no empty boast. When another Connery loyalist met a fatal end, Kallum deftly jumped aside to keep from tripping over the felled warrior.

Alastair took the opportunity to slice at Kallum and caught him across the biceps. "Aha, MacNeill!"

Kallum countered with a slice of his own, though Alastair managed to avoid the cut.

Swords crossing, the two men battled, and Alastair kept up his boisterous prattle. "You know you cannot win. You are severely outnumbered."

A noisy ruckus drew the men's attention to a contingent of Connery soldiers storming around the corner of the manor to enter the fight. When two warriors jumped upon the porch to stand beside a weary Coen, Kallum understood the laird's reinforcements had arrived after all. Though the new arrivals did not even out the numbers, they gave the resisting forces renewed strength.

Kallum grinned at Alastair, whose annoyance over the reinforcements showed on his face. Unable to resist, Kallum made a taunt of his own. "Mayhap, Connery, but you'll not survive this day to enjoy the spoils."

Abruptly, he went on the offensive again. He may not be able to defeat the entire forces who stood against the Connery laird, but he could dispatch this usurper to hell.

Driven back, Alastair weaved between his men, fending off Kallum with deft counters and well-timed thrusts. When they reached the center of the courtyard, Alastair disengaged and made a stance. "Coen's reinforcements will not make a difference, MacNeill. Surrender now, and I'll make sure your wench is not here to see you die." The man postured with a grisly smile. "'Tis the least I can do for my dear cousin afore she returns to her station as the princess's lady's maid."

Alastair's gaze flicked momentarily over Kallum's shoulder, and Kallum followed the direction of that pleased glance. The sight of Hendrik dragging Ailsa toward the king's captain made a fear Kallum had never experienced grip his gut. Ailsa struggled, but gripped in such a way, she could not reach her dagger; she could not break free of the traitor's hold. Alastair forgotten, Kallum spun to race after her, but Alastair's men encircled him to block his retreat.

Surrounded, Kallum turned in the center of the closed circle and let forth a mighty roar of rage that made several soldiers take a step back. Giving them no time to recover from their startle, Kallum launched himself at a soldier to his left and ran him through. Quickly, Kallum pulled his sword from the man's torso and simultaneously snatched the dying man's sword from the soon-to-be corpse's falling grip.

The captain took Ailsa from Hendrik and passed the mongrel a pouch, likely heavy with coin. With the captain, Hendrik, Alastair, and Alastair's henchmen all working to eliminate Ailsa, Kallum's only hope to protect her was to get her off Connery land immediately.

A sword now in each fist, Kallum brandished the weapons to keep the remaining soldiers at bay and tucked his lower lip between his teeth. He gave a shrill whistle to call his war horse from the hills, then gave the battle cry known across the Highlands to drop feeble men where they stood from an arrested heart. Today was no different. Half the remaining soldiers who faced him retreated from the challenge. Those who failed to retreat, he slashed through with a relentlessness worthy of the rebellious demon from whence he derived his satanic epithet.

He fought with the strength of ten men, and his double onslaught of parries and thrusts made short work of those bold enough to cross his path. They encountered not Kallum MacNeill, army commander, but *Auld Dubh Mahoun*, the Black Devil who felled men with deceptive ease while himself seeming to float across the field invincible.

The Connery loyalists were waning, but Kallum could not focus on their plight. His one goal, his only thought, was to free the woman he loved and place her on the back of his steed so she survived this ordeal, even if he didn't.

The sound of horse's hooves drew near, and Kallum knew Ailsa's way out was fast approaching. He quickened his pace, determined to reach the king's captain afore he could whisk Ailsa away on his royal destrier.

The sound of Ogun's gallop grew louder and louder still, until the pounding of one stallion's hooves morphed into the building rumble of intense thunder. The ground began to shake, and the roar of thunder deepened. The ominous sound made many a man in the courtyard halt their battle to glance nervously around but sent a spike of adrenaline through Kallum's body.

Ogun came over the rise, and, anticipating what else was coming, Kallum thrust his sword into the air, then gave a fierce battle cry at what followed after: hundreds of mounted MacNeill soldiers led by a bellowing Inan.

Kallum's cousin rode straight to him and dismounted with a flurry of flying limbs. "You couldn't have waited for me to return?" he snapped.

Turning to fight back-to-back with Inan, Kallum answered, "I did not have time to wait. Ailsa needed me."

"You're determined to let that lass get you killed," Inan grunted through his exertion, and they each dispatched a member of the royal guard, which had entered the skirmish upon the arrival of the MacNeill reinforcements.

The cousins pivoted to switch places.

Kallum eyed the crowd to locate the man who dared profit from betraying his goddess but took the time to respond to his cousin's inane comment. "Did you come here to aid me or to nag me yet again about Ailsa?"

"Can't I do both?" Inan offered between a breathy huff and the felling of another opponent.

Spotting the traitorous MacNeill now turned Connery, Kallum moved to hurry things along. "Well, I'm kind of in the middle of something. Can the nagging wait?"

Spotting the source of Kallum's interest, a Hendrik now decked out in Connery colors, a frowning Inan nodded. "Aye. Carry on."

Kallum disengaged from his cousin's side and made a direct line for the soon-to-die wretch who had dared cross his own clan.

• • •

Ailsa watched hundreds of mounted MacNeill soldiers rush over the Connery hills and down into the courtyard. The MacNeills threw themselves into the battle, and the tide quickly turned. Those traitorous infidels who weren't quickly dispatched began to flee.

Sensing his hold on Ailsa about to slip away, the king's captain ordered his best men to protect his flank while he tried to make a way to his horse. Ailsa ceased her struggles when she caught sight of Kallum battling his way to her. Calm replaced her anxiousness. Her life and freedom once again rested in his hands, and she knew without a doubt he was the one person she could always count on to stand by her, fight for her.

She'd seen him lift a second sword from a fallen opponent, and enlightenment had clicked along with her steadfast confidence.

Her question to him on their journey from Stirling Castle and his riddle of an answer.

Why carry you two swords?

Because I know how to use them.

The times she had watched him spar with his men and switch his sword to the opposite hand depending on the man he battled.

The day at the falls when he'd been upset and executing elaborate sequences of thrusts, parries, and roundabouts with a sword in each hand.

It all made sense now.

*Mighty Olorun...*had been her only possible thought.

The man could fight with either hand or both, *at the same time.*

Even now, he fought his way to her with two swords exacting restitution, vengeance, and appropriate justice. When he came upon an unsuspecting Hendrik from the rear, Kallum called the man's name. Hendrik whirled wide-eyed, bounty still in hand, only to lose the hand to a slice from Kallum's right-handed weapon. When Kallum spun immediately into a roundabout that brought the blade held in his left hand around to Hendrik's neck, Ailsa averted her gaze, not wanting to witness the impending decapitation.

The sound of Hendrik's maudlin gurgles made the captain glance up to see death come for him next. He shifted Ailsa and drew his sword, but he was too late to hold off Kallum's strike. The blow knocked the captain's claymore from his hand, and in desperation, the man reached for his short blade. Kallum's sword point at the center of the captain's throat dissuaded him from pulling the blade free.

Not yet willing to concede defeat, the captain straightened to his full height, though he still stood not as tall as Kallum. "How dare you assault me thus. I am the captain of the king's guard. Remove your weapon at once!"

"You are a reprobate and an assaulter of women. You deserve not the position you hold nor that uniform you wear," Kallum said to the smaller man.

"You are one to talk, MacNeill. I note you fight with two swords at once. An unusual skill, that." The captain smirked. "Know who else is known to travel with two swords? The wanted thief and mercenary known as the Shepherd. What think you the king will have to say to that?"

Kallum pressed his blade deeper into the flesh of the captain's neck. "I'd say, you'd have to stay alive long enough to tell him."

The captain's eyes widened, and he began to sputter. "Y-you'd not d-dare kill the king's man. You'd be executed for your crime." Trying to muster some bravado to cover his stutter, the guardsman added, "Or should I say *crimes*?"

Kallum grinned at the captain, that mirthless tilting of the lips that meant the opposite of merriment. "That sounds like a challenge, captain. You know the only thing I like more than a challenge?"

The nervous guard swallowed noticeably, but the wary tilt of his head was his only response.

Kallum sheathed one sword and reached for Ailsa. The captain thought to restrain her, but the hardened press of Kallum's remaining blade to his throat loosened his misguided hold. When Ailsa was out of the captain's reach, Kallum stepped close to the soldier without lowering the sword he still held at the man's neck, grabbed the guard's dagger from the man's belt, and shoved it deep into his gut.

As the man collapsed, Kallum gave the answer to the question he'd posed. "Killing people who deserve to die."

Kallum dropped the second weapon and wrapped Ailsa in his arms. Safe in his embrace, she felt able to breathe again. Hendrik was dead, and the king's captain wasn't long to follow. Then an ominous thought hit her, and she tensed.

She pulled back from Kallum. "Where's Alastair?"

"He got away from me when I made to save you from Hendrik."

Worry immediately flooded her. "Coen!" She turned to run back toward the manor, but Kallum grabbed her around the waist. She fought his hold with furious clawing. "Let me go! I cannot lose him. I have only just found him."

Kallum grabbed her face between his large palms, forcing her to look at him. "Ailsa." He waited until he had her full attention to continue. "I love you. Trust me to also take care of those you love. But I need you safe and away from this fracas until all is settled. I'll take care of Coen. I want you to get on Ogun and ride with one of my men into the hills until I come for you."

She pulled away. "Nay!"

Lifting her off her feet and striding toward Ogun, Kallum huffed in frustration. "Woman, for *once*, could you please do what you are asked?" He kissed her hard but briefly, then placed her on the back of the massive black stallion. Motioning to a mounted MacNeill soldier, he sent her off toward the hills in the soldier's care.

With reluctance, Ailsa rode away, looking back toward Kallum the whole time. He picked the second sword back up and slashed his way toward the manor. He scanned the crowds of fighting men and came upon the sight of Coen not far from the manor steps. One of Alastair's henchmen stalked Ailsa's brother from behind while Coen fought head-on with two other traitorous Connerys. The still-recuperating laird's strength waned noticeably.

Rushing through the litter of bodies strewn about, Kallum abandoned finesse and settled for brute carnage to make his way to Ailsa's newest and only true remaining family member. After dispatching the last of the men that stood in his way, Kallum glanced up to see Inan at a distance stumble to one knee. Alastair approached stealthily behind his cousin, and Kallum had to make a decision.

Hesitating only an instant, he leapt onto the stone porch and shouldered Coen out of the way of the henchman's downward slash, which surely would have relieved Coen of his head. He made quick work of the henchman and looked up to see Inan, still stunned from his prior blow, unable to push to his feet. Alastair crept closer to Inan and, with a triumphant grin at Kallum, lifted his sword above his head.

"Nay!" Kallum's cry of outrage exploded across the courtyard. He was moving afore the sound dissipated, though he was too far away to stop the impending blow. "Inan!" he shouted in warning.

Inan glanced up, and the clang of a dropped sword beside him made him adjust in time to prevent being squashed by a collapsing Alastair. With a dagger piercing his chest directly beneath the shoulder of his sword-handling arm, Alastair pressed at the blood gushing from his wound.

Kallum pulled up short, stunned to recognize the jeweled dagger impeding Alastair's use of his dominant arm. Perplexed, Kallum searched the field. No doubt looking for her, the woman who was supposed to be safely tucked up in the hills. Ailsa met his gaze from a few meters away, where she sat astride Ogun.

Inan looked down at the moaning Connery and then back up at an approaching Kallum. "Is that the dirk awarded you by the king?"

"Aye," Kallum replied.

"I didn't think you carried that dagger."

"I don't."

Inan dislodged the weapon from Alastair's chest, after first giving it a meaningful twist, and gave Kallum a perplexed stare.

Kallum grinned at him afore delivering the bad news. "I gave it to Ailsa."

She slid from Kallum's horse and started to run. She leapt into his arms, and he caught her, unmindful of the two swords that clanked to the ground at his feet.

"Ah, hell," Inan groused. "I'm never going to live

this down. Am I?"

Kallum crushed her to him, and they both laughed at Inan's grumble but otherwise ignored him.

"You daft lass. I ordered you to remain aloft." Kallum kissed her with a hunger born of his relief and likely some residual fear.

"Aye," she breathed against his lips. "And I tried to stay aloft. I really did. But you needed me."

"Ah, lass, I had only need for your safety."

"True, but you also had need that your cousin not die this day."

He pulled back to look at her.

"You had a choice to make, and I saw you choose to keep your promise to me. I have only just found my brother, and I know the anguish I would feel should I lose him this soon. You have had Inan most of your life. He is the brother of your heart. Although there have been times I wanted to kill him, I could not very well allow you to save my brother and not at the least try to save yours. I love you, too, after all."

His lips returned to hers, the kiss passionate and possessive. Unmindful of those who stood in observance, Ailsa returned the kiss with equal fervor. When her tongue sought his, the taste of him nearly made her forget the precipice they'd recently escaped with their lives, but the sound of the king's fanfare upon the hill brought them back to the looming reality. Looking up, they saw the king mounted aside Laird MacNeill with the remaining portion of the king's guard spread out behind them.

Ailsa took notice of the king, then surveyed the carnage around the courtyard. The day of reckoning had dawned. She tensed, and Kallum rubbed calmly between her shoulders. Understanding his silent message, she glanced up into soft sable eyes that promised her a forever champion. This time when she pled her birthright of emancipation, she'd not stand alone.

Kallum motioned to Inan, who came to stand by her side while Kallum walked out to greet his descending laird and the king.

Ailsa glanced over at Inan. "Thank you," she said quietly.

He looked back at her. "You understand that I did not do it to save you?"

"Aye, I know it." She turned her head to gaze at Kallum as he strode across ground littered with the Connery dead. "You did it to save him."

Out of the corner of her eye, Ailsa saw Inan give a single, resolute nod. He followed the act with an awkward clearing of his throat. The sound caused her to glance at him once more.

Sheepishly, he said, "Thank *you*."

Ailsa suppressed a grin. She understood the twinge to his pride it must have taken for Inan to thank her for saving his life. She opted not to gloat but could not resist returning his sentiment. "You realize I did not do it for you?"

He turned fully to face her. His head canted, and his lips twitched at her bold repartee. "Aye, I know it."

Facing forward again, they both watched the reason they tolerated each other bow to the king. Standing silently beside a more amiable Inan, Ailsa took into account the two lairds present to stand witness to her freedom—her brother and the influential Laird MacNeill. Most importantly, she allowed herself to feel all it meant to have the love of a powerful Highland warrior. Though she'd have to face His Majesty, she no longer feared the outcome. Whatever happened, she was a free Highland lass, and thanks to her newfound family, she had no doubt she would forever stay that way.

EPILOGUE

Two weeks later, a naked Ailsa laid in bed with a naked Kallum in the Connery chamber for privileged guests. Ailsa had been loath to leave her brother after the fight with Alastair's men on top of his close call with the poison he had ingested over time.

Truth be told, Coen had seemed loath to let her out of his sight as well.

Both had been raised only children and found the existence of a sibling comforting, since neither had either parent left alive. They had spent much time in each other's presence, getting to know each other and coming to terms with what Ailsa's existence meant for the Connery clan.

At their audience with the king, Laird MacNeill had played a suave diplomat who made it impossible for the king to claim Ailsa as an enslaved servant without massive scandal upon the monarchy. The threat of possible en masse uprising from every laird in the Highlands with a daughter had led the king to capitulate on his claim. Thereafter, Ailsa had vehemently refused to claim the Connery lairdship despite her brother's sincere encouragement. The last thing she wanted was to rule a clan, any clan, even with her status as heir having played a major role in her guarantee of unconditional and unfettered emancipation from the crown.

Coen had taken some convincing, but Ailsa had made him understand the burden of all he asked of her.

Alastair's bid for the lairdship and the traitorous behavior of many Connery soldiers would already be
much for their clan to overcome. To ask them to accept
a new laird who was not only a woman and illegitimate
but also of mixed blood would place her at the center
of much contention. Not to mention, she was now
mated with the army commander of a clan that had
until mere weeks ago been the staunchest of Connery
enemies, and the possibility still loomed of assassina-
tion attempts from any of Alastair's followers who had
not yet been uncovered. 'Twas not a task she relished
nor a position she remotely wanted to assume.
Stratagems and diplomacy existed not amongst her
skills, and she had no true desire to develop them, irrespective of the legacy of her birth.

Ailsa had lived most her life as an outsider; she
need not undertake an endeavor that would force her
to remain at the center of mistrust for the foreseeable
future. Thanks to Caitrin and Florie and several soldier
wives of Clan MacNeill, she had experienced what it
felt like to truly belong. And thanks to Coen himself,
she had been handfasted to the match of her heart to
defeat Alastair's claims. She'd not set that man aside.

'Twas her last point about her intentions with the
MacNeill that finally swayed her brother. Her concerns
about being a female laird were dismissed summarily
when he informed her that she'd not be the clan's first
female laird. That honor, to her astonishment, had gone
to the great-great-grandmother whose brooch she
owned. He also would not entertain any concerns
about her lineage. 'Twas what 'twas, and their people
would deal. And, to his mind, be all the better for it.

The obligation of the laird to make a marriage

match that put the needs of the clan above his or her own, on the other hand, was held a sacred trust in the Highlands. Coen had long been set to make such a match himself in the name of securing beneficial allies. Ailsa would do no such thing. Any union her clan would readily accept of her would likely not include a MacNeill, even with the nascent allyship. Too much ingrained suspicion still abounded betwixt the two clans.

She'd been independent too long to be obligated to make self-sacrificing decisions for the advancement of politics. Unfathomably, she, the woman who thought she'd never fall in love nor marry, had found a love match. Despite her newfound place in her clan and her desire to see them thrive, no sense of duty to Clan Connery could ever make her give up her MacNeill.

Realizing Ailsa spoke honest and true about her lack of ambition to rule, Coen had finally been content to retain the mantle of leadership. He had made her decide the fate of their wayward cousin afore reclaiming his title, however, insisting that she had been the one most harmed. Unable to give the sentence for death, Ailsa had condemned the wounded—and villainous—Alastair to imprisonment for life.

Luckily, Kallum had avoided facing any criminal accusations of his own. The king's captain had expired without opportunity to share his suspicions about Kallum leading a secret life as the Shepherd. The king had been so appalled by his man's role in Ailsa's enslavement that he had pardoned Kallum in full for his hand in the guard's death. Kallum was free to carry on his mission as the Shepherd, and Ailsa had assured him she supported his continuance of this most important role.

She rolled onto her side and looked into Kallum's eyes, a part of her still not believing they were meant to be one. An army commander and a laird's daughter—'twas an unusual match. "You never told me how you knew. When did you figure out I was the former Connery laird's daughter?"

Kallum pushed his hands into the full waves of her hair, which she had left unplaited this eve on a rare whim. "The morn you disappeared. I realized afore I left you that I'd seen the crest on your brooch afore, but not simply because it was the Connery crest. I had encountered your father at several summits attended by Laird Aymer. He had such a special crest on his fly plaid brooch, and only him. The other Connerys' adornments displayed the standard crest. 'Twas only with that memory I also recalled the man had the same light hazel eyes as you. I doubted it to be a coincidence, especially knowing some Connery had gone to a lot of trouble to make you disappear."

Her hand found its way to his chest, and she played lightly with the hair beneath her palm. "Coen gave me our father's journal to read. 'Tis odd. I spent so many years hating the man for forgetting me when, in truth, he thought of me almost daily and was as miserable as me over the separation." Her voice broke, and she had to clear her throat to continue. "It hurts a bit to know I had a loving father but never got to meet him."

He squeezed her tight. "I'm sorry, lass."

She snuggled into his hug. "I still don't understand why Alastair went to so much trouble to get rid of me. No one would ever have noticed me in the village."

"Ha. You fool yourself. You had not plans to stay a quiet, unassuming village lass. You had plans to rise to the laird's main healer. Someone would have noticed you. Mayhap young Coen himself. He's already admitted to trying to find you in the past. I suspect 'twas merely happenstance Alastair succeeded where Coen did not."

"Hmm."

He looked down at her absent response. "What is it, my sweet?"

"The Connery healer, understandably, is no longer able to engage in healing practices. At least not in this world." She looked to see his expression. "Coen offered me the position."

Kallum stiffened but fought to keep his face neutral. He was aware that being lead clan healer had been her primary goal all along. To be home in the Highlands, become lead healer, and find the missing family she used to search for would seem to give her all she'd ever wanted.

"I see. What did you say?"

"Well…" She made circles in his chest hair until he grabbed her hand and growled at her.

"Stop that. You know I cannot think straight when you touch me thus." He flipped her onto her back and pinned her arms beside her head. "Answer my question."

She grinned at his impatience but chose not to keep him in suspense. "I told him now that he has handfasted me off, that man had a want to be my forever husband and may have ideas about his wife serving as healer to other than his own clan."

The smile he gave her was glorious. She never realized what a thrill it was to make a man smile who had seemed determined to live his life without ever displaying a true one.

"Aye, you have the right of it. Your *forever* husband also has ideas about what he'd rather do with his wife in bed than talk about the confounding clan of her birth." He kissed her neck, then slowly kissed down to the center of her chest.

Taking his time, he sucked one of her nipples into his mouth, then the other.

She reached for his face and rubbed the scruff of his beard against her palms. Mischievousness grinned up at her—her only warning he intended to rub that scruff in her other favorite place to feel its tantalizing rasp.

He slid down and planted his shoulders between her spread legs. Purposefully and languidly, he bunted his face against the soft flesh inside her upper thighs. The feel of his beard sent tingles up her pelvis, right to her nipples, which hardened into tight buds. Anticipation dampened her internal heat, and when his mouth finally touched her sex, the intensity of the pleasure from his flicking tongue near erupted the rapture already building inside her.

A hand caressed up her torso, then clamped the beaded tip of a breast between finger and thumb while Kallum's tongue slowed to lave a deep path between her intimate petals. Her limbs began to tremble. The quaking lured him to focus on the bud of sensation high in the folds of her womanhood. Kallum sucked it deep, and her woman's pleasure exploded. Shaking and moaning, Ailsa twisted away from his marauding lips and tongue, but he held her firm and pushed a hand against one of the thighs that had clamped against his ears.

Kallum repeated the whole until he caused the spike and release of her woman's pleasure twice more, then moved hurriedly up her body to slide his hardened flesh deep inside her still-pulsing internal walls.

He moved inside her, slow and intense, holding her gaze captive with his mesmerizing sable orbs. "You realize, my goddess, now that we have consummated our union—multiple times—subsequent to Coen's joinder of us, you are bound to me forever due to the promise of our handfast."

Her head fell back, and she tried to hold back a little longer the returning rapture building inside her. "You know the church frowns upon such clandestine marriages."

"If 'twas good enough for James IV and Margaret Tudor…" His hips thrust, rocking his pelvis high against her sensitive bud.

She was becoming breathless, but she could not leave off the tease she had started. Having not discussed with him the marriage portion of her conversation with Coen, he knew not of her decision to honor the handfast. "Their clasping of hands was followed by a bridal mass. 'Tis not the same. Besides, I rather like the legendary ways of the Western Highlands whereby I have a year and a day to set you aside if I so choose, regardless of consummation."

"Nay," he said adamantly and choked on a laugh. "Nay, and again nay. Now that I need no longer withhold the spilling of my seed inside you, I guarantee, unless you use your herbs or other methods to prevent becoming with child, within a year we shall have an offspring. To wit, you are setting no one aside."

She pulled his head down to kiss him, lifting her legs to seat him deeper. The acute ecstasy was more than either could stand, and they found their release together.

He dropped his forehead to her chest, and she whispered in his ear, "Ah, Kallum, I thought you knew."

"Knew what, my love?" he asked, lifting his head to look deep into her eyes.

She had known that first day on the princess's balcony that her life depended on the arrival of a particular Highland clan. But what she had not known was that 'twas the wrong clan she had been seeking. What she had truly needed was not to reclaim a staid and limited Highland life but to find an expansive one. And she had found that and all else she needed with Kallum MacNeill, a man who gave her the independence to be herself while offering her all that a true love match had to offer.

She raised her hand to cup the side of his bearded jaw. "I have been yours forever from the moment I first saw you in the king's courtyard and you spoke to me with a voice that even still makes me tremble inside."

He rolled over, pulling her atop him. "'Tis fitting, then."

"In what way, my warrior?"

"For I have been yours forever from the moment I first saw you, mysterious and poised upon a castle balcony."

She smiled at his words and fell asleep where she laid, with the strength of his warrior heart—his being—beating fiercely beneath the hellion heart he had set free.

AUTHOR'S NOTE

"Absence of proof is not proof of absence."
~James W. Loewen
(From *Lies My Teacher Told Me: Everything Your American History Textbook Got Wrong*)

This is a complete work of fiction. The hero is not based on any known person, nor is this meant to be a fictionalized version of some actual event in history. While there are records of Africans in Europe—including Scotland—dating back to the early fifteenth century, revealing the total populations and exact locations of those Blacks is not the intent or focus of this work. I've written this work as entertainment only, sprinkled with some historical truths.

Admittedly, I had no story concept in mind when I told my editor I wanted to write a historical romance about a Black Highlander. I love to read Highlander romances, so having never discovered one with a Black hero, I thought I'd write my own. Because my undergraduate degree in Comparative Literature was paired with a concentration in African American Studies, I understood the broad nature of the African diaspora, though it had been some time since I focused on the displacement of Africans outside the United States.

Similar to other European countries' history of African enslavement, Scotland played a large role in the slavery-driven economies of the Caribbean—Jamaica in particular. Like those brought to the

Americas, Africans enslaved by Scots fought to escape, accompanied their enslavers on sojourns to their native land (on occasion), and sued for or sought (and sometimes acquired) emancipation. As I revisited the presence of Blacks in Europe during the fifteenth through eighteenth centuries, one tidbit in particular caught my fascination: pirates. Yep, pirates.

When pirates grabbed ships carrying enslaved Africans, they kept and disposed of that human cargo along with any other bounty on the vessels. Information varies as to the fate of those seized as part of pirate raids. Some writings suggest there were pirates who considered the enslaved Africans worthless cargo. (I have to wonder about that theory.) Other writings indicate there were pirates who sold captives to Scots or Brits, who kept the captives as domestics as a symbol of their affluence.

The knowledge that Scottish pirates regularly raided slavers made me ask "What if?" as we writers often do. What if some of those Africans escaped or were set free? Where did they go? What if they were given sanctuary amongst Highland clans? And from there this story was born.

Note that the story starts at Stirling Castle because I find this castle particularly fascinating. I've taken a few liberties with the timeline of the residency of King James VI and I in the castle. Historical accounts indicate he lived in England after the Union of the Crowns, and I found only one documented sojourn in Scotland thereafter (in 1617 on occasion of the 50th Anniversary of his accession to the Scottish throne). Interestingly, King James did spend time at Stirling Castle during that 1617 visit, and only the devoted King James scholar will likely notice that his presence at my fictional Stirling Castle has been fudged by a few years. And, yes, this is the James I who granted a charter to the Virginia Company for colonial pursuits in North America and authorized the English translation of what we know as the King James Bible.

The idea for the Black trumpeter who so enthralled our heroine came from records that indicate the presence of Blacks in the court of Henry VII and Henry VIII. Of note was John Blanke, a Black trumpeter for whom two images exist that are said to date back to 1511. Other records show royal payments to persons of African descent—thought perhaps to be free—for various services.

Because the study in the U.S. of African enslavement frequently begins in 1619 with the British colonists, many Americans do not learn the extensive nature of the African diaspora. It is rarely taught, if at all, in U.S. elementary schools or high schools that the Portuguese were granted the "right" to enslave sub-Saharan Africans by Pope Nicolas V in the mid-1400s (to extend Christianity and deter paganism). Over time, this edict led to late–fifteenth century and early–sixteenth century trade in captives with other Europeans and transport of captives across the Atlantic. Accordingly, Caribbean plantations owned by Scots and Spaniards and other Europeans during this period used enslaved African laborers. In fact, the Spanish brought enslaved Africans to North America (to present-day Florida) around the mid-1500s, about a half century *before* the settlement of Jamestown by the British colonists.

I encourage you to learn more on your own. A good

place to start for little-known U.S. history is the book from which the epigraph for this author's note was taken: *Lies My Teacher Told Me: Everything Your American History Textbook Got Wrong* by James W. Loewen. A good resource for a general global account of African enslavement is *Black Cargoes: A History of the Atlantic Slave Trade, 1518-1865* by Daniel P. Mannix.

Yours in romance and curiosity,
Lisa Rayne

ACKNOWLEDGMENTS

I am eternally grateful to my innovative publisher and editor, Liz Pelletier, without whom it is doubtful I would have ventured into writing historical romance, at least not anytime soon. I'm even more grateful that when I told her I wanted to write a romance featuring a Black Highlander hero, she didn't hesitate or bat an eye and trusted me that there were Blacks in Scotland during the seventeenth-century period in which I planned to set my story. Thanks for taking this journey with me and being patient through a few side trips down a research rabbit hole or two.

To patient and uplifting Lydia Sharp, your eye for story and push to develop deeper the emotional connections in this story have made this a much better book. Thank you for your encouraging words and the emails sprinkled with an occasional smiley face that arrived just when I needed them most. To the rest of the Entangled Publishing behind-the-scenes support network—Jessica, Heather, Riki, Meredith, Curtis, Katie, Hannah—thank you for your hard work, your dedication, and your warm welcome into the Entangled family. A special shout-out to Bree, LJ, and the graphics team. This cover…oh, how I'm in love!! You *totally* rocked this.

To my Entangled "Corset Clutch" writing crew—Lexi Post, Sapna Bhog, Eva Devon, Heather McCollum, and Michelle McLean—you ladies helped keep me sane during my debut entrée into historical romance writing. Our monthly chats or text message exchanges have been a godsend, and I consider you all not just colleagues but newfound friends. Lexi and Eva, you have particularly helped me tame my research angst and focus on only what I need to write the *current* story. Much gratitude! And Ms. Michelle, I can't tell you how much your messages, your voice, or your face across a computer screen have been my lifeline during these trying times. I loved your books before I knew you because they made me laugh out loud. Now that I know you personally, what an honor to get to share those laughs with you live and in real time. Looking forward to plotting, planning, and even cursing over many more stories with you.

To the legendary Ms. Beverly Jenkins, you are a goddess who has paved the way for other romance writers of color. Although I've only met you a few times while fangirling at book signings or conferences and you may not remember me, know that finding your books changed my life. To have read romance for over twenty years before I learned a writer existed who wrote historical romances featuring Black main characters sent me on a monthlong binge of reading through your entire back catalog (and, yes, even the contemporaries!) over a dozen years ago. To this day, *Indigo* is still one of my all-time favorite historical romances. If I can give readers even a fraction of the joy, escape, and "edutainment" you've given me, I'll consider myself more than lucky. Dare I say, even a bit accomplished?

Ally and Jordan, my fierce, independent daughters, you inspire me. Thanks for constantly being my cheerleaders. Maria, every woman needs a friend like you—someone who encourages and gives support ceaselessly, without thought or hesitation. No matter how long it's been since our last chat, it always feels like it was only yesterday. Know that your encouragement and praise help fuel my heart. To those other family members and friends who have been in my corner since I revealed my intent to write romance (especially my first readers, Karol and Bonita), I love you. While I cannot name everyone here, I hope you all know who you are and that I appreciate you every day.

Finally, to you, dear reader: thank you for taking a chance on this book. As a lifelong bookworm, I know the preciousness of your reading time. I hope you found some pleasure, some laughs, and maybe learned a tidbit or two. May we meet again between the pages of one of my stories.

Never Cross a Highlander is a historical action-adventure romance full of sarcasm, witty repartee, and irreverence. Although the story ends with a happily-ever-after, the novel includes some elements that might not be suitable for all readers. Sword battles, dagger play, blood, death, and infrequent strong language appear in the novel; there are also mentions of the deaths of family members in the characters' back stories and references to physical assault. Readers who may be sensitive to these elements, please take note.

Without mercy, there is no love in this third installment of the Sons of Sinclair historical romance series by USA Today *bestselling author Heather McCollum*

HIGHLAND JUSTICE

SONS OF SINCLAIR

As the new chief of Clan Mackay, Gideon Sinclair knows the importance of maintaining order at any cost. To keep the conquered clan in line, Gideon must mete out ruthless justice or risk losing their precious new peace. But from the moment he meets Cait Mackay— aye, from the moment the sweetness of her lips captures his—all of Gideon's careful objectivity is well and thoroughly compromised.

Cait knows that kissing the brawny Highlander is a dangerous game. It was bad enough she picked his pocket to feed the children in her care, but sometimes a desperate woman must disguise her crimes any way she can. Only her act of deception has made things worse... Because one kiss with the Highland's most brutal chief leaves her breathless and out of her depth.

Now Gideon must choose between his duty and his heart when his lovely thief is accused of treason against the king himself.